Misplaced Loyalties ™

"The Assassinations of Marilyn Monroe & the Kennedy Brothers"

Victor E. Justice

First edition published in 2005 by Trafford Publishing,
Misplaced Loyalties logo is a trademark of the author.

Printed on paper with minimum 30% recycled fibre. Trafford's
print shop runs on "green energy" from solar, wind and other environmentally-friendly power sources.

Offices in Canada, USA, Ireland and UK
This book was published on-demand in cooperation with Trafford Publishing. On-demand publishing is a unique process and service of making a book available for retail sale to the public taking advantage of on-demand manufacturing and Internet marketing. On-demand publishing includes promotions, retail sales, manufacturing, order fulfilment, accounting and collecting royalties on behalf of the author.

Book sales for North America and international:
Trafford Publishing, 6E–2333 Government St.,
Victoria, BC v8t 4p4 CANADA
phone 250 383 6864 (toll-free 1 888 232 4444)
fax 250 383 6804; email to orders@trafford.com
Book sales in Europe:
Trafford Publishing (uk) Limited, 9 Park End Street, 2nd Floor
Oxford, UK ox1 1hh UNITED KINGDOM
phone 44 (0)1865 722 113 (local rate 0845 230 9601)
facsimile 44 (0)1865 722 868; info.uk@trafford.com
Order online at:
trafford.com/05-1804

10 9 8 7 6 5 4 3 2

Contents

Acknowledgments

For reasons that should be obvious, I will not name anyone who participated in the preparation of this book. But that will not keep me from giving thanks where credit is due.

Thanks to those who believed in what I was doing from the start, who supported me along the way, especially my family and close friends. Thanks to those who offered opinions and suggestions on how to improve _Misplaced Loyalties,_ and those who read it carefully to ensure its readability and historical accuracy.

And most of all, thanks to John and the others who, after forty years, entrusted me with their stories, and for their patience and understanding while I worked to get it right.

Thomas Jefferson once said, _"We must not be afraid to follow the truth, wherever it may lead."_

Dedication

Misplaced Loyalties is dedicated to agents of the FBI, CIA, Secret Service, the Department of Homeland Security, and members of the U.S. military services who risk their lives every day to protect American citizens and their rights, and do so in a constitutional manner. You are the best of the best!

Victor E. Justice

"We sleep safely in our beds because rough men stand ready in the night to visit violence on those who would do us harm."

George Orwell

"...and ye shall know the truth, and the truth shall make you free."
(John 8:31-32)

This biblical scripture from the New Testament book of John is the CIA motto, which is inscribed at the entrance to CIA headquarters in Langley, Virginia - now known as the George H. W. Bush Center for Central Intelligence.

Important Definitions

Republic, from Latin *res,* **matter** + *publica,* **of the people,** is a state in which the supreme power rests in the body of citizens entitled to vote, exercised by representatives chosen directly or indirectly by the citizens.

Misplace
Function: *transitive verb*
A) To put in a wrong or inappropriate place "She *misplaced* the keys."
B) To set on a wrong object or eventuality "His trust had been *misplaced.*"

Loyalty
Latin, *legalis* - legal
A) Faithful in allegiance to one's lawful sovereign or government.
B) Faithful to a private person to whom fidelity is due.

Coup d'etat
Middle English: *to strike,* from Middle French: *couper*
A) To overturn [the state]
B) To upset

A Note to the Reader

Misplaced Loyalties is a work of non-fiction. It is the portrayal of actual events in history and, in the opinion of most who have read it, is much closer to the truth than what we have read in history books. The murders of Marilyn Monroe, John F. Kennedy and Robert F. Kennedy are some of the most significant and heinous unsolved crimes in modern history. They are significant, because we know intuitively that history would have been been altered tremendously had President Kennedy lived to be reelected as was predicted by the polls at the time of his death. History would have also been altered if Senator Robert Kennedy had been elected as President of the United States, rather than Richard Nixon. The murder of RFK prevented that eventuality and Nixon finally went to the White House.

Bobby Kennedy might have also served two terms as President of the United States. Marilyn's death has historical significance, not just in terms of Hollywood lore, but also because her murder led to the demise of the two Kennedy brothers. These crimes are heinous in a constitutional sense, because all three murders were planned in the White House, and all three murders involved multiple agencies of the U.S. federal government, while two of the murders involved the American Mafia.

In November of 2000 I met a man who presented first-hand evidence to me about the methods and the people employed to kill Marilyn Monroe. I refer to him as John. The plan to kill Marilyn had been developed in the lab where my contact worked. John and his colleagues were scientists whose primary function was to develop equipment and methods in support of CIA assassination operations. The plans developed there in the early 1960's included OPERATION MONGOOSE, the failed attempt by the CIA and the Mafia to assassinate Fidel Castro. The assassinations lab was operated by a contractor for the CIA, in the Edison laboratory, located in Schenectady, New York.

In his early twenties, John was a pioneer in the field of wave optics. He was employed to design and create the first night-vision scope, which was used by the CIA to locate Che Guevara in the forests of Bolivia. Guevara was one of Fidel Castro's closest lieutenants. On the following day, Guevara and his men were executed.

When I asked John how he designed the scope, he answered that he used available light from the stars and the moon at night to illuminate the image in the scope. I later learned that the first night-vision scopes used by the CIA and the U.S. Army and Marine snipers, as well as the U.S. Air Force, in its large, C-130 class gun ships were called, StarScopes. First-generation sniper StarScopes can still be purchased commercially today. You can see a current photo of a first-generation StarScope in the exhibit section of this book.

During a late night dinner the first week of November, 1963, John was told by a drunken CIA colleague that President Kennedy would be killed in Dealey Plaza in Dallas, with shooters firing from tall buildings. Two weeks later the assassination was carried out, just as John's co-worker had described.

John resigned from the lab and then moved his family out of the state, shocked and devastated with the realization that the CIA was involved in the planning and execution of the assassinations of Marilyn Monroe and President Kennedy. I interviewed John again at length in 2004 to ascertain the validity of his testimony, and to authenticate his credentials. His testimony on that day, three years later, was amazingly consistent with his previous testimony, and his scientific knowledge is extensive. There is no question in my mind that John is who he says he is.

John has lived over 40 years carrying this horrific information in his mind. He wants the public to know the truth, and asked me to tell his story. The transcript of our interview is *Exhibit B* following the *Afterword*. What John told me forms the basis of _Misplaced Loyalties,_ and my first hearing of his involvement created the impetus for me to join in this often frustrating, and potentially dangerous pursuit of the truth.

I don't like scary movies, yet I will watch films like *Saving Private Ryan* and *D-Day* if I know they are historically accurate. Likewise, the material in this book is deeply disturbing. But I hope you will find solace in the fact that _Misplaced Loyalties_ brings you closer to the truth.

In order to deliver these historical facts and events to you in a coherent and interesting way, I have written dialog and a storyline that supports the delivery of the factual information. The words spoken by Marilyn Monroe, the Kennedys, Richard Nixon, LBJ, and other historical figures represent what I believe was said behind the scenes. Of course, they are not direct quotations that can be documented. Through this theoretical dialog we can better grasp the motives for these high-profile murders. I have also quoted directly from several speeches, and you will most likely recognize the quotations when you read them.

The fictitious characters of Henry Atherton and his editor, Charlie Montrose, Henry's former wife Andrea, and others are used to assemble all the pieces of the puzzle, and to give you a chronology of the actual events. The interviews conducted by Henry Atherton are often direct portrayals of my interviews, and they aptly convey the amazing stories that have been told to me by former employees of the CIA, FBI operatives, and veterans of the conflicts in Korea and Vietnam, since November of 2000.

Is my portrayal of what happened in Dealey Plaza the absolute truth? Of course not! There have been hundreds of books written about this subject, and I cannot claim to have a better understanding than any other author. However, you will be able to determine how close I come to the truth by the degree to which this book is attacked.

Homicide detectives and prosecutors create plausible scenarios and pursue associated theories before arriving at the truth. Based on the evidence I have collected, the Dealey Plaza scene is what I believed to have happened. What is most important is not whether or not I am wrong. In the final analysis, what is most important is what you believe about the activities of our top elected and appointed officials when you have finished reading this book. So, in the words of the French playwright and philosopher, Francois-Marie Arouet Voltaire, I ask you to *"Love truth, but pardon the error,"* and as you consider my work, that you will, *"Judge a man by his questions, rather than his answers."* I cannot give you all the correct answers, but I will do my best to recount the facts and to help you to ask the right questions of yourself.

While reading *Misplaced Loyalties*, bear in mind that covering up the murder of John F. Kennedy represents the most elaborate, expensive, ongoing misinformation/disinformation campaign of all time. Connecting the dots is difficult, because considerable resources have been invested to prevent the truth from coming out. Therefore, you can be sure that some of my suppositions and implications will not be totally accurate, but I have done all I can to avoid untruths. Perhaps no one will ever know the full truth of what happened during this critical period in our history, but well-intentioned researchers and some brave participants are sharing information on your behalf, because they know how important these facts are to people throughout the world. I have been privileged to become associated with some of those scholars and witnesses along the way. I have also encountered some people who are employed in the process of keeping the truth from you. They can be identified rather quickly.

Just one example of the ongoing propaganda effort is the Sixth Floor Museum in the Texas School Book Depository in Dallas, Texas. Visitors are shocked when the keepers of the sniper's nest do not acknowledge the possibility that anyone other than Lee Harvey Oswald might have fired a shot on November 22, 1963 in Dealey Plaza. This, even though the federal government has formally announced that JFK's death was the result of a conspiracy.

One JFK assassination author provides a glaring example of why you must be constantly testing author's assumptions, including mine, and why you must always be on your guard. In his voluminous book about LBJ, entitled, _Flawed Giant_, the highly esteemed presidential historian, Robert Dallek, states at the top of page 49, _"He (LBJ) had absolutely nothing to do with JFK's assassination."_ Why would an expert who has sat on assassination panels, who has been called upon to judge the validity of JFK assassination researcher's work, make such a blanket statement about the man who had the most to gain by JFK's death? Lyndon Johnson controlled the subsequent investigation. LBJ not only had the motive, but the means and the opportunity in Dallas to facilitate the murder of President Kennedy. Authors such as Dallek write their tomes of 600 pages, filled with facts, then insert such bold statements as this one that can never be proved, to keep us off balance and to divert us from the truth. Be alert, and remain vigilant! Ask yourself the hard questions.

On the other hand, _Misplaced Loyalties_ will be attacked because it employs fictional elements in the telling, and this is to be expected. What you must decide is if the facts and suppositions I pose to you have more of a truthful ring than the other 'factual' books that have been foisted upon you, some of which contain boldfaced lies disguised as facts. At least I am delineating my fictional and supposed elements!

Additionally, I hope you will forgive my use of a pen name, and my decision not to name any of my witnesses, or those who assisted me in this effort. I trust you will judge my anonymity not as cowardice, but rather as a rational and prudent approach under the circumstances. My concern is not so much for me as it is for those who have been brave enough to come forward after all these years, who have told me their stories in the belief that I would do all I can to get the story straight. It has taken five years, and I am finally ready to release this book for public scrutiny.

In life there are historical events about which we hold a morbid curiosity, and although we are curious to know the truth, we really don't want to hear it. It's like being in denial of a terrible disease, such as alcoholism. Anyone who has struggled with alcoholism will tell you the first step toward declaring victory is to admit denial of the problem. America has been in denial regarding its assassination activities during the 1960's. Those practices and institutions paved the way for the terrible murders explored in this book. Prior to 1976, political assassinations were not considered illegal in America. It was not until 1976 that President Gerald Ford issued Executive Order number 11905 stating, *"No employee of the United States Government shall engage in, or conspire to engage in, political assassination."*

President Ford had pardoned his predecessor, Richard Nixon, the man who had appointed Ford as President of the United States, for crimes he committed, or <u>may</u> have committed. When in history has a man received a presidential pardon for undiscovered crimes? What could Nixon have done that required such a carte blanche pardon; perhaps some assassinations?

I believe in the ability of the American public to sort out fact from fiction. As you read, think about our constitutional right to bear arms *(the Second Amendment)*, the limitations imposed upon the President of the United States by the U.S. Constitution, relating to declarations of war and committing troops to battle, as well as the role assassinations have played in American presidential politics and foreign policy. Ask yourself why President Gerald Ford signed an executive order making it illegal for the United States to commit assassinations for political purposes. Think about how the Constitution contains a motive for murder, in that upon the death of the President of the United States, the vice-president ascends immediately to the presidency without the evaluative process of an election. What lessons can we take from the 1960's that apply to our lives today? I believe there are many.

Hundreds of books have been written about the events covered in this book. No author can claim to know the whole story, but we can continue in the hope that enough brave Americans, such as John, Judyth Vary Baker and James Files will speak out to tell what they know before they are gone, so we can piece the puzzle together. I have had the assistance of several experts who helped me eliminate factual errors, but I will not claim my portrayal is totally accurate. To do so would be folly.

If you agree this version of history is more credible than what you have previously been told, then you must decide how you will respond to the new historical facts revealed in this book. Our form of government is meant to be government of the people, by the people, and for the people.   The executive, legislative and judicial branches of our federal government were designed to provide the checks and balances that are meant to keep us safe. No one, not even the President of the United States, is above the rule of law.

Victor E. Justice
Washington, D.C. - July 4, 2005

"Government is not reason. Government is not eloquence. It is force. And, like fire, it is a dangerous servant and a fearful master."

George Washington

Foreword - Misplaced Loyalties

As a republic, the United States is founded upon the democratic principle that the executive branch is accountable to Congress and thereby, to the people. The president and his cabinet are charged with governing in a manner that reflects the will of the people. That is why most, if not all, federal government employees, enlisted and commissioned military staff, elected and appointed officials swear an oath, *'… to preserve and protect the Constitution of the United States.'*

So what could happen if senior officials decided to pursue objectives that were contrary to the will of the people? What sort of crimes could government executives commit with impunity if their loyalties were misplaced? Based upon new, first-hand evidence, *Misplaced Loyalties* is a portrayal of actual historical events, using creative literary means to describe what is more likely to have taken place than what historians (and those who don't want us to know the truth) have led us to believe.

"I do solemnly swear (or affirm) that I will faithfully execute the Office of President of the United States, and will to the best of my ability, preserve, protect and defend the Constitution of the United States."

The Presidential Oath of Office
Constitution of the United States - Article 2 , Section I

Chapter 1
The Assassination of Marilyn Monroe

"Everybody is always tugging at you. They'd all like a sort of chunk out of you. I don't think they realize it, but it's like 'grrr do this, grrr do that...' But you do want to stay intact--intact and on two feet."
Marilyn Monroe

Jackie Kennedy was the glamorous new First Lady from Boston high society. Her coming to the White House, not the advent of her husband, heralded the beginning of Camelot. The Camelot label was created when Jackie impressed the idea upon a journalist named Theodore H. White. The President liked to fall asleep listening to the musical score from the Broadway show by the same name. As with many wives, this First Lady instilled in her husband the class and polish that made citizens throughout the world believe this couple represented American royalty. It was the first and last time in American history when the phenomenon would occur. And like most seemingly ideal marriages, there were problems lurking underneath the surface.

Jacqueline Bouvier Kennedy was the majestic daughter of a wealthy French-American businessman. When she met the young congressman from Massachusetts, she was a journalistic photographer. Now, as First Lady, she was playing her self-designated role as national patroness of the arts extraordinaire. Never before had the White House seen such elegance and artistry. The President, however, often found it difficult to pay attention. After one too many instances of clapping at inappropriate times in the middle of a movement, the First Lady arranged to have an aide stand just offstage to let the President know when to applaud.

On this particular morning in August of 1962, Jackie Kennedy left the residence quarters in a hurry. As she strode through the halls of the White House, faster than her characteristically regal gate, her cheeks were flushed, although she had on no makeup. Adrenaline was pumping through her veins. She brushed past Mrs. Lincoln, the President's appointments secretary and the Secret Service agents posted at the door of the Oval Office, then stood in front of her husband, while a dark and foreboding look spread across her face. She passed the agents so quickly, and hit the dual doors to the President's office so hard, that the agents were startled and embarrassed that anyone could get by them in such a way...even the First Lady.

For the past few months, Jackie Kennedy had been absorbed in an ambitious endeavor to renovate the White House. The project was nearing completion. She had recently invited television cameras into the White House to give her fellow

Americans a tour, to see how their tax dollars were being used to restore a national treasure.

"*After all, the government belongs to the people,*" was the statement she used to end the broadcast, which was received around the world with wild enthusiasm.

But at this moment she was on a different kind of crusade – a fight to save her family. In her hand was a love note to the President, written on pink parchment paper, scented with Chanel Number 5. It was signed by Marilyn Monroe, the glamorous Hollywood actress.

"*Jack, I want to know what this is!*" the First Lady exclaimed, in a cracking, high-pitched voice.

"*You know what it is,*" the President replied, "*You have obviously read it.*"

"*You know what I mean, Jack Kennedy, now I want to know precisely what is going on between you and Marilyn Monroe!*"

"*Well, we have seen each other a few times, in the past. But I have told her I will not be seeing her in the future. Bobby can verify that for you.*"

The First Lady's expression and tone changed from anger to disgust, "*Jack, I cannot bear to be with you when everyone knows you have been sneaking around with Marilyn Monroe. I know she was brought to you during the Democratic National Convention on the eve of your nomination, and when you were in New York on presidential business, and that you had several liaisons with her later in Los Angeles and in Palm Beach. I knew she was going to be singing for your birthday party at the Garden, and that's why I didn't attend. Your mother was shocked at Marilyn's behavior, and you seemed to enjoy the spectacle she created that night!*

It's an embarrassment to your administration and to your family, Jack. You should be ashamed! You must get rid of her. Once she is out of your life I will consider whether or not I can forgive you. And by the way, I know that Bobby has been spending a lot of time in Los Angeles as well. You tell Bobby that if he's involved with Marilyn also, I'll go straight to Ethel."

"*Jackie, my dear,*" the President replied, "*I have told Marilyn that I'm putting an end to it, and I have. I am no longer taking her calls, and I am not calling her. So that is that! I'll talk with Bobby, and I can assure you there will be no more problems with Marilyn Monroe.*"

"*That's not all,*" Jackie Kennedy continued, "*I'm leaving today for Italy to visit my sister, and I am taking Caroline and John, Jr. with me. I am sure you will want to invite all your little girlfriends over to play while I am gone. You do so at your own risk. But mark my words; I will not consider returning until I'm convinced that Marilyn Monroe is permanently out of your life.*"

"*Come now, Jackie,*" the President implored, "*…think about how this is going to look to the public. You enjoy being the First Lady. We have to start planning now for the reelection campaign. If you leave now for Italy, it would be embarrassing. Think how it will look.*"

"*Think how it will look, you say!*" Jackie retorted, "*Embarrassing, you say. You should think about how I feel when I hear comments about you with Marilyn Monroe!*

Think of how I feel when I see articles in magazines and newspapers about the two of you. I can't think of anything more embarrassing than that!"

"All right, Jackie, you win," the President conceded. *"I'll speak with Bobby right away, and we will put a stop to this."*

"I thought you said you had already put a stop to it," Jackie replied.

"Well, she is being difficult."

The First Lady turned to leave. *"You'll figure something out, Jack. You always do, and you are a very persuasive man."* She opened the door, stepped through it, then poked her head back in. *"The kids and I will be at my sister's. I'll leave the number where I can be reached in Italy with Mrs. Lincoln. Goodbye, Jack!"* The First Lady slammed the door, hard.

* * * * * * * * * *

The following evening, Robert Kennedy had a highly irregular conversation with his wife. The Attorney General needed a plausible reason for being in California that weekend to deal with the Marilyn Monroe crisis. Time was running out, and this job had to be done in person. The President and Joseph P. Kennedy, Sr. had decided that for appearance's sake, Bobby should take his entire family for a weekend vacation to Northern California. From there, he would shuttle down to Los Angeles via helicopter to oversee the covert operation that had been planned by the CIA on the orders of the President, should its execution become necessary. Breaking the news to Ethel would not be easy, but there was no way around it now. Robert Kennedy decided he needed to pull Ethel out of the house for this conversation. It took place in the backyard of their home in McLean, Virginia, just across the Potomac River from Washington, DC, a few miles from CIA headquarters in Langley, Virginia. It was all about appearances. The perfect home. The perfect wife. The perfect family. The perfect career.

RFK was pacing in front of the large palladium window overlooking the spacious backyard of Hickory Hill, a tumbler of scotch in his hand, when his wife answered his shout to come downstairs. He grabbed her by the hand, then put his forefinger over his lips in a 'shushing' position. The music volume was turned up. Robert Kennedy quickly walked his wife out across the patio and into the backyard.

He began with an apology for his suspicious behavior, *"Ethel, I am sorry to pull you outside away from the kids like this, but we need to have a serious talk."*

"What's the matter, Bobby? I need to get the children to bed!"

"I know, but just give me a couple of minutes, will you? This is really serious here!" The Attorney General motioned for his wife to sit down at the picnic table. He looked deeply into her eyes, in an effort to gain her trust and confidence, both of which were about to take a big hit.

"Okay, but why are we talking outside?" she asked, giving him a sideways glance.

"You know the work I am doing at the Justice Department to fight the Mob?"

"Yes?," the inflection of her response sounding more like a question than an answer.

"Well, I think Jimmy Hoffa or Sam Giancana may have bugged our house!"

Mrs. Kennedy was so startled she jumped up from the table, *"Bobby, you are the Attorney General of the United States!"*

"All the more reason to wire my home."

"What makes you to believe the house is bugged?"

"That's what we need to talk about, Ethel..."

"I'm listening Bobby. You have my attention now!"

"Jack and I are in some serious trouble."

"This is not about Marilyn Monroe, is it?"

"Yes, it is." Robert's head fell.

"Damn it, Bobby, how could you be so stupid!"

Bobby looked up again at his wife, *"You know Jack and I have taken several trips to Los Angeles in the past year."*

"And Palm Beach too, Bobby."

"Yes, and to Palm Beach as well. You see, Jack got tangled up with Marilyn, and he asked me to help him disengage. The only problem was, I ended up having an affair with Marilyn also. But I have since cut off all communication with her..." the Attorney General continued to look into Ethel's eyes, seeking affirmation.

"And what did you expect me to do while you were gallivanting around with Marilyn Monroe? I have been one step away from leaving you, Bobby, for the last several weeks. Have you not seen that I have been crying when you come home from the office? She is a beautiful and seductive woman, Bobby. But you have jeopardized your career and this marriage by carrying on with her like this. Do you think I didn't know? Jackie and I have been grieving in private, wondering for months when you and Jack would come to your senses about fooling around with this woman. Don't think for a minute people don't know that you and Jack have been sleeping with her. So why are we discussing this in our backyard at 8:00 PM, when we should be tucking our kids into bed?"

"I just found out Sam Giancana has audio tapes of me in bed with Marilyn." Bobby's head fell again.

"What? Tell me you are joking!"

"I wish I was joking. But there is more. Jimmy Hoffa has tapes of Jack in bed with Marilyn at Peter's home in Malibu."

"The Lawford mansion is bugged?"

"Apparently so."

"Bobby, we have spent many weekends there, and vacations too! The President has spent a considerable amount of time there. Wait a minute! Your office at the Justice Department must approve all phone taps. How did these get through?"

"All legal wiretaps, Ethel. Everybody is bugging each other. It's out of control. Microphones planted by the Mafia are starting to interfere with bugs planted by the FBI, producing feedback. It has really gotten out of hand."

"I don't believe this!"

"Wait a minute. You haven't heard the worst of it."

"You just told me two of the most notorious Mafiosi in America have tapes of you and your brother having sex with the most famous actress in Hollywood! How could things be any worse than that? I told you your father's escapades with actresses like Gloria Swanson would come back to haunt you someday!"

"Marilyn plans to hold a press conference on Monday, August 6th."

"So, she held one a few days ago and got her movie part back."

"The agenda for this press conference is Jack and me."

"Marilyn Monroe is going before the press to tell them she has been having sex with you and the President?" Ethel walked to the edge of the lit porch, as if searching for unreachable answers. In her anguish, she picked up a globular glass citronella candle container, and smashed it on the brick patio. Glass flew everywhere, and the Attorney General's eyes grew wide at the sight of his wife in such a rage.

"I am afraid so. She has dug her heels in, thinking she can influence me and Jack by disclosing her relationships with us to the media."

"Influence you in what way?" she turned back toward her husband.

"Well, she's upset that Jack and I will no longer return her calls."

"Aaahhh!" she yelled, her arms out-stretched toward heaven, as if she was pleading to God for help. The stress and anguish was starting to overwhelm her. Ethel Kennedy spun on her husband. She wagged her forefinger in front of his face, her eyes squinted and her nostrils flared, "And you won't have anything else to do with her, now that you've confessed the affair to me. Bobby, you will be impeached and run out of office!"

"And so will the President."

"So, as usual, Joe and Jack are having you do the family's dirty work!"

"Ethel, the President should not be involved in this!" Bobby pleaded.

"He's already involved! He created this nightmare! We will have to move to Massachusetts or New York! What are we going to do, Bobby?"

"I need to go to California to talk Marilyn out of this thing before Monday. I'm not sure what the President may have said to her that might compromise national security."

Ethel Kennedy wagged a finger in her husband's face, "If you think I'm going to let you be alone with that woman again, you are crazy!"

"Listen. I have arranged for a friend to invite our entire family to his home in San Francisco for the weekend. He's agreed to say I was there with the family the whole time. We'll take the kids with us. He has planned a bunch of activities for you and for them. It will be fun! I've chartered a private helicopter to take me from Northern California to Los Angeles, and the LAPD will send a couple of detectives over to Marilyn's place with me, so you don't have to worry about me being with her alone."

"Why are the police involved? Has Marilyn committed a crime?"

"Marilyn may be a threat to national security. She's come into some information about operations surrounding Fidel Castro that would seriously damage the country and this administration if the details were disclosed."

"And how, pray tell, did she get access to such classified information?"

"You know, Ethel, don't make me explain it." Robert Kennedy cast his eyes downward again.

"Listen, Bobby, for years I've looked forward to standing beside you on a cold January day as you are sworn in as President of the United States. Until this moment, I've never doubted it would happen. At this rate, you'll be lucky to end up as a state senator. I will stand by you on this, because I love you, and because so much is at stake. But after this weekend, I don't want you to have anything to do with Marilyn Monroe, or any other woman for that matter, or I am gone! I know that Jackie went to Italy. She called me just before she left. Don't think for a minute that I will not leave too if something doesn't change soon. I am going inside now. I've got all our children to tuck in, and it looks like I need to pack them for a trip to California!"

* * * * * * * * * *

August 3rd, 1962 was a sultry Friday evening in the Los Angeles suburb of Brentwood, like most summer evenings there. The sun continued to radiate hues of crimson and salmon outward to the edges of the cirrus clouds of Southern California as it gave up on the day, and sank into the horizon of the Pacific. Earlier that morning, James Files, a Mafia driver and former U.S. Army sniper, drove Sam Giancana's top hit man, Charles Nicoletti, to Palwaukie Airport just outside of Chicago. Nicoletti was catching a private flight to Los Angeles. The sinister and deadly work Nicoletti would be doing with Johnny Roselli in Los Angeles that night would be revisited in Dallas the following year.

U.S. Attorney General Robert Kennedy quietly closed the door of the dark, unmarked sedan, then buttoned his suit jacket with his left hand while tucking his conservative tie inside his coat with the right …trademark Kennedy mannerisms he had subconsciously picked up from his older brother. The Attorney General pushed his bangs away from his forehead with his fingers and crossed the street as the two LAPD detectives stepped out of the car. Robert Kennedy had never felt so conflicted in his life.

Homicide detectives Edwards and Calvert had never been assigned to visit the scene of a murder before the crime had taken place before, either. But when the highest-ranking law enforcement officer in the country suddenly shows up and tells you to get into the car, and your superior officer nods his head, you don't ask too many questions. Robert and his brother had both been seen entering the house of the most famous actress in Hollywood many times before, and this would be no exception. But tonight would be the last time.

Attorney General Kennedy arrived that Friday evening on a mission. President Kennedy had sent his brother to talk Marilyn Monroe out of the press conference she had scheduled for the following Monday. She had just aborted another of her many pregnancies. This time it was under pressure from the Kennedys, after which they had terminated all communication with her. She was going to make her affairs with them known to the public on Monday, during which she would share her diary with the press. The Kennedy Brothers could not allow that to happen. The result would be a swift end, not only to their political careers, but to their marriages as well. In their minds, everything they lived for would come to an abrupt end because of one hysterical movie star. The fact that it was their fault never seemed to enter their minds.

Edwards and Calvert caught up with Bobby Kennedy as he approached the front door. Stepping onto the front porch, something lodged in the wall caught his eye. RFK froze in his tracks.

"What is it, sir?" Detective Edwards inquired.

The Attorney General pointed to an illuminated ceramic tile mounted next to the front door of Marilyn Monroe's bungalow.

"Do you know what that says?" Robert Kennedy inquired.

"I think it's Greek or something," Calvert replied.

Robert Kennedy's face became ashen, "It's Latin," he said flatly, "It says cursum perficio. It means, my course is perfected, or my journey is finished. It's like she has a death wish."

"Well, I just want to get in there and get this over with," detective Edwards replied, "I am trained to solve murders, not plan them. I don't want to be seen by the neighbors."

"All right," Robert Kennedy began to direct them, "While I am having a talk with her, you two figure out how this is going to look like a suicide. Got it?"

The detectives exchanged worried glances. "Got it," said Edwards.

"Yeah, we got it," echoed detective Calvert.

Robert Kennedy stepped to the door and gave his characteristic knock. Marilyn took longer than usual to reach the door. The sedatives her psychiatrist, Dr. Greenson, had given her earlier that day were beginning to take effect.

"Why Bobby!" she exclaimed as she threw the door open, "What brings you all the way here from Washington? You've not been returning my calls! But it sure is nice to see you!" she said with a smile on her face and a squeak in her voice. She reached for the back of his neck, pulled him in to her bosom, and gave the Attorney General a firm kiss. RFK could smell the Chanel on her neck, but he pushed her away and replaced his smile with a stern expression.

"It's great to see you too, Marilyn," he replied, pulling away from her, "but I have something serious to speak with you about. By the way, I would like for you to meet my new Secret Service detail, agents Edwards and Calvert."

"Nice to meet you both!" Marilyn squeaked again, "If you go into the kitchen, Mrs. Murray will fix you some sandwiches. Oh, not that way guys, that's my bedroom! The kitchen is down the hall and to the right."

"Thank you ma'am," Detective Edwards replied. They had already gotten a good look at Marilyn's bedroom.

A few minutes later the detectives were returning from the kitchen when they heard the sounds of Marilyn and Robert raising their voices. As they turned the corner into the living room, Marilyn was waving her diary at Bobby Kennedy.

"Get rid of it, right now!" he yelled at Marilyn as he pointed a finger at her. *"I told you to destroy it several days ago, and you have not done it yet."*

"And why should I?" Marilyn retorted. *"What difference is it going to make? Will you take my phone calls if I do?"*

"Marilyn, you know I can't do that," Robert Kennedy replied, *"My career is at stake here!"*

"Your career?" she shrieked, *"My whole life is at stake here. You promised to marry me, Bobby!"*

Suddenly, the yelling stopped and the combatants turned toward the two men, who had stopped eating their sandwiches, and were now standing in the living room, their mouths open in disbelief at what they had just heard. The detectives quickly retreated back into the kitchen to find Mrs. Murray. It did not take long for the arguing voices to return to a feverish pitch.

After several more minutes, Robert Kennedy entered the kitchen with a frustrated expression on his face.

"Come on guys," he said, *"Let's get out of here."*

As they reached the door, Marilyn intercepted them with a final threat,

"And you tell that almighty brother of yours that he'd better start taking my calls too!"

Detectives Edwards and Calvert followed the Attorney General out to the dark sedan. They got in and quietly drove away. Not a word was spoken in the car. The Attorney General was lost in thought. He stared out the window, focusing on nothing, during the entire drive back to police headquarters.

Upon their return to the LAPD station, RFK entered a small conference room with a secure telephone that had been set up for him by the White House Communications Agency, in cooperation with his office at the Justice Department. It was programmed to dial only one telephone number, and only he knew that number.

"Hello, Mr. President," the Attorney General began, *"She is determined to go ahead with the press conference on Monday."*

The President replied, *"Well, Bobby, then I'm afraid we have no choice. If she goes to the press with this, we can kiss the reelection, our marriages and our political careers goodbye. We have to put the contingency plan into motion tonight. I have spoken with Father, and he agrees. The CIA has developed a plan that will be carried out by Giancana's people in Los Angeles. Johnny Roselli will be the front guy. You need to remain in the area to make sure it gets done right. Then you get out of there as fast as you can."*

Robert Kennedy was desperate, *"Jack, is there something we can do that is not so drastic?"*

The President answered, *"I have been wracking my brain, and it's the only solution I can produce. Damn that Marilyn! She has forced us into this. Doesn't she realize what she is doing? I am sorry, Bobby, I really am. I know you are in love with her."*

"For God's sake, Jack, she had been carrying your child!"

"I know. That's why this has to be done, and quickly. What do you think will happen when she tells the world on Monday what she has been doing with you and me?"

Robert Kennedy replied in a resigned tone, *"Well, we may live to regret this, but I'll get things started. Goodnight, Mr. President."*

"Goodnight, Bobby, and good luck."

About an hour later, Johnny Roselli knocked on Marilyn's door. The actress recognized Roselli from the parties they had attended together at the Lawford residence on Malibu Beach. The Mafia had claimed stakes in Hollywood years before. It was a convenient way for the crime dons to launder large sums of money while mingling with the beautiful people. Thugs, mixing with heroes of the silver screen, each searching for life's meaning while living a life of extremes. The absurdity of it all added to the mystique of Hollywood. Peter Lawford, the handsome and famous actor, a member of the Rat Pack, had married the President's sister, Patricia Kennedy, on April 24, 1954. Lawford often played host to the President and the Attorney General on their frequent visits to Los Angeles. There were certain privileges and responsibilities inherent in being brother-in-law to the President of the United States.

"Good evening, Marilyn," the white haired Roselli intoned.

"Oh, Johnny, it's so wonderful to see you! Please come in and have some tea. I will have Mrs. Murray make some tea for us. I am feeling very sleepy for some reason. Perhaps some caffeinated tea will perk me up."

Roselli noted that the sedatives given to her by Dr. Greenson were making Marilyn drowsy. Her eyes and her speech gave her away. Roselli watched her movements carefully. She was using her bedroom voice now. Not for effect, but because she was now uncontrollably sleepy. Her eyes would close occasionally then fly open again as she conversed with him. Marilyn was struggling to stay awake.

She proceeded to tell Roselli how upset she was with the Kennedy brothers, and how she was about to get even with them. To Marilyn, Jack and Bobby Kennedy were not two separate men, but a monster with two heads. Just one more demon in her life that had used her, wanting only temporal pleasure and not interested in building the family life she so desired. Roselli and Marilyn were chatting on the living room couch about 15 minutes later when Charles Nicoletti burst through the door at the pre-established time. Roselli grabbed Marilyn tightly in his arms from behind while Nicoletti took a cloth saturated with chloroform out of a plastic bag. He pressed it tightly over her nose and mouth. Marilyn did not struggle for long. Philip Alderisio, also known as, 'Milwaukee Phil,' entered close behind Nicoletti. Nicoletti and Alderisio had teamed up on several previous hits. Alderisio was carrying a thermos bottle containing a solution of Nembutal and chloral hydrate. Based upon the volume and concentration of the liquids, there was enough barbiturate in that thermos bottle to kill ten people.

The mobsters carried Marilyn's unconscious body to the guesthouse located behind the main residence. They stripped her naked, laying her face down on the guest bed.

"Our instructions say to hold her down with her ankles together," Roselli ordered. *"Be sure to keep her face down."*

Nicoletti and Milwaukee Phil worked together to fill a condom with the deadly solution while Roselli held Marilyn's unconscious body down on the bed. They lubricated the condom with petroleum jelly, then inserted a plastic penis into it, causing the end of the condom to swell with pressure from the lethal fluid. They then pricked the condom several times with a needle, which created small geysers of the liquid that sprayed in several directions. They quickly inserted the deadly condom into the rectum of the famous actress, and shoved the penis up as far as they could into her body. Marilyn Monroe would absorb the barbiturate-laden solution in a matter of minutes. Using this method of poisoning would provide a plausible explanation of suicide. But Marilyn refused to die.

Marilyn's psychiatrist, Dr. Greenson, who had given her the oral sedatives earlier in the evening, was standing by. As the poison moved from Marilyn's rectum through her colon and into her bloodstream, Greenson and the mobsters collected the supplies of Nembutal and chloral hydrate pills that were stored in Marilyn's medicine cabinet. Following instructions provided by the CIA's scientists in Schenectady, New York, they emptied the prescription containers into disposal bags for removal from the house, placing the empty pill bottles on the bedside table in Marilyn's bedroom. Dr. Greenson checked Marilyn's vital signs. As the oxygen in Marilyn's blood neared exhaustion, her life began to ebb away. Greenson yelled, *"Everyone out, right now!"* Marilyn's housekeeper, Mrs. Murray, was known to give Marilyn an occasional 'dietary' enema. Acting on orders from Dr. Greenson, Mrs. Murray had given Marilyn an enema on the night she died, which cleared out her rectum, accelerating the absorption rate of the barbiturates into her blood. Greenson had convinced Marilyn to hire Mrs. Murray as her housekeeper in November of 1961. From the beginning, Marilyn had not trusted her.

Monroe had told friends that she would, *"...get rid of the spy who is living in my house."* Mrs. Murray's son-in-law, Norman Jeffries, was visiting her at Marilyn's house that night. He was a witness to the events of that evening.

* * * * * * * * * *

Robert Kennedy appeared at the house again, later that night, accompanied by detectives Edwards and Calvert. The Attorney General made it clear that Murray and Jeffries were to vacate the house immediately. Mrs. Murray and her son-in-law went to a friend's house nearby. When Mrs. Murray and Norman Jeffries saw Robert Kennedy leave with the two detectives for the second time that evening, they made their way across the courtyard, through the open gates. As they approached the guesthouse, they saw Marilyn's body through the open door. Her nude, seemingly lifeless body was stretched across the daybed. According to Jeffries, her breathing appeared to have ceased, and her skin was turning dark blue. *"It did not look good,"* he recalled later.

More than an hour passed before Mrs. Murray made a call to the Schaeffer Ambulance Company regarding, *"...a private emergency"* Mrs. Murray was taking her time, and did not want to draw the attention of the neighbors. No sirens or flashing lights were to be used. However, several neighbors did witness the strange comings and goings of that night. Within a few minutes of receiving the call, James E. Hall of the Schaeffer Ambulance Company pulled into Marilyn's driveway. Riding in the ambulance with him that night was another Schaeffer Ambulance employee, Murray Liebowitz.

As soon as they stepped out of the ambulance, they were met by a woman in the front yard. She was screaming hysterically, *"She's dead, she's dead! I think she took some pills!"* This was Patricia Newcomb, Marilyn's publicist. For several minutes, Newcomb hampered the attempt to save Marilyn's life by trying to climb over the medical technicians to get to her. Finally, Hall noticed that a man with a familiar face appeared, placed his arm around Newcomb, and, *"...calmed her right down."* That man was Peter Lawford, brother-in-law to the Kennedys. The Kennedy brothers had attended many parties at Lawford's mansion on Malibu beach. It was the perfect safe house for an occasional rendezvous with Marilyn Monroe. Jack and Bobby had taken turns.

At first, Hall was shocked to see the naked body of the most famous actress in Hollywood, splayed face down across the daybed in the guesthouse. But as soon as Hall said, *"Oh my God, it's Marilyn Monroe,"* then he realized he had a patient in critical condition and he needed to move fast. Hall noticed that Marilyn did not demonstrate the characteristic breath odor, or the white pasty substance that usually surrounds the mouth of an oral drug overdose victim. Hall inserted a breathing tube into Marilyn's throat, and began to breathe air into her oxygen-depleted lungs. Although she was in a deep, barbiturate-induced fog, Marilyn still had some fight left in her. She began to respond, her color improving. Hall then removed the breathing tube, and began to give Marilyn mouth-to-mouth resuscitation. Hall felt relieved and encouraged as Marilyn's vital signs and color continued to show progress.

It was at this moment that a man appeared, with dark circles around his eyes, carrying a large black doctor's bag. *"I am Marilyn's doctor. Give her positive pressure,"* the man said. Indeed, it was her psychiatrist, Dr. Greenson. Hall stopped breathing life back into Marilyn, and started to massage the heart, as Dr. Greenson had ordered. Hall doubted whether heart massage was indicated since the increased blood flow would speed the distribution of poison throughout Marilyn's body. Then Hall watched in disbelief as the psychiatrist reached into the doctor's bag, extracting a heart syringe, with a long heart needle already in place. But this syringe was not filled with adrenaline, used to stimulate the heart. Instead, it contained a solution of Nembutal and chloral hydrate; barbiturates intended to stop the heart from beating.

'*Psychiatrists don't carry around doctor bags with heart syringes,*' Hall thought to himself. Greenson ordered Hall to step aside, saying, "*I'm supposed to make a show out of this.*" Greenson counted five ribs down from Marilyn's collarbone, pushed her breast aside, and drove the needle into her chest. But since Greenson had never performed this procedure, he had the wrong entry point and the wrong angle. The needle stopped abruptly upon impact with one of Marilyn's ribs. The CIA's instructions to Greenson said there could be only one needle mark in her chest, so instead of backing the needle out, Hall's disbelief turned to horror as Greenson leaned on the needle, broke Marilyn's rib with a snap, and drove the barbiturate filled needle into her heart. Dr. Greenson immediately pronounced the death of Marilyn Monroe. Hall and Liebowitz were instructed to take their empty ambulance back to their offices. They could not believe they had just witnessed a murder – the murder of the most famous actress in Hollywood.

Marilyn's dead body was then moved from the guesthouse to her bedroom at the opposite end of the house. During the hour between Marilyn's death and the first official call to the LAPD, a swarm of detectives had descended upon the house. The Chief of Intelligence for the LAPD was present in Marilyn's home that night, orchestrating the cover-up. They decided upon the 'official' story that Marilyn had locked herself in her room to commit suicide. The LAPD staged the death scene in Marilyn's bedroom, wiped the entire house clean of fingerprints, and then left as quickly as they had entered.

On the night Marilyn Monroe died, a police cruiser stopped a car as it hurtled away from Los Angeles toward a private airfield used by small, fixed-wing aircraft and helicopters. When the officer stepped to the car window, he leaned in to see not only Peter Lawford, the actor, but also the Attorney General of the United States! No speeding ticket was issued on that traffic stop, and the Attorney General declined the officer's offer of a police escort to the airfield. The escaping conspirators did not want to draw any attention. The cop was dismissed with instructions to omit the traffic stop from his daily report.

* * * * * * * * * *

When the call was made to the officer on duty at 4:25 AM, Marilyn Monroe had been dead for over one hour. Sergeant Jack Clemmons took the call. Clemmons proceeded directly to Marilyn's home. Many years later, a videotape was made of Clemmons telling his recollections of the night Marilyn Monroe was killed.

When Sergeant Clemmons arrived at the address in Brentwood, Marilyn's naked body was on the bed, not in the guestroom, but in her own bedroom at the opposite end of the house. Clemmons was troubled by several aspects of the crime scene – certain items were out of place, and did not look right to him. Marilyn's body was lying face down on the bed, with her hands at her sides. According to Sergeant Clemmons, *"She was in a soldier position, standing at attention, only she was face down on her bed."*

Her friends said she always slept in the nude, on her back with the covers up to her neck. Those who were close to Marilyn knew she would not sleep in such an awkward position. Sufficient time had passed after her death for gravity to pull Marilyn's blood down into her face and chest area. This dark blue lividity would hide the needle mark in her chest.

When a person's dies, and the heart stops pumping, all available blood flows downward to the lowest point of the body. Gravity pulls the blood down, causing it to pool, creating visible bluish-purple stains. Lividity does not begin until three hours after the time of death, and since internal blood dries at approximately twelve hours after time of death, an investigator must look for the lividity effects during that period. When Clemmons pressed his finger on the bluish areas, the blood flowed away from the depression, and her skin changed to its natural color. Had the discoloration been a bruise, blood released from the broken blood vessels would have had no where to flow, and Marilyn's skin color would have remained the bluish color. So Clemmons knew she had died facing downward.

Had Marilyn been lying on her back in her normal sleep position, the drugs would not have penetrated so deeply into her body, and the puncture mark caused by the needle would have been visible.

Although it was before 5:00 AM on Sunday morning, Clemmons noticed that Mrs. Murray was washing sheets from the guestroom bed. A rather odd behavior at that hour, he thought, considering that her employer had just died. That is, unless you knew that Marilyn had been given several lethal doses of liquid drugs via her rectum the night before, while sprawled across the guest bed. Those bedclothes contained evidence of the crime, such as Nembutal, chloral hydrate, and Marilyn's urine and fecal material. Marilyn had defecated, in spite of the preemptive enema, which was how she had fought so long to stay alive. Forensic analysis of the sheets would have proven that rectal poisoning had occurred in the guesthouse the night before, and Mrs. Murray was busy before 5:00 A.M., destroying critical evidence of the murder.

Dr. Greenson explained to Officer Clemmons that Marilyn had locked her door when she went to bed that night. Mrs. Murray testified she could see that the light remained on in Marilyn's room late into the night. When it was pointed out to Mrs. Murray that the carpet was too thick to allow the passage of light, Mrs. Murray changed her testimony and said she saw the telephone cord pulled into Marilyn's room. A detective who interviewed Mrs. Murray noted that her behavior during the interview was *"evasive."* Greenson claimed he had to break Marilyn's window to gain access to her bedroom. But Marilyn's friends and private investigators noted that most of the broken glass from the window was lying on the ground outside her bedroom, indicating the window had been broken from the inside.

Standing in Marilyn's bedroom, while her lifeless body lay on the bed, Greenson said while making a sweeping motion with his arm, *"She must have taken all these pills."*

Officer Clemmons noted there was no water glass on the table next to the empty pill containers. Greenson's gestures seemed cold and rehearsed, considering the circumstances. What bothered Officer Clemmons most was Greenson's strange facial expression during the entire interview. It was a pained look - the expression of a man who was under extreme stress.

* * * * * * * * * *

A few days later, Marilyn's friends gathered to pay homage to an urn filled with Marilyn's remains, which had been reduced to ashes. Included in the congregation were two of her former husbands: Arthur Miller, the celebrated playwright, and Joe DiMaggio, the famous baseball player. Although they had been married for only ten months, DiMaggio honored his former wife for twenty years by sending flowers and making visits to the mausoleum where her urn was placed on the day of her funeral.

The crowd gathered at the Corridor of Memories at Westwood Memorial Park in Los Angeles, and listened to the words of Lee Strasberg, Marilyn's acting teacher, as he delivered the eulogy;

"Marilyn Monroe was a legend. In her own lifetime she created a myth of what a poor girl from a deprived background could attain. For the entire world she became a symbol of the eternal feminine. But I have no words to describe the myth and the legend. Nor would she want us to do so. I did not know this Marilyn Monroe, nor did she.

We, gathered here today, know only Marilyn - a warm human being, impulsive and shy and lonely, sensitive and in fear of rejection, yet ever avid for life and reaching out for fulfillment. I will not insult the privacy of your memory of her - a privacy she sought and treasured - by trying to describe her whom you know, to you who knew her. In our memories of her, she remains alive, not only a shadow on a screen, or a glamorous personality.

For us, Marilyn was a devoted and loyal friend, a colleague constantly reaching for perfection. We shared her pain and difficulties and some of her joys. She was a member of our family. It is difficult to accept the fact that her zest for life has been ended by this dreadful accident.

Despite the heights and brilliance she had attained on the screen, she was planning for the future; she was looking forward to participating in the many exciting things which she had planned. In her eyes and in mine, her career was just beginning. The dream of her talent, which she had nurtured as a child, was not a mirage. When she first came to me, I was amazed at the startling sensitivity which she possessed and which remained fresh and undimmed, struggling to express itself despite the life to which she had been subjected. Others were as physically beautiful as she was, but there was obviously something more in her, something that people saw and recognized in her performances and with which they identified.

She had a luminous quality - a combination of wistfulness, radiance, yearning -that set her apart and yet made everyone wish to be part of it, to share in the childish naiveté which was at once so shy and yet so vibrant.

This quality was even more evident when she was on the stage. I am truly sorry that you and the public who loved her did not have the opportunity to see her as we did, in many of the roles that foreshadowed what she would have become. Without a doubt, she would have been one of the really great actresses of the stage.

Now it is all at an end. I hope that her death will stir sympathy and understanding for a sensitive artist and woman who brought joy and pleasure to the world. I cannot say goodbye. Marilyn never liked goodbyes, but in that peculiar way she had of turning things around so that they faced reality - I will say au revoir. For the country to which she has gone, we must all someday visit."

Less than one week after Marilyn's funeral ceremony, President Kennedy took a small group of family and friends sailing off the coast of Maine. A beaming President Kennedy was at the helm. Sitting directly next to the President on his right was Pat Newcomb, Marilyn's publicist, wearing the President's jacket displaying the presidential seal. Soon thereafter, Pat Newcomb and Mrs. Murray the nurse left for Europe on separate itineraries. When Patricia Newcomb returned from Europe, she started work at her new job, working as a public affairs specialist for the United States Government in Washington, D.C.

Marilyn Monroe had taken on the President of the United States, just as she had taken on her employer. She intended to embarrass the Kennedy brothers by holding a press conference, during which she would disclose her diary and the details of her affairs with John Kennedy and Robert Kennedy. But the ploy failed in this case, and the cost to Marilyn was her life.

Years later, Peter Lawford was asked by his former wife, Deborah Gould, how Marilyn had died. Jack and Bobby Kennedy's brother in law, who was at Marilyn Monroe's house on the night of her murder, said, *"Let's just say, Marilyn took her last big enema."*

Chapter 2
Absence of Evidence

Henry Atherton awoke in his Manhattan apartment at 3:00 A.M. His body, bed sheets and boxer shorts were drenched in sweat. A successful investigative reporter for the *New York Tribune*, Atherton was a multi-year recipient of the *Best Investigative Reporter* award bestowed annually by the National Reporters Guild. Atherton's reputation had been built upon his unique ability to tap sources and locate evidence that eluded other investigative reporters. He did not hesitate to air his controversial views regarding senior politicos in his articles and his opinion and editorial features. Through the years Atherton had secured many exclusive interviews with key witnesses regarding high-profile scandals in the political arena. The alleged suicide of actress Marilyn Monroe had grabbed his attention immediately. Hollywood was not his beat, but there had been rumors of Marilyn having liaisons with political players in Washington. High-level politicians were fair game for any reporter, and there had been numerous sightings of the President and his brother, the Attorney General in Los Angeles. Approximately one month had passed, and the story of Marilyn Monroe's suicide was headed for the history books without a challenge.

But after studying reports of Monroe's death, a disturbing pattern had emerged. Regardless of the source, every depiction Atherton encountered was disturbingly similar. Monroe had locked herself in her bedroom, taken too many pills, and did not wake up in the morning. No variations to the theme. It was as if someone had gone to great lengths to keep the story consistent. After poring over official reports and news articles for several nights, Atherton had dreamed a different version of Monroe's death, and then found himself wide awake, drenched in sweat at 3:00 AM. But the dream was too terrifying to believe. Atherton was so shaken that it was futile to attempt getting more sleep. The dream was so vivid, so real! Atherton took a shower, and then recorded the major elements of his dream while downing a cup of hot coffee.

Atherton had not adjusted well since Andrea had left. He did not realize the degree to which he depended upon her, or the degree to which he had taken her for granted. Henry had always found it easy to lose himself in an investigation. His total absorption earned him the highest praises from his peers, and likewise, had recently cost him his marriage. Thoughts of Andrea were crowding his mind, and his grief over the loss was making it difficult to concentrate on his present case. The dream of the previous night continued to haunt Atherton. After skipping breakfast, he headed out to the gym for a workout, arriving early at the office.

By late that afternoon Atherton had decided what he must do. *"I am flying to L.A. tomorrow to investigate Marilyn Monroe's death,"* Atherton called out to Charlie Montrose, his editor, as he headed for the elevator.

"Why are you going to Los Angeles? Monroe's death was a suicide, plain and simple!" Montrose griped as Atherton bolted past him.

"If I believed everything that was in the press, I wouldn't be able to make a living, would I?" yelled Atherton.

"Well, you've got me there. Hurry back so that I can get you to do some real reporting. Keep me posted, okay?"

* * * * * * * * * *

Marilyn Monroe's autopsy was performed in Los Angeles by Dr. Thomas Noguchi. When Noguchi made the standard "Y" incision in Marilyn's chest, opening the chest cavity for the inspection and removal of vital organs, the injection mark created when Dr. Greenson drove the needle into Marilyn's heart was destroyed. This was intended by the assassination planning team at the CIA lab in New York. The autopsy notes showed no indication of a broken rib. Noguchi's examination results stated the presence of only 20 cc's of water in the stomach, and no residue of food, pills, or capsules of any kind. But Marilyn had enough drugs in her system to kill five people!

A spokeswoman for Abbott Laboratories, the manufacturer of Nembutal, said Marilyn would have had to take 75 to 90 capsules to achieve the toxicity levels that were in her bloodstream.

"That's just not possible," the spokeswoman for the drug company had said.

Atherton interviewed a psychiatrist at UCLA, who said, *"She would have been unconscious before she could ingest the amount needed to achieve that degree of barbiturates in her bloodstream."*

Atherton wanted to know why there was no residue of pills or capsules in her stomach. *'How could she have swallowed all those pills while in bed if there was no water glass by her bedside?'* Atherton wondered. *'Marilyn's stomach contained very little water.'*

The following afternoon, Henry Atherton sat waiting for an hour beyond his appointed time to interview Dr. Noguchi. He was about to leave the office when the disheveled doctor came out of his meeting with a group of men wearing dark suits. To Atherton, these men appeared to have the expressionless faces of agents for either the Secret Service, or the FBI. He had seen the look many times before.

"I am so sorry to have kept you waiting, Mr. Atherton," Dr. Noguchi apologized, *"What does the* New York Tribune *want to know about a suicide in Los Angeles?"*

Atherton replied, *"Marilyn Monroe was the most famous actress in Hollywood, and there were rumors of liaisons with the President of the United States and the Attorney General. That makes it a national news story."*

The visitors looked somber. Their expressions did not change during the entire conversation.

Noguchi shot back, *"Now, Mr. Atherton, I am the coroner for Orange County. I would not know about such things. You might want to talk to the gossip columnists."*

To that Henry Atherton replied, *"I tend not to believe what members of the press say or write unless I can corroborate their information. Well, good doctor, I have been waiting for some time now. Can we meet alone in your office? Then I will be on my way."*

Noguchi said goodbye to his visitors, led Atherton to his office, then settled into a leather chair behind his mahogany desk while Atherton consulted his notes. The most bizarre interview of Atherton's career began.

Atherton opened with, *"Dr. Noguchi, there was a notation scratched in the margin of the autopsy report, possibly written after the fact, that states, 'No nacelle marks.'"*

"That means there were no needle marks found on the body," commented Noguchi, letting pass the implication that he had altered the autopsy report.

"I interviewed Mr. Hall, the ambulance driver, who says Dr. Greenson drove a needle, that was probably filled with barbiturates, into Marilyn's heart shortly before midnight," countered Atherton. *"He said Greenson broke one of her ribs in the process. There was no mention of a broken rib in your autopsy report."*

The doctor replied in a calm tone, *"The ambulance driver is lying. He must be one of those opportunists who wants to sell a fabricated story to the tabloids."*

To that Atherton replied, sternly, *"I would like to be given access to photos of the body prior to the autopsy."*

Noguchi locked his gaze on Atherton, *"I am afraid that would be impossible. There were no photos, and furthermore, the body has been cremated."*

"What? How can that be?" Atherton exclaimed, *"Marilyn had purchased a burial site for a casket here in Hollywood! Her former husbands have each told me she wanted a traditional burial in a casket!"* Atherton began to backpedal, *"Well, certainly you took samples of the liver, kidneys and stomach for conducting toxicological studies! And what about the diary Marilyn kept?"*

Noguchi rubbed his eyes, *"I was very disturbed to learn yesterday that the organ slides and the diary were stolen from our vault here in the coroner's office."*

Atherton queried, *"How many keys exist for that vault?"*

"Only three...," Noguchi answered, *"...and I carry one of them."*

* * * * * * * * *

The Los Angeles Coroner's Aide, Lionel Grandison, phoned Atherton several days later, saying they should meet to discuss concerns about how the coroner's office handled Marilyn's autopsy. Grandison did not want to discuss that subject on the phone, so they arranged to meet at an outdoor café.

"How was your meeting with Dr. Noguchi?" Grandison began.

"Frustrating and upsetting, to say the least," Atherton replied.

"Why was it upsetting?"

"The doctor told me that organ samples and Marilyn's diary have gone missing, after they had been locked in the coroner's office safe! I have been in this business a long time, and I have never heard of such inept behavior by a coroner's office."

"What if it wasn't ineptitude, but obstruction of justice?" Grandison asked.

"What do you mean?"

"At first, I refused to sign the autopsy certificate for Marilyn Monroe. I was shocked by the fraudulent handling of the autopsy evidence and the paperwork in this case. There were too many inconsistencies and obvious violations of autopsy procedure. I didn't want to be a party to it. I wanted you to know this. But because I am putting my job in jeopardy by speaking with you, this conversation will be the extent to which I can help you. I wish you the best of luck in finding out the truth in this case. Just be careful."

"Thanks, I appreciate the information and your concern," Atherton replied.

With that, Grandison rose from the table and strode away from Atherton, blending quickly with the sidewalk traffic. Atherton was starting to believe that his dream about Marilyn's death was closer to reality than the official story.

* * * * * * * * *

Several days later, Atherton met with Jim Walston, who worked for the Schaeffer Ambulance Company. Walston was a Marilyn Monroe fan who had concerns about the way his company had handled its reports on the night of Marilyn's death.

"I am responsible for central dispatch," Walston said. "One of my duties is to log in all calls and communications with our ambulances. Within a few days of Marilyn's death, I noticed the log book for that night had been rewritten. It was not in my handwriting, and the only change I could see was that it portrayed fewer visits to Marilyn's house than actually occurred. No one will discuss it with me, and I have been told not to ask again. I don't like it at all."

"What do you think it means?" asked Atherton.

"I think it means that Marilyn did not commit suicide. Why else would logbooks be doctored? Hall's partner on that night, Murray Lieberman, told me that he had come into a large sum of money soon after Marilyn's death. He said it was hush money. Lieberman also told me that he owns several car washes in Los Angeles, and only maintains his job with Schaeffer as a cover. Something's not right here, Mr. Atherton."

"It sure seems that way, doesn't it?"

The following day Atherton placed a call to Mrs. Murray, the nurse who had been hired by Dr. Greenson. "Hello, Mrs. Murray, my name is Henry Atherton with the New York Tribune."

"I know who you are," came the guarded reply.

"I would like to ask you a few questions about what happened on the night of Marilyn's death."

"I am not supposed to talk to you," Murray answered abruptly.

"It's a free country, Mrs. Murray. The Constitution guarantees your right to freedom of speech."

"I don't give a damn about that. I care about being able to live in peace, and staying alive, for that matter!"

"Mrs. Murray, there are those who believe that Marilyn Monroe did not commit suicide. You were there that night. What do you think really happened?"

"I am weary of having to keep my story straight, Mr. Atherton. I don't want to talk about this anymore, so don't call me again. Goodbye!" The phone line went dead.

* * * * * * * * * *

For several days, Henry Atherton filed brief, mundane articles focusing on the death of Marilyn Monroe. He had cracked so many big cases in the past, his following waited anxiously to learn what Atherton would do for an encore. It seemed to the reporter that the public's appetite for crime and corruption was insatiable. Their desire for blood had drained the life and passion from Atherton's marriage. He did not have the energy to sustain both. He had vowed to himself his next marriage would be more balanced; his wife would know she was his priority, not the next hot story. But readers could tell the mighty Henry Atherton was being stonewalled in Los Angeles. He had little new information to report.

Then Charlie Montrose relayed a phone call. *"Henry, you definitely need to meet with this guy,"* Montrose implored.

"What's the big deal, Charlie?" Atherton asked. *"I've got my hands full here, and nothing is panning out."*

Montrose said curtly, *"I don't want to discuss this over the phone. Just meet with him!"*

The following day Henry met John at LAX airport. John had flown to L.A. from upstate New York, wanting to be as far from New York as possible when he told his story. John asked if they could sit in the noisiest part of the airport for their conversation. Atherton said he usually looked for quiet spots, but conceded, since John seemed agitated. Even so, a CIA counter-intelligence agent had followed John from the TOP SECRET facility, and was sitting nearby in the airport during the interview.

Atherton opened, *"Thank you for coming all this way. It's obvious you have something important to tell me. Is it about Marilyn Monroe?"*

John then told Atherton his story, *"I am a physicist who works in a laboratory, run by a contractor for the CIA in upstate New York. The lab employs America's brightest scientists who produce devices and plans to assassinate foreign leaders, like Fidel Castro. They are patriots who believe they are helping America fight communism.*

But some recent events in the lab have caused great concern. I was told about the plan to kill Marilyn Monroe, two weeks after she died! It must have been developed in a hurry. My associate who saw the plan said the document was dated two days before Marilyn's death, it looked very official, and was marked, CLASSIFIED.

My colleague told me the plan to kill Marilyn Monroe said;

Get liquid barbiturates, must be Nembutal and chloral hydrate,
Mix with a small amount of water,
Pour liquid into condom and lubricate,
Pierce several holes in the condom,
Shove it up her ass!
No autopsy...
If rectal poisoning fails use heart syringe filled with same solution
Insert syringe between ribs 5 and 6, directly into the heart.
No more than one needle mark!

The CIA made arrangements with the Mafia to carry out the murder plot, so the Agency could deny involvement. I was shocked when I heard this because Marilyn had died just two weeks before! I thought her death had been a suicide! I am endangering my life by giving you this information," John warned.

"Then why are you doing it?" Henry asked.

"Because my friends and I signed up to fight communism, not to kill innocent Americans," John replied. *"There is just one thing. I cannot be named as a source for this information. If you mention my name to anyone, I will deny ever having contact with you. Furthermore, you cannot print what I have just told you."*

"What are you saying" Atherton complained. *"You drop a hot story into my lap and then you tell me I can't print it?"*

"You have to look at this from my perspective," John replied, *"I am sorry, but this is the way it has to be. If you print this, they will identify your sources and people will die. You must find another way to corroborate my story."*

Stunned, Atherton thanked John for the meeting, and then hustled to his hotel. Sitting in the back of the cab, the reporter stared blankly out the window as his mind wandered, *"Why was the CIA involved? Why would the CIA want to kill an actress? Who would have issued such an order? Would the CIA cooperate with members of organized crime?"* Upon reaching the hotel, Atherton's head ached, so his first stop was the lobby bar.

When Henry returned to New York City several days later, he felt as though he had been defeated for the first time in his career. *"Atherton won't be winning any journalism awards for cracking the Marilyn Monroe case,"* he thought.

As he entered the lobby of his apartment building, the concierge called out,

"Mr. Atherton, this package was in today's mail, but it's too large to fit into your mailbox."

"Thanks, Edward," Atherton said as he tipped the concierge. The postmark showed that the envelope was mailed by John from Schenectady, in upstate New York. Atherton opened it, and scanned the documents.

"Unbelievable!" he exclaimed, as he raced up the stairs, rather than waiting for the elevator. After reading the contents thoroughly, Atherton ran the documents through his shredder. John was cooperating by sending corroborating materials, despite what he had said about his own safety. Apparently, John's desire for his countrymen to know the truth about the wrong doings of their Government was stronger than his sense of self-preservation.

* * * * * * * * * *

Andrea Atherton, an assistant district attorney in New York City, had accepted Henry's invitation to dinner that evening. When they met at Princeton, Henry was studying English, and Andrea, Psychology. Shortly after their marriage, Andrea was accepted to law school, and everyone wondered what Henry was going to do with a degree in English. Although Henry invited Andrea to dinner on short notice, she accepted since she had no other plans, but she dare not disclose that to Henry.

Her former husband rose to greet her, *"Andrea, you look lovely this evening!"*

"Thank you Henry," she replied, *"You on the other hand, don't look so good."*

"My trip to L.A. was a frustrating experience, to say the least."

"So what did you learn in Los Angeles?"

Henry replied in a hushed voice, *"I learned there is such a thing as the perfect crime."*

Andrea chided, *"Henry, every crime leaves behind a trail of evidence. You know that!"*

Atherton scanned the restaurant to see if anyone was paying particular attention to their conversation, *"Yes, but what if the perpetrators have the power and the ability to suppress and destroy that evidence?"*

Andrea raised an eyebrow. Giving Henry a stern look, she asked, *"And just who are these people who you claim are above the law?"*

Henry replied in a stern, yet quiet voice, *"Those who make and enforce the laws."*

"What?" Andrea almost shouted in disbelief. She lowered her voice and uttered through clenched teeth, *"Henry Atherton, are you saying that Marilyn Monroe was killed by elected officials or by law enforcement officers?"*

Henry's face fell, and then he looked around the room again. *"Andrea, please keep your voice down. I don't like the way that waiter keeps looking over here. I am sorry to say it, but I believe she was killed by both, with an assist from the Mob. It's the only conclusion that makes sense."*

"Henry, you are talking crazy! By the way, that waiter just wants to know if we are ready to place our order."

"I know it seems crazy, but it's what I believe," Henry replied.

"And just what kind of evidence do you have to substantiate such a claim?"

"That's just it, Andrea. I don't have one shred of evidence." Henry just knew that bit of information would convince his former wife, the attorney. "That's what makes me believe _they_ did it."

"Okay, so you are going to write an article about elected officials conspiring with the Mafia to kill Marilyn Monroe, and you think the cops in L.A. are corrupt. Good luck getting that one published. Henry, you look so tired. I am concerned about your job. When was the last time you checked in with Montrose?"

Henry scoffed, "Ahh, don't worry about Charlie, he knows what I'm doing."

Andrea pressed the point, "Oh really? When was the last time you spoke with him?"

"He doesn't make me check in with him, Andrea. Charlie is okay as long as I file my stories before deadline, which I have been doing."

Andrea's voice took on a more motherly tone, "Henry, I strongly advise you to see a counselor."

"You advised that during our marriage, and I never went. What makes you think I will go now?"

"You just seem to be under tremendous stress right now. Perhaps a few sessions with a therapist would give you some peace."

"Well, okay, I will give it some thought. Now, if you are ready to stop therapizing me, how about we just engage in idle chat until our dinner arrives? I'll wave that sinister looking waiter over here now, okay?"

"All right Henry, I just worry about you sometimes, that's all. I hope the lamb is as good as you say."

Chapter 3
The Kennedy Era

Henry Atherton was fascinated with John Kennedy, this seemingly youthful president with the perpetual tan, who was elected based on promises to make sweeping social changes in America, and to reduce tensions with the other nuclear superpower, the Soviet Union. Henry agreed with many of Kennedy's ideas, but he believed there were powerful forces arrayed against the Kennedy Brothers. There was a strength and determination in JFK's personality, which was most prominently displayed during his speeches.

Few Americans knew the President usually wore a back brace, that he suffered from Addison's disease, a degenerating condition of the adrenal glands, and that the famous padded Kennedy rocker was the only chair in which JFK could sit without suffering acute pain. He took daily doses of painkillers and steroids. His back pain was so severe that he often found it unbearable to walk up the steps of Air Force One. A mobile service elevator was staged at Andrews Air Force Base in Maryland. It traveled with the President so he could be hoisted to the top step of the ladder used for boarding Air Force One. Photographers were asked not to photograph this procedure, as it might send a message to the people that their President was not a strong man, able to carry the burdens of the presidency on his shoulders. One photographer disregarded this request, capturing and image of the President being lifted to the entrance of Air Force One.

Franklin Delano Roosevelt had successfully camouflaged his polio, and most Americans were not aware of his paralytic condition. This was only because television was not prevalent during his four terms in the White House. It was the famous presidential debate between JFK and Richard Nixon that ushered in the powerful visual medium of television that would forever change political strategy and presidential politics.

On the return flight to New York from Los Angeles, Atherton reviewed Kennedy's inauguration speech, which the young president gave on that cold, snowy day in Washington, D.C.;

"The world is very different now. For man holds in his mortal hands the power to abolish all forms of human poverty and all forms of human life. And yet the same revolutionary beliefs for which our forbearers fought are still at issue around the globe - the belief that the rights of man come not from the generosity of the state, but from the hand of God.

We dare not forget today that we are the heirs of that first revolution. Let the word go forth from this time and place, to friend and foe alike, that the torch has been passed to a new generation of Americans - born in this century,

tempered by war, disciplined by a hard and bitter peace, proud of our ancient heritage - and unwilling to witness or permit, the slow undoing of those human rights, to which this nation has always been committed, and to which we are committed today, at home and around the world."
President John Kennedy, Inauguration Day, 1961

When the Kennedys moved into the White House, it was a time of celebration throughout the United States, and around the globe. Preceding administrations had built up a military industrial establishment of unprecedented lethality. This was the height of the Cold War. If unleashed, the nuclear weapons of Russia and the United States could destroy all life on Earth. The planet would be a nuclear wasteland.

But Jack and Jackie Kennedy were symbols of a new era. Kennedy was taking steps to reverse the massive arms buildup, and reducing tensions between the superpowers. In June of 1963 he had a bright red telephone, called the hotline, installed on his desk to contact only one person, the Soviet Premier. Kennedy and Khrushchev agreed that in the event of an unauthorized nuclear missile launch, one could immediately contact the other to coordinate its destruction, and to avoid a nuclear holocaust. The President was also reaching out to civil rights leaders like Dr. Martin Luther King, Jr. He promised the American people that 1,000 soldiers would return home from Vietnam by Christmas. Kennedy issued National Security Action Memorandum number 263 to put that plan into motion. America would not be putting citizens' lives at risk in what French President General Charles de Gaulle told Kennedy, was the *"quagmire"* of Vietnam.

Henry liked the philosophy of this new President. Reporters are trained to maintain an attitude of impartiality, but Henry found President Kennedy's words to be much to his liking;

"We seek a free flow of information...We are not afraid to entrust the American people with unpleasant facts, foreign ideas, alien philosophies, and competitive values. For a nation that is afraid to let its people judge the truth and falsehood in an open market is a nation that is afraid of its people."
John Kennedy

When the Kennedys were able to spend a weekend away from the White House, they rarely went to Camp David, the heavily guarded weekend home provided by the citizens for the presidential family. Jackie informed the President that she would find a suitable retreat in the suburbs of Virginia. Glen Ora in Middleburg, Virginia, was the ideal weekend home for the Kennedys, due to the First Lady's penchant for horses and riding, and the President's desire to be close to the White House.

Glen Ora was located less than 20 miles from Phil and Kay Graham's place, called Glen Welby. Located in Warrenton, Virginia, Glen Welby was where the owners and publishers of *The Washington Post* spent their weekends, when they were not at their home in Georgetown. So at home, and on the weekends, the Grahams and the Kennedys were always close to each other.

A local historian, Jane McIlvaine McClary, researched the Kennedy house and grounds and penned a lengthy feature article about the historic property. The historian wrote;

> *"Some houses, like humans, are destined for celebrity. Fate, circumstance, singles them out, giving them a special aura. Such a house is Glen Ora. Actually, Glen Ora's provenance is pretty common by "Middleburgian Standards" which was surveyed by sixteen-year-old George Washington (his first job). During the fifties and sixties, Glen Ora entertained many celebrities including film stars, ambassadors, cabinet secretaries and luminaries from the arts. Artist Whitfield Walston was one such guest, who also happened to be a close friend of newly elected President John Kennedy. When Walston heard the Kennedys were looking for a weekend retreat, he convinced the young president that Glen Ora was an appropriate 'Camelot away from home.'"*

On a bright Sunday afternoon, Atherton flew into National Airport, located on the Virginia shore, just across the Potomac River from Washington, D.C. He then drove to Middleburg, in Virginia's horse country, to hear a unique Kennedy story from a young man named John Faulk. Faulk had called into the *Tribune* seeking Atherton. He claimed to have witnessed a frightening and potentially embarrassing incident involving the First Lady. Since the personal life of the First Lady was more closely guarded than the President's, making an effort to record such a story might indeed be worthwhile. The story could give Atherton's readers a unique perspective of the new occupants of the White House. Atherton met with Faulk to discuss the event in downtown Middleburg at the Red Fox Inn.

Over a dinner that included Virginia delicacies such as roasted quail, Chesapeake Bay crab cakes, and Virginia chardonnay, Faulk relayed his story;

> *"Last year I was tending a gate during one of the many horse races that take place each year in Middleburg. Jackie Kennedy was there. Her guest that day was a gentleman who rode just behind her the entire day. He did not appear to be a Secret Service agent, although there were plenty of them there. I think he was a businessman friend of the First Lady's. Anyway, I was tending my gate when a group of riders came over a fence near me. Several of the horses stumbled, but they cleared the fence line and went straight up a hill from there. None of the riders fell, and they continued with the race. Just moments later, Jackie Kennedy came over the fence at full speed, with her friend right behind her. The First Lady's horse was not so lucky.*

When Jackie Kennedy's horse stumbled and went down, she fell forward, fortunately clearing the horse as it rolled on the ground, as the horse would have crushed her. Since Jackie Kennedy's friend could not see her, he came charging in behind and jumped the fence, unaware that he was placing the First Lady in extreme danger. As her companion cleared the fence, he saw his lady friend and her horse sprawled on the ground. He could see the fear in her eyes as his horse was crashing down on her. The man had no choice but to drive his horse into the ground before its awesome weight and pounding hooves could inflict certain damage upon Jackie Kennedy. But he didn't have much room with which to work. In midair he quickly reached for the bit and forced the horse's head toward the ground with all his might. Having just achieved maximum jumping speed to clear the fence, bringing the horse's head down resulted in a bone crushing summersault for both horse and rider. When his body came to a stop, the man was sprawled, scratched, dirty and bruised, but otherwise unharmed, tangled up with the First Lady on the ground. As any woman might have felt in such a situation, she was overcome with emotion, and very thankful for the bravery of her friend. Tears of joy rolled down their cheeks. They embraced each other as they lay on the ground, happy to be safe after such a traumatic experience.

A friend of mine who worked in Middleburg as an amateur photographer was riding about a minute behind the First Lady. He was an unofficial chronicler of the event, a freelance photographer who hoped he might have the good fortune to take a memorable photograph of the First Lady. As he came over the fence, he got more than he had bargained for. The First Lady was in the embrace of this man who had just saved her life, and they were laughing and crying at the same time. Gone was the majestic aura that Jackie Kennedy displayed in the White House. Here she was, sprawled on the ground, her riding clothes soiled, in the embrace of another man, vulnerable, and overflowing with emotion. The public would eat it up! My friend quickly captured this intimate moment with his camera, consuming an entire roll of film in just a few seconds.

My friend left the property that day without his camera and the film containing images of the First Lady lying on the ground in the embrace of her friend. But he was content with his loss, since he had driven to the farm that day in his dated Volkswagen Beetle, and drove home in the man's new Jaguar. I am fairly certain that film was never processed. The gentleman probably exposed it to the sun in Jackie Kennedy's presence that day before leaving the farm!"

Atherton was taken by Faulk's account, as it demonstrated the great lengths to which the First Lady would go to defend her honor, her privacy, and no doubt, the integrity of the presidency. She would later fight just as fiercely to protect the privacy of her children, Caroline and John F. Kennedy, Jr. 'This, despite Jackie Kennedy's knowledge of the President's infidelities,' Atherton thought. Faulk became a frequent guest at Glen Ora, as the Kennedys enjoyed having other folks around. Several days after the riding accident, President Kennedy handed his movie camera to Faulk, asking Faulk to film his romp with John, Jr. and Caroline's mean-spirited pony which she had named, Macaroni, just outside the stable at Glen Ora. As the President rolled on the ground with John John, the pony tried to reach the sugar cubes he could smell in the President's pockets. It was a happy moment for the Kennedys at their weekend retreat.

* * * * * * * *

When Jackie Kennedy returned to Washington, the lights of Camelot shone brightly once again on the Kennedy White House.

The First Lady walked into the Oval office as her husband rose to greet her, *"Darling, I am so glad to see you. What brings you home at this time?"* Jackie Kennedy had a habit of returning home ahead of schedule. She never knew who she might bump into on her way back into the White House.

"It's good to see you too, Jack. I'm just back from christening that new submarine, the USS Lafayette. Its number is SSBN 616, I am told. The Lafayette is a nuclear -powered submarine, isn't it?"

"Yes, that's what the N stands for. SSBN means it's a nuclear ballistic missile submarine. The Lafayette is the first in our ballistic missile fleet with nuclear warheads targeting multiple Russian cities."

"Jack, you know I don't like to hear such things. Given my heritage though, I think it's great that I was asked to christen a submarine that's named after the Marquis de la Fayette, the French general who helped us win our independence from Great Britain. Well, I'm glad to be back now. I'm very troubled about what happened in Los Angeles, Jack. I can't imagine you would involve yourself in such a mess. I feel that something terrible happened with Marilyn, but it is so horrible, I would rather not hear any details. But the problem no longer exists now, does it?"

"No, it doesn't, and I appreciate your patience with me, Jackie."

"Jack, I don't want to hear any details. I just want to know that you will never endanger our marriage and our family like that again."

"You have my word. Say, Lyndon has convinced me to go to Dallas in November. Will you go down there with me?"

"Dallas is not a friendly place for us, but I'll support you, Jack. We need to pull together if we're going to get you reelected. I read the polls say you are going to win!"

"I wouldn't count on it just yet, my dear."

* * * * * * * * *

In 1963, there was serious unrest within the Democratic Party in Dallas. The President was perceived as being soft on communism, and the Dallas/Fort Worth area was one of the most important regions in the nation for producing war materiel. Oil and weapons formed the economic base in Texas. There was not much love in Dallas for this presidential dove who sought to make peace with the Soviets, and who was about to pull out of Vietnam. The diplomatic trip to Paris had schooled the President regarding the political value of having the First Lady attend political events. The President was so enthusiastic that the First Lady would be going to Dallas that he participated in selecting the specific outfits she would wear.

As preparations got underway for the trip to Dallas, President Kennedy received a phone call from his dear friend, the Reverend Billy Graham. *"Mr. President, Billy Graham here,"* the respected minister began.

"Hello, Reverend, it's always a delight to take your call," the President replied, *"To what do I owe this pleasure?"*

Graham's voice deepened, *"Mr. President, my soul is troubled by the notion that you plan to visit Dallas. I am praying for you night and day, but I have been led to make this call to beg you not to go."*

The President took a deep breath, *"Well, Reverend, I cannot thank you enough for your concern and for your prayers. But I must go to Dallas. The Vice President has insisted that I go down there to deliver a unified message. The Democratic Party there is in disarray, and my administration needs strong support from Texas in the upcoming election. I plan to speak with the defense community down there to give them some assurances, even though I am planning to pull our troops and advisors out of Vietnam, which they are not likely to take kindly. What would Americans think if the President was afraid to visit one of our major cities?"*

Billy Graham surrendered, *"I understand, Mr. President, but I want you to know that my congregation will be in constant prayer for you and the First Lady."*

The President concluded, *"You don't know how much I appreciate those prayers, Reverend. Please tell your congregation that for me, will you?"*

Then, in a somber voice, the Reverend Billy Graham prayed, *"Dear Lord, place your protective hand upon Jack and Jackie Kennedy. Guide their steps and those who will be around them on this trip to Dallas. Let them wear the full armor of God so that they might be safe. For this and for all your mercies, we are thankful, Amen. Good night, Mr. President."*

"Good night, Reverend, and thank you again,"

"Remember, Mr. President, all thanks be to God."

"Yes, of course, Reverend. Good night, now."

Jackie Kennedy had entered the Oval Office near the end of the conversation, and now was sitting on the chair closest to the President. *"Was that Reverend Graham?"* the First Lady inquired in her small voice, a warm smile was spreading across her face.

"Yes it was," replied the President.

Jackie Kennedy probed further, *"What was on his mind?"*

"Oh, he was just calling to bless us on our upcoming trip. Prayers are like votes, Jackie; we need every one we can get."

"Jack, you should not be joking about prayers like that. It can result in some unfortunate consequences."

"Look, Jackie, if they are going to get me, then they are going to get me. I have excellent protection, so let's stop worrying about it, okay?"

The next morning, Jackie Kennedy visited her husband again in the Oval Office. She entered with a look of grave concern on her face, *"Jack, your doctors are telling me you have increased your medicine dosages, and the frequency of application."*

"Really Jackie, you worry too much. I feel fine."

"If you were fine, you wouldn't have increased your medication, now would you?"

"I was not feeling well at the time, but you are here now, and the world looks wonderful."

"My main concern, Jack, is you are taking so many different kinds of medication. I'm told you may be using more than one doctor to prescribe medications. Is that true?"

"Don't worry, Honey, I have never felt better."

"That's exactly what concerns me. Not enough testing has been done on these steroids you are taking. We don't know what the long term side effects will be," the First Lady insisted.

"As I said, Honey, I will be fine."

* * * * * * * * * *

As fall approached, the President and Jackie Kennedy enjoyed having a nightcap on weekend nights, after Caroline and John John had fallen asleep, as they sat on the back porch of Glen Ora. The President would sit upright in his custom-made rocker that provided extra support for his sensitive back. It seemed to Jackie this was the only time when she was truly alone with her husband. She treasured these moments. It was also the only time they could have intimate conversations without the fear of being overhead by agents of the Secret Service, or by listening devices that might be planted inside the house.

It was on one such evening that Jackie Kennedy decided to respond to a question that had been posed weeks before by her husband. *"Jack,"* the First Lady began, *"I have been thinking about the time you asked what I would do if something were to happen to you."*

"Yes, Dear, and what have you decided?"

"Well, you know that I don't like to think of such things in the first place."

"I know, Jackie, but I am the President of the United States, and that makes me a target. We are living in trying times. So what have you decided?"

"You know that Aristotle Onassis has always acted kindly toward me – well, there is a good chance that if, God forbid, you were to be taken from me, I would go to live with Aristotle on his island in Greece. Whenever he attends a Kennedy function, he asks me to contact him if ever he can be of service."

"Aristotle Onassis! Why, that man is a criminal! Of all the men in America who would give their right arm to be with you, why would you want to go to Greece to live with him?"

"Jack, you are one to talk. I met Aristotle through your father. Joe and Ari have done business together for years."

"Yes, you have a point there. But why would you go to live with that oaf?"

"Darling, you yourself have said the Kennedy family has made enemies here in this country."

"Yes, I have said that."

"And if something were to happen to you, my first concern would be the welfare of our children. The Kennedys have no enemies in Greece, and what would be safer than living on a private island? The best thing I could do in such a situation would be to leave the States."

"My God, what a tragedy it would be for a President's family to flee the country after his death!"

"No less a tragedy than if the country, your children, and I were to lose you."

"Thank you for saying that, Jackie. Let's just hope and pray you will never be faced with such decisions."

The couple sat in silence for some time. "On a business note," the President began, "...have you had an opportunity to size up the White House press corps?"

"Yes, I have been monitoring the way they interact with Pierre, and I have identified one that we might want to recruit. He is not a member of the White House corps, but of the mainstream press. Which is why I think he can be useful to us."

"Is he friend or foe?"

"On balance he likes you, but more importantly, Jack, his columns are highly acclaimed. I am speaking of Henry Atherton, the New York Tribune reporter who covered Marilyn Monroe's death."

"Well then, by all means, we should develop a relationship with this man."

"Do you want me to have a conversation with him, Jack?"

"No, let me have a chat with him first. There are a few political hints I would like to drop that might conveniently show up in his column."

A few days later, President Kennedy made one of his frequent trips to New York. Atherton had received an invitation to meet personally with the President. 'What could this be about?' Atherton wondered. Atherton took the elevator to the top floor, marked as the presidential suite. As he passed the final perimeter of Secret Service agents who were posted by the door, a woman rushed past him looking quite disheveled. 'She looked vaguely familiar,' Atherton pondered for a moment. 'Kind of like someone that I know from the movies. Anyway, I need to get focused. I am about to meet the President of the United States.'

"Hello, Mr. Atherton," President Kennedy smiled as he moved forward to greet the reporter.

"Hello, Mr. President. Please call me Henry."

"Very well then, Henry. I appreciate you dropping by to see me."

"It's not every day that an investigative reporter is invited to meet with the President of the United States."

"It does seem a little odd, doesn't it?"

"You know that I am not a member of the White House press corps, nor am I plugged into the scene in Washington."

"That is exactly why I wanted to speak with you. Actually, it was Jackie who suggested this meeting."

"The First Lady, Sir?"

"Yes, she thinks you might be interested in conducting a few feature interviews with the President and the First Lady."

"It would be an honor, Mr. President."

"The First Lady has been impressed with your work. She is quite the patron of the arts, you know."

"Yes, I am aware of that."

"Perhaps you will attend one of her upcoming tours of the newly renovated White House. We are reaching out to a few selected reporters who are not tainted by the gossip of Washington. We want to make sure certain stories are told without the partisan politics that permeates everything on Capitol Hill."

"I understand." Atherton's head was swimming, *"When do we start?"*

"Give my secretary, Mrs. Lincoln, a call at this number. She will get you on my schedule within the next week or so."

"Thank you, Mr. President. I will look forward to this project, sir."

Although several presidential aides, and John Kennedy himself, had dark premonitions about the Dallas trip, the entire staff was delighted that Jackie Kennedy had terminated her absence from the White House, and had cheerfully chosen to accompany the President on what would probably be a challenging trip. President Kennedy was aware of the dynamic dimension his wife brought to his public endeavors, and he was deeply involved in every aspect of her preparations. In fact, the First Lady brought so much attention and spectacle to their joint appearances that JFK often felt overshadowed by his sophisticated spouse, as when they had traveled to France. But her charms would be very helpful in the political challenges that lay ahead. And so it was, that the reunited king and queen of Camelot began to prepare for their trip to Dallas.

Chapter 4
The Great Ideological War

"Now the trumpet summons us again. Not as a call to bear arms,
though arms we need. Not as a call to battle, though embattled we are. But a
call to bear the burden of a long twilight struggle against the common
enemies of man – tyranny – poverty – disease – and war itself."
John Kennedy

<u>New York Tribune, December 3, 1962</u>
Opinion/Editorial by Henry Atherton, Staff Writer

World War II is known in the United States as *The Great War.*
America now finds itself in the midst of a *Cold War,* as the specter of
communism spreads over the Earth, encroaching upon the Western
Hemisphere. There is another, brutal and bloody war being waged here
now in the United States. The combatants are two factions possessed of
diametrically opposed ideologies.

This war is being fought in front of us on television, but it is virtually
impossible to recognize the identities of the combatants. I refer to this
covert, civil conflict as *The Great Ideological War.* It is being fought at the
highest levels of our federal government. It took shape during the
administration of President Eisenhower, as the United States and the Soviet
Union amassed their vast nuclear arsenals, and the civil rights movement
caught fire here in the States. Conflicting ideologies erupted into battle, not
only in Washington, but also on the streets and college campuses of
America. Clashes between protestors and police, as well as heavy drug
usage, have become signs of the times.

The more organized of the two factions consists of men who want to
fight communism with every available weapon, anywhere communism
appears on the face of the earth. They are devout believers in *The Domino
Theory.* In their view, the loss of any country to the communists will result
in a chain reaction of neighboring countries that will fall to communism in
rapid succession. They are certain the loss of Vietnam would result in the
losses of Laos, Cambodia and Thailand to communism. They are war-
makers. These bellicose men hate anyone who wants to negotiate peace
with the Soviets. They refer to anyone who does not agree with their
worldview as 'unpatriotic.'

Underlying the ideological rift regarding communism are two
domestic conflicts that affect us all. They are the struggle of blacks for
racial equality and the struggle of women for gender equality in America.
The men in this group are out of control. The name I have given to the war-
makers is *OCAAU,* which stands for *Out of Control Americans Against
UnAmericans.* The OCAAUs want to fight the communists despite the

consequences. They do not want to see blacks integrated into American society, or allow women to have equal rights with men.

UnAmericans are what the members of *OCAAU* consider members of the opposing faction to be. According to the *OCAAUs*, President Kennedy is an UnAmerican because he is 'soft on communism,' and wants to pull the U.S. out of Vietnam. Kennedy served in the U.S. Navy and was wounded in combat. He has been tempered by war. Dr. Martin Luther King, Jr. is an UnAmerican, because he wants to give blacks the same rights as whites in America. Reverend King has said that America has a, *"schizophrenic personality,"* that we say one thing, yet do another. Robert Kennedy is an UnAmerican, because he supports détente with the Soviets. He is also a strong supporter of the civil rights movement.

Adlai Stevenson is an UnAmerican. John Kennedy's rival for the Democratic Presidential nomination, Stevenson has become a key figure in the Kennedy administration as the U.S. Ambassador to the United Nations. He challenged the Soviet Ambassador during the Cuban Missile Crisis, saying he would wait for the Soviet Ambassador's reply regarding the presence of offensive nuclear missiles in Cuba, *"...until Hell freezes over, if necessary."* During Stevenson's bid for the presidency, the Republican Party sent Joseph McCarthy and Richard Nixon out to spread anti-Communist rhetoric to scare the public away from Stevenson's peaceful policies. Stevenson is revered by many Americans, and considered the elder statesman of the Democratic Party. He is known by many as '*the voice of conscience in America.*' Adlai Stevenson gave a well-received speech before a predominantly black crowd in Washington on September 22nd of this year to commemorate the centennial of the Emancipation Proclamation. He has made strong arguments for the non-proliferation of nuclear weapons. Adlai Stevenson is a peacemaker.

But when Stevenson's presidential aspirations evaporated, President Kennedy decided not to appoint him as Secretary of State. Instead the President named him Ambassador of the U.S. to the United Nations, where he became known as '*the voice of America to the world.*'

"It is often easier to fight for one's principles than to live up to them."

Adlai Stevenson

The animosity between Richard Nixon and Adlai Stevenson represents the epitome of the conflict between the *OCAAUs* and the UnAmericans. Stevenson has characterized "Nixonland" as, "*...a land of slander and scare, of sly innuendo, of poison pen and anonymous phone call, and bustling, pushing, shoving – the land of smash and grab and anything to win.*"

What will be the outcome of the conflicts between the OCAAUs and the UnAmericans is anyone's guess.

* * * * * * * *

"Did you get a load of this newspaper article?" Attorney General Kennedy asked his older brother, as he strode unannounced into the Oval Office, holding a copy of the *Tribune*.

"Yes," replied the President, not looking up from his paper, *"But I'm not sure yet what to make of it."*

"What to make of it, this guy is in our camp!"

"I hope he is, because Jackie tells me he holds a lot of sway with his readers. Bobby, shut the door, will you?"

The Attorney General approached the President, *"Why the concerned look, Big Brother?"*

"Atherton is the guy who's been investigating Marilyn's death."

"Oh! I see what you mean."

"Jackie told me recently she was going to meet with him. We had discussed finding a sympathetic reporter on the outside to facilitate the release of our political messages."

"What an uncomfortable coincidence. I don't think getting those two together is a good idea," Bobby suggested, as the blood drained from his face, leaving a pale expression of guilt and grief. He crossed his arms and began pacing the plush carpet which bore the presidential seal. Immediately, thoughts of Marilyn began to crowd his mind; conflicting, disturbing, and distracting thoughts. But mostly he felt regretful. Bobby grew sullen, staring out the window into the Rose Garden as if his brother were not there. *"What a disaster that could be,"* Bobby ventured out loud, his voice trailed off to a whisper as he stared blankly over the Rose Garden, toward the Tidal Basin.

The President's next comment regained Robert Kennedy's attention, *"I have a meeting set up with him this week. Perhaps you should join us."*

"No, Jack, I think you should perform this task yourself. You are more emotionally distanced from this situation than me. I am not up to reliving that chapter of my life, so you can fly solo on this one. Right now I have to get to the Justice Department for a hearing. I'm going to put Hoffa on the stand today, to have some fun with him."

"Remember, Bobby, these guys play hardball. I don't want your vendetta with Hoffa to boomerang on us someday."

"Yeah, I know. I just have a few curves I want to throw him, that's all. The other day, I asked him a question, and there in front of the television cameras, he giggled. I could not believe it!"

"Well, Bobby, just be careful, okay?"

"Relax, everything will be fine! See you later Mr. President," Bobby chuckled as the backed out the doors of the Oval Office, thinking about the fun he would have, questioning the president of the Teamsters Union later that day.

President Kennedy punched a square, white plastic button on his phone and the President's secretary responded, *"Yes, Mr. President?"*

"Need you to get a reporter on the phone for me. His name is Henry Atherton, with the New York Tribune."

"A reporter, sir? Are you sure you don't want Pierre to handle the call?"

"Just do it, please, Mrs. Lincoln. And let me know when you have him on the line."

"Yes, Mr. President."

Chapter 5
National Security, Communism & Plausible Deniability

"Having worked in the White House for some time, I can assure you that most of the stuff that is classified is flagrantly over classified and a good deal of the secrecy system is a means, not of hiding things from the enemy, but of covering up mistakes, errors and criminality, and concealing them from Congress and the American people."

Dr. Arthur M. Schlesinger, Jr.

New York Tribune, February 15, 1963
Opinion/Editorial by Henry Atherton, Staff Writer

There are many reasons why details of scandalous incidents involving government executives have not been disclosed to the American public. The most common excuse is *national security*. Information that U.S. citizens want to know is withheld because it is *classified*. There are certainly instances when every government must protect information that if released proximately to the time when the information is developed or learned, could harm the interests of the nation. As a country, we should give our full support to such legitimate cases of compartmentalized information and secrecy, as they exist for our benefit. However, the passage of time usually results in the declassification of classified material, once the threat to national security has decreased or has been eliminated. Yet there are numerous cases in American history where substantial evidence has been withheld from Americans for decades, regarding events that pose little or no threat today or never posed a threat to the American people. Such classifications are due to the political fallout, embarrassment and criminal liability such revelations would assign to those persons who were in positions of authority at the time, or to those who became accomplices after the fact. <u>At what point does withholding, tampering with, or destroying key evidence relating to a national tragedy leave the realm of protecting the security interests of the United States, and move into the domain of defrauding the people?</u>

During this decade America has suffered from an identity crisis of epic proportions. Overshadowing every aspect of national importance is the specter of communism. The Russian bear is rambling all over the globe, swimming in the oceans in the form of nuclear submarines, intelligence ships lurking off our shores disguised as fishing trawlers, and through the establishment of nuclear missile bases within striking distance of the United States. In the minds of many Americans, there is a communist behind every bush. Paranoia has spread across this land, with the underlying assumption that everything that is not good in the U.S. is the result of a communist plot. Most members of the Eisenhower and

Kennedy administrations, including President Kennedy, subscribe to *The Domino Theory*. This theory portrays a line of dominos, representing neighboring countries that might topple due to communist aggression. Such a line would be represented by Vietnam, Laos, Cambodia, Burma, Australia, and New Zealand. *The Domino Theory* hypothesizes that if the first fell, the others would easily fall as a result, just like a line of dominos.

Many Americans are stockpiling canned goods in underground shelters, preparing for a nuclear holocaust. We rehearse air raid drills, during which our children crawl under their desks at school, as if that might protect them in some way from a nuclear blast. The most dramatic manifestation of our national fear of communism was portrayed by the hearings led by Senator Joseph McCarthy, who officially interrogated U.S. citizens in the Capitol building, seeking possible connections between Americans and the communist movement. No American who has heard the audio recording will ever forget the words of Senator McCarthy while acting as the Chairman of the House Committee on Un-American Activities, when he bellowed the questions *"Are you now a member of the Communist party? Have you ever been a member of the Communist party?"* Doesn't this seem like the behavior of a government that fears the people?

As the communist threat takes shape in such far-flung countries as Korea, Vietnam, Laos and Cambodia, and closer to home in South America and Cuba, the civil rights movement in the United States is igniting the fires of hatred within our borders. It is during this time of unrest that social change seems imminent, but political and ideological differences fracture the solidarity of the nation, and the United States is divided. There are those in positions of power who do not agree with the views of John Kennedy, Robert Kennedy, Adlai Stevenson and other social reformers such as Dr. Martin Luther King, Jr. They cover their war-making diatribes with calls for unity and national security. They call any voice of dissension unpatriotic. To this, I say what Dr. Samuel Johnson said in 1775, *"Patriotism is the last refuge of a scoundrel."*

The dissension over how to handle Russia, Cuba, Vietnam, and the integration of blacks as equals into our society has created such intense political and ideological tension within our government that the over-zealous faction could resort to drastic means as a way of subverting the democratic process. My hope is the two sides will find peaceful ways of settling their differences. Otherwise, the stakes are too high for the United States, and for the world.

"This Atherton fellow seems to have a good sense of what is happening on the Hill," the First Lady commented to the President over breakfast as they looked out over the South Lawn.

"Mmm, I don't like what he said about classified information. That's a presidential prerogative. But he got the communism thing right."

"I'd forgotten I had planned to meet with this man to see if he could be of some help to us," the First Lady reflected.

JFK was frustrated that his wife picked this timeframe to become so involved in the politics of his administration. *"It's okay, Dear. I'm taking care of that. He's already on my calendar for a few interviews. You just focus on the work you're doing here to remodel the White House. How is that coming? From what I've seen, you appear to be doing a great job."*

"I think the project is proceeding very well."

"I'm glad to hear it. Now what is our schedule for the day?"

* * * * * * * * * *

Based on a number of quiet discussions with his top military leaders, President Kennedy called a special meeting of his national security team, and a panel that had been formed to study the theoretical effects of entering a period of time when America would not be fighting a war. Although Kennedy said the concept was, *"...full of nonsense,"* his military advisors convinced him to commission a study on the topic. They were summoned to the Situation Room beneath the White House to deliver their findings.

The President began, *"Gentlemen, the previous generation has fought two world wars, and another in Korea. Now we are engaged in a nuclear arms race with the Soviet Union. I'm concerned about many aspects surrounding this situation, and have asked for your study and recommendations in this area. I am looking forward to your findings and recommendations. Mr. Chairman, are you ready?"*

"Yes we are, Mr. President."

"You may proceed." John Kennedy sat in his firm leather chair with his right foot resting on his left knee, even though his doctor warned him repeatedly that doing so would aggravate his back. The President always chuckled at his doctor's chidings, replying that his frequent sexual encounters provided adequate toning of the lower back muscles to compensate for any deficiencies.

"Mr. President, the panel assigned to this task is composed of some of the best economists, strategists, and military minds in the United States. Most of these men you know personally. Our proceedings have been classified."

Kennedy nodded in affirmation.

The Chairman continued, *"The document I present to you today is the result of that study. Here are some of our findings, Mr. President. First, as long as the country has* an enemy, we will remain strong. Our economy, our military, and our foreign policy all benefit from having to remain vigilant against our enemies. We believe, however, that future conflicts may not be characterized by long wars fought by huge forces, but more as limited engagements with highly specialized soldiers."

"Yes," Kennedy replied, "I am familiar with this concept. I witnessed a demonstration of this capability at Fort Bragg. I believe you call them, Special Forces. Very impressive!"

"That is correct, Mr. President. It's our contention that our nation will be its strongest, and least vulnerable if we are always engaged in a war, or training due to the threat of war. This will also support the military budgets required to maintain military superiority. We have made an extensive study of natural energy resources within our borders, however, and have concluded that in the coming decades our national security will be dramatically affected by the availability of foreign oil, particularly from the Middle East. We will only be able to protect our stockpiles if there is a constant flow into the United States from elsewhere around the globe. We recommend that our strategic defense planning and foreign policy always maintain access to these sources as a high priority.

Our next point has caused some consternation. You no doubt recognize the fact that American presidents have waged wars without a declaration of war granted by the Congress. Only five such declarations have been issued in America's history, and we will leave it in the hands of constitutional scholars and legislators to debate the constitutionality of this process. But you should always be aware that you can arbitrarily commence a conflict simply by allowing an enemy to commit an act of aggression, giving you support from the citizenry to commit military forces. We are not advocating a 'first strike' policy, just a convenient way to start a war in response to a provoked attack. No doubt you are familiar with instances where presidents have allowed such acts to occur, providing the cause of retaliatory action that would be supported by most Americans."

The President straightened in his chair and pointed his finger at each of the panel members, "If I ever find out that any of my generals kept critical intelligence information from the National Command Authority in a situation such as that, heads will roll. Am I understood on this point?"

"Yes, Mr. President" the advisors responded in unison.

The panel chairman concluded, "Our message for you on this, Mr. President, is you have a tool that can be used to commence a conflict, against Cuba perhaps, or some other communist threat. In fact, Sir, General Lemnitzer has prepared a plan labeled, OPERATION NORTHWOODS which would involve sinking a U.S. Navy ship in Guantanamo Bay, or paying Cuban exiles to attack our Marine base there. We could even detonate the next Apollo rocket upon launch when John Glenn is scheduled to go. These dramatic acts could be easily blamed on the Cuban communists, providing the public support you would need to commit U.S. forces against Castro."

"I'm not interested in a debate over the situation in Cuba at this time, or a discussion of covert operations within our borders to antagonize our own people and bring harm to them. On that note, General Lemnitzer!"

"Yes, Mr. President," the Chairman of the Joint Chiefs replied.

"It was recently brought to my attention that you have a battalion of Marines at Camp Lejeune, South Carolina, that is rotating 25 percent of its troops to the island of Vieques in Puerto Rico every six months, and that they are forward-deployed there in preparation for an invasion of Cuba. Is that true?

"Yes, Mr. President," the Chairman answered, "We have the Marines there in case you order an invasion."

"Well, I have not been briefed on this deployment, nor did I approve it. It is a provocative move, and could be construed as an act of war, or a prelude to war. Therefore, you will recall those men immediately, and cancel any further rotations."

"Yes, Mr. President, it will be done immediately."

"Please proceed with your briefing."

"Mr. President. We are concerned that a lasting peace would have serious negative effects on the nation and on the federal government. In short, wars keep our military trained and fit, and our economy strong. The threat of war keeps our citizenry in check."

"What do you mean by...' in check?'"

"As long as Americans believe they are threatened by an enemy, they will rely on their government to protect them. Fear is the most powerful tool that government has in managing the populace. The threat does not have to be real, so long as it is perceived by the majority of the population to be real. Citizens will even submit to restrictions on their civil liberties in exchange for protection. However, we don't expect Americans to give up their guns."

"I should say not," the President barked, as he bolted upright in his chair. "The precedent for the Second Amendment to the Constitution, the right to bear arms, originated in my home state of Massachusetts when the King of England sent his Redcoats to seize the militia's weapons at Lexington and Concord. It exists in case Americans ever find themselves being ruled by a tyrannical government - they can rise up in force to replace that tyranny with a democracy. The Second Amendment has never been exercised in America during modern times to take back the government, but based on the way some of you are leaning, I'm not certain that record will stand."

"Rest assured, Mr. President, we have the best interests of Americans in mind here."

"I am not so sure that you do," retorted Kennedy. "Well, gentlemen, I thank you for your work. I must say that I never expected this group of scholars and military thinkers to make such unconventional recommendations, but I will give your report due consideration. You are dismissed."

"Thank you, Mr. President" the advisors chanted in unison. As the senior military officers passed down the vacant, tiled hallway, General Lemnitzer, the Chairman of the Joint Chiefs of Staff, said under his breath, "That Ivy League punk is a spoiled brat, and he is soft on communism. Based on his approval ratings, we probably have to put up with him for six more years. And after that comes his brother, who is even more of a hard ass. We can take them both out at one time. I think we should kill the bastard!" Lemnitzer snorted.

Chapter 6
Profiles in *OCAAU*

"Democracy is three wolves and one sheep, voting on what to have for supper."

Anonymous

In 1947, California Congressman Richard Nixon's office came to the aid of a mobster who was collaborating with Nixon as an informer and a clandestine operator. Jack Rubenstain (the spelling used at the time by Congressman Nixon's office) had grown up as a member of a Jewish family in Chicago. When Rubenstain was called by the Justice Department to give testimony before a congressional committee, Nixon's office intervened via the FBI, saying that Rubenstain should be excused from testifying, so as not to "*...compromise our source of information.*" In fact, Nixon was concerned about the illegal activities Rubenstain was conducting on Nixon's behalf while operating on the CIA's payroll. Subsequently, Rubenstain would go to Greece to illegally purchase arms in support of the Bay of Pigs Operation. Born, Jacob Rubinstein, the mobster moved to Dallas where he ran guns and drugs for the CIA, while posing as owner of a strip club known as, The Carousel. Jacob Rubinstein *(the correct spelling of his name)* was known in Dallas as 'Jack Ruby.'

In 1960, Vice-President Nixon was defeated in the presidential election by a young senator from Massachusetts, named John F. Kennedy. Kennedy's campaign was architected by his brother, Robert, whom the President would appoint as U.S. Attorney General at the insistence of their father, Joseph P. Kennedy, Sr. Robert Kennedy was grossly under-qualified to be U.S. Attorney General, but President Kennedy probably ended many of his days in the White House reflecting on the fortuitousness of the appointment. Nixon realized the aid Kennedy had received from mobster Sam Giancana of Chicago had secured the victory for Kennedy. Thus, another shadowy figure, Bebe Rebozzo, would play an active, visible and permanent role in Nixon's professional career, his financial dealings, and his personal life. The present-day headquarters of the United States Coast Guard in Southeast Washington, D.C. on the Anacostia River is housed in a building that was acquired by the U.S. Government during the Nixon administration. The building had been owned by Bebe Rebozzo.

When they took the White House, John and Robert Kennedy decided to turn on the Mafia, after which the Attorney General launched a tireless campaign against organized crime. In one of his most memorable quotations of that period, FBI Director, J. Edgar Hoover said, "*... the Mafia does not exist.*" Nixon relished clandestine operations. He particularly enjoyed his role in supervising the assassination of heads of state. As vice-president under Eisenhower, Nixon had been the senior political officer who oversaw numerous assassinations as a key instrument of American foreign policy. Prior to the escalation of U.S. forces in Vietnam, Vice-President Nixon was the highest-ranking American official to visit the embattled country. He met with Special Forces troops and CIA personnel in Saigon, and was briefed on illegal, covert operations that were taking place in Laos and Cambodia. By commanding U.S. military special operations forces, the CIA, and through his Mafia connections, Nixon could assemble a trained team and execute an assassination plan with amazing speed and accuracy.

"The top officials of both parties should set an example of propriety and ethics which goes beyond the strict minimum required by law."

Richard Nixon

When Nixon took office as president, staff members and even journalists would receive telephone calls after midnight from Nixon, during which he would rattle off unintelligible statements, speaking in slurred sentence fragments, which would often trail off into silence. The recipients of these calls were horrified and alarmed by the President's behavior and his state of mind. Several times during his presidency, Nixon fell asleep during these bizarre phone calls. Secret Service agents would receive a frantic call, and then rush into Nixon's quarters to find him asleep with the phone still clutched loosely in his hand. Nixon's psychiatrist stated several times that he harbored serious doubts about Nixon's emotional ability to manage the pressures of the presidency. Perhaps the most colorful and memorable of Nixon's many outbursts was a public incident that occurred aboard Air Force One. During a return flight to the White House, the ever-supportive First Lady, Pat Nixon, asked if she could join her husband and his aides for a drink. Nixon leaned across the aisle in front of his associates, and in a strong, harsh tone, said to his wife, *"Shut your fucking mouth!"*

According to the staffers and reporters, the silence following that remark was deafening.

"In matters as sensitive as guarding the integrity of our democratic process, it is essential that not only rigorous legal and ethical standards be observed, but also that the public, you, have the total confidence that they are both being observed and enforced by those in authority and particularly by the President of the United States."

Richard Nixon

Lyndon Johnson was the consummate Capitol Hill politician. No one could work legislation through Congress like LBJ. His Texas drawl would lull his adversaries into the comfortable notion that he was as stupid as he sounded, then, he would pounce. If Lyndon Johnson could not beat you directly in getting his way, he would cash in on previous favors and have someone else deal with you. Johnson had a habit of physically overwhelming other politicians with vigorous handshakes and backslapping, violating their personal space until they acquiesced to whatever the agreement was that Lyndon wanted to extract from them.

As vice-president under the young John Kennedy, Johnson was miserable. Whenever Johnson would throw a fit, the President would call his brother the U.S. Attorney General, and say, *"Bobby, Lyndon was just in my office crying again. Can you take care of this please?"* Johnson's power base was in the Houston oil market and the military industrial complex of the Dallas/Fort Worth area. In his mind, his biggest challenges were the ongoing issue of Cuba and how to deal with the turmoil being raised by 'colored people' in the Deep South. More than anything else, Lyndon Johnson wanted out from under the young Kennedys, and to hold the reigns of power himself.

* * * * * * * * *

President Kennedy and his brother, the U.S. Attorney General, conversed in hushed tones while playing nine holes at the Army-Navy Country Club in Arlington, Virginia. The President wanted to be clear of any listening devices that were installed in the Oval Office, and to get outside the earshot of the ever-present agents of the Secret Service. *"Bobby, I brought you out here because I need to talk with you about some topics I didn't want to discuss in my office, or over the phone."*

"Sure, Jack, what's up?"

"The CIA is going around the world assassinating world leaders against my direct orders. They are creating conflicts to incite wars…wars that get American boys killed. I had a special phone installed on my desk with a direct connection to Premier Khrushchev. We've agreed to keep these phones on our desks in case some crackpot general officer from either side launches a nuclear missile.

As vice president, Nixon provided oversight for the assassination attempts while General Eisenhower was president. Most soldiers find assassination gruesome, even those who are trained to carry them out. Nixon relishes the task. I think he gets some kind of morbid satisfaction from seeing dictators come to a violent end. We beat him in the presidential election, but that Nixon gives me the willies."

"You don't think he cut his ties with the CIA when he left office, do you?"

"They have a saying, Bobby, 'Once you are inside the CIA, you can never leave,'" the President replied.

"Yep, I have heard that one. And I imagine it's true."

"It goes deeper than just the CIA, Bobby."

"What do you mean?"

"You know how much Hoover despises you. He hates working for you."

"I get such a kick out of making him wait forever in the lobby. Hey, guess what I am going to do. I am having Carlos Marcello picked up in New Orleans and I'm deporting him to Guatemala."

"You better be careful, Bobby. One day all this fighting with the Mob could come back to haunt us. Anyway, Hoover is making noise through back channels that he will oppose any moves we make to enforce his mandatory retirement from the FBI, which will take effect after his next birthday. He wants full control of the CIA, and is lobbying to have CIA functions transferred to the Bureau."

"Jack, I am Hoover's boss. How do you know these things when I don't?"

"Let's just say I have some beautiful connections."

"Can you imagine Hoover rambling around in his home with no dossiers to keep, no political sex lives to research? What would he do? Did you hear about his testimony to my committee? He had the gall to say there is no such thing as the Mafia in America!"

"Well, Bobby, as Dad taught us, Hoover knows the best way to make a living fighting organized crime is to have the Mafia leaders in your pocket. But the CIA and the FBI don't get along."

"Jack, I have a hard enough time trying to keep the FBI under control. The FBI and the CIA are always keeping intelligence information from each other. To them, information is power."

"Information is power; that's for sure. I guarantee you; the potential exists for them to cooperate. What it will take is a mutual goal...a unified mission."

The President and the Attorney General made small talk while standing on the tee box for the fifth hole, since the Secret Service agents were close at hand. Always the competitive brothers, the President out drove his brother on the dog leg left, placing a nice draw spin on the ball that placed it squarely in the fairway.

"You should have been a professional golfer, Mr. President," Robert Kennedy beamed with unmasked pride in his brother's prowess on the links. As they walked briskly toward their golf balls, the President returned to the business at hand.

"Today is April 11th, 1963, isn't it?" JFK inquired.

"Yes, why?"

"Because yesterday was April 10th, and it's a date we both need to remember. Two events took place yesterday I want you to know about. You know what the Thresher is, don't you?"

"Yeah, Thresher is our latest nuclear attack sub. Thresher is the fastest, deepest-diving, and most quiet attack submarine in our fleet, right? If memory serves, she was designed to carry out special missions inside Soviet territorial waters."

"We lost her yesterday."

"Thresher is missing?"

"No, Bobby, the exercise went terribly wrong, and she went down with all hands about 200 nautical miles off of Cape Cod. There were 129 men aboard, including staffers from COMSUBLANT who were observing a classified weapons exercise Thresher was conducting."

"Oh my God! What a sad day for the Navy."

"The event is classified, and there will be an investigation by the Navy. That's all anyone needs to know. Got it?"

"Got it. What else did you want to talk about?"

"Last night in Dallas, someone fired a shot through General Walker's den window while he was working on his income taxes. I am told the shot must have come from the corner of his backyard fence. The bullet was fired from a high-powered rifle, but the shooter missed, and the bullet lodged in the wall just over Walker's head."

"You mean the same General Edwin A. Walker we removed from command for his role in the anti-communist indoctrination of his troops?"

"The very same one."

"Isn't he heading up some ultra right wing conservative group now?"

"Yes, the John Birch Society," the President replied.

"Not that I would mind seeing him gone, but who would want to take Walker out?"

"That's what I am trying to figure out. I certainly had nothing to do with it. It's interesting that the Dallas Police Department has not booked anyone yet. I thought maybe the FBI would have some information."

"Geez, this is the first I am hearing of it. I will see what I can find out."

"Bobby, this does not look good. Someone might accuse us of doing this, so the sooner we know who the shooter is, the better."

"What makes you so concerned about the Walker incident, Jack?"

"This shooting seems contrived to me. It might have something to do with the trip I am taking there in November. I'm afraid someone in Dallas is trying to set me up."

Chapter 7
The Legacy of Joseph Kennedy, Sr.

Senator Mark Andrews placed a call to Henry Atherton. Andrews was a senior member of the Republican Party. He chaired the Senate Defense Appropriations Committee. Andrews had learned that Atherton was conducting interviews to gather information about the new president. During their brief phone conversation, Andrews indicated he wanted a meeting to relay some information about the President's family.

"Your work would not be complete without the information I can relay to you," Andrews cautioned over the phone.

The two men described the clothing they had on, and agreed to meet on the west lawn of the Washington Monument, on the grassy hill that slopes toward the White House.

After a few pleasantries, Andrews began, *"By all accounts the patriarch of the Kennedy family, Joseph Kennedy, Sr., is a ruthless, driven man who would stop at nothing to get his son, any son, into the White House. A compelling argument can be made that since John Kennedy has been in the White House, it is his father who pulls the strings. He taught his boys to win at any cost. Joseph Sr. showed his boys how to compete at everything, including the pursuit of women. It's not unusual for the Kennedy boys to fight over a woman, or exchange phone numbers with a brother when it is time to change partners. The Kennedy sons came by this behavior honestly.*

One day during his youth, John Kennedy stowed away aboard the family sailing yacht while Joseph Kennedy took Gloria Swanson, the famous Hollywood actress, out for a sail at Hyannis Port. When young Jack popped his head up from below deck, he stumbled upon his father 'in the act' with Ms. Swanson. Young Jack was so traumatized by seeing his father having sex with their visitor, he jumped overboard! A naked Joseph Kennedy had to dive in to fish him out.

Joseph Kennedy invested heavily in Hollywood, in partnership with his Mafia connections, which had a strong hold on the moneymaking enterprises in Hollywood. Due to the large sums of money involved, the movie business is an excellent vehicle for money laundering. Joe Kennedy is enamored with the stunning women who live there. He established a legacy of fascination and entanglements with actresses in Hollywood that is being passed to his sons."

Atherton replied, *"I have heard rumors that the President has mistresses, but there seems to be an unspoken code with the White House press corps that the extra-marital sex life of a president is off the record. So if the Kennedy clan is as dirty as you indicated, how did they get into the White House?"*

Andrews continued, *"Joseph's first son, Joseph P. Kennedy, Jr. was the chosen one. At his birth, Joseph, Jr.'s grandfather, Bostonian mayor 'Honey Fitz,' declared that Joseph, Jr. was, 'The Future President.' From that day on, 'The Future President' was Joe, Jr.'s nickname, and Joseph, Sr. would have had it no other way. Good-looking and* smart, Joe, Jr. was groomed for the presidency. But the older brother was jealous and agitated by the attention young Jack received for his alleged heroics aboard PT boats in the Leyte Gulf.

John Kennedy's sexual exploits in Washington began before he entered the world of politics. Knowing that the Army and the Marines would not take Jack due to his back injury, and because of his history of poor health, Joseph Kennedy flexed his diplomatic muscle and got Jack into the Navy. Upon entering the Navy, Ensign Kennedy was detailed to the Office of Naval Intelligence in Washington, D.C. Jack took up residence near his older sister, Kathleen. Everyone close to Kathleen calls her, 'Kick.' Jack became infatuated with one of Kick's friends. The friend's name was Inga Marie Arvad. Arvad was a blonde, Danish journalist, who had once interviewed Adolph Hitler. Arvad had been friendly with Hitler while she was covering the 1936 Olympics in Berlin. FBI Director Hoover suspected Arvad of being a spy, so he had her house bugged. Jack and Inga decided to give the FBI agents who were listening to their moments of passion something to talk about. The Navy then shipped Jack off to South Carolina. From there, JFK went to the Melville PT boat school in Florida, serving there as an instructor. After being passed over numerous times for deployment to the front, Jack convinced the Navy to assign him as a replacement officer in command of a PT boat in the Pacific theatre. It was there in the Leyte Gulf that Jack Kennedy got his first command of a PT boat as a lieutenant, junior grade."

"Can you tell me about the President's PT boat accident? There seems to be some controversy about what exactly happened that night," Atherton commented.

"On that particular night, Lieutenant Kennedy's PT boat was stationed in a picket line crossing one of the busiest shipping lanes for Japanese supply convoys. The PTs were to idle their engines, listening for the destroyers that would lead the Japanese ships home from their re-supply mission. Kennedy made several serious mistakes that night. He set off on his mission without the life raft aboard which is required by Navy regulation. He allowed several of his men to sleep while they were on duty station. Worst of all, Kennedy shut down all but one of his four engines while waiting on the picket line. By the time a lookout shouted a warning that a Japanese destroyer was bearing down on them, Kennedy was not able to start his engines to avoid being rammed. The destroyer sliced through the PT boat, cutting it in two. You know, the worst thing that can happen to a boat's captain is to lose his ship! He should have been court-martialed! I guess becoming president can lead to forgiveness for all kinds of sins.

The death and hardship suffered by Kennedy's crew will haunt him for the rest of his life. The experiences Kennedy had in the Leyte Gulf, and the back injury he aggravated in the collision, reminds him every day of his presidency that war should be avoided at all costs. A young boy once asked the President how he became a war hero. 'It was easy,' the President replied, 'They sank my boat!' The President knows the worst thing that can happen to a Navy captain is the loss of his ship, and he was not comfortable when his father wanted to make PT-109 a major promotional theme for his son's campaign.

During his campaign for the presidency, John Kennedy downplayed his heroism in the way he saved the lives of his marooned crew. With the tethers of Ensign McMahon's lifejacket in his teeth, Kennedy swam for miles through the shark-infested waters of the Leyte

Gulf, and then led his crew over coral reefs that lacerated their feet, soaking the water with blood. Each night Kennedy would brave the ocean currents, swimming out in hopes of signaling an American ship. This must have been meant to soothe his guilt, because Kennedy broke Navy regulations once again by leaving his crew unattended.

A few times, other crewmembers took his place when he did not have the energy to swim. Finally, Lieutenant Kennedy got an idea to convince an island aborigine to take an inscribed coconut to an Australian watcher, who radioed the U.S. Navy that Jack and his crew were alive, and relayed their coordinates. John Kennedy recovered that coconut and had it encased in plastic. He displays it prominently in the Oval Office today as a constant reminder of that harrowing experience.

Joseph Jr. died soon after Jack's triumphant return home. He had volunteered to pilot missions for the British well after his tour had ended. Competing with his brother the war hero, Joseph Jr. volunteered to pilot a bomber filled with explosive materials that he was supposed to crash into a virtually impenetrable, underground German V-2 launch site. At that time, Hitler's V-2 rockets were falling on London, killing many citizens and driving fear into their hearts. Joseph Jr. and his co-pilot were to be escorted across the English Channel into France, where they would guide the flying bomb into the steel blast doors of an underground V-2 installation. The explosives would be detonated by one of the accompanying aircraft just after Kennedy and the co-pilot had jumped clear and their parachutes had opened. But as the flight made its final turn over the English coast to cross the channel, someone in the formation broke radio silence. The resulting transmission triggered the explosives, and the 'Future President' died in a fireball. At the moment Joseph Kennedy, Jr. died, the crushing obligation of becoming the first Irish-Catholic president fell to his woman-chasing younger brother, Jack. Jack knew the family had already reserved the White House for his older brother. Jack Kennedy aspired to be a journalist."

Andrews added, "Joseph Kennedy, Sr. had political aspirations of his own. He had served in London as U.S. Ambassador to England."

"Yes, I was aware of that," interjected Atherton, "...but he didn't fare well in London, did he? He was the U.S. Ambassador to London at the Court of Saint James."

"You're right about that. Joseph, Sr. was ridiculed for arguing the Nazis would easily win the war, and the United States should not get involved. His diplomatic career ended when in frustration, President Roosevelt recalled Joseph Kennedy, Sr. from London. Meanwhile, young Jack had studied the rise of Adolph Hitler. Jack disagreed with his father's position on the Nazis, arguing that America should enter the war to rid Europe of the fascist dictatorial regimes of Hitler and Mussolini.

Realizing that much of the Kennedy fortune rode upon the shipments of intoxicating liquors from Europe gives me pause as to why Joseph Kennedy endorsed neutrality by the United States, when entering the war meant the certain targeting of American supply ships by German U-boats as the freighters crossed the Atlantic. Since such an operation required lucrative contracts with the shipping giants operating in the Atlantic and the Mediterranean, it is likely that Joseph Kennedy, Sr. had extensive dealings with Greek shipping magnate Aristotle Onassis during this period. Onassis is a man of untold wealth. He lives on a secure island. Although Onassis is not a very attractive man, he has the knack *of attracting beautiful women. I have it on good authority that he communicates with the First Lady on a frequent basis, by the way. I think she likes his money.*

While at Harvard, Kennedy wrote a paper about the war in Europe. It was the result of observations and the opinions he had formulated during his travels throughout Europe in connection with his father's ambassadorship. Jack's Harvard thesis on why England did not recognize the threat imposed by Hitler, in which he was able to state some of his own views on the war, was published in 1940. The book is entitled, <u>While England Slept.</u> Young Jack was not afraid to disagree with his father in philosophical terms, but his father dominated the relationship and to this day, Joseph has a tremendous influence on the President.

Another concern is that the Pope will have an undue influence on this young President, since he is the first Irish-Catholic president in American history.

I wouldn't worry too much about the religion issue. Although a lot gets made of that topic in the press, I don't think the President's decisions are swayed by his religious beliefs any more than his predecessors. To answer these questions, though, it helps to know the history of the Kennedy clan.

The father of Joseph Kennedy, Sr. was a saloon keeper in Boston. It's not difficult to see how the Mafia would have taken an interest in the activities of the Kennedy clan, as the Mob controlled most of the illicit speakeasy liquor business during Prohibition, which began with the passage of the 18ᵗʰ Amendment to the Constitution, known as the Volstead Act. There is speculation that Joe, Sr. plied his trade during the prohibition period, but no one knows for sure. Sam Giancana of Chicago became a member of the internal Kennedy circle when he foiled a contract that another mobster had placed on the life of Joseph Kennedy, Sr."

"My research indicates that both the Democrats and the Republicans are tangled up with the Mafia," Atherton posed.

"You are probably right. Before the Securities and Exchange Commission was formed to regulate trading on the stock market, there were instances of tremendous manipulation of the market for selfish purposes. Joseph Kennedy, Sr. was hired to orchestrate such manipulations. One of Joseph Kennedy's clients was the owner of a taxicab company. When his client was in danger of a hostile takeover by a rival taxi company, Joe Kennedy was hired to fix the problem. Kennedy told his wife and children that he would be gone for a month then moved into a hotel room with his secretary. During that month, Kennedy manipulated the market in such a way that the stock prices of the two cab companies were influenced to suit the purposes of his client. Kennedy's plan succeeded and his client's company was saved. Joseph Kennedy also made a fortune by selling short on many of his stock holdings just prior to the stock market crash. Kennedy was so in tune with the workings of the stock market, he knew it was going to crash. In spite of these shady activities, Joseph Kennedy, Sr. was appointed by President Roosevelt as the first Secretary of the U. S. Securities and Exchange Commission!"

Atherton reflected, *"Well, you have to admit, there is no one better suited to regulate a system than someone who has proven he can manipulate it!"*

"There is one more thing," Andrews concluded, *"Joseph Kennedy, Sr. was determined to get one of his boys into the White House. And even if Jack failed, there was*

always Robert. The covert operations, ties to the Mafia, fixing of markets and elections mixed with marital infidelity, created a legacy of perversion… a cocktail in the Kennedy household that none of the compliant sons could stand to drink. I thought some of this information might provide some balance to your reporting."

"I think my reporting is balanced, but I will certainly consider what you have told me for future articles," Atherton replied.

Atherton thanked Andrews for meeting him and bid him goodbye. After a few steps, Andrews turned around to face Atherton and said, *"You know that we cannot discuss this topic again!"*

"Yes, I am getting used to hearing that from people," Atherton nodded his head slightly as he shook hands with Andrews.

Atherton was being forced to live in a world of compartmentalized information. People were eager to speak with him, and they were telling him amazing stories, but it was his job to figure out how it all fit together. The life of a reporter becomes complicated when there is not opportunity to follow up with a source for verification of facts, for clarification, or additional information, because the witnesses are fearful. It made him feel quite alone. Atherton shrugged and made his way down Constitution Avenue to his parked car.

Chapter 8
Kennedy's Women: Ornaments or Liabilities?

"A man can be so fascinated by the beauty and the wonders of the sea, that he can be blind to its dangers. So can he also be blinded by the beauty of a woman."

Victor E. Justice

Henry agreed to a phone interview with a man who called, claiming he was an agent of the U.S. Secret Service. The man's assignment since the 1961 inauguration was as a member of the protective detail for the President of the United States. Although Henry had a steadfast policy of dismissing telephone interviews, since he got more than his share of crackpots, Henry understood why a Secret Service agent would not want to be seen with a well-known investigative reporter. He decided to take the chance this source might be legitimate.

The voice on the phone had given detailed instructions, directing him to a pay phone on one of the busiest street corners in Manhattan. He also provided the number of a similarly situated pay phone across the river in Newark, New Jersey. If Atherton did not call the number at precisely 11:52 AM on the following day, the interview would not happen. There would be no opportunity to reschedule, and the voice did not provide a call back number.

Atherton arrived with time to spare. He sipped sparingly on his large coffee, realizing he should have used the restroom before leaving his apartment. *'Too late now,'* he thought. Atherton stood at the prescribed phone booth with the bi-fold doors open and one foot planted inside. Anyone approaching who looked remotely interested in using the pay phone received a look of such intensity that each hurried down the sidewalk to the next booth. At 11:51, Henry began the process of dialing the number in New Jersey. He had brought more change than he would need to insure against incomplete calls.

The phone was picked up on the first ring. *"The rockets red glare,"* a familiar voice said.

"God bless America," Henry responded. At first he thought this procedure was childish, but realized it did facilitate the process of identity authentication. Perhaps he would use this technique for phone interviews in the future.

The man wasted no time getting into his story. *"Mr. Atherton, based on our previous conversation, you remember what I do for a living?"*

"Yes I do!" Atherton replied, *"And I suppose I am not going to get any further corroboration."*

"I am sorry, but that's just not possible, and you understand why we cannot meet in person," the voice responded, *"I believe that by the end of this conversation, you will believe my story is authentic, and you will believe I am who I say I am."*

Atherton was ready for the details, *"Okay then, tell me what you have to say."*

"I have come to you because my associates and I believe the President is a threat to national security."

Henry could not believe what he had just heard. *"What are you talking about?"*

"Now, I can tell by reading your articles you are a Kennedy admirer. But would you believe that presidents usually have two personalities? The public persona is one. The private personality can be quite different."

"Yes, history has shown this to be the case."

"And would you agree my associates and I are in the best position to witness the private persona?"

"Without a doubt," Henry replied in an acquiescent tone.

"As I tell you what I know, keep in mind the President has been heard to say, 'If I don't have sex every couple of days, I get headaches.'"

"Wow. Okay, I will keep that in mind," but Atherton was not ready for what he was about to hear.

"Can you imagine what it feels like for us to be standing outside the locked door of some actress, socialite, Mafia mistress, or a whore, while the President of the United States spends hours with her, totally exposed, vulnerable, and without our protection? Invariably, there is a lot of alcohol involved. What if one of these dames slips him a mickey and poisons his drink? What if the Russians recruit one of the President's mistresses, tempting him to reveal our most highly classified information? I have been told that Marilyn Monroe was preparing for a press conference during which she intended to reveal liaisons with both Kennedy brothers, as well as what the President had told her about Fidel Castro. If that's not a breach of national security, then I don't know what is!"

Henry pounced on the reference to Marilyn Monroe. *"What else can you tell me about Marilyn?"*

"Nothing," the voice answered, flatly.

"But surely if you're so close to the President, you know a great deal about Marilyn Monroe!" Henry pleaded.

"I will not comment on that subject. If you inquire further, I will hang up, and you will never hear the rest of my story."

Henry surrendered, *"Please continue."*

"For example, the President keeps two buxom secretaries in the White House. Their names are Priscilla Wear, and Jill Cowan, but we refer to them as Fiddle and Faddle, respectively. There was a memorable day when Jackie Kennedy made a surprise return to the White House, arriving home sooner than she had been expected. At that moment, the President was drinking a high ball, while cavorting with Fiddle and Faddle in the White House pool. When the word was given that the First Lady's helicopter was landing on the lawn, the President bolted out of the pool, handing one of our guys his drink as he headed for the shower."

As this new, tantalizing evidence was revealed, Atherton wondered if he would ever be able to print the incredible story that was being laid out for him.

The voice continued, *"Judith Campbell is not only a regular sexual partner for the President, she also carries money and messages from the President to Sam Giancana, the mob boss in Chicago. Few people know this, but the 8,000 extra votes Kennedy got in Illinois, which sealed his election over Richard Nixon, were largely attributable to the efforts of Sam Giancana's people in Chicago."*

"The President himself is connected with the Mafia? That's quite an allegation. How do you know this?" Atherton demanded.

"It's our business to know everything about everyone who has contact with the President of the United States. Also, Giancana and Joseph Kennedy, Sr. go way back."

"I guess that makes sense," Henry admitted in a resigned manner.

"The President has other mistresses," the voice continued. *"I know for a fact the Attorney General has paid off at least one of the President's mistresses, Judith Campbell, to keep her quiet about a pregnancy. She had to have an abortion, because the President had gotten Campbell pregnant the last time he slept with her. It was hush money to keep her from going public regarding her affair with the President. And get this; Campbell was sleeping during the same period with one of the top Mafia bosses in Chicago, Sam Giancana. The President has also been having an ongoing affair with Helen Chavchavadze. An East German woman, Ellen Rometsch, had been having an affair with JFK, and we deported her before the story hit the mainstream press!"*

"The President's favorite mistress is simply in love with him. She is definitely the President's favorite, and ours as well. Mary Pinchot Meyer is a socialite in Georgetown, who has taken the President by storm. She is gorgeous, and she is smart! It may sound crazy, but the guys always look forward to Mary Meyer's visits to the White House living quarters when the First Lady is away. Jackie Kennedy is pretty, but Meyer is off-the-charts beautiful, and she's not stuck up! Mary has been in the President's private quarters at least thirty times. She introduced the President to marijuana, and possibly even LSD. You can see why this would be a matter of concern for us."

"And to show you what a good friend she is, Mary Meyer once had a young woman, Pamela Turnure, stay with her for a while because Congressman Kennedy had been seeing her, which got them both tossed out of the rooming house!"

"The President was smoking dope in the White House?" Atherton was incredulous.

The Secret Service agent continued, *"Not long ago, I had to accompany the President in his convertible with the top down, as he drove from the White House into Georgetown, where he entered the home of a particular lover who lives directly across the street from the church he now attends. He then had sex with this lady while I waited outside in the car! This president is out of control."*

"And still, there are cases of infidelity on the part of the President that I don't know about. A journalist by the name of Bob Pierpoint told me he saw the President exiting a cottage in Palm Beach, getting into a limousine with Mary Meyer, and he saw them hugging as the light went out."

"Let me tell you how crazy it can get around here. Mary Meyer is a painter. I suppose that's why she likes to fool around with experimental drugs. When a modern artist

named Tom Wesselmann brought his paintings to town, the board of trustees at the *Washington Gallery of Modern Art almost rioted during the preview. Apparently, Wesselmann had painted a portrait of President Kennedy, standing next to Marilyn Monroe in the nude. Several trustees, including Marie Harriman and Katherine Graham of the* Post *wanted the painting removed from display. Mary Meyer quickly intervened with the President, who laughed and said he wanted the painting to remain."*

"In this particular case we have been able to do some damage control and keep her in check," the voice indicated.

"How is that?"

"Meyer's former husband is Cord Meyer, one of the CIA's masters of covert operations. And, Mary Meyer's sister is married to Ben Bradley, editor of The Washington Post. *We are friendly with him. Check it out! That's all I have to say...goodbye, Mr. Atherton."*

And with that final comment, the line went dead.

As an American citizen, Atherton found this information discomforting. But for a reporter, it would be difficult to conceive of a story that would generate more curiosity and interest. Certainly, his editor would want to know about this hot lead right away.

"Now Henry...," Montrose chided, *"...you know there's an unwritten code among journalists that we do not publish anything about the private lives of presidents while they are in office. But I have an idea. How about I give you a six-month sabbatical to write a book on the topic? I know a publisher who would jump on a book deal like this. I can have him call you..."*

Atherton cut him off, *"No thanks, Charlie. I really appreciate the offer, but I need to keep piecing this puzzle together. There are several large chunks missing that I need to find."*

"All right then," Montrose sighed, *"Let me know if you change your mind."* Montrose hung up the phone, shut the door to his office, then plugged a special communications handset into a non-standard plug installed under his desk, and spoke in muffled tones.

* * * * * * * *

Jackie Kennedy could often be found in the White House performing in her self-fashioned role as the consummate patron of the arts. The televised tour she gave Americans of the newly redecorated White House displayed the poise of a queen, as well as her appreciation for art and aesthetics. But she most enjoyed the time she spent with her family at Glen Ora.

As the First Lady continued to take trips away from Washington, and during his own trips, the President found numerous women who were taken by this dashing young man, the leader of the free world. On a trip to Hawaii, for instance,

15 women were made available, and the President was given the opportunity to choose who the lucky girl would be to spend some intimate time with him.

* * * * * * * *

The young, bronze-skinned Hawaiian woman named Malika flopped down on the bed next to the President. She turned her head on the pillow, and smiling at him, her breathing was accelerated as her breasts rose and fell. A glow of slight perspiration appeared on her forehead.

"Wow! That was incredible, Mr. President. I must say you have excellent technique. I'm so glad you picked me to be with you today, since you had such a large group to chose from."

"Thank you, Malika," John Kennedy flashed his famous smile, and Malika instantly felt more at ease.

"Have another pina colada," the President suggested. *"Your skin is so soft, and such a beautiful amber color. Your hair feels like silk on my skin. It shines like the ocean at night, and it smells like heaven."*

"That's because I rub my skin every day with coconut oil, and I wash my hair with a shampoo made with balsam and other native products."

"By the way, since we have so quickly become intimate friends, please call me Jack."

"If you say so, but it's awkward referring to the President of the United States by his first name, since everyone else calls you,' Mr. President.'"

"Well, this will make that dilemma easier to handle. When you volunteered for this duty, you agreed you would never speak about this with anyone. There are many reasons for this, but the two most important reasons are your personal safety, and national security."

"I understand, Jack. Well, if we will never speak to each other again, we might as well make today a memorable experience."

"That's the main idea!"

"You can be on top this time," Malika offered.

"No, I need for you to be on top because of my back injury."

"You have a back injury? You should have told me!"

"I injured it a long time ago, but it acts up periodically."

"In that case, I will just have to make you forget that pain." With that, the young Hawaiian woman reached under the covers and totally disappeared.

"Oh my God," the President moaned.

* * * * * * * *

President Kennedy's most famous and mysterious mistress was Marilyn Monroe. President Kennedy was quite taken with Marilyn. She, in turn, was impressed with John Kennedy's power, his looks, and his intellect. The Kennedy brothers had frequent and easy access to Marilyn through their brother-in-law, actor

Peter Lawford. Lawford had married Patricia Kennedy. He was close to Jack and Robert Kennedy. Frequent trips from Washington to Lawford's mansion gave the President and the Attorney General many opportunities to tangle with mistresses in Hollywood.

Joseph Kennedy, Sr. had invested heavily in the burgeoning movie business, in cooperation with Mafia figures in Los Angeles. These ties and their interests in fostering extra marital relationships with women in Hollywood such as Marilyn Monroe, frequently brought Jack and Robert Kennedy to Los Angeles. A regular guest at parties hosted by Lawford at his mansion in Santa Monica, the President was able to fraternize with Marilyn under a cover that provided plausible deniability of an untoward relationship with Hollywood's hottest sex symbol. On at least one occasion, Lawford arranged to borrow a house in Palm Springs, not far from the Kennedy compound, where the President and Marilyn could indulge in their lust for each other. According to a caterer in Los Angeles, Marilyn was brought to JFK's hotel room, during the Democratic National Convention on the night he won the presidential nomination. The most famous, most lusted-after woman in the world was brought to the presidential candidate's suite by the Secret Service, and was soon ushered out the back door of the hotel like a prostitute. It did not sit well with her.

* * * * * * * * *

As the furor of the Democratic National Convention came to a climax, Adlai Stevenson conceded his bid for the presidential nomination to John Kennedy, who then emerged victorious over Lyndon Johnson. Kennedy would later appoint Stevenson as U.S. Ambassador to the United Nations, to Stevenson's dismay. Now Kennedy had to select his running mate. JFK's father pushed for Johnson to fill the vice-president position on the Democratic ticket to secure more votes in the South. JFK quickly realized that for political reasons, Johnson must be given the first right of refusal, so he sent his brother Robert to make the offer, despite the fact that Bobby vehemently opposed the notion.

"Lyndon can help us in the South," John Kennedy said, *"For God's sake, he is the majority leader in Congress! Think about how much political capital that buys for our legislative agenda! Anyway, he will probably turn it down. His ego won't let him take that job."*

"I'll go down to his suite to represent you, Jack, but I just don't like it."

"It will all work out, Little Brother, don't worry."

What followed was a series of visits and phone calls that resulted in massive confusion, and a decision that would have a tragic impact on American history. Johnson insisted on negotiating directly with John Kennedy, while Bobby tried to create the illusion that the Kennedys were in the process of selecting Johnson. Johnson called in his close friend and advisor, Philip Graham, publisher of *The*

Washington Post, to assist him with the negotiations. Graham had worked closely with both Johnson and Kennedy.

For hours following Senator Kennedy's offer of the vice-presidency, Lyndon Johnson fumed over whether or not he should take the job.

"Don't even think about it," yelled Mrs. Johnson, *"You deserve better!"* Johnson's daughter made a speech on the convention floor, saying that her father and his constituents would live to fight another day. Totally uncomfortable with the concept of being vice-president, Johnson spoke with his aides, advisors, and supporters. The vast majority counseled him that Majority Leader was a much more powerful position than vice-president, and that he should go for the Democratic nomination in 1964.

Then came the fateful call from his lawyer. Edward A. Clark, Johnson's longtime attorney in Austin, Texas, called and told Lyndon to take the call alone in his bedroom. As always, Johnson carried out Clark's instructions.

"Hello, Lyndon!"

"Yes, Ed."

"Sounds like things are getting pretty interesting there at the convention."

"Yeah, that young brat Kennedy got the nomination for president and in ten minutes I have to give him my final decision about whether or not I will take the vice-presidency."

"You should take it, Lyndon."

"Dammit, Ed, the vice-presidency is a crock of shit! It's the most insignificant job in the world. All the vice-president ever does is sit on his ass and listen to the Senate, and fly to god-forsaken places to attend funerals of men he has never met. It's a fate worse than death. I don't want to be vice-president, I want to be president. And the way things are going in Washington, there may never be another chance for me. I might just end up in jail instead."

"No, Lyndon," Clark replied in a matter-of-fact tone of voice in a futile attempt to calm him down, *"...the firm is taking care of those problems for you. You just leave all that to me."*

"Well, I hope so, 'cause that crap is keeping me up at night."

"Lyndon, you are going to be president," Ed Clark continued with an ominous tone, *"Remember what we did for you in Texas. According to the Constitution, there is an expedient way for a vice-president to become president without having to face the scrutiny of a presidential race or even a confirmation hearing, which you might not survive right now."*

"You don't mean we would..."

"I am already rounding up a team and working on the plan. I've been talking with Giancana. He is really pissed at the Kennedys for double-crossing him. The new president will have to visit the South at some point. Now go down to Kennedy's room and accept the vice-presidency, before he offers it to Smathers!"

A few minutes later, Senator John Kennedy walked into his suite.

"Darling, you look like you've just seen a ghost," Jackie Kennedy exclaimed.

"Well I don't believe it, John Kennedy gasped, *"Lyndon just accepted the vice-presidency. I never thought for a moment he would take it!"*

Before Bobby knew what had happened, Senator Kennedy appeared in the 'Bowl,' a room where important announcements were made to the press and delegates of the convention. Senator Kennedy announced that Lyndon Johnson would be the vice-presidential candidate on the Kennedy ticket. And with that announcement, John Kennedy sealed his own fate.

Kennedy could now turn to focus his attention on beating his Republican opponent, Richard Nixon. As support for Kennedy grew, the Senator came to understand Nixon's methods and the way Nixon thought about world issues, and how he interacted with people. He questioned whether Richard Nixon, who was raised a Quaker, had a heart at all.

One day, JFK turned to Ted Sorenson, his highly talented speech writer, and said, *"Do you realize the responsibility I carry? I am the only person standing between Nixon and the White House!"*

One night as JFK prepared for a dinner party at the White House, the President invited Ben Bradlee of *The Washington Post* to visit with him. Sitting on the side of his bed, pulling his pants on, JFK said, *'Ben, can you believe that J. Paul Getty* [the richest man in America at the time] *only paid $500 last year in federal income taxes? It's probably illegal for me to know that, much less tell you,"* the President said with a gleam in his eye. Bradlee knew better than to publish such politically explosive material.

* * * * * * * *

Those who witnessed Marilyn Monroe, wearing her sequined, transparent dress without underwear, singing her lusty rendition of *Happy Birthday* to Kennedy during his birthday party in 1962 at Madison Square Garden, said there must have been intimate relations between the two of them. The sense of intimacy and sexual innuendo in Marilyn's voice and body language was too strong for it not to be the case.

> *Happy Birthday.........to yoou!*
> *Happy Birthday............to yoou!*
> *Happy Birthday.........Mr. President,*
> *Happy Birthday......to yoou!*

Although she was playing to the attending crowd of thousands of screaming Democrats, in Marilyn's mind there were only two people in the arena that night.

As Marilyn's song subsided, a beaming President Kennedy made his way to the podium, *"I can retire from political life…,"* Kennedy chided, *"…now that I have had Happy Birthday sung to me in such a wholesome manner."*

The First Lady had known what was going on between her husband and Marilyn Monroe, and for that reason, she did not attend the President's party. Rose Kennedy, the President's mother, was sitting behind him, probably cringing at the thought of how her sons were following in their father's philandering footsteps.

Rose Kennedy once said to Jackie, *"Great men have great flaws."* But Jackie didn't buy that philosophy.

Hugh Sidey, the prominent journalist, wrote; *"When Marilyn Monroe appeared in a sheer dress to sing for the President, her sexual power was overwhelming."*

One observer said that Marilyn showed up wearing *"…skin and beads."*

"That's the trouble, a sex symbol becomes a thing. But if I'm going to be a symbol of something, I'd rather have it sex than some other things we've got symbols of."

Marilyn Monroe

RFK had paid off Judith Campbell for suppressing the news of being impregnated by the President. Campbell had aborted the pregnancy with the financial assistance of Sam Giancana at Grant Hospital in Chicago. When RFK approached Marilyn Monroe with the same type of proposition, he was met with a different response. *"Fuck off,"* Marilyn spat at Bobby, *"I am having my baby and no one is stopping me from having it."*

* * * * * * * * *

The President and the First Lady came to know Philip and Kay Graham, owners of *The Washington Post*, quite well, attending social functions, private parties, and benefiting from the advice given by Phil, much as he had done for Johnson in the Congress. President Kennedy handpicked Philip Graham to lead the development of COMSAT in Maryland, a new and exciting enterprise that combined the best of industry and government, making an early foray into space through satellite communications.

One night in early 1963, President Kennedy received a late night call from Philip Graham. *The Washington Post* publisher was talking nonsense, and the president became very concerned. The president hung up and immediately picked up the phone again. After several more calls, he dialed an internal extension.

"Operator, this is the President," JFK announced to the White House switchboard operator from his bed. *"Patch me through to Bobby Kennedy's home please. And after that call ends, I want to you ring up Kay Graham at her residence."*

"Bobby, Jack. I am sorry to bother you at such a late hour, but there's something seriously wrong with Phil Graham. I just got a crazy call from him, and I've spoken with

some folks with him at the American newspaper editor's conference in Phoenix. They all say Phil is out of control. He was not supposed to speak tonight, but he got up to the podium anyway and started babbling about my relationship with Mary Meyer. Then he started to take off his clothes! There are two doctors, named Farber and Cameron, who have been attending to Phil in D.C. I want you to spin up a government plane to get those doctors as close as possible to where Phil is staying. This could be a matter of life and death, I am told."

"Jack, I know Phil is your friend, but I'm not sure this a legal use of a government aircraft."

"Bobby, stop being attorney general for a minute, okay? Phil is an asset to this administration, and as such he is an asset to our country! This is being done on my authority. If anyone gives you a hard time, tell them to call me."

"I'll get on it right away, Jack."

A few days later, President Kennedy received a note from Kay Graham, saying that he was a wonderful friend, and quite literally, *"...a life saver."*

The unexpected outburst by Phil Graham in front of his peers, which was not printed by any of the executives at the editorial conference, heralded the end of the hot romance between the President and Mary Meyer, the sister-in-law of *Washington Post* Editor, Ben Bradlee. The night JFK informed Mary Meyer of his decision to break off the affair, she got drunk, left the White House party in a daze, and wandered around the White House grounds in the snow for over two hours. Bradlee would later write an article acknowledging the relationship between Mary Meyer and President Kennedy. The article ended Bradley's relationship with his sister-in-law, and Mary's sister Tony subsequently divorced Bradley.

Jackie Kennedy recalled that her husband often went to sleep listening to a recording of the Broadway musical *Camelot*. The lines he most loved were those of the king, played by Richard Burton, *"Don't let it be forgot, that once there was a spot, for one brief shining moment that was known as Camelot."*

Camelot was a fantasyland, where the climate was perfect, and everything was made idyllic by order of the king. Lest we forget, the fabled story of King Arthur and the Knights of the Roundtable ended in marital infidelity and death.

John Kennedy was a dreamer. He had visions of a new world order of peace, where America's race with Russia would be restricted to putting a man on the moon. And perhaps there might even be collaboration in that mission as well. But while Kennedy's head was in the clouds, thinking of how he could save the world from World War III, and distracted by his many girlfriends, the OCAAUs led by Johnson and Nixon were plotting against him.

Chapter 9
Politics by Assassination

*"If I could find a way to get Saddam Hussein out of there, even
putting a contract out on him, if the CIA still did that sort of thing, assuming
it ever did, I would be for it."*

Richard Nixon

As General Eisenhower's presidency was coming to an end, Sam Giancana held a series of meetings with his son in preparation for work his family would be doing in conjunction with the CIA.

"Listen, son," Giancana began, *"Sometimes our government cannot do shit on the up and up. So by early 1954, my folks and the CIA were two sides of the same coin. Sometimes they need a little trouble, or sometimes they need a bastard taken care of. They can't get caught doing shit like that. What if people found out? But we can. Guns, a hit, muscle...whatever dirty work needs to be done. Right now, we're working on Asia, Iran, Latin America...we got this deal all sewn up. Eisenhower, all he does is play golf. Shit! He is a pigeon. It's Vice-President Nixon that's got the power. I've been meeting with the CIA guys since last August. We're gonna hit the prime ministers of Cuba, the Dominican Republic, and the Congo."* Of those three prime ministers, the only one to survive assassination attempts was Fidel Castro.

* * * * * * * * *

Atherton had begun to recognize some patterns that were developing in his research. The untimely death of Marilyn Monroe, the missing evidence, the convenient suicide story. The Kennedys had definitely been involved with Marilyn. Could her death have been politically motivated? Could it have been an assassination? Atherton proceeded to research the role assassination had played in world history. He was fascinated by a scholarly paper written by Professor Thomas White of The George Washington University. The paper was titled, *"Being Popular in Democratic Politics Can Get You Killed."* The professor agreed to meet the investigative reporter at the Willard Hotel in Washington, D.C.

As Atherton waited for the professor in the hotel lobby, he found himself studying the text of a speech written by Dr. Martin Luther King, Jr. during his stay at the hotel. It spoke of how blacks in the South should continue their practice of non-violent protest in the spirit of Gandhi, so that America could finally achieve the constitutional premise that all men are created equal. Atherton had been in the predominantly black crowd in Washington on that day, August 28, 1963, when Dr. King delivered his, *'I Have a Dream,'* speech from the steps of the Lincoln Memorial. *'That was without a doubt, the most powerful speech I have ever heard,'* Atherton thought to himself. *'His speeches are as articulate as President Kennedy's, and even more moving. King's peaceful agitation must be making the right wingers miserable. If Dr. King can motivate and lead the blacks of this country the way Gandhi led his followers in India, the OCAUUs must have Dr. King near the top of their most-wanted list. His life could be in danger.'*

Atherton might not have been surprised to learn that Bobby Kennedy had agreed to let J. Edgar Hoover tap Dr. King's phones. Atherton snapped out of his stupor as the professor entered the lobby, wearing the bright green tie they had agreed upon. It seemed silly to Atherton when the professor made the suggestion, but the green tie certainly stood out in a hotel where folks were dressed in the drab business fashion of the nation's capitol.

As the men shook hands, the professor was clearly uneasy. *"I would prefer it if we could meet in your suite,"* the professor said in a pleading tone.

"That would be fine," Atherton replied, *"I appreciate you meeting with me on such short notice."*

Once the men were comfortably seated in Atherton's hotel room, the professor was more forthcoming. *"Before we discuss some of your historical findings,"* Atherton began, *"I would like to ask you a specific question about the President. How does President Kennedy feel about the use of assassination?"*

"This is a very good question. The U.S. has used assassination more often than most Americans would like to believe. In the case of President Kennedy, he certainly knows this, and he does think about it a lot."

"In what way?"

"Mostly, that it might happen to him."

"How do you know this?"

The professor shifted forward in his soft chair, using his hands to tell the story, *"Let me give you an example. One day, when the President was in church, there were several reporters sitting behind him. The President turned to them and said in a matter-of-fact way, 'You know, if someone took a shot at me, he would hit one of you first.'"*

"Interesting!"

Shifting back and deeper into his chair, an intense expression appeared on the professor's face, his eyes growing wider, with lines appearing on his forehead, *"Mr. Atherton, my research has shown that throughout history, dirty politicians have used assassination as a method of eliminating their more popular opponents from the political landscape. In a democracy, how can a vicious politician gain power and supersede his rival when the rival is more popular? History has shown that such politicians will sometimes commit murder to achieve what they cannot gain through a popular election. Furthermore, what do rulers do with people who are so popular with the masses that they endanger the authority of their government? You should bear in mind what President Theodore Roosevelt said about the assassination of President McKinley,* 'It was in the most naked way an assault not on power, not on wealth, but simply and solely upon free government, government by the common people, because it was government and because it yet stood for order as well as for liberty.' For me, that is the best characterization of what a presidential assassination means."

Atherton was intrigued, "Historically, what are some of the most illustrative examples of assassination, in your opinion?"

"The assassination of King Philip II of Macedonia, the father of Alexander the Great, is an excellent example," the professor replied. "Of course, this was not an example of subverting a democracy. Rather, it was an ambitious son getting his father out of the way before the son of Philip's second wife, Cleopatra, could come of age and inherit the kingdom. According to the Greek author Diodorus, King Philip had ascended to the position of leading the Corinthian League, an assemblage of Greek states that intended to conquer Persia. In October of 336 BC, Philip hosted an elaborate celebration to honor Cleopatra. To demonstrate his omnipotence, Philip made his entrance alone, telling his bodyguards to remain behind. At this vulnerable moment, one of Philip's bodyguards by the name of Pausanias rushed forward and drove a dagger between Philip's ribs. Pausanias was killed immediately in the ensuing chase, so his testimony about the conspiracy would never be heard.

The most interesting assassination case to me is the death of Jesus Christ. The death of Jesus of Nazareth was the result of an odd conspiracy. There is little doubt that Christ's own people, the Jewish elders conspired with their Roman captors to force Pontius Pilate into having Jesus killed. No story during that period of history has been recorded by more people with amazing consistency as the life and death of Jesus. That crucifixion was a fantastic manipulation of the Roman legal system, since Jesus was not found guilty of any crime. It also required that the conspirators convince the people of the validity of their criminal activity. The Jewish priests found it expedient to work with their Roman captors, because Jesus was a tremendous threat to the power they held over the people. Jesus had influence over the Jews. He was an instrument of social change, who drove fear into the hearts of the priests. So, they had him killed by the Romans, giving the Jewish priests plausible deniability for his death."

"What you're saying is the conspirators don't always have to be on the same side," Atherton observed.

"Exactly!" replied the professor. "In fact, political assassinations are often carried out by a recruit from another party or nationality to divert attention away from the conspirators. Another commonality is that assassinations usually involve the participation of persons close to the victim. We know that in the case of Jesus, it was Judas Iscariot who betrayed him. A final point to note about the assassination of Jesus is that his death was meant to strike fear into the hearts of the people. Such a brutal death by suffocation on a cross in a public place told the Jews not to make trouble, or they would meet the same fate. Assassination not only eliminates rivals, it can be used to control the people."

Atherton decided to get directly to the question at hand, "What can you tell me about politically motivated assassinations in American history?"

"First, I am sure you know that John Wilkes Booth shot Abraham Lincoln at Ford's Theatre on April 14, 1865. Booth had originally intended to kidnap Lincoln, then he was going to exchange him for Confederate troops. Booth died when shots rang out two weeks later, *after Federal troops cornered him in a Virginia barn. Then in 1901 on September 6th, a Polish immigrant named Leon Czolgosz went to the Pan-American Exposition in Buffalo, New York, where he shot President McKinley. McKinley died eight days after the shooting."*

"Yes, I had forgotten about McKinley," Atherton commented.

"People also tend to forget about the assassination of President James A. Garfield. Garfield lived for 80 days after he was shot by Charles Julius Guiteau, which took place on July 2nd 1881, at the Baltimore and Potomac Railroad Station in Baltimore. Finally, it is not well known that Giuseppe Zangara fired a shot at President Franklin Delano Roosevelt on February, 15, 1933. The shot missed President Roosevelt, but it struck and killed Chicago Mayor Anton Cermak."

"Apparently," Atherton reflected, *"...our country has seen more assassination attempts on presidents, and we have committed more assassinations, than we care to remember. I can see how we might be living in collective denial of these facts."*

"That is indeed my premise," the professor replied. *"Now, you need to know about an important and diabolical alliance, the one between the CIA and the Mafia. American intelligence ties to organized crime go back to the OSS. The Office of Strategic Services was the predecessor of the CIA. The OSS employed mobster Meyer Lansky's men to protect the docks in New York harbor from sabotage by Nazi agents during the mid-forties. The CIA also used mobsters to break up labor strikes in both the U.S. and France. But during the Eisenhower administration, the Mob came to the forefront of America's most clandestine operations. Vice-President Nixon and the CIA found in these criminal elements a most useful component of any assassination team. All this while J. Edgar Hoover, the Director of the FBI, claimed there was no such thing as organized crime in the United States. If there was no organized crime, then how could it be helping the CIA? Quite convenient, don't you think?*

I know that during this so-called 'Cold War,' the United States is training members of its Special Forces and covert operations agents to assassinate foreign leaders. Mind you, I have no problem with assassinations of foreign leaders when we have declared war; my concern is with covert operations against heads of state when we have not declared war against those nations. I know the CIA developed and tested several creative ways to kill Castro. One was to blow his head off by packing his cigar with plastique explosive. Another was to mix cyanide into his milkshake. A third method was to use an ink pen with a special needle to inject Castro with poison. Finally, the CIA and the Army developed an umbrella that can shoot a rocket powered poison dart that dissolves undetected in the body of a dog, or a human. These initiatives were strongly supported by Robert Kennedy, the Attorney General."

"How do you know that?" Atherton inquired.

"I was told by an employee of the CIA who is in a position to know. Don't even ask me who, because I won't divulge that information because I intend to protect that individual. The attempts on Castro's life were part of an operation within the CIA known by the code name OPERATION MONGOOSE. The mongoose is a mammal that kills snakes by attacking them in their underground lairs.

I know that while he served as vice-president under General Eisenhower, Richard Nixon provided oversight for numerous attempts by the United States to assassinate foreign leaders. Several of those attempts were successful. As an example, the United States would go to great lengths to ensure its ability to move warships and freight through the Panama Canal quickly and cost-effectively, rather than taking the long southern route around Argentina. But the Eisenhower administration was worried about communist influences that were affecting the policies of Jose Antonio Remon, President of Panama. As an increasing number of intelligence reports from the CIA showed that Remon's activities were moving in a manner that was contradictory to the Eisenhower administration, Nixon was sent to solve the problem.

On January 1, 1955, at a meeting in Honduras, Nixon was briefed by a squad of assassins made up of U.S. Special Forces personnel, CIA operatives, and Mafia hit men. According to one of the attendees, the agenda for that meeting was dedicated to a detailed discussion regarding plans to assassinate the President of Panama. Travel records show that everyone in that meeting left Honduras the same day. The next morning, Jose Antonio Remon, President of Panama, was murdered in a hail of machine gun fire. He was ambushed on January 2, 1955, at a racetrack outside Panama City. The CIA also sponsored the overthrow and assassinations of Prime Minister Rafael Trujillo of the Dominican Republic, as well as Congolese leader, Patrice Lumumba. On the night Lumumba was killed, a CIA agent ended up driving around Lubumbashi after curfew with Lumumba's body in the trunk of his car! In order to complete the cover-up story, Lumumba's death was not announced for several days."

Atherton was writing everything down furiously. Suddenly, he grasped upon the most critical issue, *"Does your research have anything to do with what happened in Cuba, at the Bay of Pigs?"*

"I am afraid it does. Richard Nixon was also the chief political officer of the National Security Council's Special Group that planned the Bay of Pigs invasion under Eisenhower. Nixon and John Dulles established secret military training bases in Guatemala for counter-revolutionary Cubans whose assignment would be to infiltrate back into Cuba, establish centers of guerrilla military resistance and wage terrorist attacks against the economic infrastructure of Cuba. The codename for this initiative was OPERATION FORTY. Moneymen and mobsters who were kicked out of Cuba by Castro were brought into OPERATION FORTY. Their job was to carry out a clandestine secondary operation, the assassination of Castro, his brother Raul Castro, Che Guevara and five other revolutionary leaders."

The professor continued, *"As Castro's ties with the Soviets deepened, the CIA gathered intelligence regarding how Castro's influence was spreading throughout the Caribbean region. If Kennedy had Titan nuclear missiles in Turkey targeting Moscow, then Khrushchev wanted his missiles in the Caribbean, targeting Washington! When the CIA and their Mafia friends failed to assassinate Castro, they turned their attention to his followers. Fidel sent his brother Raul and a loyal revolutionary named Che Guevara into neighboring Latin American countries to spread the communist gospel according to Moscow. If the CIA could not kill Castro in Havana, then they would get his lieutenants!*

One day, I was working in my office on assassination research, when I was visited by a man who provided sufficient proof to me that he worked for the CIA. He gave me permission to tape his story. Would you like to hear it?"

"Of course, please do!" Atherton replied.

The voice on the tape was clear, 'We knew in 1960 that Che Guevara was somewhere in the forests of Bolivia, but we could not pinpoint his location. The CIA developed the first night vision apparatus with the best optic lenses available at the time. The first night vision lens captured starlight and intensified it in the scope. It came to be known as the Starlight Scope. With this new device mounted in a helicopter, we were able to locate Guevara's camp in the black of night from an altitude of one mile above the forest. We were able to discern Guevara and his men quite well with the night vision camera. The next day we inserted a squad of CIA operatives who commanded the Bolivian military police squad that conducted the search. As soon as Guevara was captured, the CIA officer ordered that Che and his men be executed. For political propaganda reasons, Che's body was displayed and filmed for several days. Following CIA orders, the officer cut off Guevara's hands, and delivered them to CIA headquarters in Virginia for positive identification.'

"The man did not give me his name," the professor said with a warning tone and expression, "And I did not ask for it. I promised I would destroy this tape immediately after you had heard it."

"Thank you for sharing that information with me," Atherton replied. "It gives me a better understanding of what American capabilities have been relative to assassination in recent history."

The professor continued, "I also know that this year, the Administration and the CIA have become very frustrated with Ngo Dinh Diem, President of South Vietnam. Diem's corrupt ways are overshadowed by the brutality of his brother, Ngo Dinh Nhu, who has been terrorizing villages in South Vietnam, and killing Buddhist monks. Diem and his brother are Catholics, and their despicable behavior is troubling and politically volatile for John Kennedy, since he is the first Irish-Catholic American President.

As South Vietnam destabilizes, it is becoming apparent to the U.S. that the communists might overrun the South, starting a domino effect in Asia. I am concerned that the conflict building in Vietnam is ripe for another assassination. This is only conjecture on my part, you understand."

"Hmmm, yes. I understand," Atherton muttered under his breath as he tried to absorb and process everything the professor had said.

* * * * * * * * *

On October 2nd, 1963, General Maxwell Taylor and Defense Secretary McNamara delivered a leather-bound, fully illustrated report of their visit to Vietnam, to the President. Much of the language in the report had been determined in advance by Kennedy, because it would serve as his basis for withdrawing American forces from Vietnam. Kennedy had been quoted as saying, *"In the final analysis, it is their (South Vietnam's) war."* Included in the Maxwell/Taylor Report was the statement, *"There is no solid evidence of the possibility of a successful coup, although assassination of Diem or Nhu is always a possibility."*

* * * * * * * *

"In high quarters here, it is the clear-cut conclusion that if [Lumumba] continues to hold high office, the inevitable result will [have] disastrous consequences . . . for the interests of the free world generally. Consequently, we conclude that his removal must be an urgent and prime objective."

Allen Dulles, CIA Director, 1960 memo

After only 100 days in office, Patrice Lumumba, the first prime minister of the free republic of the Congo nation in Africa, was turned over to soldiers of the former imperialist controlling government of Belgium who were working with the CIA and soldiers of General Suharto. Lumumba was maliciously beaten, moved several times, then lined up against a tree and shot. General Suharto's coup and the purge that followed resulted in the deaths of close to a million Congolese citizens. The policy of the United States was that these losses were necessary to prevent the Congo from falling to communism.

* * * * * * * *

On November 1, 1963, President Ngo Dinh Diem of South Vietnam, and his notorious brother Ngo Dinh Nhu narrowly escaped a coup by generals of the South Vietnamese army. It was just three weeks before President Kennedy went to Dallas. The CIA-supported military police were dispatched to the Catholic parish where Diem and his brother were hiding. The general's aides arrested the head of state and his brother, loaded them into a waiting van, and shot them both in the head. President Kennedy had applied his tacit support for the coup, but had been given assurances by Henry Cabot Lodge, the U.S. Ambassador to Vietnam and Kennedy's former political rival, and the CIA, that Diem's life would be spared. President Kennedy was so overwhelmed when he learned that Diem and his brother had been assassinated, he immediately left the Cabinet Room, then ran to the Oval Office bathroom to vomit.

Chapter 10
The Beginning of the End

"The covert training of Cuban exiles by the CIA was due in substantial part, at least, to my efforts. This had been adopted as a policy as a result of my direct support."

Richard Nixon, <u>Six Crises</u>

The corrupt regime of Fulgencio Batista, prior to Castro, was a boon to organized crime in America. Every form of vice was readily available to Americans in Havana, including drugs, gambling, prostitutes, rum…an ideal Mafia haven for smuggling and money laundering. It was a racketeer's paradise. But when the revolutionary forces led by Castro ousted Batista in 1959, all Cuban and American assets were seized and businesses were stripped from their owners. Many Cuban businessmen escaped to Miami. Some came to Washington to develop a plan with the CIA in cooperation with the Mafia to reclaim what they had lost.

The Cuban exiles expected to have the full support of the United States in reclaiming their government. The leader of the Cuban exiles, and the presidential designate of the provisional Cuban government-in-exile, was a Cuban investment banker, named Mario Garcia Kohly, Sr. The CIA established an office for Kohly in Washington. He would often hold meetings there with the Cuban exiles who would form the new government of Cuba once Castro was eliminated. CIA scientist Robert Morrow once met Mafia dons Sam Giancana and Johnny Roselli in Kohly's Washington, D.C. office. This was the same Sam Giancana who helped Kennedy win the presidential election, and the same Roselli who helped the Kennedy brothers murder Marilyn Monroe. These events all transpired during the early days of John Kennedy's administration.

During that period, Mario Kohly received legal representation from an experienced Washington politician, working from his law offices in New York. As Kohly waged his public relations war against President Kennedy, making speeches, radio addresses and television appearances to provoke an invasion of Cuba by the United States, and while Robert Morrow of the CIA helped Kohly avoid Kennedy's agents, Kohly's lawyer worked overtime keeping Kohly out of jail. Kohly's lawyer was the former vice-president, Richard Nixon. Kohly and Nixon entered into a pact regarding Cuba that would ultimately lead to Nixon's downfall.

Prior to Kennedy's inauguration, Kohly had cut a deal with the devil. There were certain liberal members of the Cuban government in exile, and in Brigade 2506, the exile invasion force, that Nixon did not want to see in power. Nixon proposed that if Kohly would agree to commit his underground forces of several hundred trained men, who were hiding in the Escambray Mountains during the invasion at Bahia de Cochinos, Nixon and his CIA agents would ensure the assassinations of Miro Cordona, Manuel Artime, Aureliano Sanchez Arrango and all the leftist Cuban Revolutionary Front leaders. The leftists in the invasion force were to be murdered by their compatriots as they landed on the beach. The conservatives would know who to kill based upon the color bandana each was wearing around his neck. The assassinations of fellow brigadistas during the invasion were to be the climax of OPERATION FORTY.

This murderous plot would lead to the burglary at the Watergate Hotel, the ensuing cover-up by President Nixon, the end of Nixon's presidency, and the beginning of heightened distrust of government by the American people. Nixon ordered the burglary of the Democratic National Committee headquarters at the Watergate office complex, during which Cuban exiles working for Nixon attempted to recover photographic evidence pertaining to Cuba related activities as part of OPERATION FORTY. Watergate would be the first step toward breaking down the wall of denial that our elected officials could betray Americans in such a fashion.

The covert operations division of the CIA worked feverishly to equip and train the Cuban exiles in Florida, and then subsequently in Guatemala for the assault that would enable them to eliminate Castro and regain the homeland for its exiles. Meanwhile, battalions of American troops were making preparations in Puerto Rico for a full-scale invasion of Cuba. President Kennedy was concerned about plausible deniability of U.S. involvement in the operation, so he moved the proposed landing site from Trinidad to a more shallow location further south, called Bahia de Cochinos. The shallow water depth at the landing site was a major contributor to the ultimate failure of the invasion. Americans would come to know it as the Bay of Pigs. The operational concept had been approved by President Eisenhower prior to the end of his term, and President Kennedy, although never enthusiastic about the plan, allowed it to move forward.

The CIA assumed that by the time of the invasion, Kennedy would agree to provide air cover by American fighter aircraft to ensure the success of the mission. What they did not count on was John Kennedy's strong aversion to war, and his desire for plausible deniability in such covert operations. An assault on Cuba with U.S. forces could ignite a nuclear war with Russia! As a former Navy man, Kennedy knew how important air cover would be to an amphibious invasion such as the one proposed at Bahia de Cochinos.

"A man does what he must, in spite of personal consequences, in spite of obstacles, and dangers, and pressures."
John Kennedy

* * * * * * * * *

Atherton's research into assassinations took him to Miami. He had located a U.S. Navy gunboat skipper who had ties to the CIA. Captain Martin had helped train the Cubans of Brigade 2506 who fought Castro's forces at the Bay of Pigs. By the time Atherton located the tiny bar in South Miami, the captain already had a few brews under his belt. The two men shook hands.

"*I might as well beat you to the punch. We will never talk again after this, right?*" Atherton offered.

"*You got it, partner.*"

'*At least he is not making me give him some secret handshake,*' Atherton mused. He had started to like the covert interviews. They were exciting. "*Okay, then let's get right to it. Why did the invasion of Cuba fail, and what is this I hear about Cuban exiles killing each other on the beach?*" Atherton inquired.

"*You cannot quote me as a source,*" the captain began, "*But I am going to tell you what I know, because you are probably the best person to figure out a way to get the truth to the American people. There were a number of reasons the attack on Cuba failed. First, Kennedy refused to let our flyboys take out Castro's warplanes, which we could have accomplished easily from the air. The exiles would have been far more successful if we had been overhead, strafing and bombing enemy aircraft, supply trucks and troops. President Kennedy did allow U.S. Navy warships to stand offshore and bombard the landing site with their big guns before the Brigadistas went ashore, but he would not allow our pilots and aircraft to get involved. Those poor Cubans were doomed before they ever hit the beach.*"

The captain took a pause to sip his beer, then went on, "*Mind you, President Kennedy did not promise air support, then reverse his position. However, the CIA repeatedly assured the exiles they would have American air support for the invasion. Kennedy allowed the Cuban exiles to conduct air strikes against Castro's minimal air force, with unmarked aircraft provided by the CIA. But Castro's remaining three T-33 jets and Sea Furies repelled the invasion. Although it took months of investigation for Kennedy to fully understand what had happened around him, he took full responsibility for the disaster.*

In an effort to provoke Kennedy into ordering strong action against Cuba, the exiles launched numerous unauthorized guerilla attacks against Cuba from Florida beaches before and after the Bay of Pigs invasion. These operations were conducted with the full support of the CIA, against direct orders from the President. In fact, the activity in Florida was so obvious and intense that newspaper articles claimed the United States was preparing to invade Cuba. Castro saw them coming, and he was ready!"

"*If Castro knew the invasion was coming, then why was it allowed to go forward?*" Atherton asked.

"*President Kennedy allowed the invasion of Cuba to take place due to political pressure applied by the CIA. Known by its codename, OPERATION ZAPATA was launched on April 17, 1961. The 1,400 Cuban exiles who invaded Cuba at the Bay of Pigs were slaughtered by Castro's forces. Those who were not killed were captured. Approximately 2,500 Cubans were jailed, including sympathetic citizens who were rounded up afterward. The freedom fighters in the Escambray Mountains, and the Cuban people did not rise up to overthrow Castro, as the CIA had promised. This was a flawed assumption of the plan. In fact, when Kohly realized his invaders were defeated on the beach, he ordered his forces in the Escambray to remain hidden in the mountains. He would not sacrifice them to the slaughter that was transpiring on the beaches and in the lowlands.*"

"You still haven't told me about assassinations on the beach?" Atherton chided.

Martin's face became dark, *"Have you ever heard of something called OPERATION FORTY?"*

"Yes, I have," Atherton said proudly, *"It was the plan to assassinate Castro, his brother, and some other revolutionaries, such as Che Guevara."*

"Guess you never heard the rest of that story."

"Perhaps not," Atherton replied.

"The CIA actually imprisoned the liberal Cuban leaders at Opa Locka, a CIA-operated air base in Florida, on the day of the invasion, with the intent to kill them. But Manuel Artime escaped through a window and called President Kennedy."

"Guess the President was really in the dark on this one. You know what Benjamin Franklin said?" Atherton mused, *'The worst lies are half-truths'"*

Captain Martin continued, *"Now, I'm going to tell you a lot of facts, and I am going to give you many names. It will be up to you to tie everything together and get all the details. But I can get you started."*

"Sounds good to me!" Atherton replied, already wondering if this guy's amazing stories were to be believed.

"Robert Morrow is a CIA scientist who works from his home laboratory in Baltimore. Morrow once rescued Mario Kohly, the U.S.- supported provisional president of Cuba, from the hands of federal agents who were sent by President Kennedy as Kohly exited a broadcast station in Washington, D.C. Kohly had participated in a live broadcast interview that directly opposed President Kennedy's statements earlier that day. Kennedy had insisted there were no nuclear missiles in Cuba. Morrow picked Kohly up in a CIA-modified performance car, eluded federal agents, and then drove to a commercial airport in Gaithersburg, Maryland, where a plane was warmed up, ready for takeoff. Morrow flew Kohly to the secret, CIA-operated airstrip in Opa Locka, Florida, to protect Kohly from President Kennedy and his agents.

Morrow is the guy who purchased four Italian-made Mannlicher-Carcano carbines with funds supplied by the CIA for use in assassinating a 'head of state.' I'm not sure why they chose that weapon, because the Mannlicher-Carcano is a carbine, a light rifle which is not very accurate and doesn't have the muzzle velocity of a high- powered rifle. It's possible they chose a carbine because of its shorter length, making it easier to conceal.

Tracy Barnes at the CIA authorized the purchase, using funds provided by Carlos Marcello, the Mafia boss in New Orleans. Marcello had an axe to grind with the Kennedys, because he had been illegally deported from the United States by Robert Kennedy.

Now, David Ferrie is Marcello's personal pilot. Morrow purchased the Italian carbines at a Sunny's Surplus store in Towson, Maryland; then, Tracy Barnes assigned Morrow the task of redesigning the Mannlicher-Carcano carbines for quick disassembly using only three screws. Once his modifications were complete, David Ferrie flew to Baltimore to pick them up from Morrow.

Morrow also has designed communication devices he calls 'walkie talkies,' because you can hold it in your hand and talk while you are walking. They operate at ultra low frequencies. These secure handheld radios require antennas that are four feet long. The antennas can be strapped to the operator's leg, and they are designed to be used by spotters during assassination operations. One of the guys in Ferrie's Civil Air Patrol unit is a fellow by the name of Lee Harvey Oswald.

Ferrie and Oswald are now working in the same building in New Orleans. It's one of those old, triangular buildings that fronts on two streets. Ferrie is working with Guy Bannister, a CIA operative and a former FBI agent. Bannister's office address is 531 Lafayette Street, and Oswald is working where Sergio Arcacha Smith used to work, at 544 Camp Street. But both offices are in the same building! Their assigned mission is OPERATION MONGOOSE.

There was a critical covert operation that took place on the day of the Bay of Pigs invasion. It was to be carried out by David Ferrie and Robert Morrow. The CIA was desperate to obtain hard data showing the Cubans had Soviet nuclear missiles ready to launch against the United States. General Cabell of the CIA had assured Morrow that if the initial assault on the Bahia de Cochinos was not successful, their mission into Cuba would be aborted. The CIA misled Morrow. Despite knowledge that the invasion had failed, the CIA allowed Ferrie and Morrow to take off from Opa Locka with orders to land in Cuba to collect telemetry data. They stopped to load some gear at Buckingham Field, an abandoned army airstrip, then flew across the Gulf of Mexico at an altitude of only 50 feet.

Once on the ground in Cuba, Morrow obtained telemetry readings proving there were indeed Soviet nuclear missiles staged in Cuba that could be programmed to attack Washington, D.C. at any moment. As Morrow loaded his electronic equipment back into the Beech airplane, Ferrie spotted one of Castro's propeller fighters, a swift WW II Sea Fury, which was bearing down on them. Ferrie was wounded in the shoulder on the first strafing run, so Morrow had to take over the controls from the co-pilot position. Morrow got the plane off the ground, but he knew the Twin Beech could not outrun the Sea Fury. Remembering a deep gorge they had flown over on their way into Cuba, Morrow lured the young Cuban into the gorge who was flying at twice his airspeed, intent on a quick kill. When Morrow pulled the Beech aircraft up over the ridge at the last possible moment, the faster Sea Fury plowed into the mountain, exploding upon impact and leaving behind a ball of fire and a cloud of dark smoke. When the CIA after- action report mentioned that the special aircraft had landed, only a few realized this was a reference to Ferrie and Morrow.

After Morrow's return to Florida, he realized the CIA had treated him as expendable, despite his loyalty and his repeated contributions to their cause. One of the reasons I am putting myself in danger by speaking with you is that Morrow told me he found explosives and an altimeter fuse attached to his plane when he returned to Florida. The CIA could have taken Ferrie and Morrow out while airborne if that had somehow suited their agenda. Morrow began to wonder if his loyalties were misplaced. President Kennedy and Attorney General Robert Kennedy ordered that the secret training bases in New Orleans and in Florida be shut down. Not long after that, a young man witnessed a frustrated David Ferrie describing to Clay Shaw and Lee Harvey Oswald at his home in New Orleans how Kennedy could be killed. Ferrie spoke of a kill zone, featuring multiple shooters in tall buildings with triangulation of fire, diversionary fire, and the 'good shot.' And with Lee Harvey Oswald sitting in his living room, Ferrie stated there would have to be a 'patsy.' Little did Ferrie know it, but Lucien Conein at the CIA was working on just such a plan for the President's trip to Dallas."

"Well, Captain Martin," Atherton began with a sigh, "I continue to be impressed with how people like you have the desire to speak with me, and the level of detail you have provided, but I am frustrated by the fact that I cannot corroborate much of this information."

"I know," the Captain replied, "But you have to live with that. Just find out as much as you can, and do your best to piece it all together. Good luck to you, Mr. Atherton. You may be the one who blows this whole thing apart. Just be careful!"

* * * * * * * *

The core group of David Ferrie, Clay Shaw, Lee Oswald and Guy Bannister in New Orleans, the team that had been assembled by Robert Kennedy as OPERATION MONGOOSE to assassinate Fidel Castro, together with their CIA/Mafia ties, was now turning its lethal knowledge and government supported capabilities against Bobby's brother, the President of the United States!

The Attorney General stepped into his brother's office at the White House, "You wanted to see me, Jack?"

"Yeah, Bobby, thanks for coming by. I know you want to get home to Ethel and the kids."

"You don't ask me over to see you in person unless it's something important."

"Well, it is. And I want you to hear it directly from me. You know I have just returned from a meeting with former President Eisenhower at Camp David. He filled me in on many of the details about the Bay of Pigs, since he approved the operation in the first place. I didn't tell him anything of what I am about to tell you. A memo has just been transmitted from me to General Lemnitzer at the Joint Chiefs. I have decided to abolish the CIA." The President paused for a moment, as he let the momentous information sink in. "I am tired of them ignoring my direction, and trying to topple regimes that end up worse off than before. I am going to smash the CIA into a thousand pieces, and scatter it to the winds, Bobby. I am firing Director Dulles, his deputy, Richard Bissell, and General Cabell, at a minimum. They will not be serving anywhere in my administration. The mission of the CIA, and its budget are being transferred to the Pentagon. I am creating a new intelligence agency, called the Defense Intelligence Agency. The DIA will take on the mission and the budget that CIA once carried."

"My God, Jack, this is a drastic action you are taking. Have you already put this in motion?"

"I thought about it carefully, and it's done," the President replied as he played with the piece of scrimshaw he kept on his desk.

"Why didn't you speak with me about it first?"

The President looked up at his brother, "Because I figured you might try to talk me out of it."

"You're damn right I would have. But if it's done, it's done."

"Okay, now go home and play with the kids, Bobby."

"*Yes, Mr. President,*" the U.S. Attorney General gave a slight bow of his head as he backed his way out of the Oval Office, drawing a smile from his older brother. The attorney general's face transformed into a dark scowl as he walked down the White House corridor. "*Langley won't take this lightly,*" Robert Kennedy said under his breath.

President Kennedy knew he must take full responsibility for the Bay of Pigs tragedy, as the Chief Executive and Commander-in-Chief. He did so in an address to the primarily-Cuban audience at the Rose Bowl stadium in Miami. During that address, he stated, "*The forces of communism should not be underestimated.*" Those around him at the time were impressed with his Presidential style, including his political rival, General Eisenhower.

When John Kennedy and Robert Kennedy became the President and Attorney General, respectively, they decided to get rid of the ghastly organization that had helped them gain the White House. There was something unseemly about the White House and the nation's highest-ranking law enforcement officer being linked directly to the Mafia. So Robert Kennedy launched an inquisition into the world of the Mafia and labor organizations, such as the Teamsters Union. Robert Kennedy's clash with Jimmy Hoffa, President of the Teamsters Union, is legendary, and the attacks from both sides got personal. RFK's 'Get Hoffa' program was intense and highly visible on Capitol Hill.

Prior to his appointment as U.S. Attorney General, Robert Kennedy served as counsel for the Senate Rackets Committee in 1958. During that time, RFK referred to Sam Giancana as, "*…the chief gunman for the group that succeeded the Capone mob.*" When Giancana refused to answer questions put to him by the Senate Rackets Committee, Giancana pleaded Fifth Amendment protection against self-incrimination and ended his statement with a giggle. To that, Robert Kennedy replied, "*I thought only little girls giggled, Mr. Giancana.*"

Robert Kennedy's pursuit of the Mafia was patterned after the infamous persecution of suspected communists by Senator Joseph McCarthy's House Committee on Un-American Activities, a committee on which Robert Kennedy had served as legal counsel.

Bobby Kennedy's relentless pursuit of Mafia bosses, including the illegal deportation of Carlos Marcello while RFK was Attorney General, provided sufficient motive for the Mob to assist the CIA, the Pentagon, and their political bosses to murder both the President and RFK himself.

The Bahia de Cochinos fiasco and its aftermath provided sufficient motive for the CIA to kill the President. Even so, John Kennedy and Robert Kennedy withheld evidence from the American people that the Soviets were staging nuclear missiles in Cuba - missiles that could destroy half of America's cities in one salvo. The Kennedy brothers withheld this evidence from the public for political reasons. Apparently, they wanted to wait to release the information at a moment that would boost the chances of achieving a Congressional electoral victory, giving the Democratic Party control over Congress. And that is exactly what happened.

Just prior to his death, President Kennedy issued several executive orders that never saw the light of day. He was going to replace the CIA with the DIA in the Pentagon. He was going to pull all American troops out of Vietnam. He was going to restructure the Federal Reserve debt by changing the backing of certain U.S. currencies with silver and gold metals. He was going to terminate the oil depletion allowance. Finally, he was going to amend certain National Labor Relations Board and IRS statutes that would prevent foreign flag shipping from being exempt from American income taxes. As a result of these policy changes, international bankers, the U.S. military/industrial complex, Big Oil in Texas, and shipping magnates like Aristotle Onassis would have lost billions of dollars. Also, the Mafia knew that killing the President would get the Attorney General off their backs.

The CIA fumed over the President's delays in exposing the missile evidence, hoping such a disclosure would prompt Americans to demand a full-scale invasion of Cuba by U.S. troops. The Kennedys held this information until John Kennedy's televised announcement of the U.S. blockade of Soviet ships delivering more missiles to Cuba. This occurred two weeks before the Congressional election, resulting in a strengthened Democratic control of Congress, and surging approval ratings for President Kennedy.

Thirteen days passed in October of 1962 during which President Kennedy and Premier Khrushchev stood eyeball to eyeball, each waiting for the other leader to blink. The President and the Attorney General held constant meetings to hammer out how the United States would respond to the threat of offensive nuclear weapons that were active on an island located just 90 miles from Florida. This special executive committee, known as Ex Com, met secretly throughout the 13 tension-filled days. The Pentagon and several cabinet members pushed for bombing of the missile sites and an amphibious invasion by U.S. Marines. Such a war would have probably resulted in an exchange of nuclear weapons. Kennedy and Khrushchev were both concerned that there were not enough safeguards on nuclear missile systems to prevent an unauthorized launch.

Because a blockade is an act of war, Kennedy borrowed a phrase from President Roosevelt, referring to this naval action as a quarantine. At one point during the resulting crisis, Nikita Khrushchev sent a note to Kennedy, saying, *"Now we and you should not pull on the ends of the rope in which you have tied the knot of war, because the more the two of us pull, the tighter the knot will be tied."* Approaching the end of the second week of the crisis, a Lithuanian bartender in the National Press Club overheard a conversation between a Pentagon reporter named Robert Warren and his boss, indicating he was preparing to accompany Marines to Cuba. Troops were being staged in Puerto Rico in preparation for an assault on Fidel Castro's forces.

While walking to their cars in the parking lot of the National Press Club, a Soviet embassy officer bumped into Warren.

"Hello, Yuriy!" Warren called out to the Soviet official. "What's going on with all those ships that are stopped in the water off of Cuba? Are they going to challenge the blockade or return to Russia?"

"I find your choice of words very intriguing, Comrade Warren. Your President has been calling it a quarantine. By the way, there are rumors President Kennedy could be making preparations to invade our friends in Cuba? Do you think he would do such a thing?"

"You better believe it! Okay, Yuriy, see you around."

Robert Warren would not have imagined it, but a telegram conveying his words was on the desk of the Soviet Premier within hours. That message provided the motivation for Khrushchev to turn his ships around.

* * * * * * * * *

Jack Scali, a reporter for ABC News, stationed in Washington, was contacted by Aleksandr Fomin, the senior Soviet intelligence officer for the KGB, with a message from Premier Khrushchev for President Kennedy. The journalist was being asked to serve as mediator between the Kremlin and the White House. No diplomats were to be involved. The President agreed with the highly unorthodox arrangement, since it suited his political agenda as well.

It provides another example of how journalists during this period were drawn into active participation in political and intelligence activities on the international level. Reporters knew significant people, they could ask tough questions, and they could move about with a certain degree of freedom.

Scali and Fomin met at the Occidental Restaurant adjacent to the Willard Hotel, located at the corner of Pennsylvania Avenue and 15th Street, N.W., one block away from the White House.

"Thank you for meeting with me on such short notice, Mr. Scali. I imagine you are not accustomed to handling such affairs, but my government wants to avoid certain diplomatic entanglements."

"I understand," Scali replied, "And I need for you to know I am not at all comfortable in this role."

"Relax, Mr. Scali. What these people sitting around us, talking about legislation, interest rates and cocktail parties do not know is that a Russian intelligence officer and an American journalist are sitting at this table discussing the fate of the world. There is nothing to be uncomfortable about. Now, let us get down to the business at hand. Have you met with the President?"

"Yes, I was in the Oval Office less than an hour ago."

"And you presented our proposal to him at that time, da?"

"Yes I did."

"And just what did Mr. Kennedy have to say?"

"It took a while for me to convince the president and his staff that the Soviet government was making an official peace proposal through me. But I told them you and I had met a few times at legitimate diplomatic functions, and that you seem to trust me."

"But, of course, I trust you. Why else do you think my government would venture to address this issue with the White House through you? It was on my direct recommendation!"

"Well, desperate people do desperate things."

"Are you saying the Soviet people are desperate?"

"No, I am saying the governments of the United States and the Soviet Union have placed the entire world in a desperate situation, during which some lunatic military officer on either side with access to launch codes could instigate an exchange of nuclear weapons that would destroy all life on Earth. So I would say that both sides are desperate, and if it means using a reporter and a spy to diffuse this insanity, then so be it."

"You are right, my friend. Although I don't care to be called a spy. I am an intelligence officer. This is a deplorable situation. And I have no more interest in dying than you. So, due to the nature of my job and the highly irregular duty you have been assigned, history may not even record the role we play in this, but I hope we will succeed in pulling this crisis back from the brink of disaster."

Scali leaned further over the table, toward his friend from the Soviet Union, "Now tell me, how did Premier Khrushchev react to our offer? We guarantee there will be no more invasions of Cuba if he immediately withdraws the missiles."

"The Premier of the Soviet Union has instructed me to tell you he will accept these terms with one condition. He wants President Kennedy to withdraw the Titan missiles installed in Turkey which target Moscow and other cities within the Soviet Union."

"We had anticipated this request," Scali replied, "And I have been instructed to answer in the following way. The President will agree to remove the Titan nuclear missiles from Turkey, but only after six months has passed and this crisis has subsided."

"Why do you wish to wait six months?"

Scali explained, "It would be too politically sensitive for the President to remove those weapons as part of the negotiation at this time. Premier Khrushchev might want to continue his formal relationship with President Kennedy for four more years, da? Therefore, you cannot publicize this decision by President Kennedy in any way."

"Ahh yes, I am forgetting that in America you have to concern yourselves with such things as elections. I do believe Premier Khrushchev would like to continue his association with President Kennedy for a second term of office. My government and I would like to say 'spasiba' to you, Mr. Scali. Thank you very much."

The KGB operative reached across the table to shake the hand of the American reporter. The agent mused aloud so only Scali would hear him, "The patrons of this restaurant can now have their dessert and cognac safe from the threat of nuclear catastrophe. The chocolate mousse here is excellent; you should try it!"

With that, the senior Soviet intelligence agent wrapped his scarf loosely around his neck, then walked out of the Occidental Restaurant to his waiting limousine. Soon after the unorthodox meeting between the reporter and the spy,

President Kennedy received a letter from Khrushchev containing an ideological message. It also tacitly confirmed the accord that had been reached between the superpowers.

October 25, 1962

John F. Kennedy

President of the United States

The White House

Washington, D.C.

Dear Mr. President:

I have received your letter of October 25. From your letter I got the feeling that you have some understanding of the situation which has developed, and a sense of responsibility. I appreciate this.

By now we have already publicly exchanged our assessments of the events around Cuba and each of us has set forth his explanation and his interpretation of these events. Therefore, I would think that, evidently, continuing to exchange opinions at such a distance, even in the form of secret letters, would probably not add anything to what one side has already said to the other.

I think you will understand me correctly if you are really concerned for the welfare of the world. Everyone needs peace: both capitalists, if they have not lost their reason, and all the more, communists - people who know how to value not only their own lives but, above all else, the life of nations. We communists are against any wars between states at all, and have been defending the cause of peace ever since we came into the world. We have always regarded war as a calamity, not as a game or a means for achieving particular purposes, much less as a goal in itself. Our goals are clear, and the means of achieving them is work. War is our enemy and a calamity for all nations.

Sincerely,

Nikita Sergeyevich Khrushchev

Premier of the Soviet Union

* * * * * * * * *

Meanwhile in New Orleans, a beautiful, young cancer researcher was tasked by the CIA with developing a deadly strain of lung cancer that would kill a man within weeks of its injection. It was widely known that Castro was a chain smoker of excellent Cuban cigars, and his accelerated death by lung cancer could have been plausibly denied by the CIA. David Ferrie, pilot to Carlos Marcello, worked with Judyth Vary Baker, a protégé of the famed surgeon, Dr. Alton Ochsner in New Orleans, in the development of the lung cancer virus. The plan was to mix the cancer with a virus that would attack the immune system. Once the two viruses were injected into the bloodstream, death would be swift.

In order to minimize the possibility of disease killing all of the white test mice during experimentation, Ferrie maintained cages of the mice in his New Orleans apartment. The esteemed Dr. Mary Sherman of the Ochsner Clinic was recruited also. Testing took place in her apartment as well as David Ferrie's apartment.

Judyth Vary Baker had arrived in New Orleans two weeks ahead of schedule. Young Lee Harvey Oswald was sent to 'bump into' her at the post office on April 26th, 1963. Oswald was having problems with his wife, Marina, and Judyth's new husband, Robert Baker, had been given an extended assignment to work on oil rigs in the Gulf of Mexico. Lee and Judyth had much in common. They both spoke Russian, they were both working on a secret project for the CIA, and they found each other attractive. As Ferrie directed the experiment to develop the deadly cancer strain to kill Castro, Lee and Judyth worked closely together, and a romance developed between them. The CIA made arrangements for the young lovers to work together at the Reily Coffee Company in New Orleans as the testing moved forward.

Oswald and Ferrie arrived together in Clinton, Louisiana, in August of 1963, in a black Cadillac driven by Clay Shaw [aka Clay Bertram]. Clay Shaw was later tried by District Attorney Jim Garrison of New Orleans Parish. Garrison accused Shaw of being associated with a CIA plot which successfully assassinated President Kennedy in November of 1963. Shaw was acquitted.

Oswald, Ferrie and Shaw were waiting in Clinton, Louisiana, for a shipment of convicts from the Angola State Penitentiary. Several selected prisoners were to be used unwittingly as human subjects for lung cancer experiments. They needed proof that Judyth Vary Baker's strain of lung cancer could kill Castro. The testing was a success, as the prisoners soon died.

Oswald was later sent by the CIA to Mexico, in an attempt to transfer the cancer virus cocktail to a trusted member of Castro's medical staff. James Jesus Angleton of the CIA had previously sent Oswald to Moscow and to Minsk, after having him trained in Russian, to give the Soviets information that was used to shoot down the U-2 reconnaissance plane flown by Francis Gary Powers.

The KGB contact sat down with Oswald in Moscow when Oswald feigned an attempt to defect to the Soviet Union. The defection story provided plausible deniability for Oswald's reason for being in Russia.

"I have some information for you about American reconnaissance flights over your country," Oswald began.

"Yes, we are aware of these flights," Oswald's contact began, *"But your U-2s fly at an altitude that cannot be reached by our surface-to-air missiles."*

Oswald continued, *"There is a specific flight scheduled that will be taking pictures of your ballistic nuclear missile sites in advance of the summit meeting with President Eisenhower. I am going to give you the coordinates over your airspace where the U-2 will experience an unfortunate flame out of its engine. The pilot will be forced to dive to a lower altitude to restart his engine. We will ensure he gets low enough for your missiles to reach him."*

The KGB man looked dumbfounded, *"And why would you Americans allow such an event to take place?"*

Without blinking, the counter intelligence agent, Lee Harvey Oswald replied, *"We want Premier Khrushchev to cancel the nuclear summit."*

The downing of the U-2 had the desired result – cancellation of the nuclear summit between the superpowers. Oswald's Mexico trip was later used by the CIA cover-up team as 'proof' that he was a pro-Castro communist.

* * * * * * * * *

In the fall of 1963, the CIA instructed mobsters Rolando Masferer and Tony Verona to orchestrate an abortive attempt to assassinate Castro. Santo Trafficante, the Mafia don in Tampa, coordinated with Carlos Marcello in New Orleans and Johnny Roselli in Las Vegas, making it look like the United States had tried to kill Castro. This gave Castro a motive to eliminate President Kennedy. Later, the CIA met with a high-ranking Cuban official in Brazil, named Rolando Cubelo, who wanted to defect to the United States. He offered to assassinate Castro himself. Cubelo was given the codename AM/LASH by the CIA. Although he was in favor of assassinating Castro, Robert Kennedy nixed the Cubelo plan based on the recommendation of the CIA's Director of Counterintelligence, James Jesus Angleton, on the premise it might be a double cross.

Shortly after the meeting in Brazil, the CIA was delighted to see the widely published warning by Castro that any further attempts on his life would put American officials in grave danger. The CIA had now secured plausible deniability for the assassination of President Kennedy.

During the first televised debates prior to the presidential election, JFK had decided to propose a planned attack on Cuba, in an effort to disclose the covert operation that was being prepared by the Eisenhower Administration, under the direction of Vice President Nixon. JFK had learned of the plan to invade Cuba, and he thought the idea was reckless. To which, Nixon later replied, *"There was only one thing I could do. The covert operation had to be protected at all costs. I must not even suggest by implication that the U.S. was rendering aid to rebel forces in and out of Cuba. In fact, I must go to the other extreme: I must attack the Kennedy proposal to provide such aid as wrong and irresponsible because it would violate our treaty commitments."*

During the fourth debate on ABC, on October 21, 1960, Nixon lied to the American people about his plan to invade Cuba in an effort to discredit Kennedy, and to keep his plan a secret. Nixon claimed that invading Cuba would be dangerous, irresponsible and in violation of five treaties between the U.S. and Latin America, as well as the United Nations' Charter. Nixon failed to mention that America's invasion of Cuba in the absence of a declaration of war from Congress, would also be illegal under federal law.

Then on October 22, 1960 at Muhlenberg College in Allentown, Pennsylvania, Nixon said, *"Kennedy called for -- and get this -- the U.S. Government to support a revolution in Cuba, and I say that this is the most shockingly reckless proposal ever made in our history by a presidential candidate during a campaign -- and I'll tell you why . . ."*

The CIA later confirmed by analysis of cargo ship waterlines [the ships should have been lower in the water] and by aerial photographs, that many of the Soviet missiles that had been installed in Cuba did not return to Russia, but were spirited away in underground bunkers. Khrushchev reneged on his promise to Kennedy, whereas Kennedy did remove the Titan nuclear missiles the U.S. had based in Turkey, which he deemed to be obsolete.

* * * * * * * * *

Several weeks after the missile crisis was resolved, General Lemnitzer, Chairman of the Joint Chiefs of Staff, called a meeting of the Joint Chiefs in a seldom-used conference room located within the innermost corridor of the Pentagon. The conference room was classified as a SCIF (Specially Compartmented Information Facility) and as such was impervious to listening devices. He posted an armed guard outside the doorway, with orders to admit no one once the meeting began.

General Lemnitzer scanned his staff sternly as he cleared his throat. *"This meeting has been called so that I can apprise you of a significant threat to our national security, and to brief you on the mission we will soon undertake to eliminate that threat. Each of you has sworn an oath to protect your country from all enemies, foreign and domestic. Here in the Pentagon we tend to focus our attention on our foes overseas. We often forget that the American people count on their government to protect them from domestic enemies as well. Americans who threaten our lives and our national security run the gamut from crazies with weapons to high-ranking government officials who would sell out America and its people to advance their own political gains. Would each of you agree that such a situation could exist in our federal government, and that when such a threat was identified, it would be our sworn duty to eliminate that threat?"*

All heads nodded in agreement, while exchanging looks of apprehension. It would be the only time the chairman would ask for consent for the rest of the meeting – what remained were his instructions and orders.

"Now, gentlemen, for reasons that will soon be clear, the proceedings of this meeting are classified at the highest level. No notes are to be taken, and your appointment calendars should not reflect that this meeting ever took place. It is a non-event – never happened. I will now disclose to you the name of the man who poses such a high risk to our national security. In fact, we have irrefutable proof that he and his associates represent a clear and present danger to the security interests of the United States. The man's name is John Kennedy!"

Immediately upon the mention of the President's name, all available air in the room was sucked into the lungs of the generals and admirals seated around the oval table. The response was totally involuntary, but the emotion was so intense and immediate - it was experienced by each individual in the room.

Lemnitzer continued, *"Some of you may be more shocked by this revelation than others. For those of you who may not be fully aware of the particulars, I will highlight just a few of President Kennedy's crimes against the people. When the President failed to support the Bay of Pigs operation, he blamed me and my staff for one of the worst military blunders in modern history; this, even though he authorized the mission to proceed while ignoring our tactical recommendations. In the aftermath of that disaster, Kennedy fired top-ranking officials at the CIA, and then ordered that their functions be transferred to me here in the Pentagon under a new command called the DIA. Following this order would have weakened America's ability to carry out clandestine missions abroad. The DIA will have a mission, but we are not going to dismantle the CIA. During the missile crisis in Cuba, the President made a secret deal with the Russians to remove American nuclear missiles from Turkey. Those missiles represent a critical first-strike capability, and a strong deterrent against the communists in the Soviet Union. By securing the removal of Russian missiles from Cuba, Kennedy's political capital increased just prior to the congressional elections, giving the Democrats control of the Congress. When he secretly removed American missiles from Turkey, Kennedy weakened our national security, committing treason against the people he is sworn to protect. In addition, we have proof that the President employed the Mafia during his election, and has employed mobsters while in office to take care of some of his dirty business. The President has disclosed the details of highly classified operations to several of his mistresses. We have tapes of these conversations. Each of these disclosures is a breach of national security. Who knows if any of these women are communist spies? General Lansdale will now brief you on the details of what will transpire in Dallas."*

* * * * * * * * *

Several days later a meeting was held in Austin, deep within the darkened offices of Clark, Thomas and Winters, Lyndon Johnson's law firm. The firm had been providing criminal aid to Johnson his entire political career, stuffing ballot boxes to steal elections, buying off circuit court judges, and masterminding several murders under the cloak of attorney client privilege; assassinations which were instrumental in helping Johnson ascend to the vice presidency. As federal prosecutors closed in on Johnson and his associates, including Bobby Baker and Billy Sol Estes, the Kennedy brothers distanced themselves from Johnson, fearing a negative impact on the upcoming campaign for reelection.

"Come on in!" Ed Clark called out to the sharp-looking Mac Wallace as he sat glumly, holding his hat in the waiting area of Clark's law firm. As Wallace entered the room, the Vice-President rose to meet him with his signature, teeth-rattling handshake and a back slap that almost took Wallace's breath away.

"Good to see ya, Mac. How is the family?" the Vice-President beamed.

"My family is just fine, Mr. Vice-President. Why do you ask?"

"Well now, I just want to be sure we have been taking good care of them as we had promised. We have kept our promises to you, haven't we?"

"Sure you have. Can I ask what this is about?" Wallace inquired.

"Sure, son," Clark replied, *"But first I want to say how sorry we are about the mess you got into over the death of that USDA agent."*

"Ya'll had promised me I wouldn't do any jail time, remember?"

"We tried to control it the best we could," Clark replied, *"...but there are a few things that are out of our control, and sometimes there has to be a guy who takes the fall."*

"So why did you call me here today?"

"We need you to do one last job for us, in the interest of national security," the Vice-President intoned, giving Wallace a somber look.

"Can't the FBI or the military take care of this one? I really don't want to spend any more time in prison."

"Don't worry," Clark waved his finger, *"We've got the entire law enforcement community behind us on this operation, at the local, state and federal levels. Only those who have a need to know are clued in, so security is very tight."*

"Okay then, who is the target?"

"John Kennedy," Clark said with a blank look on his face.

"You want me to assassinate the President of the United States? You gotta be kidding me!"

"We are deadly serious," Clark retorted, a grin of relief spreading across his face. *"You will be one of several sharpshooters."*

"And now we're going to tell you the plan," Johnson sat down and put his hands together as Wallace sat down in a daze. *"It will definitely be worth your while."*

As the plot was laid out for him, Wallace began to replay memories of the other murders he had committed for LBJ and Ed Clark, including those which helped to cover-up LBJ's criminal activities. One of Johnson's associates, Bobby Baker, would later be tried and convicted on seven counts of tax evasion and larceny. But LBJ's ties to organized crime had long and deep roots.

* * * * * * * *

In September of 1962, a wealthy Cuban exile by the name of Jose Manuel Aleman, sought out Santo Trafficante, Jr. in Tampa to make arrangements for a loan from Jimmy Hoffa's pension fund at the Teamster's Union. They met at Miami's Scott Bryan Hotel, and the proposed loan was in the amount of $1.5 million. Trafficante was talking about life in America - how things would be better once John Kennedy was no longer in the White House.

After a couple of drinks and some good Caribbean food, Trafficante asked Aleman, *"Have you seen how his brother* (Robert) *is hitting* (Jimmy) *Hoffa, a man who is a worker, who is not a millionaire, a friend of the blue collar? He doesn't know that this kind of encounter is very delicate. Mark my words, this man Kennedy is in trouble, and he will get what's coming to him!"*

"Come, Santo," Aleman replied, *"You know that Kennedy will be reelected, so we need to get used to dealing with Bobby."*

Trafficante looked sternly at Aleman, and stated flatly, *"No, José, he is going to be hit."*

Frank Ragano was a Sicilian-American, born in 1923, who had served in World War II and had received the Bronze Star while fighting in Germany. After completing his legal education, Ragano worked as a clerk for the Florida Supreme Court. In 1948 he started representing the Mafia boss for Florida, Santo Trafficante, Jr. In 1961 he defended Jimmy Hoffa against claims by Robert Kennedy that Hoffa had embezzled from the Teamster's Pension Fund. Ragano was sent to jail at least twice for tax evasion, and lost his license to practice law.

Early in 1963, Jimmy Hoffa sent Frank Ragano to the Royal Orleans Hotel in New Orleans, with a message for Carlos Marcello and Santo Trafficante. During that meeting, Ragano said to the Mafiosi, *"You won't believe what Hoffa wants me to tell you. Jimmy wants you to kill the President!"*

* * * * * * * *

A few days later on a brisk fall afternoon, President Kennedy slipped out of Washington with Mary Meyer to Arlington Cemetery, just across the Potomac River from the White House, for a walk among the quiet memorials to the nation's fallen military heroes. Jackie was in the hospital preparing to give birth to their second son, Patrick, who died soon thereafter, bringing the couple closer together than ever before.

The President asked his Secret Service detail to wait and watch at a distance as the lovers walked up the sloping hill toward the Custis-Lee Mansion, home of

Confederate General Robert E. Lee, the man of faith who was revered by Virginians. Meyer linked her arm with John Kennedy's as they strode silently up the steep hill. The President winced a few times due to the pain in his back, but he was determined to continue on. At one point, the President looked up and saw the American flag waving defiantly on top of the hill, in front of the Lee Mansion. He turned on his heel to see that the place where he stood was in a direct line between the flagpole in front of the Lee Mansion and the Lincoln Memorial across the Potomac River. A breeze blew over the water and tousled JFK's hair.

At that moment, a wistful look washed over President Kennedy's face. He brushed his bangs away from his eyes and he whispered to Mary, *"I could stay here forever."*

November 10, 1963

To: Commanders of the U.S. Army & Army Reserves
    National Capitol Region
    Dallas/Fort Worth Region

From: Chairman, Joint Chiefs of Staff
      The Pentagon

Intelligence has uncovered rumors of possible riots in several major cities, in the aftermath of recent racial incidents across the country. You are ordered to maintain the highest levels of readiness during the period commencing November 21, 1963 and sustaining that level of readiness through December 1, 1963, in both the National Capitol and Dallas/Fort Worth districts. Your men must be prepared for rapid deployment, equipped with full riot gear including gas masks. Such deployment would be to quell civil disturbances that could take place during that timeframe.

The Dallas reserve units that would normally provide increased presidential protection during President Kennedy's visit on November 22nd will stand down. Their services will not be needed, and will be engaged in drills as their commanders see fit. You will maintain high-alert status until the order has been given to return to standard operations.

In the case of Washington D.C., forces should surround the White House in protection of our Commander-In-Chief. Each unit should be equipped with wireless communication, since land- based telephone systems may not be reliable under such circumstances.

This order is a matter of national security. It carries the highest level of classification, and is 'eyes only' for the recipients listed above. You are to pass this order on to your subordinates without comment or discussion, with orders to read this order, then destroy it.

"Hello, Mrs. Paine? This is David Phillips. The Agency needs a favor from you. We need you to go to New Orleans to bring Marina and Lee's kids to Dallas. Since Michael is not living with you now, we thought you might like to have Marina as company. If you put them up in your home, we'll be happy to compensate you for it. Don't tell either of them you spoke with me. Just tell them you have found a good job for Lee, and that Marina and the kids are welcome in your home."

"Mr. Phillips, I understand what you are asking, but you need to be aware that Marina and Lee are fighting a lot right now. He is a very angry man."

"Yes, I know that, but we need Lee in Dallas for the next few months, and we want to keep close tabs on Marina, to make certain her KGB ties have been cut. She's become active with some communist organizations since she arrived here from Minsk."

"Well, Marina and I get along fine, but I don't want Lee living in my house. If he shows up here, I want someone from the Agency to be watching. My address is 2515 Fifth Street in Dallas."

"Okay, he will have to find a room somewhere. Your knowledge of the Russian language might be comforting for both of them, since they're having problems communicating right now. Part of the problem is Lee seems to be quite taken by a young cancer researcher named Judyth, who is working for us. A few days ago, Marina called over to the 500 Club in New Orleans, asking for her husband, and the lady who answered said she didn't know where Lee was. A few minutes later, in walks Marina who finds Lee there with Judyth. It was not pleasant at all."

"So why does the Agency need Lee to be in Dallas?"

"I can't comment on that, but I need you to bring them here as soon as possible. Tell Lee you have a friend named Roy Truly, who might be able to get him a job at the book depository downtown on Elm Street. Be sure to write that name down. After that, I'll instruct Lee to check in with Special Agent Hosty over at the Bureau. Thanks for your help, Mrs. Paine. The Agency really appreciates it. Goodbye now."

Chapter 11
The Assassination of President Kennedy

"There are causes worth dying for, but none worth killing for."

Albert Camus

John Kennedy had the reputation within the CIA and the Pentagon of being soft on communism. In their view, the President's decisions with regard to the Russians were un-American. But with mainstream America, John Kennedy's administration was seen as a new hope, the dawn of a new generation. Americans believed that a brighter future lay ahead. Kennedy was going to negotiate peace with the Soviets, pull out of Vietnam, eliminate the Oil Depletion Allowance, reduce the nation's dependency on the internationally controlled Federal Reserve System, and work towards achieving equal rights for black Americans. Even the opposition party acknowledged this; and they were angry.

Some Republicans actually admired President Kennedy. Former President Eisenhower once exclaimed, *"There is an air of high drama about John Kennedy. He has become the darling of the population."*

* * * * * * * * * *

President Kennedy went to Fort Worth and Dallas shortly after a Miami trip that was to include a motorcade was cancelled. The CIA/Mafia team had been training, and they had their supplies. One of the key players was David Morales, a tall Cuban with a dark complexion. Morales was chief of operations for JM/WAVE, the large CIA station in Miami that coordinated the Bay of Pigs operation. Morales had the reputation of being the CIA's top assassin for Latin America.

The CIA/Mafia team had aborted previous attempts to assassinate JFK in Chicago, Houston, and finally, Miami. It was common knowledge that the anti-Castro Cuban exiles in Miami were furious with John Kennedy. It would have been very plausible for the Agency to deny involvement in an assassination of JFK in Miami, and blame it on agents of Castro, or anti-Castro sympathizers. Although it is not well-known, two Cubans had planned to shoot down Air Force One on takeoff as President Kennedy left his vacation home at West Palm Beach on November 17, 1963 – just five days before his trip to Dallas.

There was plenty of Kennedy hatred to go around in Miami, following the Bay of Pigs. An FBI contact mailed Atherton the transcript of an interview that took place in Miami during the timeframe when President Kennedy had been scheduled to visit the city of Cuban exiles in America. The witness worked in the Parrot Jungle gift shop in Miami Beach. Atherton sat down with a cup of coffee to read the transcript;

The FBI agent opened with a question to the gift shop attendant, *"Tell me about the suspicious man who visited your shop."*

"I was working at my gift shop in Miami," the elderly lady began. *"A man of Mexican or Cuban origin came into my shop, and he began to just talk crazy. He said, 'I am a sharpshooter. I can write with both hands simultaneously. I hate President Kennedy, and I can put a bullet between his eyes. I have a friend named Lee. He is also a sharpshooter. He lives in Texas or Mexico. Lee speaks German and Russian.' It was the strangest thing I had ever heard. I was just glad when he walked out of my shop. I knew that Kennedy was not popular with the Cubans in Miami, and I had heard that he was scheduled to visit Dallas. That's why I called the FBI, but they didn't take me very seriously. They told me to forget about it, and not to discuss it with anybody."*

* * * * * * * * *

Jack Ruby [aka Jacob Rubenstein], owner of the Carousel strip club in Dallas, sent one of his dancers named Rose Cheramie, to serve as entertainment for the assassins who failed in their attempt to mount an assassination against President Kennedy in Miami. When she heard the rebuking of JFK while riding with the conspirators in the car, Cheramie had an attack of conscience. She pleaded with the men to abandon their plans to kill the President in Dallas. They drugged her, and tossed her out onto the highway near Eunice, Louisiana on November 18th, 1963. As she came out of a coma on November 20th, she told her doctors at East Louisiana Hospital that President Kennedy was to be killed in Dallas on November 22nd. She was heavily sedated by her doctors, recovered and was sent home. She was silenced after the assassination as the result of a hit-and-run in a suburb of Dallas. She was shot, and then run over by a car.

* * * * * * * * *

During one of Vice-President Johnson's trips to New York City, a meeting took place that would have caused tremendous interest, had anyone other than the Secret Service known about it. Former Vice-President Nixon, FBI Director Hoover, Vice-President Johnson, and General Lemnitzer, Chairman of the Joint Chiefs, met to discuss their political futures. It had become apparent that their lives were tied together by a mutual desire – the elimination of John Kennedy and his cronies from the political landscape.

"Thank you all for visiting me here in the Big Apple. I don't get to Washington often these days," Nixon began.

"Well, I feel much more comfortable being out of D.C., but I'm not sure why you insisted that we meet right away," Vice-President Johnson inquired.

"Some information has come to my attention that affects each of us, but you most of all, Lyndon."

Questioning looks were exchanged around the room.

Nixon continued, "You all know I have continued my close relationship with the CIA since leaving the White House. The Agency will sometimes forward information to me that might affect me and my political friends. We know that recent polls are showing that President Kennedy is positioned to win his bid for re-election. But I have just been given evidence that confirms your fear, Lyndon. The President intends to drop you from his ticket."

Johnson picked up the conversation, "I have a Secret Service agent friend who meets me in the White House driveway every morning to give me the latest about what is going on with the Kennedy brothers. I anticipated the Kennedys might do this, and I've tried to look as far as I can down the road if the current trend continues. The picture does not look good. If the President drops me from the ticket, I will never be president. You, Dick, will have to wait a long time to get another shot at the White House, if you ever get a chance at all. Edgar, the President intends to force your retirement from the Bureau at the mandatory age, which will soon be upon you. And General, you know the President is soft on communism and he intends to pull us out of Vietnam. I think we are all in agreement that Kennedy's reelection is not in the best interests of our country, or for us personally. In fact, based upon his recent behavior with lady friends and his worsening medical condition, I've come to the conclusion that we have only one option to protect our country and ourselves – we must assassinate the President."

Johnson continued, "I have an expert marksman named Wallace lined up in Texas who has agreed to come aboard. Now Dick is the expert in these kinds of operations. I recommend that he work with the covert operations group at CIA to iron out the details. They are still hopping mad over the President's lack of action during the Bay of Pigs. I've communicated through back channels to the CIA that I will not allow the President to dismantle the Agency, as he has threatened to do. They should be motivated to reciprocate, but I can't hold off the President for long before he will become suspicious. Edgar, if you will cooperate, I'll see to it you keep your job at the FBI for as long as you care to work. The FBI will be in charge of gathering evidence and giving expert testimony after the assassination, so your cooperation is imperative. General, I know from reading White House transcripts that your post is in jeopardy as well. Certain military personnel will be needed to perform the autopsy and guard against riots and uprisings. Dick, you will need to sit out one term, then I will not seek reelection. I will then step aside so you can become president."

Hoover asked, "What if the Attorney General tries to interfere with the swearing in of Lyndon as president?"

Johnson replied, "There is nothing he can do. The Constitution clearly states that upon the death of the president the vice-president shall be the president. No swearing in is required, from a constitutional perspective. It's merely a formality."

"Don't you just love that old Constitution?" General Lemnitzer teased.

Johnson beamed, "Yeah, it really comes in handy sometimes."

General Lemnitzer continued, *"What you speak of is treason, Lyndon, but I have to admit, I like the idea."*

"Not to mention premeditated murder," Johnson replied coldly.

"So how are we going to avoid prosecution?" Hoover asked.

"By making sure your boys do a good job of handling and mishandling evidence," Johnson replied. *"A key element of Dick's plan is to set up a patsy, one man who will be the fall guy – a lone gunman if you will. Several shooters will be involved to ensure success. They won't even know who the other shooters are. But it will be conducted to appear as if it's the work of one looney tune. And that looney tune will die soon thereafter, because dead men tell no tales. The CIA has been grooming a guy for this part for years. They even sent him to Moscow and Minsk, where he repudiated his American citizenship. We'll convince the American public that he is a commie before we have him killed. By that time, the court of public opinion will want him dead."*

"Where and when do you propose this would take place?" asked Director Hoover. The Vice-President replied with a smile creeping onto his face, *"I'm pushing for President Kennedy to visit Dallas in November. As you know, I have a few friends down there."*

* * * * * * * * *

Many members of the Kennedy Administration, and several of John Kennedy's friends and acquaintances, pleaded with him not to go to Dallas. The political and social climate was too volatile for Kennedy to travel there, they claimed. U.S. Ambassador to the United Nations, Adlai Stevenson, had been accosted in Dallas in the recent past as he made his way through picket signs toward his car. A woman spat in Stevenson's face, and he was purposely hit on the head with one of the picket signs.

Meanwhile, Johnson went to the press, saying, *"The President must take his message to the South,"* in a successful effort to goad Kennedy into making the trip.

Johnson won the struggle, convincing Kennedy that the President of the United States should be able to visit any state in the nation if he so desires. And now that Marilyn Monroe was out of the picture, Jackie Kennedy was enthusiastic about supporting her husband in the political scene, even in politically hostile territory such as Dallas.

Shortly before the trip, a small contingent of Secret Service agents met with President Kennedy for the usual arm-wrestling meeting, prior to any public appearance, that pits the president's desire for exposure to the people against his own personal safety.

"Mr. President," Agent Kellerman began, *"We strongly recommend that the bubbletop be installed on the presidential limousine when you and the First Lady drive through downtown Dallas."*

"Yes sir," Agent Greer continued, *"We don't know what the weather will be in Dallas, and we know Mrs. Kennedy likes the bubbletop because it keeps her hair in place."*

"Well, we are going to Dallas to be close to the people, so there will be no bubbletop on this trip. I will tell Mrs. Kennedy to wear a hat," the President replied.

As the agents walked to their waiting car, they exchanged knowing glances and smiles. *"We did it, Greer,"* Agent Kellerman whispered.

Although it would have added negligible protection for the president from rifle fire, the bubbletop would have provided conclusive evidence about the number of incoming bullets and the direction of fire.

* * * * * * * *

On the night of Thursday, November 21, 1963, a party was held at one of the many residences owned in the Dallas area by oil magnate Clint Murchinson. Murchinson was one of the wealthiest men in America, and the owner of the Dallas Cowboy football team. Attendees that night included Richard Nixon, Lyndon Johnson, FBI Director J. Edgar Hoover, former CIA Director Allen Dulles (he had been fired by JFK) and John J. McCloy, Chairman of the Chase Manhattan Bank. Dulles and McCloy would later be selected by LBJ to serve on the Warren Commission. Nixon, a Republican, was in charge of planning and coordinating the assassination team, and Johnson, a Democrat, was about to become the President of the United States.

Madeleine Duncan Brown was LBJ's lover at the time. Johnson also had long-term affairs with Alice Glass and Helen Gahagan. Late in life, Madeleine Duncan Brown published a book which detailed some of the particulars of the Murchinson party. Brown claimed that LBJ joined the party, sat next to her briefly at the bar, and then ordered a drink. Shortly thereafter, LBJ was called into a closed-door meeting with Nixon, Hoover, Dulles, McCloy, and others in the library. While Brown was still seated at the bar, Jack Ruby from the Carousel Club entered the room, accompanied by a prostitute. It was Ruby's duty to deliver loose females to such events when powerful men visited from Washington. Ruby escorted his guest to the appropriate room, returned to have a drink with Madeleine at the bar, and then left the party.

According to Madeleine Brown, Lyndon Johnson was visibly excited and agitated when the men came out of the library. He sat down next to Madeleine at the bar, gave her hand a painful squeeze with his giant hand, and said, *"After tomorrow, those goddamm Kennedys will never embarrass me again – that's no threat – that's a promise."*

On that same evening, Lee Oswald left his boarding house room, located at 1026 N. Beckley Street in Dallas, and took a walk to a local pay phone, where he would call his mistress, Judyth Vary Baker. It was the favorite part of his day.

"Well, Judy, my suspicions were correct. There's going to be a bad scene tomorrow when President Kennedy comes to town."

"I just don't like seeing you messed up in all of this, Lee! You gotta get outta this," Judyth pleaded. *"You shouldn't report for work tomorrow, so you aren't there when the*

President drives by your building." Baker knew that Lee would not back away from the danger he was in. He had never done it before. This, even though Lee had confessed concerns to Judyth that he might be set up to take a fall.

"If I don't show up for work, there will be one less bullet aimed at Kennedy. Judyth, no matter what happens to me, never forget the name, David Atlee Phillips."

"I know Mr. Phillips. What about him?"

"Phillips is a traitor."

* * * * * * * *

Jack and Jackie Kennedy flew into Fort Worth to spend the night with Lyndon and Lady Bird on the Johnson ranch before heading to Dallas the following day. Johnson made arrangements to have all of John Kennedy's favorite foods for dinner that night. It was to be John Kennedy's last supper.

The President and the Vice-President had an unspoken pact that they would keep their extramarital affairs quiet. So on this evening, the two couples spoke of family while enjoying New England food served Texas style, with Southern hospitality.

The President commented to the First Lady that night before retiring, *"Did you notice, Dear, that tonight Lyndon was in an uncharacteristically generous mood?"*

The next morning, President Kennedy woke up with a wry sense of humor about the day ahead. *"You know, Jackie, some rifleman could get me today from a high building."*

"Now stop that, Jack. You know how much that kind of talk bothers me. The Secret Service has gone to great lengths to plan your visit to Dallas," the First Lady said comfortingly.

In fact, the Secret Service had done more planning than usual on this trip - with the intent to eliminate the final protective perimeters surrounding the President.

* * * * * * * *

Atherton could not understand why the exact route of the motorcade was printed in two Dallas newspapers two weeks before the visit, and again on the morning of the motorcade. And he was curious about the rerouting of the motorcade through Dealey Plaza, which would require slowing down to a speed that would not provide as much protection for the President. When it comes to motorcades, speed means life. He learned later in the day that the White House press corps and their photographers, usually positioned one car away from the President, was moved by the Secret Service to the rear of the motorcade. They would be several blocks away and unable to record the drama that was about to unfold. This resulted in a strong protest from the reporters, which fell onto the deaf ears of the Secret Service. When the President flew into Dallas, the city was buzzing with activity.

Approximately two hours before the President's plane landed at Love Field, Atherton was waiting at Love Field near the tarmac when he saw former Vice-President Nixon preparing to board American Airlines flight 82, bound for New York. *'I wonder what Nixon's got going on in Dallas today?'* Atherton mused. The day before, Nixon had attended a convention for his client, Pepsi Cola, as a cover for attending the final planning session at Clint Murchinson's party the night before the assassination. It was just like old times for Nixon. The future President's flight landed at Idylwild Field in New York. Just one month later, on Christmas Eve, 1963, it would be renamed JFK Airport.

Everywhere he went Atherton overheard conversations anticipating the arrival of the President and the First Lady. There was a mysterious and exciting air about the city as the king and queen of Camelot paid a visit to their subjects in the South. The President would give a defense-related speech in Fort Worth, then fly to Dallas to speak at the Trade Mart later that day. It was Friday, November 22nd, 1963. The weather that morning revealed light rain and overcast skies. As noon approached, the skies over Dallas began to clear, and the sun shone brightly.

The men of Dallas wondered what the President would say, and the women talked excitedly about what the First Lady might wear. When Jackie Kennedy made her preplanned, late entrance into the ballroom in Fort Worth where the breakfast meeting was underway, the audience erupted. The ladies were delighted to see her wearing a pink outfit and matching pillbox hat. The First Lady had upstaged the President, as usual, and it suited him just fine.

Once the commotion had subsided, and with JFK's artistic sense of comical timing, the President who had accompanied his wife to Paris, opined, *"No one ever seems to care what Lyndon and I wear."*

The President was pleased to have his wife in Dallas supporting him. They had just lost their second son, Patrick, whose birth was premature, and so he had lived just a few days. The President had been more involved in this pregnancy than Jackie's previous pregnancies. Now, JFK and Jackie were the closest they had ever been during their marriage. To those around them who knew them well, their newfound intimacy was evident in their body language on that fateful morning in Dallas.

On the plane to Dallas from New York, Atherton had again reviewed the FBI transcript of the gift shop owner in Miami. *'Whoever that man was, he wanted to go on record as being involved in a plan to kill the President,'* Atherton thought. *'And why did he make it a point to mention the name, Lee? He said that Lee lived in Texas. Maybe he lives in Dallas!'*

Then, suddenly, it all became clear to Atherton. It was like the Marilyn Monroe case all over again.

'They are going to kill him today!' The thought was a voice like a sledgehammer, slamming into his brain. *'But who is involved? Whom can I trust? Who should I tell? And who would believe me?'*

Chauncey Holt had arrived in Dallas at daybreak on November 22nd. He had driven to Dallas from the Grace Ranch in Arizona. Located just outside of Tucson, Grace Ranch was owned by Cleveland Mafia boss Pete Licavoli. Grace Ranch was a remote mansion with a landing strip. It served as a base for drug smuggling and CIA covert operations. Together with Holt were Charles Nicoletti from Chicago, and Leo Moceri, Licavoli's second in command. The fourth passenger was Joe Canty, a CIA contract pilot who was to fly Chauncey Holt back from Red Bird airport.

Charles Nicoletti was Sam Giancana's most trusted hit man. Holt was told they were going to New Orleans to meet with Mafia boss Carlos Marcello, the one who had been deported by Robert Kennedy. Originally, Holt was to fly to Dallas with his own plane, but Licavoli had sent him a note to stop by the ranch to pick up Nicoletti and Moceri. They wanted to fly to Dallas with Holt. But their luggage was extremely heavy, and the Cessna was too underpowered to carry the four men and their bags.

The decision was made to drive to Dallas in one of Licavoli's cars, an Oldsmobile station wagon. They were expecting a fourteen hour trip, so they took turns driving. They drove the speed limit at all times to avoid attention from highway patrols along their route. It was standard operating procedure for the Mafia, to avoid unwanted interactions with police.

The mobsters had planned to arrive at the Dallas Cabana Hotel in the afternoon on Thursday, November, 21st, giving them time to prepare for the assassination attempt on the President. But a severe sandstorm had delayed them. The storm was so strong it severely affected visibility, slowing them down. The blasting of sand had taken much of the paint off the car. The Mafiosi finally pulled into the Cabana Hotel in Dallas at sunrise on November 22nd, 1963.

Chauncey Holt was to deliver a set of forged Secret Service lapel pins to Homer Echevarria, an extreme Cuban exile who was vigorously anti-Castro. Holt was supposed to meet with Charles Harrelson and Carlos Montoya in the parking lot near the railroad yard, behind the Texas School Book Depository. Holt gave Harrelson a set of forged identification badges from the Alcohol, Tobacco, and Firearms division of the Treasury Department. If they were caught during the ensuing moments after the assassination, they would be covered as ATF agents, and they could say they were working in the railroad yard as undercover agents, seizing a train full of stolen weapons.

Chauncey Holt's instructions came from his CIA contact, named Philip Twombly. Twombly had been a vice-president for Coca Cola. Twombly was an informer for the CIA in the Caribbean and South America. Twombly had instructed

Holt to take part in an anti-Castro demonstration to create a diversion during Kennedy's visit.

Holt was instructed to dress casually to blend in with the railroad workers. In case of problems, he was to seek refuge in boxcar number 22 of the Rock Island train, which would appear to be sealed from the outside. After the assassination, Holt was joined in the boxcar by Charles Harrelson and Carlos Montoya. The train was to be driven out of the train yard.

The scheme to rescue the three men in the boxcar did not take place as planned. Chauncey, Harrelson and Montoya would be detained by the Dallas Police, but they were not booked, and no record was kept of their arrests. The photos of Holt, Harrelson and Montoya being escorted through Dealey Plaza by two shotgun-toting officers would be known as 'the three tramps.'

* * * * * * * * *

Johnny Roselli had just flown into Dallas on a CIA-supported flight. According to James Files, Roselli [aka Colonel Ralston], was the liaison between the CIA and the Mob. Emanuel Rojas and Tosh Plumlee, CIA pilots, flew the military air transport service [MATS] plane that brought Roselli from Miami to Dallas. Nicoletti had ordered his driver and protégé, 21-year-old James E. Files, to pick up Roselli at the Cabana Hotel at 7:00 AM.

James Files [born James Sutton] began his career with the CIA after he killed two of his own men in the US Army 82nd Airborne Division in Laos. He had shot both of his men in the head as they were running away from him. Files did this to earn favor with his allies in Laos, while he was fighting an illegal war there. Files had been recruited to the CIA by David Atlee Phillips, who was his controller on the day of the JFK assassination.

David Atlee Phillips [aka Maurice Bishop] had sent Lee Harvey Oswald to show Files around Dallas the week before the assassination, making sure Files knew all the getaway routes, ensuring that he would not be chased into any dead ends. If that happened, Files was well armed with a Colt .45 pistol and a grenade. But shooting his way out of Dallas would be a last resort.

As Files pulled up to the Dal-Tex Building, Roselli was standing outside speaking with another man. Roselli gestured to Files, indicating that he needed to wait for a few minutes.

"Hey, Johnny!" said Files as Roselli hopped in, "Who was that?"

"That's Jim Braden, one of our guys in California," Roselli replied. "Now, take me to Fort Worth. I need to pick up something from Jack Ruby. Do you know him?"

"No I don't," Files said, as he stepped on the gas.

"He runs the Carousel Club for us here in Dallas. It's a strip joint. You should go there for some fun!"

"Mr. Nicoletti doesn't want me to have fun while I'm on a job," Files explained. "But why all the way to Fort Worth, if he's from Dallas?"

"Because I don't wanna be seen with him. Everyone knows this guy. He acts like a fucking celebrity. By the way, are you packing?"

"Have you ever known me to be without a weapon?" Files asked with a smile.

"Okay! We're going to the pancake house in Fort Worth. I want you to cover my ass in case anything happens. Just think like I'm Chuck, okay?"

"Don't worry, Johnny, I'll cover you like I do Mr. Nicoletti. He told me to take good care of you."

"I am going to be sitting at that table in the back, Jimmy," the immaculately dressed, white-haired Roselli whispered to Files with a nod as they walked through the door of the pancake house, "Station yourself where you can see us and the door, and be ready for anything."

Files sat at the coffee bar, nursing a cup of strong coffee when Jack Ruby entered the restaurant, wearing dark glasses and one of the ubiquitous dark hats worn by most businessmen in Texas. Files had his .45 caliber pistol tucked into his belt. Ruby was carrying a manila 8 by 12 inch envelope, which he quietly passed to Roselli. Files watched carefully as Roselli and Ruby spoke for less than five minutes. After Ruby walked out, Files followed him to make certain the parking lot was clear. Roselli took his time exiting the restaurant, while Files pulled the car up to the front door.

On the way back to Dallas, Roselli pulled the contents out of the envelope. As he was driving, Files glanced over and quickly recognized the Secret Service badges, and a Secret Service map of the final route the presidential motorcade would take through downtown Dallas. Files kept his mouth shut, although proof of involvement on the part of another agency of the federal Government raised many questions in his mind. Especially the guys whose job it was to protect the President.

"Excellent! They only made one change in the route," Roselli commented, "They are going to slow down to make this turn into Dealey Plaza from Main Street onto Houston, and then left onto Elm before getting onto the Stemmons Freeway. It's perfect. Kennedy will be a sitting duck!"

As the men arrived back at the Cabana Hotel, Roselli stepped out and told Files to wait outside for Charles Nicoletti. It took several minutes for Nicoletti to come down. Nicoletti ordered Files to drive to Dealey Plaza where they parked the car in front of the Dal-Tex building. As the men walked around the plaza on that damp, grey morning, the sun broke through the clouds, and the sky began to clear.

"Jimmy," Nicoletti said carefully, "How would you feel about backing me up on this one?"

Files was surprised by the question. "What happened to Johnny?" he asked. "I thought he was going to be your backup!"

"Johnny is a little paranoid on this one. Johnny will be with me, but he doesn't want to be a shooter. He will be my spotter. Some of the wrong guys at the CIA got wind of the plan and want the hit stopped. Johnny just flew in and gave that information to Mr. Giancana."

"And what do you say?" inquired Files.

"Screw them! It's a go anyway! Only Sam can stop this now. I spoke with Sam this morning, and we are going!"

"Jesus, Mr. Nicoletti, I would be honored to back you up! That bastard Kennedy had all of my Cuban friends slaughtered at the Bay of Pigs!"

"Okay, Jimmy, what do you think would be the best spot for you?"

"I'll station myself behind that fence on the knoll there. With my jacket I could pass for a railroad worker and that large tree gives me good cover. I'll stand just to the left of it where that branch is hanging over."

"That's exactly the spot I had in mind for you. Now remember, Jimmy, we want everything from behind and we're going for a headshot. So you must only shoot if I miss, or if I don't hit him in the head. Kennedy cannot leave Dealey Plaza alive. You're just my insurance in case I blow it. Got that?"

"Don't worry Mr. Nicolleti! Headshots are my specialty, as you know. The Army trained me good, and that's why the Agency recruited me."

"What weapon will you go with?"

"I'll go with the Fireball."

"The Fireball? Why? The Fireball is a single shot weapon!"

"If you miss, Mr. Nicoletti, a single shot is all I'm gonna get. I've been practicing all week with the Fireball, it's a very accurate weapon. It's my favorite gun for a hit like this, and from that fence as he approaches, Kennedy will be a fish in a barrel. I'll use one of the mercury rounds Wolfman made for me. That should split Kennedy's treacherous head open like a melon."

"Okay Jimmy, it's your call. I trust it won't be necessary. What would you say is the best spot for me?"

"I think in that building where we parked the car."

"Super! The Dal-Tex building is the place we had picked."

"But how do you get in there?"

"Don't worry, we have someone to get us in. He's one of our people in California that you don't know."

"Is that the guy I saw with Johnny this morning? Braden or something?"

"Yes, that was him. I need you to park the car where we are parked now - with the trunk to the building, so I have quick access and can put the Marlin in without being seen. And one more thing, Jimmy, when you walk out of there, head for the car, and just walk relaxed, no running. We've got this thing covered. There will be people covering you. You won't know who they are, and that's the best way."

"Okay, Mr. Nicoletti. I'd like to say one more thing. You've got to aim a little higher, because Kennedy's car will be moving away from you. This is not like a normal job when we pop a guy between the eyes."

"I know, Jimmy, you explained that to me before with moving targets. I haven't forgotten. Your military background and your marksmanship is why I am asking you to help me on this."

"I won't let you down, Mr. Nicoletti. But there is one thing that bothers me. "

"What is it, Jimmy?"

"It's about Lee Oswald."

"Why are you worried about Lee Oswald?"

"He's with the Agency, one of David Phillips' guys. Phillips sent him over to my motel to help me out here. I've spent the whole week with him. I'm a little nervous about him, because he's a tie back to me. And I am a tie back to you and Sam, if you catch my drift."

"Don't worry about Oswald, Jimmy. Oswald will be taken out of the picture by the end of the day today. You just worry about making your shot count if it's needed."

* * * * * * * * *

Eugene Hale Brading [aka Jim Braden] had a contact in the Dal-Tex Building, located across Houston Street from the book depository, who gave the assassins access to the second floor window Nicoletti needed for a clear shot at President Kennedy from behind. The Dal-Tex location had a better line of fire than the sixth floor depository window, allegedly used by Oswald on that day. The sniper's nest window was partially obstructed by a Texas live oak tree.

The CIA had given Files a brand new weapon that had just passed the prototype stage of development. Files had spent several days with Oswald near a landfill outside Dallas, training with the weapon, and perfecting his aim with the scope. Remington had developed a miniature rifle that looked and operated like a handgun. The Remington XP-100 Fireball was a bolt-action, single-shot weapon with a 3X scope that fired a reinforced .222 round. Files had a friend nicknamed Wolfman, who was an expert at making ammunition and modifying guns for Giancana's men. Wolfman had drilled into the tip of the bullets, filled the cavities with liquid mercury, and sealed the bullet nose with wax. When this fragmentary round strikes a man's head, the heavier mercury rushes forward forcefully, like water inside a fast-moving balloon, causing the bullet to explode. This would send metal fragments and a spray of mercury poison throughout the target's brain, resulting in certain death.

* * * * * * * * *

Atherton did not know who he should talk to, but he needed to get from Love Field to downtown fast! He hailed a taxi at the airport, and asked the driver to give him the time. It was already noon.

Meanwhile, Mac Wallace was working on the sixth floor of the Texas School Book Depository. Helping him move book crates and boxes was Lee Harvey Oswald. At the time of the shooting, there were several Cubans working on the sixth floor of the Texas School Book Depository, in adjacent windows, and at the opposite end of the hall. Wallace had just finished eating his lunch of fried chicken, and had left the bag of bones by the window.

"Hey, Lee, help me move these boxes over by the window," Wallace called down the hall. Wallace swore under his breath, *"Damn, I forgot my gloves."*

Wallace quickly took his handkerchief and wiped his fingerprints off the boxes he had been handling. He thought he had gotten them all, but one never really knows...

Oswald walked through the doorway. *"They will be turning onto Houston soon,"* he said.

Wallace answered gruffly, *"Now listen, Lee, you go down to the snack room, buy yourself a soda pop, guard the door, and make sure no one comes up those steps until I come down."*

"No problem," Oswald replied, *"You gonna take a shot at the President?"*

"Yeah, Mr. Giancana wants to scare him, so he will see things more Sam's way. Now remember," Wallace chided, *"If anything unravels, you exit the back door, go home and get your pistol, then meet David Phillips at the movie theatre, got it?"*

"Got it," Oswald replied, as he headed down the stairs to the employee lunch room of the Texas School Book Depository.

* * * * * * * *

Jack Ruby, the CIA/Mafia runner of guns and drugs, working undercover as the owner of the Carousel nightclub in Dallas, was chronically late in paying for his advertisements with the Dallas newspapers. In the weeks leading up to the assassination, he placed his ads well in advance. He always paid in cash. On the morning of November 22, 1963 President Kennedy thumbed through a Dallas paper, stopping on the page carrying a large advertisement that featured profile and frontal photos of the President, imitating police mug shots, with the ad copy being a single word; 'COMMUNIST!'

The President lamented to Jackie Kennedy as they got dressed that morning, *"We are going into real nut country now!"*

Another advertisement depicted a wanted poster with the President's portrait and profile images. The caption read, 'Wanted, dead or alive!'

The Secret Service even leaked a statement that the motorcade would '...*move slowly through downtown Dallas, so the people could get a good look at the President and First Lady.'*

Whenever the President traveled, without fail, the nearest military special operations unit would be mobilized to assist in policing the areas through which the motorcade would pass. Their duties included checking out tall buildings with open windows, and beefing up the Secret Service detail by placing snipers in strategic locations. On this day, their superiors in the Pentagon ordered them to stand down! Their services would not be needed in Dallas.

As workers prepared Dealey Plaza on the morning of November 22nd for the motorcade to pass through, Judith Ann Mercer was stuck in traffic. While waiting in her car for traffic to move, Mercer noticed Jack Ruby behind the wheel of a green Ford pickup truck that was pulled up on the curb of Elm Street, just before the triple underpass that ran under the Stemmons Freeway. She had seen Ruby and another man get out of the pickup dressed in plain clothes. Ruby's companion pulled a long, wrapped object out of the pickup truck with two hands, in such a way that it could only be a rifle.

'Boy,' Mercer thought, 'The Secret Service isn't very secret.'

When the President (codename: LANCER) and First Lady (codename: LACE) landed at Love Field in Dallas, after the short, thirteen-minute flight from Fort Worth, the First Lady was presented with a bouquet of red roses. As they made their way shaking hands to the waiting limousine, the king and queen of Camelot showed their growing affection publicly by loving touches, knowing smiles and glances at each other.

"How odd, Jack," the First Lady observed, "Every where we go in Texas they give me yellow roses. But here in Dallas the roses are red. By the way, Darling, I had asked for the bubble top to be on the car today. I don't want my hat to blow off and my hair messed up."

The presence of the bubble top could have averted bullets slightly, and would have proven their points of origin, with absolute certainty.

"Don't worry, Jackie," the President consoled, then chastised her, "The sun is going to come out, and we want the people of Dallas to get a good look at us. Jackie, please take off your sunglasses so people can see you!"

When the dark blue, 1961 Lincoln Continental presidential limousine left the airport, the top was off, the hydraulic back seat had been raised to its full height of 10.5 inches, and the Secret Service agents perched on the rear footrests of the limo began to fall back to the follow up car. The Secret Service had instructed the Dallas Police that no motorcycles would be placed in front of the presidential limousine, or to the sides, which was standard operating procedure.

The President and First Lady did not know it, but four of the seven Secret Service agents in the follow-up car had stayed up drinking until about 4:00 AM that morning in a Fort Worth bar called, The Cellar, before taking the flight to Dallas. The agents knew that such behavior was grounds for immediate dismissal from the Secret Service, but the 'night before' celebration went unpunished.

As the presidential limousine exited Love Field, Secret Service Agent Henry J. Rybka stepped off the follow-up car to take up a protective position on the limousine rear right bumber, shadowing the President in his limousine. Being in this position would protect the President from any would-be assassins who attempted a shot from behind.

But before Rybka could reach the X-100 presidential limousine, Senior Agent in Charge Emory P. Roberts rose from his seat in the follow-up car, rebuked Agent Rybka, and ordered him to fall back. Agent Rybka was a fully trained, weapon-carrying protective agent, and when he realized he was being waved off of protecting the President, he raised his arms twice in protest and disbelief. The interaction was captured by a movie camera.

Although another agent made room for Rybka on the right side running board of the follow-up car, Rybka chose at that moment to remain behind with the Secret Service contingent tasked with protecting Air Force One. He would not be a party to whatever was going on in Dallas.

At approximately 12:15 PM, an incident was staged in Dealey Plaza, on Houston Street, which drew the attention of the people who had come to see President Kennedy and the First Lady pass through, on their way to the Trade Mart. A man pitched a fit, faking a *gran mal* epileptic seizure on Houston, distracting the attention of the onlookers. This diversion enabled the assassins to take up their positions unseen on a verbal command from Lucien Conein, the CIA covert operator and controller for this mission, using the ultra-low frequency walkie-talkies that were adapted for this mission by Robert Morrow, the CIA scientist in Baltimore.

During the distracting incident, and while the assassins took aim from their positions, Lee Harvey Oswald was seen by Carolyn Arnold in the second-floor lunchroom, eating his lunch. Arnold saw Oswald often at that time of day. She was the secretary to the TSBD vice-president, and Oswald would visit her to exchange dollar bills for coins to use in the lunchroom soda machine. Arnold was pregnant at the time, so she stopped on the second floor for a drink of water since the day was warming up, before going outside to watch the motorcade.

While Oswald was eating lunch, Wallace finished moving boxes and piling books, building a firing position that would come to be known as, 'the sniper's nest.' A fingerprint lifted from 'Box A' was later conclusively identified as belonging to Malcolm Wallace. While Wallace built the sniper's nest, two Cuban exiles took up a firing position in the sixth floor window closest to the grassy knoll.

At this moment, the last Secret Service agent standing on the running boards of President Kennedy's limousine released the handrail and stepped onto the pavement, leaving the President vulnerable to the snipers who were taking up their pre-assigned positions in Dealey Plaza, their sights zeroed in on Elm Street just before the triple overpass at the Stemmons Freeway. The agent joined the large contingent of his peers on Vice-President Johnson's car.

Conein's plan called for seven shooters. However, none of the shooters knew where all the other shooters were located, or who they worked for. Like all sophisticated covert operations, the most critical information was compartmentalized. In counterclockwise rotation, Charles Harrelson was positioned on the roof of the Dallas County Records Building on Houston Street. Charles Nicoletti was the second shooter, looking out from the second floor of the Dal-Tex Building, also on Houston Street, with Johnny Roselli acting as his spotter. Mac Wallace was by himself in the sniper's nest. Hermino Diaz Garcia, a Cuban who survived the Bay of Pigs invasion, was on the sixth floor of the Texas School Book Depository on Elm Street, at the opposite end of the hall from the sniper's nest. Sergio Arcacha Smith, a leader of one of the CIA-sponsored anti-Castro groups, was standing to the right and behind where Abraham Zapruder was standing. Arcacha Smith was shielded by the structure of the ornate pergola that stood between the TSBD and the Northern grassy knoll. James Files was shooter number six. Files was standing just to the left of a tree trunk, under an overhanging branch behind the stockade fence at the top of the famous grassy knoll on the north side of Elm street. He had been chain smoking Pall Malls, and had paced in the muddy soil for so long he had to scrap the mud off his shoes several times on the steel rail at the perimeter of the railroad parking lot. The seventh shooter was the Cuban exile Antonia Veciana, who had taken up a position behind the fence at the top of the grassy knoll at the south side of Elm.

As the killers patiently waited for the President's limousine to divert from Main Street onto Houston, and then turn left onto Elm Street, James Files practiced what he had learned during his Army sniper training. He detached the 3X scope from his Fireball, and used it like an old-fashioned telescope to seek out people he knew in Dealey Plaza that day. Making a couple sweeps of the plaza, he recognized a number of familiar faces related to organized crime, the CIA and Cuban exile organizations. He also saw one of his young CIA buddies standing on the curb of Elm Street, about to open an umbrella.

Suddenly, the assassins heard two distinct clicks over their walkie talkies. *"Approaching,"* the wireless radio called out in a whisper. As the dark blue X-100 limo rounded the corner with the presidential and American flags waving, the sights of six high-powered Mauser and Marlin rifles, and Files' Fireball came into focus on the spot where their first shots would be fired at President Kennedy.

For some unknown reason, Vice-President Johnson ducked down in his limousine, seeking protection underneath the agents who were swarmed around him.

Mac Wallace used a German Mauser, the precise rifle used by most snipers of the time who fired from long range. The Cuban who fired from the opposite end of the hall used one of the Mannlicher-Carcano rifles that were purchased at a surplus store located in Towson, Maryland. Robert Morrow purchased and modified the rifles under orders from Tracy Barnes at CIA headquarters in Langley, Virginia. Barnes ordered Morrow to modify the Italian rifles for easy disassembly. Morrow purchased the Italian rifles with funds provided by Jack Ruby's counterpart, Mafia don Carlos Marcello, who operated the 500 Club in New Orleans.

The Mannlicher-Carcano, not the Mauser, was supposed to have been left behind in the sniper's nest. But someone made a mistake in that aspect of the planting of evidence to frame Oswald, and the swap did not take place in time.

Just before the motorcade made the slow turn from Houston onto Elm Street, Joseph Milteer was standing midway down Houston Street, with his arms crossed while others clapped and cheered for John Kennedy and the First Lady. As the presidential limousine passed, Milteer gave the high sign, raising his arm in a 90-degree angle with his fingers pointing upward, as if to signal a clear field of fire. The limousine slowed, then turned left onto Elm Street.

President Kennedy sat in his elevated seat, waving to the crowd, as the Governor's wife, Nellie Connolly, turned and shouted from the middle seat, *"No one can say they don't love you here in Dallas, Mr. President!"*

"No they caan't," the President replied in his Bostonian accent, smiling, as he leaned on the right side of the car and waived at the crowd.

As the motorcade passed the midpoint of Elm Street in Dealey Plaza, a young man (known as *Umbrella Man* by the Warren Commission) was standing on the sidewalk by the curb in front of the grassy knoll. The President would be only 12 feet away from Umbrella Man when the motorcade passed by.

The skies were clear and blue by noon, the temperature was a cool and breezy 68 degrees, yet this young man was standing on the curb, holding an open umbrella over his head, and the umbrella pivoted clockwise, tracking with the President as his car moved down Elm Street. Such a situation is entirely contrary to Secret Service policy, and should not have been allowed by the agents who were on the scene.

Sighting down the launch tube that protruded through the webbing of the umbrella, the young man fired a self-propelled flechette dart that pierced President Kennedy's tie, then entered his throat. The rocket powered dart from the M-1 umbrella weapon injected it's paralyzing drug into JFK's body, and began to dissolve completely, leaving only a 4 mm hole in Kennedy's throat and clothing. Immediately, John Kennedy's hands clenched into fists, his head snapped forward, and his mouth was frozen in an open position. As bullets began to hit John Kennedy, not a sound came from his throat. When a round struck the President in the upper back, his paralyzed arms flew upward from the impact, but he did not fall forward. This was because Kennedy's muscles had tensed and locked into position as a result of the paralyzing drug, and he was being held upright further by his back brace.

The U.S. Army had developed the 'dog projectile' weapon at Fort Detrick, in Frederick, Maryland. The inventor, Charles A. Senseney, had demonstrated a prototype of his invention for Colonel L. Fletcher Prouty in the Pentagon. Prouty had flown by helicopter to Fort Detrick to observe a demonstration of the top secret weapon system on July 29, 1960. U.S. Special Forces intended to use the weapon to completely paralyze a large guard dog before he could bark, enter a facility, then escape undetected while the dog regained consciousness. It was never used in Vietnam.

The CIA asked the Army for this technology, and they inserted the barrel inside an umbrella to disguise it for use on humans. The solid rocket propellant, battery, and trigger were located in the handle, with wires extending to the launch tube which was the size of a drinking straw. The CIA had provided specifications stating that the flechette must be able to penetrate clothing, enter human muscle, paralyze the target completely within two seconds, dissolve without a trace, and be undetectable in an autopsy.

* * * * * * * * *

The Umbrella Man's accomplice, a Cuban exile, stood close behind him. When he saw the flechette hit the President, he raised his hand high in the air, and communicated a signal with his walkie talkie, indicating that the shooters could fire the first volley. Now the target was immobilized, sitting in an elevated seat, wearing a back brace, traveling in an uncovered limousine at low speed.

At 12:30 PM, on a verbal radio signal from Lucien Conein, the first volley was fired at President Kennedy. Shots one, two and three were fired from behind President Kennedy at the same moment.

The **first shot** was fired by Hermino Diaz Garcia, a Cuban exile, from a westerly window on the sixth floor of the Texas School Book Depository, at the opposite end of the hall from the sniper's nest, which was at the eastern end of the building. Diaz Garcia had been a bodyguard for Mafia boss Santo Trafficante in Cuba, who had been expelled by Castro to Miami. He had also been involved in the CIA-backed assassination attempt on Castro that was coordinated through Johnny Roselli.

As the presidential limousine emerged from behind the large Texas live oak tree that obscured the firing angle from the sniper's nest, Diaz Garcia fired a shot that struck President Kennedy in the upper back. It entered approximately six inches *below* the mastoid bone at the neck, which is where the Warren Commission said it struck Kennedy. The mastoid bone was in approximate alignment with the spot where the paralyzing flechette dart had entered Kennedy's throat. The bullet fired by Garcia penetrated only a few inches into JFK's flesh, as planned.

Diaz Garcia was using a Mannlicher-Carcano, medium-powered carbine with a modified sabot cartridge, [pronounced sabo, French for 'wooden shoe']. Sabot cartridge technology enabled the assassins to take a bullet that had previously been fired from Oswald's Mannlicher-Carcano into bales of cotton and retrieve them in pristine condition for reuse by the assassins. The presence of a bullet fired from Oswald's rifle in the President's body protected the lone gunman theory.

These sabots used fewer powder grains than a normal cartridge, so the bullet traveled at a lower velocity. The bullet did not penetrate deeply into the tissues of John Kennedy's back, and was removed from Kennedy's body prior to the official autopsy. Too many bullets meant more than one shooter. More than one shooter meant a conspiracy. A doctor at Bethesda Naval Hospital would probe this wound with his finger during the autopsy. FBI agents and military officers, including Rear Admiral George G. Burkley, the President's personal physician, instructed the doctors at Bethesda Naval Hospital to *"...ignore that wound."*

The first bullet in President Kennedy's upper back would certainly not have been fatal.

The **second shot** was fired by Charles Nicoletti from the second floor of the Dal-Tex Building. On that day, the Dal-Tex Building housed offices of the Dallas Police Department. This bullet was meant for the President's head. It flew over the limousine's occupants and between the heads of the Secret Service agents sitting in the front seat, and struck the sidewalk near the triple-overpass of the Stemmons Freeway, then ricocheted into the lawn where the force of impact created a mound of soil and grass. A fair-haired FBI agent was later captured on film, taking this slug from the grass with his left hand, and dropping it into his coat to disappear forever.

The shots emanating from the second floor of the Dal-Tex Building varied only slightly from the trajectory of shots that were supposedly fired from the sixth floor of the book depository, where the sniper's nest had been built.

The **third shot** was fired by Charles Harrelson from the roof of the Dallas County Records Building, located on Houston Street, next to the Dal-Tex Building. Harrelson took aim at President Kennedy's head and fired. This shot also flew over its target, striking and lodging itself in the metal flashing located at the top of the limousine's windshield. The assassins quickly chambered another round. These three shots, and the next volley as well, were all fired at the same instant.

On Conein's next command, shots four, five and six were unleashed simultaneously. Governor Connolly, who was sitting well inboard of John Kennedy in the front seat, upon hearing the first set of shots, turned around to see if the President had been hit. The **fourth shot** was fired by Mac Wallace from the sniper's nest on the sixth floor of the Texas School Book Depository. Wallace aimed at the back of John Kennedy's head, as the President had begun to lean slightly forward. The shot went high, missing Kennedy and struck the turning Governor Connelly in the back, near his right arm pit. The bullet passed through his chest, shattered his 5th rib, exited under his right nipple, then struck and shattered his right wrist as he held his hat. At that point, the impact with Connolly's wrist deflected the bullet downward, creating a shallow wound in the muscle tissue of his left thigh.

There was little left of this bullet after it struck Connolly's ribs and wrist, yet the Warren Commission would have us believe this *magic bullet* passed through the skin and bones of both Kennedy and Connolly, and then somehow showed up on Connolly's stretcher at Parkland Hospital in pristine condition! A pristine bullet would display distinctive ballistic markings that would tie the bullet to Oswald's rifle, which it had been fired from previously. A bullet that had broken into fragments would not have provided the same kind of evidence that would tie back to Oswald.

Charles Harrelson, who was laying face down in a prone position on the roof of the Dallas County Records Building, took aim again at the President's head. As Kennedy leaned slightly forward from the impact of the previous bullet, Harrelson fired the **fifth shot**, which overflew its target and struck the curb on the south side of Elm Street near the triple underpass, at the feet of James Tague, a car salesman. Fragments of concrete sprayed into Tague's face. His cheek bled after the concrete fragments broke his skin.

Sergio Arcacha Smith, who had been standing as a spectator behind the pergola, pulled a .45 caliber pistol from his belt, and fired the **sixth shot**. The bullet struck the right posterior of the President's head as he turned to his left. The bullet traversed the back of JFK's brain, exited the left side of his head, and embedded itself near a manhole cover on the south side of Elm Street to be photographed and recovered later.

At this point in the limousine, John Kennedy was slumped slightly forward, his paralyzed arms were raised with his elbows pointing outward.

When the shots first rang out, Secret Service Agent John Ready jumped from the follow up car to protect the President, but he was quickly ordered back by Agent Emory Roberts. Five seconds had elapsed since the first shots rang out and no Secret Service agents had left Vice-President Johnson's car to protect the President. As the President turned left stiffly to look at Jackie, and as Jackie leaned over to comfort him, his right temple presented the perfect target for James Files who was standing behind the stockade fence at the top of the northern grassy knoll, just before the triple underpass. The train yard was behind Files, which afforded him an open and easy escape route, as long as no one blocked his way.

Most gun shot victims would have fallen forward in such a condition, but the paralyzing drug, and the President's back brace kept him in an upright and vulnerable position. Files could tell that Arcacha had hit the President's head, but he could not be sure the injury would be fatal. Although Files was not assigned to the hit until two hours before the shooting began, he was the *failsafe* assassin. He would have to take the critical shot.

Agent Greer applied the brakes, steering slightly to the left to give Files a clean headshot. If the President was not killed in this attack, the Vice-President would not become president, and the conspirators would be exposed and tried by the U.S. Attorney General, Robert F. Kennedy, for attempted murder and for treason! Johnson would have to face the consequences of the TFX Fighter scandal, and he would have to explain his close dealings with the criminals Bobby Baker, Billy Sol Estes, and Jack Halfen, an associate of Carlos Marcello.

As Files peered into the scope of his Fireball, he confirmed that President Kennedy had not received a confirmed fatal headshot by the time JFK emerged from behind the large Stemmons Freeway road sign, from the vantage point of the stockade fence. Files had received orders from Charles Nicoletti that Jackie Kennedy was not to be harmed. This instruction had originated with Aristotle Onassis. Onassis was protecting his shipping interests, and he had designs on the First Lady as well. Files aimed for the right eye of President Kennedy and squeezed off the **seventh shot**. The high velocity, .222 missile traveled less than 100 feet at over 3,180 feet per second before striking the President's exposed right temple. When the mercury-filled round impacted Kennedy's skull, the liquid mercury slammed forward, causing the bullet to explode.

The hollow-point bullet entered the President's head with so much force that the right side of the President's face flapped open like a gruesome flag waving in the breeze. The bullet flattened, opened and exploded as it passed through the bone plates of John Kennedy's skull, spreading droplets of poison mercury and metal fragments throughout President Kennedy's brain…he never had a chance. The resulting exit wound was a gaping hole, with a diameter of 13 centimeters (approximately 5 inches) in the left rear of the President's head.

When this bullet struck President Kennedy, it snapped his head violently backward, and to the left. He had been leaning slightly forward before he was hit. The force of impact raised his entire body upward, hurling him against the back of his seat in the limousine. The dying President then collapsed into the First Lady's lap.

As the bullet exited the left-rear portion of John Kennedy's skull, a pinkish fog of brain matter and blood sprayed Jackie Kennedy and the motorcycle cop who was riding at his assigned station in the motorcade, to the left-rear of the presidential limousine. Eyewitnesses and those who have viewed the Zapruder film said, "… *John Kennedy's head exploded."*

As these events transpired, Lee Bowers was sitting in the control tower of the train yard located behind the pergola of Dealey Plaza. Bowers saw what he later described as a "…*puff of smoke, and a commotion,"* just behind the stockade fence as the first shots were fired. Jean Hill, who was waving to the President by the curb, heard Jackie Kennedy scream, *"My God, they have shot my husband!"*

When Jackie Kennedy saw that her husband's brains had been splattered onto the rear of the car, she instinctively reached out from the relative safety of the backseat, crawling onto the exposed trunk of the limousine to retrieve John Kennedy's brain material. Mrs. Kennedy had done what any spouse would do instinctively when a loved one loses a body part.

At that moment and later that day when they compared notes at Parkland Hospital, Kennedy aides Kenneth O'Donnell and Dave Powers wondered why the Secret Service agents surrounding Vice-President Johnson had not sprinted toward Kennedy's limousine which had obviously come under attack. Only when Jackie Kennedy was seen crawling on the trunk of SX 100 did Secret Service Agent Clint Hill run to the car to keep the First Lady from falling under the wheels of the next car in the procession. Such an accident would have halted the motorcade and kept the conspirators from making their getaway to Parkland Hospital where the cover-up began.

There can be no question, based on the video evidence, the movements of the President's body, the head wounds, and the blood splatter pattern, that the fatal headshot was fired on a fairly level trajectory from in front of the President, and that the exploding bullet entered his head in the area of the right temple.

Agents were nowhere near the limousine until after the fatal shot had found its mark. Agents Greer and Kellerman in the front seat of the President's limousine showed little surprise or reaction when they turned to look at the President after the fatal headshot was inflicted. Rather than looking horrified, it seemed more like they were checking to ensure the deed had been done.

A young news reporter affiliated with CBS had posted himself just past the triple underpass. A native Houstonian who had been living in Dallas, the reporter had been brought into the strange world of Lyndon Johnson at an early stage of his presidential aspirations. He had endured the characteristic tirades and backslapping for which Johnson was known. After the fatal shot, when the motorcade accelerated and headed for the hospital, the CBS film, which might have captured some important aspects of the assassination, such as the abandonment of the President by his protective detail, was tossed to the young reporter from a truck that was traveling at 50 miles per hour. The film might be considered quite valuable by the American people. The reporter who caught that film was Dan Rather.

* * * * * * * * *

Upon arriving at Parkland Hospital, a stunned, widowed Jackie Kennedy murmured to a doctor, *"I have my husband's brains in my hands."*

Jackie Kennedy handed the pinkish gel over to him, turned, and walked away in silence.

* * * * * * * * *

Using the low-frequency radios provided by CIA operative Robert Morrow for communications, the assassins had coordinated their fire so that the number and direction of the shots would be nearly impossible for the shocked eyewitnesses to ascertain. By firing in volleys, six sharpshooters had fired seven shots such that witnesses would be hard-pressed to testify accurately as to where the shots originated from, and how many there were, when even trained soldiers in the crowd were ducking for cover. Unfortunately for the conspirators, there were several private movie cameras rolling when the shots rang out. The shooting transpired in approximately six seconds of elapsed time, commencing at 12:30 PM in Dallas, Texas on November 22, 1963.

At first, Dallas Police motorcycle officer Joseph M. Smith thought he had been hit by a bullet, due to the intensity of the impact of blood and skull matter that struck him in the face. When he realized the blood was John Kennedy's, he dismounted and drew his service pistol, charging up the grassy knoll, since he *knew* the shot that sprayed him with the President's brain matter had come from that direction.

Several of the assassins waited safely inside a freight train, after which officers of the Dallas Police Department came to collect them. As the 'tramps and hobos' were escorted with their heads down along the protective perimeter by shotgun-toting police officers, General Edward Lansdale, Chief of Special (Covert) Operations in the Pentagon, walked past them in the opposite direction, giving them nods of approval and a slight wave of the hand for a job well done. The officers escorted the 'tramps' to Sheriff Decker's office in the Dal-Tex Building, where they were released immediately without questioning or booking. On November 22, 1963, the mayor of Dallas was Earle Cabell, brother of General Charles Cabell whom President Kennedy had fired from the CIA in the aftermath of the Bay of Pigs fiasco. Earle Cabell would later become a member of Congress where he would lobby successfully to have the ornate casket that returned on Air Force One destroyed at sea, with no forensic testing allowed.

Less than two minutes after the firing stopped, Dallas Police Officer Marion Baker rushed into the Texas School Book Depository lunchroom, accompanied by the TSBD Building Operations Supervisor, Roy Truly. Baker pointed his pistol at Oswald, who was drinking a cola, and asked Supervisor Truly if Oswald worked in the building. Truly vouched for Oswald, then told Oswald that the President had been shot. Oswald waited a few minutes before walking out of the Texas School Book Depository.

A CIA operative known to James Files had been given the assignment to kill Oswald as he exited the book depository. Oswald had been instructed to leave by the rear entrance. But as the shooting began, Oswald realized he was walking into a trap. He remembered what David Ferrie had said in his New Orleans apartment, about the need for a patsy. So, Oswald calmly exited through the front door, eluding his would-be assassin. Oswald now was certain he was the fall guy, something he had been suspecting for some time, and he had shared his concerns with his lover, Judyth Vary Baker. His controllers had been too controlling lately!

As Oswald ran to catch a bus to his boarding house, a CIA operative who looked similar to Oswald, wearing the same maintenance outfit, saw one of his compatriots, a husky Cuban by the name of David Morales by the pergola. Oswald

2 whistled, getting the Cuban's attention, as well as the attention of several onlookers, and they ran together to the light green Rambler that was parked behind the stockade fence. The escape of Oswald # 2 and Morales was witnessed by Dallas Deputy Sheriff Roger Craig. Morales and Oswald # 2 got into the Rambler station wagon, then drove to the dry Trinity River Basin, which is located within the Dallas city limits.

The young CIA operative who was waiting behind the TSBD realized he had missed Oswald, so he proceeded to the Oak Cliff area to intercept him at the safe house location that had been assigned to Oswald by David Atlee Phillips. The operative would have to kill Oswald at the Texas Theatre. Because the operative's description was similar to that of Oswald, the young CIA man was stopped by Dallas Police officer, J.D. Tippit. Tippit was patrolling Oak Cliff, searching for the man who had just killed the President, who was reported to be in the area, supposedly attempting to escape on foot. Officer Tippit pulled his patrol car over to the curb next to the man who was assigned to kill Oswald. Witnesses observed the police officer and the assassin talking through the open window on the passenger side of the patrol car. When Tippit stepped out of the car to question the suspect further, the CIA man fired several shots into Tippit, who fell to the ground immediately. Tippit died moments later. Several witnesses watched the killer walk swiftly away. One witness heard the CIA man mutter, *"Dumb cop!"*

As Tippit lay dying in the street, a citizen grabbed the squad car radio handset and called to inform police headquarters that one of their own had been shot and was in need of immediate medical attention. The police dispatcher indignantly told the citizen to stay off of the radio.

A traumatized Lee Oswald made his way to the theatre where he had been told to go if '*...things turned sour.*' He walked past the theatre manager and entered the establishment without purchasing a ticket. While he was sitting in the darkened movie theatre, Oswald's confusion turned to shock when approximately 30 officers of the Dallas police force arrived to arrest him for the murders of Officer Tippit and President Kennedy. After a brief scuffle, during which Oswald slugged a police officer, Oswald was taken into custody. This event was chronicled by Hugh Aynesworth, a reporter for the *Dallas Morning News*, who had also been standing on Elm Street, watching the motorcade at the time of the assassination. Aynesworth had intercepted the police transmission, and claimed to have raced to the Texas Theatre where he had witnessed the capture of Lee Harvey Oswald.

The CIA man who had actually murdered Tippit, showed up later at the hotel room of James Files. He asked Files to help him by disposing of his gun. He confessed to Files that he had murdered Officer Tippit. Files refused the request to help dispose of the murder weapon. He had bigger problems to worry about. Files had just killed the President of the United States!

Atherton had abandoned the taxi, and had been running for several minutes before he arrived in Dealey Plaza. Traffic was heavy in Dallas, and a number of streets had been blocked off in preparation for the President's visit. A chaotic scene greeted Atherton as he staggered, breathlessly into Dealey Plaza. Men were standing around with shocked looks on their faces. Some were chasing after ghosts, thinking they might capture one of the well-trained assassins, from this well-coordinated operation. Several women were weeping, sitting on the ground with their heads in their hands. Some were praying audibly, and Catholics were clutching their rosaries. Armed police officers and agents took cameras from witnesses and escorted several people to the police station. Atherton heard the receding sounds of ambulances, and knew his premonition had been correct. Men in suits and trench coats were questioning witnesses, and confiscating film from cameras. But many photographs taken in Dealey Plaza survived the purge by law enforcement on that day.

Primary and secondary escape routes had been determined in advance. Charles Nicoletti and Johnny Roselli quickly got in the car James Files had driven to the Dal-Tex Building. Files immediately got some grief from his mentor.

"Hey, Jimmy, don't you think you over-reacted a bit back there?"

"Mr. Nicoletti, you told me only to fire if I didn't see a significant headshot. When the target emerged from behind the freeway sign, I saw no real head damage through my scope, so I took the shot. I missed my target, though, because I was aiming for his right eye."

"Don't worry about it, Jimmy. Just get us out of here, okay?"

* * * * * * * *

On the morning of the assassination, Sergeant Robert G. Vinson was the sole passenger on a strange flight that originated from Andrews AFB, bound for Lowry AFB in Denver, Colorado. The regularly scheduled shuttle flight to Ent AFB in Colorado Springs, where Vinson worked for NORAD, had been cancelled, so he jumped at the chance to get on the flight to Denver. He was the only passenger.

Vinson immediately noticed that the C-54 did not have the usual USAF insignia and tail number. The pilot and co-pilot wore non-descript jump suits, and no one said a word to their confused, but thankful passenger.

Somewhere over Nebraska, the pilot made an announcement at 12:30 Central time, that the President had been shot. Nothing else was said. The C-54 immediately banked 90 degrees, heading due South. Vinson recognized the B-29 bombers on the tarmac at Offutt AFB as they passed beneath him. At approximately 3:30, the pilot made a rough landing on the dry and flat floodplain of the Trinity River, which is located inside the city limit of Dallas. A tall Cuban and a short, Caucasian man climbed aboard, and the C-54 took off again within 15 minutes of landing; the engines remained running the entire time the aircraft was on the ground. The two new passengers remained silent the entire flight. They both wore unmarked, beige coveralls, like a repair man would wear.

When the plane landed, the crew and the two new passengers rushed to get out of the plane, and did not return. Vinson did not recognize where he was. He was on a secret air force base in New Mexico, where a CIA station existed at the time. He had to take a bus to return to his home in Colorado Springs, but only after the alert status was lifted from the base, which prevented anyone from leaving.

Several days later, as they watched the television coverage that served to find Lee Harvey Oswald guilty before he was assassinated, Vinson leaned forward and said to his wife, *'That's the little guy who was on the flight from Dallas!'* To which Vinson's wife replied, *'That's impossible. Oswald is in jail.'* The subsequent decades would reveal there were several men posing as Oswald around Dallas, inciting events that would assist in the unjust media trial of Oswald that was to follow.

After suffering through scary and embarrassing surveillance and monitoring efforts by the CIA, Vinson and his wife were ordered by the Air Force to sign secrecy agreements, even though Vinson held a top level 'crypto' clearance with NORAD. The couple knew of no precedent for a spouse having to sign a secrecy agreement. Vinson was flown on secret orders to Washington, where he was 'interviewed' by the CIA and repeatedly offered a job with the Agency. Vinson repeatedly refused, as he was near retirement. But before retirement could arrive, Vinson was ordered to transfer to a secret base in Las Vegas, operated by the CIA. The agency kept Vinson busy and quiet, as he worked as a logistics officer in support of the U-2, the SR-71, and other U.S. spy planes. At one point during the 18 months he was stationed there, Sergeant Vinson had breakfast with one of the pilots whose name would go into the history books – Francis Gary Powers. Powers had always believed his handlers at the CIA orchestrated the shoot down of his U-2 plane over Russia, which caused the summit meeting between the two nuclear powers to be cancelled. Lee Oswald would have been the perfect source for the information, since he was sent to the Soviet Union prior to the shoot down, and he had intimate knowledge of U-2 operations due to his prior experience in Japan.

There is little question in Sergeant Vinson's mind as to the purpose of the mysterious flight, and why the CIA was so concerned that he or his wife might discuss their experiences on November 22, 1963 with others. Vinson is a very credible witness.

* * * * * * * *

At 12:40 PM in Dallas on November, 22, 1963, at Parkland Hospital, a white male patient was admitted who was suffering from a gunshot wound to the head. The patient, number 2470, who was immediately sent to Trauma Room # 1, was the dying President Kennedy. The surgeon made an incision in the dying President's throat, inserting a tracheotomy tube to assist his breathing. This incision would cause confusion later at Bethesda Naval Hospital because it destroyed the entrance wound in John Kennedy's throat, caused by the flechette dart used to paralyze the President. At 1:40 P.M., Central Standard Time, just seventy minutes after James Files fired the fatal headshot, Secret Service Agent Ready called for Father Huber to administer last rites of the Catholic Church to John Fitzgerald Kennedy.

After the President was pronounced dead, the county coroner, accompanied by a justice of the peace, began to make arrangements for an immediate autopsy. Kenneth O'Donnell, and the entire contingency of Secret Service agents, their weapons drawn, argued with the coroner, saying the autopsy must be performed in Washington, D.C. The coroner stated that the body could not be legally removed from Dallas prior to an autopsy. The Secret Service insisted that the President's body was going back to Washington, and those in the room were afraid the Secret Service would run over the coroner with the gurney that now carried the casket containing the body of John Kennedy. All this while Jackie Kennedy stood there in shock, soaked with the pinkish mist sprayed on her by the fatal shot, and mixed with the dark-red stains of the blood-soaked head of her Jack that she held in her lap all the way to the hospital. Despite the pleas made by the attending physicians, Jackie did not want to leave her husband's side. At one point, she slipped the wedding ring from her finger and gently put it on her dead husband's hand.

The nation came to a halt as normal television programming was interrupted at approximately 1:15 PM Central Time; the world witnessed a news flash during which the revered Walter Cronkite informed us, *"Three shots were fired at the President's motorcade as it traveled through downtown Dallas. Apparently, the President has been wounded by this shooting."*

Cronkite may not have known it, but the famous announcement he made, just minutes after the shooting, was an important 'fact' to be planted in the collective mind of the public, since it was the premise of the lone-nut story the Warren Commission would publish, stating that Oswald had fired three shots.

Fifteen minutes after his first announcement, an obviously upset Walter Cronkite appeared again on our television screens. He removed his glasses, shed a tear, and said with a voice that was choked with emotion, *"From Dallas, Texas, the flash - apparently official - President Kennedy died at 1:00 P.M. Central Standard Time, 2:00 P.M. Eastern Standard Time, some 38 minutes ago."* The CIA propaganda wizard, David Atlee Phillips, was using the classical approach of 'authentication by association.' If Cronkite said it, then it must be true!

At that moment, there were thousands of American soldiers in the air over America and on the ground, who were on alert in case they would be called upon to defend the new shadow government against their fellow Americans if riots broke out in Washington, D.C., or elsewhere in America. Although such measures would have been necessary for their physical and political survival, those orders would have been a direct violation of the Posse Comitatus Act of 1878. Posse

Comitatus [says the Army cannot be used as a police force] was the direct result of the occupation of the South during the reconstruction period after the Civil War in the United States. When Rutherford B. Hayes signed the Posse Comitatus Act on June 18, 1878, there was tremendous political pressure on him to do so, because the Northern military presence in the South was having a direct impact on voting results, due to intimidation. The reply sent to the South from the federal authorities in Washington, was that the troops were there only to keep the peace during the election.

The only exceptions to the Posse Comitatus Law are the law enforcement powers of the U.S. Coast Guard, the ability of an individual state to employ National Guardsmen to enforce federal and state laws, and such acts as are authorized by Congress. Since it is unlikely the conspirators in the assassination of JFK secured congressional approval to use the Army as a police force within the borders of the United States, doing so would have added yet another crime in the indictments that should have been brought against them, but have not been filed to date.

"No free man shall ever be debarred the use of arms. The strongest reason for the people to retain the right to keep and bear arms is, as a last resort, to protect themselves against tyranny in government."
Thomas Jefferson

Secret Service Agent Sorrells placed a call to the flight control tower of Andrews A.F.B. in Camp Springs, Maryland.

"Flight Control, Specialist Thompson speaking, how can I help you?" the young voice offered.

"Specialist Thompson, my name is Sorrells with the Secret Service. I'm in charge of the presidential protective detail."

"Yes sir, I know your credentials, Mr. Sorrells. What can I do for you?"

"I need you to get Air Force One in the air as soon as possible. The President has been shot."

"The President has been shot? How can that be? Don't you think he will need to stay in the hospital in Dallas for several days?"

"Listen, Thompson, I don't have time to argue with you. Just get the President's plane into the air, ASAP, okay?"

"Yes sir, roger that, sir."

Andrews Air Force Base, the home of the presidential and vice-presidential aircraft, was now buzzing with activity, as mechanics finished whatever routine maintenance they were doing and the tanks were topped off on Air Force One.

"Uhh, Andrews Tower, this is Gambit five five zero," the naval pilot called to alert the tower to what he had just seen as he passed over Andrews Air Force Base in his Navy, F-8 Crusader.

"Go ahead, Gambit."

"Yeah, I just saw Air Force One take off from the taxiway, and then she went vertical. They weren't even on the runway yet! Besides, they were not supposed to take off until tonight. What gives?"

"The President has been shot, Gambit. We need to keep this frequency clear. Tower out."

"Roger that. Gambit, out."

At approximately 1:20 PM Central Standard Time, presidential assistant Kenneth O'Donnell walked into the hospital room where Johnson was waiting, and said, *"Mr. President, the President is dead."*

* * * * * * * * *

Within a few hours of the assassination, Richard Nixon arrived in New York on the flight that had left Dallas that morning. Nixon took a taxi from the airport to his apartment in Manhattan. As he entered, his wife Patricia was transfixed by the television, like most Americans on that day. *"Pat, what's all this hysteria on the news? Why are people crying in the streets?"*

"Haven't you heard, Dick? John Kennedy was just assassinated in Dallas!"

"Good God! How did it happen?"

"He and Jackie were riding through downtown Dallas, and some lunatic shot him. Dick, you were in Dallas this morning!"

"Yes, Dear, I was there yesterday for a Pepsi convention. You know they are clients of mine."

"Dick Nixon, did you have anything to do with this? That man was your political enemy, but I swear to God, I could never forgive you if..."

"My dear Pat, how could you even say such a thing? John Kennedy was a friend of mine! Now I am going to fix a drink and get some client work done in my study...if you will excuse me."

* * * * * * * * *

At the moment of John Kennedy's death, Lyndon Johnson became the 35th President of the United States. Johnson despised John Kennedy and his brother, Robert Kennedy, the Attorney General of the United States. In a few seconds he had eliminated one, and removed the power base from the other. Robert Kennedy could no longer hinder the endeavors of the CIA and the Mafia.

But the Congress, and thereby the People, did not take action to pursue the criminals. Instead, they abdicated their responsibilities under the Constitution and allowed the criminals to preside over and manage the investigation. In fact, there was no trial in the murder of John F. Kennedy until U.S. District Attorney Jim Garrison tried Clay Shaw of the CIA for conspiracy to kill the President in New Orleans. Jim Garrison diligently pursued his case, even though several witnesses were murdered, and his offices were bugged. The jury deliberated for less than one hour before acquitting Clay Shaw.

> *"So, let us not be blind to our differences - but let us also direct attention to our common interests and to the means by which those differences can be resolved. And if we cannot end now our differences, at least we can help make the world safe for diversity. For, in the final analysis, our most basic common link is that we all inhabit this small planet. We all breathe the same air. We all cherish our children's future. And we are all mortal."*
> John Kennedy

The reporters and photographers milled around at Parkland Hospital, kept well away from the presidential limousine and the hospital entrance by the Dallas Police Department, the FBI, and the Secret Service. The Secret Service and the Dallas Police Department wasted no time in washing the blood and brain tissue evidence off the trunk of the limousine. Photographs of this evidence, and forensic analysis such as blood splatter samples would have proven the multiple directions of fire, and that the fatal shot came from in front of the President. As reporters followed the hearse carrying the deceased President's coffin and the former first lady to Love Field, an anxious Lyndon Johnson was waiting on Air Force One with its engines running.

Several times, Jackie Kennedy was asked if she wanted to change out of her pink outfit, which was now stained dark red with her husband's blood. Each time, she replied, *"No, I want Dallas to see what they have done to my Jack."*

As Atherton watched the solemn process of loading the ornate bronze casket into the rear of the aircraft, he noticed a commotion on the starboard side of the plane. A brown van had pulled up to Air Force One and it appeared that a long gray plastic box was being hoisted into the cargo hold. The box was about six feet long and three feet across. It looked to Atherton like it could be a rudimentary casket. Plainclothes agents surrounded Air Force One with submachine guns.

White House Communications Agency personnel aboard Air Force One placed a phone call to a traumatized Robert Kennedy.

The phone was then handed to Johnson, *"My God, Bobby, I am so sorry,"* the President whined.

"Lyndon, what happened?"

"I don't know. Do you think it was Castro?"

"Who could do this? The whole world loves...loved my brother."

"It's crazy, Bobby. Listen, I need to ask you an important question. If I am sworn in here in Texas does that create any problems in terms of the legitimacy of my presidency?"

"Geez, Lyndon, my brother's head was just blown off right in front of you and you're asking me constitutional questions?"

"Now, Bobby, you are the Attorney General of the United States. It's your job to answer such questions when they come from the President."

"Well, not for long perhaps."

"What do you mean by that?"

"Never mind, I am fairly certain you have to be sworn in by the Chief Justice."

"All right Bobby, I want to meet with you first thing tomorrow morning. We have a lot to discuss."

President Johnson turned to Secret Service Special Agent Kellerman, and said, *"We better keep a close watch on Bobby."*

"The CIA is headed over to Hickory Hill right now. Don't worry, we're keeping tabs on him, Mr. President," the agent replied.

"Mr. President! Gee, I like the sound of that," the unelected President remarked. *"Tell Jackie to come forward,"* Johnson said, *"I'm not going to be sworn in until she is standing next to me. The people need to see the peaceful transition of power."*

Johnson was sworn in as President on Air Force One at Love Field with a traumatized, blood-stained Jackie Kennedy standing next to him.

Regardless of how painful it was for Jackie Kennedy, Johnson insisted upon the appearance of White House approval, showing Americans that the queen of Camelot consented to his actions. Judge Sarah T. Hughes, A U.S. District Court Judge for Northern Texas, was conveniently on board Air Force One to administer the oath of office. Johnson would not wait to have the Chief Justice of the U.S. Supreme Court accomplish the task, as prescribed by the Constitution.

At the conclusion of the swearing in ceremony, an obvious grin spread over Mrs. Johnson's face. The President looked over his right shoulder and saw Congressman Albert Thomas from Texas. They exchanged grins and winks as if to say, *"We did it!"*

All this while, Jackie Kennedy stood next to them in shock. As darkness closed in around her with the realization that her Jack was gone, she was oblivious to the knowing looks being exchanged inside the presidential aircraft.

"Let's get the Hell back to Washington," Johnson roared.

As Air Force One increased power and lifted off from Love Field, the final stage of the carefully planned getaway from Dallas was complete. During the flight to Washington, Johnson's mood became more somber.

When he thought no one was around to overhear, Johnson became sullen and muttered to himself, *"I may be the first chief executive to end my presidency in prison."*

When Air Force One landed at Andrews Air Force Base, little attention was given to the military helicopter that hovered for about 90 seconds outside the starboard cargo door of the presidential jetliner. While the pomp and circumstance and media attention were focused on the fancy Britannica coffin that was unloaded ceremoniously from the rear of Air Force One, the helicopter containing a plain gray shipping container, used to transport corpses to the morgue, carried John Kennedy's body to Walter Reed Army Hospital in Washington, DC. The stop at Walter Reed Army Hospital was for the purpose of conducting pre-autopsy surgery to reshape the entrance and exit wounds in John Kennedy's skull, and to remove bullet fragments and mercury droplets from Kennedy's brain that could prove the presence of multiple assassins. The surgery was performed by U.S. military doctors, with high-ranking officers and FBI agents supervising the operation. A proper sectioning of John Kennedy's brain [normal autopsy procedure when a gunshot wound to the head is in evidence] would have proven conclusively the direction and trajectory of the bullet that passed through President Kennedy's head.

John Kennedy's brain was traumatized by two things, the high-velocity, .222 mercury-filled bullet that was fired by James Files from behind the stockade fence, and the pre-autopsy surgery at Walter Reed Hospital, during which most of the metal fragments and mercury droplets were extracted from his brain tissues. Little was left of John Kennedy's brain once the pre-autopsy surgery was completed at Walter Reed Army Hospital. President Kennedy's brain was not missing, as many claim; it was destroyed.

Walter Reed is located just 7.5 miles from Bethesda Naval Hospital in Maryland by car, and only 4.2 miles on a direct path by helicopter. As the motorcade carrying the Britannica coffin slowly made its way from Andrews AFB, John Kennedy's surgically altered body entered the back door of Bethesda Naval Hospital, almost thirty minutes before the motorcade arrived at the front door. These events were witnessed by several U.S. Navy personnel working at Bethesda Naval Hospital on that fateful day.

As a federal agent escorted a medical technician carrying X-rays of John Kennedy's skull through the halls of Bethesda Naval Hospital, Jackie Kennedy and Robert Kennedy came through the front door, unwittingly accompanying the casket carrying the body of Officer Tippit. By the time the fancy casket made its way to the morgue, the official autopsy of President Kennedy was well underway. According to the naval medical personnel who observed the autopsy process, there was much consternation between the agents and military brass supervising the autopsy, and the doctors who performed it.

It was at this point when the conspirators made a serious mistake. In order to perpetuate the illusion that entrance wounds were exit wounds and vice versa, the head of the murdered President was photographed, but when the film was processed, the images were reversed and flipped. These gruesome photographs were made public to convince the people that the President had been shot from behind. What no one noticed at the time, but a Scandinavian researcher was later to prove, was that JFK had a distinctive, Y shaped scar on the right side of his nose, explaining why he liked to have profile photos taken of only the left side of his face. As a result of the flipping and reversing of the autopsy photos, this characteristic scar appears on the left side of Kennedy's nose in the autopsy photographs. This photographic evidence is irrefutable.

No one noticed the director of Bethesda Naval Hospital's Education and Training Division who surreptitiously videotaped the autopsy proceedings from the observation chamber above the autopsy room. The result of his filming was an unofficial record of the autopsy, including the highly contradictory and controversial conversations that transpired during the operation. The director's name was Lieutenant Commander William B. Pitzer. Although it was standard operating procedure at Bethesda Naval Hospital to film autopsies, no such order had been given in this unique case. Pitzer knew the intrinsic value and national importance that such a film would have, so he recorded the event and kept it a secret.

The doctors immediately concluded that the fatal shot entered the right temple area, and exited the left posterior portion of the skull. This was obvious due to the position of skull bone fragments, which delineated the path of the fatal bullet. The bone fragments in Kennedy's right temple wound were directed inward, indicating entry, while the fragments around the left posterior wound were outward, indicating exit. Despite the surgery performed at Walter Reed, the right anterior wound was significantly smaller than the left, posterior wound.

FBI agents argued with the doctors, saying, *"That is wrong!"* and registered other similar protestations.

"Dr. Humes, this is Attorney General Kennedy speaking."

"Yes, Mr. Attorney General. I am very sorry for your loss, Sir."

"Thank you, Doctor. Now listen, I am sitting upstairs, attending to my sister-in-law. As you can understand, she is quite upset."

"Yes, I understand. If you would like, I can send a nurse to check her vitals to make sure she doesn't go into shock."

"No, that won't be necessary, but thank you for your concern. Listen, Humes, is it normal procedure during an autopsy such as this to take samples of the liver and the adrenal glands?"

"Yes, it's standard operating procedure to open the abdominal cavity and take samples of the stomach, the liver, and the adrenals.. But why do you ask?"

"Because I must ask you on behalf of the Kennedy family, and the American public, that you not dissect the adrenal glands or the liver."

"Admiral Burkley has just given me the same instructions. Mr. Kennedy, it's a mad house down here. I've got military brass and agents climbing all over me, giving me orders about how to conduct this autopsy, and I am not even a professional pathologist!"

"Just trust me, Doctor, that sampling my brother's adrenal glands will cause you more grief than not sampling them. This request comes, not only from me, but also from Jackie Kennedy. I am representing her in this matter also."

"Yes sir, I will do as you say. Good day to you, Mr. Kennedy, and please extend my condolences to the First La...er, to Mrs. Kennedy, I mean, and to the rest of your family."

"That's okay, Doctor. Thanks, and I will pass on your good wishes to my sister-in-law."

Rear Admiral George Burkley and Robert Kennedy did not want the American public to find out about the advanced stage of Addison's disease that was having a degenerative effect on JFK's adrenal glands. Additionally, a toxicology test of President Kennedy's liver would have revealed the high levels of cortisone and steroids that were being injected into him by Admiral Burkley and Dr. Travell on a daily basis.

As they sat alone together in the quiet chapel at Bethesda Naval Hospital, Robert Kennedy moved closer to Jackie Kennedy as she cried and prayed. He felt as though he was going to be sick. *"Jackie, there's something I need to tell you,"* RFK whispered.

Despite her own shock, kneeling next to her brother-in-law in a pew, still wearing her pink outfit which displayed the dark stains of her husband's blood, Jackie could tell there was something that was disturbing him deeply. *"What is it, Bobby? Tell me what's wrong!"*

He looked up, took Jackie's hand, and with tears in his eyes, looked directly into hers. *"I may have gotten Jack killed,"* he said with a crack in his voice.

"Bobby, that's crazy! What are you talking about? Of all Jack's brothers, you loved him the most."

"That may be so, but I need to tell you this."

"Okay, Bobby, what do you want to say?"

"I had approved an operation to get Castro. It was called OPERATION MONGOOSE. It operated out of New Orleans, and it involved the CIA, the FBI, and a bunch of Cuban exiles. You know that I've been after all the Mafia bosses, Giancana, Marcello, Trafficante, Roselli, and people who are linked to them, like Jimmy Hoffa."

"Yes, that isn't a secret; everyone knows about that."

"Well, from what I have been able to gather thus far, the people who are responsible for Jack's death may be the same team we put together to go after Castro. They might have gotten frustrated with me and Jack, and decided to take us out at the knees."

"Oh, Bobby, please don't trouble yourself with such thoughts right now. I know you will get to the bottom of this, and you will see that justice is done. But right now, we need to grieve for Jack. I need you to be strong, to help me with Caroline and John John. His birthday celebration is tonight, you know. John John is expecting his birthday party tonight. If I change it to another date, he won't understand!"

"I know, Jackie. I promise you that Ethel and I will be there."

"I need you, Bobby, now more than ever."

* * * * * * * * * *

The chief surgeon who performed the autopsy, Dr. Humes, was later compelled to burn his original notes, and rewrite them from memory, drawing different conclusions than he had previously. Humes later testified that his associates did not take notes during the autopsy. But his associates did take notes. Humes called the surgeon at Parkland Hospital to confirm that he had used the flechette entry wound in the front of President Kennedy's throat to begin the tracheotomy incision. The dart that entered the throat was not found during the autopsy at Bethesda Naval Hospital, because it had dissolved quickly, as the Army had designed it to do.

At 1:22 PM, less than an hour after the assassination, a rifle was found by the law enforcement officers searching the sixth floor room in the Texas School Book Depository where the sniper's nest was constructed. The next day, at a televised press conference, Assistant District Attorney Wade repeated what Deputy Constable Seymour Weitzman had said, that he and Sheriff Boone had found a 7.65 German Mauser rifle with a 4/18 scope. This was in direct conflict to the Warren Commission Report, which stated that the gun found near the sniper's nest was the same as owned by Oswald, an Italian Mannlicher-Carcano 6.5 carbine. The authorities had to scramble to cover-up the Mauser evidence that had been printed in newspapers and reported elsewhere. With enough repetition about the lower-powered Mannlicher-Carcano, the Mauser would be forgotten.

Atherton's readers were calling him in record numbers. The country was obsessed over the death of their beloved President. Everyone had an opinion and a theory. Henry's job was to sort them out. One particular call got his attention. The man indicated that he wanted to relate a conversation that took place two weeks before the assassination that predicted exactly how and where the murder would take place. Atherton sensed the serious tone of this man's voice on the phone, and felt he was legitimate. Atherton agreed to meet with the man at a restaurant in Manhattan. Atherton arrived early, and when the hostess escorted the man to the table, Atherton rose to shake his hand.

The man did not crack a smile. *"I am here because I am carrying a story that needs to get out, and I think you are the man to do it,"* he began.

"Thank you for having faith and trust in me," Henry responded.

"I have read your work for years, and I believe you are worthy of my trust. I'm betting my life on it."

"I understand."

"You can call me, John. I work in a special laboratory operated by the CIA in Schenectady…perhaps you have heard of it."

"Yes, in fact, I have."

"I was invited to a dinner at a restaurant along with another CIA scientist, and our program manager from the lab. We were taken to dinner at a nice Italian restaurant to recognize us for our previous work, and to perhaps check us out regarding potential future assignments. Since our working areas are compartmentalized, we do not know each other well, and we all go by code names. Often they are the names of Hollywood actors. We never use our real names. I am just a young, quiet scientist, trying to do my part for the cause of freedom, and to fight communism. But I have seen and heard evidence in the lab of events that worry me about how the CIA is using my expertise. Although I don't remember the exact date, I do remember the dinner was during the week of November 4th and it was definitely sometime before November 8th.

We were joined by a CIA operative who we refer to as 'the Moneyman' from CIA headquarters in Langley, Virginia. The Moneyman is a flamboyant Hungarian national. Hungarians make great operatives for the CIA because they hate the communists more than they hate Americans; due to the way the Russians devastated their people and their country.

If a cover was blown, the CIA could easily disavow them, since they are not American citizens. The Hungarian will visit with us to describe a particular device he needs, and he asks us if we could design and manufacture such a device. We respond by saying that it might be feasible, using certain types of technology, depending upon the functionality he required. He would then ask us to formulate a budget that details the amount of funding needed to manufacture the device, and a timeline of how long the entire process of design, manufacture, and testing will take. The Hungarian would then return in a few days with the amount of cash needed to complete the project. I'm continually amazed at how the CIA can supply whatever amount of cash we request, no matter how outlandish our figures might seem. Where do they come up with all that cash? We purchase the best transistors, optical equipment, and testing devices. Cost is not relevant, suitability for the mission and precision timing in execution is everything to us!

On this particular evening, the Hungarian was accompanied by two buxom blondes. By 2:00 AM the next morning, much food and alcohol had been consumed, and the restaurant was virtually empty. I was probably feeling a bit sleepy when the Hungarian made a statement that startled me, making me sit upright. 'President Kennedy should be killed,' the Hungarian blurted out. Someone at the table sheepishly asked him why. 'He is a communist sympathizer,' was the Hungarian's reply. If we were not awake at this point in the conversation, the next comment gave us a jolt, 'It's OK,' the Hungarian continued, '…it will be taken care of in the next few weeks.'

Then, to our utter amazement, the CIA operative described the following scenario. 'When Kennedy goes to Dallas, the motorcade will take a detour from the main road, through Dealey Plaza. The setup will be multiple shooters, some in buildings firing from behind the President, and one will be firing from the front. The whole thing will be covered up because we will plant a patsy to take the heat.' When President Kennedy was killed two weeks later during his trip to Dallas, the words of the Hungarian came flooding back to me. I have been haunted by those statements ever since. This is the first time I have ever spoken of it. I believe its important now for the American people to know what really happened, and who is responsible for the murder of President Kennedy."

"I can see why you are upset," Atherton said, reassuringly. "Rest assured I will do all I can to make sure Americans learn the truth about what happened in Dallas."

* * * * * * * *

On November 22, 1963, Phil Willis witnessed the assassination and took a series of twelve photographs around Dealey Plaza just before and just after the assassination of President Kennedy. Willis was a decorated World War II hero, who fought at Pearl Harbor on the day America was attacked. He also served two terms in the Texas legislature.

Willis was quoted in an interview, saying, "All the Warren Commission wanted to hear was that three shots had come from the Texas School Book Depository. I am very dead certain at least one shot, including the one that took the President's skull off, had to come from the right front. And I'll stand by that to my death. Over my mother's grave."

A newsman, who worked for decades in radio broadcasting and had served as a White House correspondent, recalled his reaction to the news of President Kennedy's death;

> "I will never forget it…I was driving my father's car, which had a steering wheel made of steel. I was so upset by the news of Kennedy's assassination that I pulled over to the side of the road. As I realized that my beloved President had been taken from me, the most profound anger started to well up inside of me, and I began to pound that steering wheel. I pounded it, and pounded it, until my shirt was soaked with tears, and my hand could no longer withstand the pain. After all this time, I still can feel the deep bruising I caused in the bones of my hand on that fateful day…it is a constant reminder."

The shock and trauma experienced in the United States was reflected around the world. A sobbing babushka who was interviewed on a street in Moscow exclaimed, "We Russians honored this man, and trusted him, like no other American president before," the old woman said with tears in her eyes. A close advisor of JFK's, MIT economist Walt Rostow was heard to say, "Today, Washington is a city of male widows. We were all so devoted to him."

Three days ago the Constitution of the United States was attacked in the most violent way imaginable. Although President Kennedy was aware that high-ranking government officials were aligned against him, he did not take the proper precautions.

An attack on the President of the United States is an attack on the Constitution, and as such, it is an attack on the American people. Our founding fathers drafted the second amendment to the Constitution to ensure our right to bear arms. Most Americans believe their second amendment right is designed to help Americans protect their families, and this is partially true. But the primary purpose of the second amendment is to enable Americans to overthrow an illegal and oppressive government by force. The American colonists ousted King George only because he could not seize their weapons, as he tried to do at Lexington and Concord. The militia came out to meet them, a shot was fired, and the American revolution began.

When Lyndon Johnson flew in haste to Washington, he had the blood of an American president on his hands. Protected by his co-conspirators, the US Secret Service and the military, he spent his first restless night in the White House, wondering if the American people would perceive what had happened and rise up against him. This would have been the time for Americans, if they were not able to prosecute and impeach Johnson, to exercise their right and responsibility to bear arms, removing Lyndon Johnson from office by force.

But on this occasion, the people were in so much shock they did not storm the White House gates. Instead, the lead conspirator is appointing an investigative body called the Warren Commission with hand-picked, anti-Kennedy representatives to question witnesses, and then explain what happened to the American people. The fact is, Americans are smart enough to perceive what happened in Dallas, and in Washington, without having to know all the facts. But are Americans brave enough to carry out the intent of our forefathers, to bear arms and protect the Constitution of the United States? That is the question before us now.

* * * * * * * *

Jackie Kennedy sat alone in a booth at the rear of the Old Ebbitt Grill restaurant, located within walking distance of the White House. She did not want to run the risk that her children might hear this conversation. The Secret Service had complied with her request to clear the neighboring tables to ensure complete privacy. Glancing up from the table, she saw the lovely blonde with a crestfallen face, making her way to the booth, escorted by an agent.

"Please do sit down, Mary" the always graceful Jackie Kennedy began, *"I appreciate your coming to see me on such short notice. First, I want to thank you for letting me know about the walk you took with Jack to Arlington National Cemetery, and how you found the spot where he is now buried - that he found it to be peaceful. It means a lot to me."*

Mary Meyer nodded her head, not knowing what to say.

"There are just a few things that I would like to know."

"Jackie, I must admit I loved Jack very much. But I am sorry I allowed our relationship to continue."

"He was a very attractive and persuasive man," replied Jackie Kennedy. A dreamy look flashed across her face, then was gone. The widow continued, *"You and I have a lot in common, Mary. I remember when we were classmates at Vassar. Jack was always cutting in on guys to dance with you."*

"I am surprised you remember that."

"You and I have both lost children to death, and that is a pain most people can never understand. When we lived next door to you at Hickory Hill in McLean, I always worried about a child being hit by a car on that street. I was so disturbed when your Michael died that way."

"I remember how caring you were during that terrible time, and I really appreciated it, Jackie."

"You will recall I made a point of seating you next to Jack at most of our formal and informal dinners at the White House."

"Yes, I wondered about that, and I thank you for that also."

"Mary, there was no question about what Jack thought of you. He loved to talk to you, and I am sure he confided in you about certain topics he did not share with me. As much as that hurts, I will leave those secrets for you to cherish." The former First Lady continued, *"Well, there is one fact I want to know, but it gives me great pain to ask it. How many times did you sleep with my husband, Mary?"*

"Jack had the tendency to call me when he was going through a traumatic experience. I think he felt I was a safe place when he was alone and he felt mortal and vulnerable. For example, he had me over for dinner the night after Marilyn Monroe committed suicide. The White House sign-in book will show that I checked in about fifteen

times, and there were at least an equal number of visits where I was logged in as 'Dave Powers plus one,' for example."

"Come now, Mary," Jackie Kennedy looked directly at Mary Meyer, "Do you really think Marilyn's death was a suicide?"

"Well, I have wondered about that also."

"When the Kennedy Library opens in Boston, I will be locking away certain documents that will not be made public until after Caroline and John John are dead and gone. Mary, don't underestimate the risks you take when you are cavorting with men such as these. Your former husband works for the CIA, and your brother-in-law is an executive at The Washington Post. Surely you are aware of the possible danger in this."

"All I know, Jackie, is that I loved Jack, and he found solace with me at times when you were gone, and he had nowhere else to turn. I'm sorry for any heartache I may have caused you." Mary Meyer dissolved into tears and brought her hands to her face, "I am so sorry, I truly am. If I could just do this all over again..."

"My dear, you're not the only one who would like to relive the past few months. I am sure many of us would do things differently. I should never have let Jack go to Dallas. Now, I have to ask you a delicate question."

The beautiful artist lifted her head, blinked away her tears, and waited for the question.

"Did my husband ever get you pregnant?"

"Well, I am not sure," Mary Meyer said with a puzzled expression on her face.

"What do you mean?"

"There was a time when I thought I might be pregnant with Jack's child, so I quickly had a dilatation and curettage procedure, just in case."

"You know, Mary, it's time for both of us to pick up the pieces and go on with our lives. For the sake of my children, I hope you will be discrete about the relations you had with my husband."

"You can be sure of that, Jackie. Have no worries on that account."

"Thank you, Mary. Now if you will excuse me I have to get back to the White House to resume my packing."

Eight days after her husband was killed, Jackie Kennedy wrote one of the last letters she would write from the White House. It was a personal letter, but one of global importance. It was not typed, but written entirely in the hand of Jackie Kennedy. The former First Lady was writing a final letter to Russian leader Nikita Sergeyevich Khrushchev, the man John Kennedy had stared down during the Cuban Missile Crisis. She did this, even though she was told, and she believed at the time, that her husband had been killed, "...by a silly little communist!"

December 1, 1963

Dear Mr. Chairman-President:

I would like to thank you for sending your representative to my husband's funeral. He looked so upset when he approached me, and I was touched by this. I tried that day to tell you some things through him, but it was such a horrible day for me that I do not know if my words were received as I wanted them to be.

Therefore now, on one of the last nights I will spend in the White House, in one of the last letters I will write on this White House stationery, I would like to write my message to you. I am sending it only because I know how much my husband was concerned about peace, and how important the relations between you and him were to him in this concern. He often cited your words in his speeches, "In the next war, the survivors will envy the dead."

You and he were adversaries, but you were also allies in your determination not to let the world be blown up. You respected each other and could have dealings with each other. I know that President Johnson will make every effort to establish the same relations with you. The danger troubling my husband was that war could be started not so much by major figures as by minor ones.

Whereas major figures understand the need for self-control and restraint, minor ones are sometimes moved rather by fear and pride. If only in the future major figures could still force minor ones to sit down at the negotiating table before they begin to fight!

I know that President Johnson will continue the policy my husband believed in so deeply, the policy of self-control and restraint — and he will need your help.

I am sending this letter to you because I am so deeply mindful of the importance of the relations that existed between you and my husband. I read that your wife had tears in her eyes as she was coming out of the American embassy in Moscow after signing the book of condolences. Please tell her "thank you" for this.

Sincerely,

Jackie Kennedy

Soviet Ambassador Dobrynin transmitted the letter from Jackie Kennedy to the Kremlin on December 4, 1963. In his transmittal, the Ambassador indicated that it might be useful to maintain contact with the Kennedy family in America through Jackie. But instead of remaining in America, Jackie and her children ended up safely on an island with her new husband, Greek shipping magnate, Aristotle Onassis.

Jackie Kennedy had just witnessed the violent death of her husband. She was angry and depressed. She wanted to get out of Washington and the United States, and she was anxious to break away from the Kennedy clan. She just wanted someone to protect her. She wanted to be with someone who could shelter her children from the terrible forces that had just shattered her world. Yet she knew she was part of a larger picture. Jackie Kennedy's letter demonstrates her awareness and compassion for a world that possessed the capability to eradicate itself. Despite her naïveté regarding the likelihood that Johnson would follow the foreign policies of her husband, Jackie Kennedy's perceptive and heartfelt letter probably went a long way to soften the soviet premier's posture toward the United States during that critical era.

* * * * * * * *

A target of assassins himself, President Charles de Gaulle of France had his intelligence agency study the assassination of John Kennedy. President de Gaulle concluded that whoever killed President Kennedy meant to strike so much fear into the hearts of Americans, that no one would dare pursue the truth. General de Gaulle knew that public executions of popular leaders are a powerful means of controlling the people.

* * * * * * * *

A few days after the assassination, a women's group met in Milwaukee, Wisconsin. One of the regular attendees of the group was a law student named Cindy Ackerman, who was working as a White House Assistant in the Kennedy administration. She was traveling with the Kennedy entourage as an intern, and was with President Kennedy on the day he was killed. Members of the women's group noticed how sullen and withdrawn she was on this particular night. It was understandable, however, since she had been on Air Force One during the escape flight from Love Field to Andrews Air Force Base.

The group's leader opened the evening by saying, *"I would like to begin tonight with a prayer. Dear Lord, we ask that you will give peace to the soul of our departed President, John Kennedy. We ask that you would give solace to his wife Jackie, their children, Caroline and John, Jr., and the entire Kennedy family, which has seen tragedy before when they lost their eldest son, Joseph, Jr. We ask that you would also bless and keep*

Cindy Ackerman, who is with us tonight. We know she carries a deep burden because of the relationships she forged with members of the Kennedy Administration, and because of her relationship to those affected by this tragedy. Amen."

During the prayer Cindy Ackerman sat stock still, hunched over in her chair with her hands clasped together. Her tears began to moisten her hands and some fell to the floor. By the time the leader closed her prayer, Cindy Ackerman's body was shaking noticeably, as she was wracked with sobs. When she looked up at the members, her face was filled with anger, not sorrow.

"What is it, Cindy? What's wrong? How can we help you?" the leader asked.

"You don't understand," Cindy cried, her hands now rose with her palms facing upward. She began to tremble with rage. Ackerman continued, *"What the White House said about the attitudes of those traveling on Air Force One during the return flight from Dallas... it's all lies! The newspapers are saying the mood aboard that plane was somber. It was not! Lyndon Johnson and the rest of them were smiling, acting as if the assassination of President Kennedy was a cause for celebration. The only thing they were worried about was whether or not the White House would be attacked by the citizens. We should have burned the place to the ground before allowing Johnson to assume the presidency. That man should be in jail, not the White House!"*

The women were so disturbed by this revelation the meeting was cancelled for that night, and the dumbfounded wives went home to be with their families.

Chapter 12
The Cover-up

"It is not necessary to bury the truth. It is sufficient to merely delay it until no one cares."

Napoleon Bonaparte

On November 24, Atherton remained in Dallas to report on the case. As with his trip to Los Angeles, Atherton found that most of the evidence he sought was either not made available to him, or had vanished entirely.

The CIA had its propaganda machine ready to go well before the shots rang out in Dealey Plaza. The research had been done, the mercenary members of the media were in place, and the machine was immediately set in motion. Merriman Smith, the White House UPI correspondent fought with another reporter for the only available phone, and called in his report within minutes of the shooting.

Soon after that call, Walter Cronkite, the most respected newscaster in American broadcasting history, interrupted regular television programming to say, *"This news just in from Dallas. There are reports that three shots were fired at the presidential motorcade as it passed through downtown Dallas. It appears that President Kennedy has been wounded by this shooting!"*

We could not have known at that moment, the importance of Cronkite's statement that there were three shots. The lone nut theory could only be substantiated by the presumption that three shots were fired. The public would have to be convinced that one bullet wounded both President Kennedy and Governor Connelly. But if Walter Cronkite said it, then it must be true. It all happened so fast, and it was so violent! The nation and the world were in a state of shock.

Secret Service Agent Clint Hill, who had sprinted to the presidential limousine and had pushed Jackie Kennedy from the trunk into the back seat, covered the President's mortally wounded head with his jacket until the President was unloaded from the car at Parkland Hospital.

As soon as John Kennedy was taken from the presidential limousine and it was parked, the FBI began to destroy evidence. The blood splatter evidence was destroyed as agents washed the car, as evidenced by photos at Parkland Hospital showing agents and police officers surrounding the limo with buckets and hoses. After the limousine was clean, the blood-soaked red roses were replaced with a bouquet of fresh, yellow roses to please the eager photographers and news cameramen.

"The tree of liberty must sometimes be watered with the blood of patriots."

James Madison

The assassins in the Texas School Book Depository had escaped from the sixth floor to the roof of the building. They waited there until they received the *all clear* signal from the CIA controller on Morrow's ultra low-frequency walkie-talkies before descending the stairs that were guarded by their co-conspirators. Leaving their rifles on the roof to be collected later, the shooters exited at street level, quickly blending into the frantic crowd.

During the chaos that ensued as the Presidential motorcade sped away to Parkland Hospital, Jean Hill and her friend, Mary Moorman saw Jack Ruby running from the Texas School Book Depository, back to where his truck was parked in the railroad yard. Thinking he must have been a shooter, and not knowing what she would do when she caught him, Jean Hill ran after Ruby in pursuit. But FBI agents and deputies were posted throughout Dealey Plaza to protect the assassins, and to intercept anyone who might interfere with the escape plan for shooters and spotters. Two agents grabbed Jean Hill, confiscated the film from her camera, and took her in for interrogation. *"That man is getting away!"* she yelled. What followed was a contentious interview with the FBI. She later told U.S. Attorney Jim Garrison that her testimony, as published by the Warren Commission was, *"…an entire fabrication…"* compared to the testimony she had given on that day in Dallas.

From approximately 12:30 PM until 1:30 PM, Central Standard Time, (1:30 – 2:30 PM EST), the entire phone system in the Washington, D.C. metropolitan area was down. Residents in D.C., Maryland and Virginia could not place or receive phone calls. Those who experienced this rare problem probably dismissed it as an overload caused by D.C. area residents calling each other about the tragedy that had just occurred in Dallas. In fact, the phone blackout had been planned and timed precisely. The *OCAAUs* predicted that Robert Kennedy, who was at home in Virginia, might realize a coup had taken place in Dallas, invoke the second amendment, and use his position as U.S. Attorney General to retaliate with force to reclaim the government. Who has the ability, the power, and the authority to terminate all phone service in the nation's capital for an hour at a specific point in time, namely, the hour immediately following the assassination of the President?

Within minutes of the shooting in Dallas, a Deputy Director of the CIA was at Robert Kennedy's house. When John Kennedy was killed, Robert, Ethel and their children were home at Hickory Hill in McLean, Virginia, just a few minutes down Chain Bridge Road from CIA headquarters. Before moving to the White House, Jack and Jackie Kennedy had lived at Hickory Hill, next door to Cord and Mary Meyer. Robert Kennedy and the CIA man were seen walking together in Robert Kennedy's yard.

The spook said, *"Don't you worry, Bobby. We'll get the communist bastard who did this!"*

At that moment, Robert Kennedy realized he was outgunned by the *OCAAUs*. There would be no retaliation. Just in case, however, the Joint Chiefs of Staff in the Pentagon had entire U.S. Army divisions in the air, ready to descend upon riots that might erupt anywhere in the country in response to the assassination of President Kennedy. There were American troops inbound from Germany and France at a high state of readiness, ready to fight a war against their fellow citizens, if necessary, although they were not aware of who their possible foes might have been at the time.

At some point, Bobby realized that the OPERATION MONGOOSE team he had assembled to kill Castro had played a key role in the assassination of his brother. From that moment on, the crushing guilt of that realization, and the resulting depression would never leave Bobby for the remainder of his life.

On the first night Johnson spent in the White House, he insisted that his speechwriter and advisor, Horace Busby, one of LBJ's most trusted aides, sit in an armchair to watch over the President and First Lady while they slept. Busby tried to sneak out several times during the night. Each time Busby would try to leave, Johnson would lurch up and say, *"Buzz, are you still there?"*

* * * * * * * * *

Prior to the arrival of the presidential motorcade in Dealey Plaza, Deputy Sheriff Roger Craig and the other plainclothes deputies were instructed by Sheriff Decker that, *"We were to take no part whatsoever in the security of that motorcade."*

A police officer in Dealey Plaza had seen where a bullet struck the sidewalk across the street from the grassy knoll, leaving a path in the concrete. It then ricocheted into the grass some five feet from the initial impact point on the sidewalk, raising the turf into a mound. He called in this observation, and was told to guard the location. Shortly after the assassination, a photo was taken of a light-haired FBI agent recovering the bullet from the grass with his left hand, and then placing it in his pocket. There were Dallas police officers standing next to him at the moment he mishandled this important piece of evidence that was never entered into the record. Several witnesses at the scene retraced the bullet's flight path via the line etched in the concrete. It did not point to the Texas School Book Depository. Instead, it pointed directly at the Dallas County Records Building. Those same witnesses were shocked when the bullet was not even mentioned in the Warren Report. When they returned to look again at the sidewalk, the bullet track that pointed to the Dallas County Records Building had been filled in with concrete!

Buddy Walthers was the deputy sheriff who had discovered the bullet track, and he was the first police officer to interview James Tague, the car salesman who was wounded, while standing beneath the triple underpass, by concrete fragments emanating from a shot that had missed the President. Walthers initially reported that he saw the fair-haired federal agent place the bullet in his pocket. The deputy later recanted his story.

* * * * * * * *

Dave Powers and Kenny O'Donnell were John Kennedy's closest aides. Both had been with him since his early days of politics in Boston. Although Powers and O'Donnell wielded a great deal of power on behalf of the Oval Office, they kept such a low profile that most observers thought they were Secret Service agents. When the President would call Evelyn Lincoln, his secretary, asking the whereabouts of *"…those clowns,"* she knew the President meant Powers and O'Donnell. Dave Power's vantage point of the assassination was especially privileged, since he rode in the Secret Service follow-up car, where the official White House photographer would normally ride, but did not on that day. While waiting for news of John Kennedy's status at Parkland Hospital, both O'Donnell and Powers found they were pondering the same question. Approximately five seconds elapsed between the time the dart struck President Kennedy in the throat, and the fatal headshot, with many shots fired in between. Any of the Secret Service agents in the second and third cars could have sprinted that distance in five seconds, but none of them moved, because Special Agent in Charge, Roberts, ordered them to remain with Vice-President Johnson.

With the exception of the mercury explosive round fired by James Files from the Remington Fireball, all of the rounds that hit Kennedy used *sabot* technology. A favorite device of assassins, the sabot is a small plastic device, which centers a round in the rifle chamber, allowing a smaller caliber slug to be fired from a larger shell casing. Using a *sabot* with a full charge of gunpowder in the shell casing, the smaller slug will have increased velocity. Conversely, powder grains can be removed from the cartridge, decreasing the round's velocity. This is the kind of cartridge that left a bullet in John Kennedy's upper back. This explains why the bullet did not penetrate deeply into, or pass through, Kennedy's body.

The sabot rounds had been previously fired from Oswald's rifle into bales of cotton, and then recovered, resulting in ballistic markings that matched Oswald's weapon. A shell casing from a powerful 30.06 rifle, indicating the use of a *sabot* to match a Mannlicher-Carcano was later found on the roof of the Dallas County Records Building overlooking Dealey Plaza.

* * * * * * * *

"Hello, Jack. This is Sam Giancana. I am still staying at the Adolphus, across the street from your club. I'll be here until we get everything cleaned up. Listen, Jack, we need you to do something for us. We need you to get into the basement of the police station when

they transfer Oswald, and take him out. We're concerned he is gonna squeal, and that would blow the whole thing."

"Hey, Sam, I might be able to get in there with my police contacts, but you can't ask me to murder a guy when there are thirty cops standing around with guns."

"Jack, this is not an optional assignment. I am afraid that if you don't do this for us, things might not go so well with your sister, Eva."

"You don't have to threaten me like that, Mr. Giancana! I will take care of Oswald, don't you worry."

"I thought you would see it my way, Jack. We'll do our best to take care of your family, until we can get you out. Chief Curry is gonna call you when Oswald is about to be transferred. Your only chance to get him will be in the basement of the police station."

* * * * * * * * *

And so it was that Jacob Rubinstein, the man Richard Nixon had protected in 1947, hung up the phone, wondering why Giancana made the comment about taking care of his family. Ruby realized that after killing Oswald to silence him, he would probably never live outside of jail for the rest of his life. Ruby liked Oswald, but they were threatening to harm his sister! Oswald knew most of the players involved in the conspiracy to kill the President, so he had to be silenced. Ruby had no choice. He knew what he had to do, and how he was going to do it.

After extensive questioning for fourteen hours without the presence of a lawyer, Lee Harvey Oswald was to be transferred from his jail cell to stand before the Court in response to his indictments for killing President Kennedy and Officer Tippit. Oswald was finally going to have his say, and make an attempt to secure justice. As Oswald was escorted through the basement of the Dallas Police Department, the deputies stepped aside while Jack Ruby stepped forward, shouted Oswald's name and shot him at 11:21 AM. Ruby had used his Colt Cobra .38 to fire a single shot into Oswald's stomach area. With immediate medical treatment, this should not have been a fatal wound.

Oswald was quickly pulled back into the elevator and taken upstairs, where he was given a lethal injection before being taken out to the ambulance on a stretcher. When Oswald emerged from the elevator on his way to the hospital, his eyes were directed upward and his tongue protruded from his mouth. According to reporters standing by in the basement, Oswald looked as if he had been drugged.

While the surgeon was operating on Oswald in an attempt to save his life, a call came into the switchboard of Parkland Hospital.

"Hello ma'am, do you recognize my voice?"

"No, I don't. Should I?"

"Well, ma'am, this is Lyndon Johnson, President of the United States, calling."

"Yes sir, what can I do for you, sir?"

"I need to speak with the doctor who is working on the President's assassin. I believe the patient's name is Oswald."

The physician was irritated at being called to the telephone while he was operating on a critical gunshot wound.

"Doctor, this is the President speaking. Do you recognize my voice?"

"Yes, Mr. President, I've heard you many times on the television and at your radio station when they broadcast your speeches."

"Okay, now listen closely to me Doctor; it is imperative to national security that Lee Harvey Oswald not survive the operation."

"But Mr. President, his blood test results look strange to me, and he is starting to come around. He might make it."

"Well he can't make it, and that is that. Do you have something that will cause him to just slip away?"

"Yes sir, I do."

"Well, use it then. It's very important for the security of this nation, understand?"

"Yes, I understand."

The physician slowly hung up the phone and quietly made his way back to the operating room. He was about to voluntarily violate the Hippocratic Oath. No one noticed that the doctor had taken a large amount of controlled anesthetics out of the medicine cabinet without signing for them. No one was in witness when the doctor added the toxic amounts of barbiturates to the patient's intravenous mixture. Within minutes, Oswald had flat-lined.

* * * * * * * *

The propaganda campaign to frame Oswald as the presidential assassin included publicity of his classified mission to Moscow and Minsk, where he had sought to become a Soviet citizen, his return with Marina as his wife, his suspicious trips to the U.S. Embassy in Mexico, during which he supposedly asked for diplomatic support to visit Castro, his distribution of pro-Castro leaflets outside the Office of Naval Intelligence in New Orleans, his radio debate with Carlos Bringuier, a Cuban exile sympathizer, and other such masquerades – all this while he was conducting secret meetings with FBI agent James Patrick Hosty. Hosty worked with a CIA counter-intelligence agent, George de Morenschildt, to 'handle' Oswald, so he would be in the right place at the right time. Oswald had been hired by the FBI as an informant, which was a convenient way for the Bureau and the CIA to keep tabs on him. Oswald was given the FBI identification number 179.

Oswald has also been named as the would-be assassin who fired a shot at General Edwin Walker through the window of his study, on April 10, 1963 as Walker was working on his tax return. But Lee Harvey Oswald, the former Marine, missed the target! Those who knew Oswald well in the military and the Cuban exile training worlds knew that marksmanship was not one of Oswald's strong points. However, listening, gathering information, and keeping quiet all the while was something in which he excelled; the perfect profile for a patsy. Just so long as he followed his orders, counted on being rescued, and remained silent until the conspirators could have him terminated...

Perhaps the best example of manufactured circumstances is the visit paid by Oswald and two Cubans to the home of Sylvia Odio in Dallas. In late September, 1963, approximately 60 days prior to the assassination of JFK, the two Cubans and Oswald called on Ms. Odio, whose father had run a successful business in Cuba prior to Castro's coup. The Cuban's asked Sylvia Odio a number of questions that belied their knowledge of her father's anti-Castro activities, and she denied their requests for information and support. She did not trust them. She noticed the American had a very limited ability to speak Spanish. In fact, the U.S. military had taught Oswald to speak Russian, and he knew only a little Spanish.

A few days later, Sylvia Odio received a phone call. The Cuban voice mentioned that the name of the American who visited her was "...*Leon. He was an ex-Marine, an expert marksman and he would be a tremendous asset to anyone, except you never know how to take him. He could do anything, like getting underground in Cuba, like killing Castro. He says we Cubans don't have any guts, and that we should have shot President Kennedy after the Bay of Pigs. He says we should do something like that."* Unprovoked, scripted comments like that could have had only one purpose, to set the stage depicting Oswald as a homicidal sharpshooter.

In the same timeframe as the Odio visit, on a Saturday morning, Oswald and a Cuban he referred to as "Hernandez," drove up to the house of Robert McKeown, who was on probation for running guns from Prio Soccares to Fidel Castro. The young, Anglo-American began the conversation by saying, *"I'm Lee Oswald."*

After some casual conversation, Oswald (or an impersonator of Oswald) stated his purpose for the meeting, *"Mac, would you do me a favor? I will not involve you in any way. I can give you $10,000 if you can get me four rifles, 300 Savage automatics, each with a telescopic sight."*

McKeown was immediately suspicious of Oswald, because he knew anyone could walk into a SEARS store in 1963 with few hundred dollars, and buy those guns.

The Odio and McKeown incidents sufficiently illustrate the lengths to which the conspirators went to set up Lee Harvey Oswald, every step of the way.

The campaign to frame Oswald was complex, disjointed, and reactionary, including fabricated letters sent to him from addresses in Havana after the assassination, and memos on the day of the assassination by J. Edgar Hoover, stating that Oswald had attempted to travel to Cuba, but would not discuss it with his agents.

Several days after Oswald's death, members of Oswald's family gathered to bury the body of the quiet man who had been convicted before his death in the eyes of the public for assassinating President Kennedy and murdering Officer Tippit. Forty reporters attended the ceremony, and they remained at a distance, and did not bother the Oswald family during the somber event. Several reporters had to be called into service as pallbearers. Sitting at the graveside were Oswald's wife,

Marina, his mother, Marguerite, his brother Robert, a fellow Marine, and his two daughters, June Lee and Rachel. An overwhelming number of plain-clothed federal agents guarded the Oswald burial site until they were certain no one could recover the body for drug testing. Oswald had served the OCAAUs well, although he had done it unwittingly.

"American spies must lead difficult lives. The most honest of them, and even their superiors, don't always know whom they're working for. "

Vladimir Y. Semichastny, Director of KGB

* * * * * * * *

Responding to a summons from the White House, Chief Justice Earl Warren entered the Oval Office, taking a seat opposite the President. Lyndon Johnson beamed a Texas smile when Chief Justice Warren entered the room.

"Thank you for visiting me, Mr. Chief Justice."

"It is always my pleasure to serve, Mr. President."

"Now that is the kind of attitude I like to hear. Not much of that on Capitol Hill, you know."

"Well now, Mr. President, the reason I have lasted so long up here on the Hill is that we justices are removed from all the partisanship."

"That is exactly why I asked you to visit with me here today. Justice Warren, you know the American people are clamoring for answers regarding the assassination of President Kennedy."

"Yes, I have read the papers, and I have heard there are numerous rumors being tossed about. I try not to give it much thought, however."

"You are wise to maintain that attitude. And that is exactly why I want you to serve the people in a capacity that will help to calm them down."

"The function of a democratic government is to serve the people. Whatever I can do to help, Mr. President."

"Splendid, what I want you to do is to form a commission that will examine the evidence and publish findings indicating that Lee Harvey Oswald was a lone assassin. I have a list here of folks I would like for you to consider. There are some sharp minds on this list."

"Now, Mr. President, I am willing to serve you and the American public in any way I can. But I will not oversee an investigative process that states the outcome as its premise. That flies in the face of the Constitution, and every precept of justice."

"I don't give a damn what it flies in the face of! The people need to be reassured that Oswald killed the President, and I cannot be the one to do that, for reasons that should be obvious. There are going to be riots in the streets if we don't publish some answers, and soon!"

"You are right, those reasons are obvious, but that does not mean I am obligated to defraud the American public for the sake of political expediency. Furthermore, if I was your lawyer, I would recommend that you stay as far away from this process as possible, Mr. President."

"This is not about politics, Mr. Chief Justice; this is about practicality and common sense. This administration cannot function properly as long as there is a cloud hanging over it. The people want answers."

"I would be happy to oversee such a commission, so long as I have the same degree of autonomy and objectivity in my work as I do as Chief Justice of the Supreme Court. But I will not serve if I am restricted to a particular outcome."

"Damn you, you will serve! Furthermore, you will serve in a manner that is in support of the President."

The Chief Justice stood to leave. *"I will need some time to consider this task before giving you an answer, Mr. President. My workload at the Court is at an all-time high."*

"You just go ahead and give it some thought, Mr. Chief Justice. I will expect your answer by 8:00 AM tomorrow morning. No later! You hear me?"

"Yes sir. Good day, Mr. President."

"Good day, Mr. Chief Justice."

During his time of service leading the investigation into the assassination of President Kennedy, Chief Justice Warren traveled to Dallas to take testimony from Jack Ruby. Ruby pleaded with Chief Justice Warren to take him to Washington for his testimony regarding the death of President Kennedy. Ruby told Warren he was not safe giving his testimony in Dallas. His request was denied. Ruby was injected with the virulent cancer strain that was developed for the CIA by Judyth Vary Baker. Jack Ruby died without ever leaving the Texas prison.

America must have been shocked as Chief Justice Earl Warren abandoned his lifetime appointment to the Supreme Court. Rather than remain until his death, Earl Warren resigned from the bench.

* * * * * * * * *

Abraham Zapruder was the clothier who took the famous motion pictures of the John Kennedy assassination. Of the many ironies of that day, one is that if Zapruder had continued panning to the right for just a moment after the limousine went under the triple overpass of the Stemmons Freeway, he would have most likely captured the image of James Files firing from under the tree branch, behind the stockade fence on the grassy knoll. When the Zapruder film was first released to the public, the frames involving the fatal headshot were doctored. By reversing only those movie frames, the FBI hoped to portray John Kennedy's head movement as forward, and to the right, instead of back, and to the left. When the doctored version of the Zapruder film was discovered to be a hoax, J. Edgar Hoover testified that the anomaly in the film was "*...a printing error.*"

As he completed his testimony before the Warren Commission, Abraham Zapruder was agitated that he was not questioned about an aspect of the assassination he thought was critical to the case. As he was about to be excused from the witness stand, he interjected a reference to his concern. Whether being interviewed on television, radio, or testifying for the Commission, Abraham Zapruder found reliving those moments in Dealey Plaza quite painful. The weight of the world had been placed upon him since he was asked almost daily to repeat what he witnessed through the lens of his movie camera. In fact, his testimony before the Commission could be characterized as apologetic. The FBI had apparently browbeaten Zapruder into testifying that the shutter speed of his camera was wrong, since careful review of his film later proved that two bullets struck targets in the limousine in such rapid succession that it would be impossible for them to have been fired from a single Mannlicher-Carcano, which takes at least 2.3 seconds to cycle. As he was about to be excused, Abraham Zapruder asked the Warren Commission attorney who was interviewing him an important question:

Mr. Zapruder: *Well, they claimed they told me it was about two frames [too] fast. Instead of 16 it was 18 frames [per second] and they told me it was about two frames [too] fast in the speed and they told me that the time between the two rapid shots, as I understand, that was determined, the length of time it took to the second one and that they were very fast and they claim it has proven it could be done by one man. You know there was indication there were two?*
Warren Attorney: *Your films were extremely helpful to the work of the Commission, Mr. Zapruder.*
Mr. Zapruder: *I am only sorry I broke down. I didn't know I was going to do it.*
Warren Attorney: *Mr. Zapruder, I want to thank you very much, for the Commission, for coming down. It has been very helpful.*

The Warren Commission only wanted to hear what it wanted to hear.

An independent researcher of the John Kennedy assassination wrote an article about her views after reading the report from the Warren Commission. Sylvia Meagher wrote," *There are no heroes in this piece* [the Warren Commission Report], *only men who collaborated actively or passively, willfully or self-deludedly, in dirty work that does violence to the elementary concept of justice and affronts normal intelligence.*"

* * * * * * * * *

When Dr. Hahn reviewed the X-rays taken of Governor Connelly's thigh at Parkland Hospital, he noted the large amount of metal fragments in the governor's leg. Considering the fragments, Hahn commented, "*I can't conceive of where they came from this missile."* Likewise, when his associate, Dr. Frick was asked if the pristine bullet could have shattered Connelly's wrist, Frick replied, *"No, for the reason that there are too many [metal] fragments described in that wrist."* A damaged bullet that had shattered bones would not have displayed the markings tying the missile to Oswald's gun, which was necessary to uphold the lone gunman theory.

* * * * * * * *

The way in which John Kennedy's casket was handled and disposed of is both alarming and probative. What makes it most alarming is that Robert Kennedy was instrumental in the disposal of this critical piece of evidence, perhaps due to his intention to run for the presidency in 1968.

The National Archives and Records Service (NARS) [as it was called in the 1960s] is a branch of the U.S. General Services Administration (GSA). In a MEMORANDUM FOR THE RECORD, dated February 24, 1966, Webster Robinson, an administrative officer for the NARS, described the casket that was allegedly used to transport John Kennedy's body from Parkland Hospital to Love Field as, *"…reddish-brown in color with a brushed satin polish and plain in appearance."* The casket had a single, curved lid, and long, fluted handles on either side. It was contained in a bluish-gray painted pine box. We have been led to believe that John Kennedy's body remained in this casket from the time the Secret Service agents wrestled it from the Dallas County Coroner, until it reached Bethesda Naval Hospital. But the chain of evidence was broken. After the casket was loaded onto Air Force One, John Kennedy's body was removed from the reddish-brown, formal casket and placed into a gray plastic shipping casket, naked, and in a transparent body bag. Another corpse had been covertly brought aboard, and placed into the reddish-brown casket. The DNA evidence in both caskets would have provided significant value as evidence in the case of the assassination of President Kennedy.

* * * * * * * *

While in Dallas investigating the assassination of President Kennedy, Henry Atherton began to form some impressions about how events were transpiring. There were gaps of information, and people who were cryptic or downright hostile when asked about the assassination. One night in Dallas, Atherton's phone rang in his hotel room. Only Andrea and Montrose had the number.

"Hello?" Atherton answered.

"You need to back off, Atherton," the voice barked. *"You don't know what you're dealing with here. Get out of Dallas and don't come back."* Then the line went dead. Atherton found it difficult to sleep that evening.

New York Tribune, February 9, 1966
Opinion/Editorial - Henry Atherton, Staff Writer

This reporter has acquired the transcript of a call from Senator Robert Kennedy, a leading contender for the Democratic Presidential nomination in 1968, to Administrator Knott of the General Services Administration in Washington, DC. In my opinion, it holds great importance for Americans who seek the truth in the assassination of President Kennedy.

Senator Robert Kennedy called on February 3, 1966 at 6:10 PM

Kennedy: *I talked over there about what we're going to do with the casket that President Kennedy came back in. I have talked to Secretary McNamara about getting rid of that so he has made some arrangements. He is not able to get release of the casket. Wanted to see if we can get that released.*

Knott: *My concern, and I have not talked to the [Defense] Secretary, but with his man Steadman, is the man who is at Dartmouth now (Manchester) and spent some time in National Archives and like so many of us, while writing this story was quite outraged about this aspect and he had planned in a biography that he is writing, which I understand will be released in 1968, to include a chapter dealing with this particular subject. If this is so, I think it is going to raise loads of questions about the release of the casket.*

Kennedy: *In what way?*

Knott: *As to how it was disposed of. More than that, the Attorney General had a letter from Congressman Cabell, urging that it be disposed of and related to an act of Congress passed last year that dealt with the rifle, tagging it as government property.*

Kennedy: *I don't think it was pertinent at all to this case.*

Knott: *The Attorney General has asked that we do nothing without clearing with him. I am held up by the Attorney General and until I could talk with you, and you could explore the possibility in 1968.*

Kennedy: *Hope that won't be published in 1968 - I don't know why we need this [the casket] around at this time.*

Knott: *I think it ought to be disposed of. I think I was one of the first to discuss the possibility of disposing of it. On the other hand, if, in 1968, someone is going to be publishing things that will raise the question...*

Kennedy: *What question?*

Knott: *The question of authority to release and dispose of it.*

Kennedy: *I think it belongs to the family and we can get rid of it in any way we want to.*

Knott: *I don't want to appear negative - just want to be sure we are clear and that we do this when the timing is right.*

Kennedy: *I've talked to Secretary McNamara. What I would like to have done is to take it to sea. Could you call them and make the arrangements with Secretary McNamara?*

Knott: *I'm held up that at this point in time for clearance from the Attorney General.*

Kennedy: *Why don't we go ahead - I will have Attorney General Katzenbach call you. I don't know what this has to do with this matter even if Manheim has a chapter on it.*

Knott: *It is a disposal of government property in one sense, although I took the position we were paying for services.*

Kennedy: *I don't think anybody will be upset about the fact that we disposed of it - I will take the responsibility for that and I will call Mr. Katzenbach and have him call you.*

Knott: *If there is no problem in your mind. . .*

Kennedy: *Will you call Secretary McNamara after you hear from Katzenbach?*

Knott: *Yes I will, and we will make arrangements from there.*

Atherton continued to gather evidence regarding the ornate casket, and he published his findings in mid-March;

New York Tribune, March 11, 1966
Henry Atherton, Investigative Reporter

There is a crucial piece of evidence in the Kennedy assassination case that has been sealed, and is now sitting in a locked, alarmed room at the National Archives in Washington, D.C. It is the casket that Jackie Kennedy accompanied on Air Force One to Andrews AFB, then was transported by motorcade to Bethesda Naval Hospital. Congressman Cabell has written to the GSA Administrator, indicating, *"I am unable to conceive of any manner in which the casket could have an evidentiary value. Nor can I conceive of any reason why the national interests would require its preservation. Consequently, I am of the view that the reasons for destroying the casket completely outweigh the reasons, if any, that might exist for preserving it."*

Edward Cabell was mayor of Dallas on the day of John Kennedy's assassination. He was later elected to Congress. Edward Cabell is the brother of General Cabell who President Kennedy had fired from the CIA over the Bay of Pigs fiasco. The murder took place in his city, and it was facilitated, then covered up by Cabell's police department. It was Congressman Earle Cabell who wrote the letter on February 11, 1966 that was referenced by the GSA Administrator. Why did U.S. Attorney General Katzenbach, the same Attorney General in the Johnson administration who pushed for evidence that implicated Oswald, write a similar letter to GSA, stating not only that the casket had no *evidentiary value*, but that it should not be preserved since the Warren Commission wanted nothing to do with it? Katzenbach referenced H.R. 9545, which provided for the acquisition and preservation of *certain items of evidence*, but its purview was restricted only to those items that were considered by the President's Commission!

Robert Kennedy is preparing for the Presidential election in 1968. He wants the casket gone before then. He is in the process of destroying evidence that does not belong to his family, as the casket clearly belongs to the U.S. Government. Put another way, that casket belongs to the people!

The casket that was purchased by the Government from the O'Neal Funeral Home in Dallas, and was allegedly used to transport John Kennedy's body to Air Force One, has been kept under tight security in an alarmed room at Pennsylvania Avenue and 8th Street in Northwest Washington, D.C., sealed within a wooden box, and then again with wrapping paper. On Thursday, February 17, 1966, acting on orders from the Office of the Secretary of Defense, the Archives Handling Branch Chief bored 42 one-half inch holes into the casket, in the top, both sides and both ends. He placed three sandbags, weighing approximately 85 pounds each into the casket. He locked the lid, sealed the casket with metal bands, and placed the casket back into the wooden crate. The lid was screwed back into place on the wooden crate, and it too was drilled with holes. The wooden crate was then secured also with metal bands, and it was made ready for transport.

On Friday, February 18, 1966 the perforated, weighted and banded casket was picked up by a military truck, which took it directly to Andrews AFB in Maryland. It was loaded onto a waiting C-130E aircraft [number 54960]. A Pentagon representative, Colonel B.R. Daughtrey, Executive Assistant to the Secretary of the Air Force, accompanied the casket to ensure its absolute destruction. The loadmaster, SSgt Thomas E. Eagle, AF 13478093, secured the cargo and the military plane took off at 8:38 A.M. The pilot was Major Leo W. Tubay, USAF, FR 42561. He was assisted by co-pilot Captain Frederick E. Clark, USAF, FV 3066163. They proceeded to the predetermined spot in the Atlantic Ocean, fixed at 38/30 North latitude and 72/06 West longitude, arriving at 10:00 A.M. The site can be described as an unexploded ordnance area, east of the continental shelf, with a depth of 1500 fathoms (9000 feet). Major Tubay descended to an altitude of 500 feet, where he gave the order, and the crate was pushed out the rear of the aircraft. According to the official report, two small parachutes deployed just prior to impact. There had been great concern that the box and casket would shatter. Tubay circled for 20 minutes, ensuring that the casket sank intact, and that it did not return to the surface.

No law enforcement or forensic investigator ever saw the inside of that casket. No blood samples were ever taken from its cloth lining.

Since February 18, 1966, the perforated casket has been sitting in deep salt water, the most corrosive natural environment, where the salinity is upwards of 35 parts per thousand, surrounded by latent explosives that would endanger any human who might attempt to retrieve the casket.

As an American, do you feel that the casket might have had value as evidence? What is your impression of government officials deciding to drill holes into it, wrap it in metal bands and push it out of a plane? Why were Cabell, Katzenbach, and even Robert Kennedy anxious to get rid of this casket? Why was it important to them? What remains is the U.S. Attorney General (a Johnson appointee) the mayor of Dallas on the day of the assassination (now a Member of Congress), and John Kennedy's brother (now a likely candidate for President) were determined to see the casket destroyed. All this is indeed worthy of note.

A reviewer of the Warren Commission report, David McDermitt, offered the following words when considering facts in cases like the assassination of John Kennedy. McDermitt says the strategy of the Warren Commission was to overwhelm the people with facts:

"Now facts are all very well but they have their little weaknesses. Americans often assume that facts are solid, concrete (and discrete) objects like marbles, but they are very much not. Rather, they are subtle essences, full of mystery and metaphysics, that change their color and shape, their meaning, according to the context in which they are presented. They must always be treated with skepticism, and the standard of judgment should be not how many facts one can mobilize in support of a position, but how skillfully one discriminates between them, how objectively one uses them to arrive at truth, which is something different from, although not unrelated to, the facts."

U.S. Attorney Jim Garrison of New Orleans pursued the only court case filed in the aftermath of the assassination of President John F. Kennedy. The OCAAUs constantly harassed his efforts, and he was not able to secure any convictions. Although Jim Garrison was able to get reelected, despite efforts from within the government to ruin him, and bribes to abandon his case, Jim Garrison was finally defeated by Hayward Colvin in a subsequent election. Colvin then proceeded to destroy Garrison's files pertaining to the assassination.

A teacher of American history wrote a letter to the editor of her local newspaper:

"America is nothing if it cannot live by its stated ideals of respect for an informed citizenry. America is nothing if it jails honest men like Mr. Redmond, who had the heroic courage to refuse to follow the bidding of his employer, [U.S.] District Attorney Hayward Colvin, and destroy historical records. The files of Jim Garrison's case against Clay Shaw in the assassination of President John Kennedy are public records funded by tax money and now mandated by Congress to be reviewed by the Assassination Records Review Board. It is our history and not the private property of any elected individual. America was conceived in order to protect us from private agendas like those of King George of England and Hayward Colvin.

Every student in our schools knows that question and hypothesis must be proved by evidence. That is basic curriculum and the foundation for *civilized progress. <u>Destruction of evidence is a deliberate act of war against</u> <u>the entire process of rational thought.</u> Destruction of evidence is what Hayward Colvin is advocating. It is sad to witness a judicial process in New Orleans that has acted as an accessory to this reprehensible action that flies in the face of law, of Congress and of constitutional protection. The public has a right to know what is in files paid for with tax dollars. Elected officials who deny that right should be promptly impeached. Too many unanswered questions remain about the murder of a President. The evidence has been withheld, and answers have been provided without evidence. That's bad science, bad governing and abuse of power. A democracy lives only when a rich diet of information is available—then let the people decide."*

Penny Gibson
Eighth Grade Teacher

  Years after the assassination, a bullet cartridge was found on the roof of the Dallas County Records Building. The cartridge had rolled to the edge of the roof, and had lodged under some roofing tarpaper. The portion of the cartridge that was exposed was weathered and pitted from long-term exposure to the elements. The cartridge bore distinctive crimp marks, indicating that it was a modified sabot round, the kind used to imitate Oswald's Mannlicher-Carcano.

  During the months that followed the assassination, President Johnson would frequently call Jackie Kennedy at her New York apartment, giving her words of reassurance and advice. Jackie Kennedy would thank the President for calling, and would tell him about her despair and depression.

  "Hello Jackie. How are you, Darlin'?"

  "Good afternoon, Mr. President. It's so nice of you to call."

  "Well, I just want to make sure my girl is okay...you are doin' okay, aren't you?"

  "I must admit I have been pretty depressed lately."

  "Your husband was a great man, Jackie. Losing him has left a large hole in your heart. It only makes sense you would have difficulty adjusting to such a loss."

  "I just can't understand why that lunatic shot Jack. What did it accomplish?"

  "It's a cold and cruel world that we live in, my dear."

  "Well I hope Lee Harvey Oswald burns in Hell!"

  "That's my girl, you have a right to be angry...it should make you feel better."

  "Right now I feel awful. I just pray there's a light at the end of this tunnel."

  "There is, my dear. Now I want you to call me if you need anything...anything now, you hear me?"

  "Yes, Mr. President, and thank you for taking the time from your busy day to check on me."

  "It is the least I can do. You take care now."

  "Goodbye, Mr. President."

"Jackie, from now on, I want you to call me Lyndon."
"Whatever you say, Mr. President. You know, I used to refer to Jack as Mr. President."
"Okay, Darlin'. I can't say anything against that, now can I? Goodbye!"

Jackie hung up the phone, lay face down on her bed, and softly began to cry.

* * * * * * * *

"How sadly our interpretations are dominated and distorted by unconscious preconceptions."
Dr. Arthur M. Schlesinger, Jr.

The cover-up ruse that carried the most devastating potential for millions of human beings around the world, was the fact that immediately upon announcing the death of the President, the Pentagon issued previously prepared orders that the Strategic Air Command and submarine forces extend their patrols, moving ever closer to Soviet airspace and waters, shifting to a military posture of DEFCON 2. DEFCON 1 is war. Submariners in nuclear subs said later the tension was so heavy at the time, this period was the closest America ever came in the Cold War to launching nuclear weapons against the Soviet Union. In order to distract the military from retaliatory efforts to help American citizens reclaim the government that had been stolen from them, the American fascist shadow government risked starting a nuclear war!

Chapter 13
Assassination by Heart Attack

"It's hard [to live with] *when you see someone who is being looked at* [an African man] *in a restaurant, and he just dies, right there at the table!"*

John, CIA scientist and inventor of the Heart Attack Machine

Henry made a call to Andrea from his hotel room in Dallas. *"Andrea, there's something very strange going on down here. I'm amazed at the number of witnesses, investigators, suspects, reporters, lawyers, and publishers related to this case who have died recently of heart attacks. It seems that every time I schedule an interview with a material witness, the person has a sudden heart attack and drops dead."*

"Henry, that's probably a good enough reason for you to stop chasing this story, don't you think?"

"Yes, I suppose so, but there's something going on here that ties all these assassinations together. I just can't figure it out."

Several weeks later, Henry received a telephone call that would provide several of the pieces to the puzzle that were missing.

"Mr. Atherton, I am calling to tell you about another aspect of the story that comes from the CIA lab in upstate New York."

"What new information do you have for me?"

"I can't discuss it on the phone."

"Where would you like to meet, then?"

The man flew to Washington. He met Henry in a Georgetown bar, just a few miles from the White House. When Henry walked in, he noticed the man sitting in a booth at the back of the restaurant, away from the bar.

"You must be part Italian," Henry chided.

"What do you mean?" the man replied as he scanned the tables.

"Usually guys who sit in the back of restaurants facing the door are Mafia," Henry said with a smile. The look on the man's face demonstrated his lack of amusement.

"Are you interested in this new information or not?" There was a tone of irritation in the man's voice, as he scanned the restaurant. With the White House just a few blocks away, Atherton questioned if he had picked the best location for the meeting.

"Yes, I am interested. I'm sorry if my attempt at humor was upsetting to you. Let's try this again. You have some new information from the lab that is causing concern?"

"Yes, I've learned of another development that might play a significant role in your investigations."

"I'm all ears," Henry replied.

"Another CIA-developed assassination device is a generator that produces a microwave pulse so powerful that an assassin can kill his target by stopping the victim's heart in a crowded restaurant, on a street corner, or while the victim is sleeping, without anyone ever knowing the victim's heart attack was artificially induced! The CIA developed this heart-shocking device for only one purpose, to assassinate with plausible deniability in a crowded area. Pistols are too noisy. At any given time, there are at least five of these devices in use by the CIA around the world, and perhaps more."

Atherton answered, *"I must say this information supports some of my findings, but how can I establish who you are, and that you're in a position to know this highly-classified information?"*

"That's the whole point," the man replied. *"You can call me, John, but that's all you can know about me. Our working conditions are so compartmentalized, my boss doesn't even know what I am doing. You can decide whether or not to believe what I say, but I will tell you I know about these heart attack machines because I am the inventor. I'm telling you about it now, at the risk of my own life, because I don't like to see how my machines are being used. I have built five for the Agency thus far, and they have the plans of my design, so they can build more of them. I was told my invention would be used to fight communism."*

* * * * * * * * *

Still unable to connect all the dots, Atherton was convinced by Montrose to abandon his *'witch hunts'* and traveling investigations, and return to regular reporting assignments in Manhattan. He needed to stabilize his life. But he continued his research and conducted occasional interviews regarding the Monroe and Kennedy cases. His relationship with Andrea began to improve as they spent more time together.

* * * * * * * * *

In July of 1965, a group known as, *Artists and Writers Dissent* delivered to Adlai Stevenson, the former Democratic candidate for president, and the current U.S. Ambassador to the United Nations, a declaration which stated;

> *"We have watched in dismay as our government, by its actions in Vietnam and in the Dominican Republic, has clearly violated the United Nation's Charter, international law, and those fundamental principles of human decency which alone can prevent a terrifying, worldwide escalation of suffering and death. We urgently ask you, as our government's representative in the United Nations and as a man who in the past has stood for the best hope of realizing American ideals, to consider your complicity in*

what this Government is doing. . . We urge you to resign as United States Ambassador to the United Nations, and, having done that, to become a spokesman again for that which is humane in the traditions and in the people of America."

Stevenson was often placed in the awkward position of making statements in the United Nations and abroad, that were in conflict with his own heart. Stevenson was forced by Johnson to present evidence to the world that supported the global conquests of Johnson and the CIA, although he vehemently disagreed with U.S. policy in Vietnam and the Dominican Republic.

On July 9th, 1965, Adlai Stevenson flew to Paris. That night, Stevenson had dinner with several journalists. Always the consummate diplomat in public, Stevenson was known to complain and grouse in private. He had a reputation of being indecisive, even about the prospect of being president. That night, Stevenson vented openly about his disagreement with U.S. policy in Vietnam, and the way the United States handled the crisis in the Dominican Republic, which he characterized as a *'massive blunder.'*

On the evening of July 13th, Stevenson stayed as a guest of the Bruces at the residence of the U.S. Embassy in Grosvenor Square, London. Earlier that day, Stevenson spoke with Britannica representatives about going to work for them, following his planned resignation from his position as U.S. Ambassador to the United Nations. That day, *Washington Post* President Kay Graham visited the American Embassy as a stopover for the vacation she was taking with Truman Capote. Adlai had dated Kay often in Washington, but her interest in him never rose to the level of his interest in her. Stevenson wanted to see Kay in London, but she was not too keen on the idea. That evening, Stevenson waited for Graham in the Embassy library. While he was waiting there, Stevenson fell into a deep conversation with Eric Sevaried, the famed newscaster. Stevenson complained again about the position of the United States in the United Nations, and his tenuous position there.

Stevenson's credibility had been negatively affected by the fact the Kennedy Administration had not told Stevenson the Bay of Pigs operation was going to be launched two days before the 'Cuban Issue' was to be discussed in the U.N. General Assembly. However, Adlai Stevenson is best known for his famous reply to Soviet Ambassador Zorin, regarding the presence of Soviet offensive nuclear missiles in Cuba. While pressing Zorin for an answer in the General Assembly, Zorin told Stevenson, *"You will have your answer in due time,"* to which Stevenson shot back, *"I am willing to wait until Hell freezes over, if that's how long it takes!"*

Since the hour was late, Graham did not want to interrupt the conversation or perhaps have an embarrassing moment with Stevenson in front of Sevaried, so she tiptoed past the study to her room. Hearing a loud rap on her door, Graham opened it to see Stevenson, who was angry with Graham for not making her presence known. The Ambassador and the publisher spoke for approximately an hour before Stevenson departed, leaving behind his eyeglasses and his tie. Later that evening, Graham quietly placed them outside his bedroom door.

* * * * * * * * *

"Hello, Dick, this is Lyndon. We are on a secure line. I'm afraid we need to execute the plan we developed as a contingency for Stevenson in London. He is talking openly about being unsupportive of our position in Vietnam. I cannot take any more of this man's damned insubordination. This is an open threat to our national security! I have tens of thousands of troops standing by, ready to go into Vietnam, and I cannot have our Ambassador talking openly against this administration. I need you to take care of this right away."

"Yes, Mr. President, I will make the call."

On the morning of July 14th, 1965 Adlai Stevenson took a walk with his dear friend and confidante, Marietta Tree. As they walked by the U.S. Embassy in the direction of Hyde Park, a cluster of people on the sidewalk blocked their way. Marietta skipped out into the street, and so was momentarily diverted away from Stevenson. This left Stevenson on the sidewalk, requiring him to navigate around the cluster of CIA agents, who appeared to be a group of casually dressed American tourists gathered in front of the U.S. Embassy. This enabled an agent on the group's edge, closest to Stevenson, to aim the heart-shocking device at Stevenson's chest, which the agent carried under his arm in a box decorated to look like a birthday present. The silent device consisted of a microwave transmitter, a resonating chamber for adjusting frequencies with a dial at the back end, a powerful battery, and a Y-shaped antenna, all contained in the birthday present box. Since the human heart generates only 20 millivolts of electricity, it takes only a moderate microwave pulse to disrupt the heart's rhythm. As Stevenson approached, the agent adjusted the dial until striking the frequency that caused Stevenson's heart to fibrillate. His heart flat-lined immediately.

As Marietta rejoined him, her friend Adlai blanched and he whispered his last words, *"Hold your head high, I am about to faint!"*

With that, Adlai Stevenson fell backward, striking his head fully on the stone pavement. U.S. Embassies are legally classified as American soil. Therefore, the U.S. Government would have had jurisdiction over deaths such as Stevenson's. Three days after Stevenson's death, President Johnson sent an additional 50,000 American troops to Vietnam.

* * * * * * * * *

"Andrea, do you remember the heart-shocking machine that I told you about? Well, there have been a number of suspicious deaths by heart attack that are connected to the assassination of President Kennedy. Enough of them to give me reason for concern. There are other similar deaths, and I cannot prove that they were not by natural causes, but I can

say that so many people connected to this case have died by heart attack that it warrants investigation. Can you imagine the implications if that machine was used by the CIA to kill Americans?"

"Henry, this all sounds pretty scary. Don't you think you should contact the FBI and let them handle it?"

"Andrea, you are not getting it! Who do you think was responsible for gathering and evaluating evidence in the Kennedy assassination?"

"Listen, Henry, you need to slow down and get some of your facts straight. First of all, the CIA does not have jurisdiction in the United States. Their work is performed in other countries."

"Don't you think I know that? Are you aware that during the Red Scare in the '50s, the CIA was opening the mail of American citizens who were suspected of being communists? Many government employees, and particularly those in the State Department, were unfairly persecuted to the point where their careers were destroyed."

"No, I did not know that," Andrea replied in a resigned tone. "I guess we will need to look into this further."

"Are you nuts? _We_ are not looking into this further. No way! I really want to crack this case, but I don't have a death wish!" Henry exclaimed.

"Okay, I am just trying to be supportive. Why are you so agitated all the time?"

"I am sorry, Andrea, I really am. It's just that this stuff is starting to get to me."

"Why don't you just drop these cases and walk away?"

"That's exactly what they want me to do. I'm not giving up that easily. Try as I might, I cannot turn away from this. My conscience won't allow it."

Chapter 14
Witness Elimination

"Those who misremember the past, are pleased to repeat it as 'proof'."
Mike Huybensz

The Warren Commission Report was released in February of 1964. The voluminous report contained no references to Castro, the Cuban exiles, or OPERATION FORTY.

Mary Meyer was President Kennedy's favorite lover. Like Marilyn Monroe, Mary had kept a diary of her more than 30 sexual liaisons and dinner conversations in the White House with the President. And, like Marilyn, it may have gotten her killed. She had sufficient time to consider the Warren Commission Report, and she was disturbed by its findings. She knew for certain that some of its conclusions were wrong, and that there were major omissions. For years, Mary had been surrounded by the top movers within the CIA. She knew how things worked in Washington. She was also close to Robert Kennedy.

By this time, RFK had visualized the links between his persecution of Castro, Carlos Marcello, Giancana, Hoffa, and the death of President Kennedy. Bobby was closing in on the CIA, and as usual, was relentless in his investigation. As a former CIA spouse and paramour of the President, Mary Meyer held a unique perspective. She was also a woman who would speak her mind. When Manuel Artime escaped imprisonment by the CIA at the airbase in Opa Locka , Florida, President Kennedy had found out about Nixon's OPERATION FORTY. Mary Meyer was able to provide Bobby with certain details about the CIA that no one else would have the courage to pass on.

In early October of 1964, shortly after the release of the Warren Report, CIA scientist Robert Morrow was hastily summoned to Paul Young's Restaurant in D.C. An attorney for Mario Kohly, named Marshall Diggs, met with Morrow. Diggs supported Kohly in cooperation with former Vice-President Nixon. Marshall indicated to Morrow that Mary Meyer was a threat, that Tracy Barnes at the CIA was worried about her knowledge of the Cuban exiles and their possible role in the assassination of President Kennedy. Kohly was hiding from a New York prosecutor, and was told by Nixon to go underground. Nixon did not want Kohly to be placed on the witness stand. Kohly might be tempted to give up OPERATION FORTY to save his own hide. Diggs did not want to invite a perjury conviction for himself, so he asked Morrow to find Kohly and warn him about Mary Meyer and the conversations between her and Robert Kennedy.

Mary was upset, not only over the loss of her beloved Jack, but also about how the American people were being misled about the assassination of JFK. Surely,

Mary Meyer had in her head, and in her diary, information about the Bay of Pigs operation, assassination plots, and other sensitive information given her by President Kennedy during their private dinners and pillow talk that would have shed light on his assassination. Once while they were smoking marijuana in the President's private quarters, he speculated, *"Our government is assassinating heads of state against my direct orders. I can't stop them. You know, Mary, they will probably get me someday with a high-powered rifle from a tall building...."* President Kennedy seemed to be obsessed with the possibility that he might be assassinated.

Then on October 12th, 1964, Mary Meyer took a break from the painting she was touching up in her art studio in Georgetown. She set the colorful canvas in front of a fan to dry the fresh oil paint while she took her midday jog by the Potomac River. As was her daily routine, she donned tennis shoes, slacks and a sweater, and then ventured out onto the famous Chesapeake & Ohio Canal towpath, owned by the U.S. Department of Interior, and managed by the U.S. Park Service as an historical landmark. She was walking on federal government property, which would have jurisdiction for any crime that might be committed there. Mary would never return home to finish that painting.

She soon passed the brownstone trolley car garage located on the D.C. side of the Francis Scott Key Bridge. Known as The Barn, the CIA used the brownstone building to train Third World police forces in the techniques of torture, interrogation and assassination. Meyer picked up her pace as she crested the hill, heading down toward the river with a view of the Virginia shore to her left. She passed the colonial era home of Francis Scott Key, the American patriot who was forced to sit out the bombardment of Fort McHenry in Baltimore Harbor, as a prisoner aboard an English warship during the War of 1812. The spot Mary Meyer passed displays a memorial that pays tribute to Key, author of America's National Anthem. Its refrain echoed in her mind.

Oh say, does that star spangled banner yet wave,
O'er the land of the free, and the home of the brave?
Francis Scott Key

As she left Georgetown behind her and moved down toward the river, Meyer entered a wooded section of the Chesapeake & Ohio Canal. The C & O Canal had been used to ferry supplies up the Potomac to Harper's Ferry. The canal never made it to Ohio; it terminates at Cumberland, Maryland.

As the strikingly beautiful Vassar graduate strode along the Potomac River, enjoying the autumn day, a man appeared next to a cottonwood tree. He wore a black sweater and black latex gloves. The CIA operative stepped aggressively toward Mary Meyer and grabbed her arm. She saw a pistol in his hand. Mary tried to fend off her attacker. The assassin fired a bullet directly into Meyer's face which lodged in her brain and would have killed her. *"Someone help me!"* she called out. For a moment, Mary Meyer grabbed hold of the small cottonwood tree.

Instinctively, her hands went to her face and were quickly covered with blood. She became disoriented and began to loose her balance. As her colorful world rapidly faded to black, the killer dragged Mary a few steps down the embankment toward the Potomac River. Summoning her last surge of energy, Meyer broke away and ran up the embankment toward the canal. There, she collapsed on the towpath. The killer ran up to her, put the pistol to her shoulder, and fired the second shot that severed Meyer's aorta from her heart. The assassination transpired in approximately ten seconds.

The operative quickly walked through the middle of the creek, leaving no footprints, to where his canoe lay on the bank of the Potomac. With one push the canoe left the rocky bank, floated out into the river and was turned downstream by the strong current. The swift waters of the upper tidal Potomac are generated by the rapids of Great Falls. The CIA man didn't need his paddle for propulsion.

'There's one less risk to national security,' the assassin thought to himself, allowing a smile to cross his face. He looked like one more fisherman on the Potomac, using the catch-and-release method. *'Whatever state secrets that lady had in her head just died with her,'* he mused.

Locating a distinctive rock formation on the shore, and after calculating the distance from the shore to his canoe, the operative stuffed his latex gloves and the pistol in a weighted iron box that was perforated with holes measuring one inch in diameter. He leaned over the Virginia side of his boat, making his actions more difficult to see from the shore, and placed the heavy mesh box in the water. He let go, and the metal cage containing the gloves and pistol plunged quickly to the murky bottom of the Potomac River. To an observer, the assassin would appear to be releasing a fish.

Using his paddle as a rudder, and with a few powerful J-strokes the assassin pulled his canoe onto the public boat ramp at Fletcher's Boathouse. He checked his canoe in, paid his bill in cash, and was back at CIA headquarters across the river before police and reporters appeared at the crime scene.

After the assassin briefed his superiors, Cord Meyer, second in command of the CIA's worldwide covert activities, dispatched the divers that would retrieve, under the cover of darkness, the gun that had killed his former wife, Mary Meyer.

At the time of the murder, Henry Wiggins and William Branch, employees of the Key Bridge Esso gas station in Georgetown, were working on a disabled Rambler on the road just above the crime scene. Wiggins testified that he saw the killer fire the second shot that shattered Mary Meyer's shoulder blade and tore her aorta. His description of the killer conveniently matched one Ray Crump, the delirious young black man found bleeding and soaked with water by the Potomac River in the vicinity where the murder took placed. Crump was acquitted through some sharp lawyering, and a motive was never established for his alleged commission of the crime. Crump claimed to not remember the events of that day, and went on to lead a violent life without purpose or direction. It is possible that Crump was another victim of the CIA's MK-ULTRA brainwashing program.

When the newspaper reporters and photographers arrived on the scene, they found it peculiar that they were not allowed near the victim. An abnormal procedure for such a situation; reporters and photographers were required to remain on the opposite side of the canal. At one point, a photograph showed eleven men gathered around Mary Meyer's body; she was lying in the fetal position on the canal towpath. Only three were uniformed officers. The remaining eight men wore suits and trench coats. It is possible they were waiting to coordinate their stories, give the actual killer time to escape, and make sure Mary Meyer's life had totally ebbed away.

The bullets were placed with incredible accuracy and were fired at point blank range, with the coldness and precision of a trained killer. And so the beautiful mistress of President Kennedy and former wife of a top CIA covert operator lost her life in a few brief seconds. She was killed by an expert assassin. Mary Meyer was murdered just two weeks after the release of the Warren Commission Report, which stated that Lee Harvey Oswald acted alone to kill President Kennedy.

"It was strange, especially the way the police and newspapers rushed to judgment about who did it. It felt wrong."

An acquaintance of Mary Meyer

When the news of Mary Meyer's death reached her close friend, Anne Truitt in Japan, Truitt placed frantic calls to both Tony Bradlee, Mary's younger sister, and James Jesus Angleton, Counterintelligence Chief at the CIA who was also Cord Meyer's boss. Angleton was later run out of the CIA for his role in OPERATION CHAOS, a program that involved spying on American citizens. What followed was an embarrassing and controversial chain of events. Anne Truitt was worried that Mary Meyer's diary might fall into the hands of the press, thus disclosing her affair and drug experimentation with President Kennedy. Ben and Tony Bradlee first went to Meyer's townhouse in Georgetown to look for Mary's diary. An embarrassed James Angleton was discovered already in the house, also seeking the diary. When the Bradlees returned to search Mary's garage, they found Angleton picking the garage padlock. Ultimately, Tony Bradlee found the diary, showed it to her husband, Ben Bradlee, Editor of *The Washington Post*, who claims to have given it to Angleton for destruction by the CIA. The contents of that diary could go a long way to determine why Mary Meyer was assassinated, and it has never been made public.

* * * * * * * * *

During his incarceration in Dallas, Jack Ruby was injected with malignant cancer cells during a routine physical. Ruby died in his cell before he could fully testify as to what he knew about the assassination of President Kennedy. As with the father of Alexander the Great, Ruby had killed the alleged patsy, and had been killed in turn to maintain the vicious silence.

On November 8, 1965, Dorothy Killgalen was found dead in her room, sitting upright in her bed. Her death was ruled a suicide, caused by an overdose of alcohol and Secenol. Best known for her role as an incisive questioner on the popular prime time television program, *"What's My Line?,"* Kilgallen had covered the trial of Jack Ruby in Dallas, and during the trial had somehow gained Ruby's confidence. Killgalen had conducted several brief interviews with Ruby, and had allegedly established connections between Ruby and Officer Tippit, the policeman who was slain that day, and also between Ruby and David Ferrie. Ferrie was the homosexual CIA/Mafia pilot who flew into Cuba during the Bahia de Cochinos assault, and the personal pilot of Mafia don Carlos Marcello, of New Orleans. Ferrie would die soon after the assassination of President Kennedy in his New Orleans apartment of 'natural causes,' while he was providing testimony to District Attorney Jim Garrison for his case against Clay Shaw, who was ultimately acquitted. Years later, a CIA director would testify that Shaw was a CIA operative.

Apparently, Ruby had told Kilgallen he and Ferrie had purchased a plane together, and of how the plane had been used. He explained how he and David Ferrie procured the arms shipments for the Cuban exiles through Centro Mondiale Commerciale S.A., and its European subsidiary, Permindex S.A. in Greece. Centro Mondiale Commerciale and Permindex were operated by Clay Shaw of the CIA in New Orleans. Kilgallen appeared at the television studio at least once with folders containing her notes from sessions with Ruby. Her producer pleaded with her not to touch the subject while on the air, and he sent her roses when she refrained from doing so. Not long after Kilgallen died of an overdose, her neighbor and friend, Mrs. Smith died of a heart attack. Mrs. Smith was supposedly keeping Kilgallen's notes of her interviews with Ruby. The notes of Dorothy Kilgallen's interviews with Jack Ruby have never been released.

On Saturday, October 29, 1966, LtCmdr William B. Pitzer, U.S.N. was found dead with a gunshot wound to his head. Pitzer had gone into his office at Bethesda Naval Hospital in Maryland, where he was Chief of the Educational Television division for the Naval Medical School. When he failed to return calls from his wife, who was calling from their home in Tacoma Park, Maryland, Mrs. Pitzer called the hospital security office. As security officers entered Pitzer's office, his body was discovered, dressed in civilian clothes, lying in a pool of coagulated blood, with a bullet wound in the right side of his head.

The autopsy showed no indication of the blunt force injury on the left side of Pitzer's head, which would have rendered him unconscious. The pistol was held a significant distance away from Pitzer's head when it was fired, based on powder burn evidence, and Pitzer's wife and friends testified that he was left- handed.

The Montgomery County Medical Examiner quickly asserted that Pitzer's death was a suicide, and rumors were spread about an affair Pitzer was allegedly having with another woman. There is no record of Mrs. Pitzer confirming such rumors.

A few weeks before Pitzer's body was found in his office, federal agents visited Colonel Daniel Marvin. Marvin was a Special Forces soldier, trained to conduct covert assassination operations as a Green Beret. The visit took place in late 1966, while Marvin was training at Fort Bragg, North Carolina. The agent informed Marvin he was being assigned to carry out an assassination.

When Marvin inquired as to the identity of the target, the federal agent replied, "*His name is LtCmdr William B. Pitzer. He is a traitor. Pitzer is Chief of Educational Television at Bethesda Naval Hospital. He told a subordinate he has videotaped proof that President Kennedy's official autopsy was rigged, and he's going to sell the film to a Hollywood producer upon his retirement, which is imminent.*"

Marvin refused the assignment, saying he was trained to kill communist officials, not active-duty officers in the ranks of the United States military establishment on domestic soil.

Marvin claims the agents then approached an associate of his at Fort Bragg, and he witnessed that conversation from a distance. Marvin never saw his fellow Green Beret again, though he made concerted efforts to locate him over the years.

During the conflict in Vietnam, Colonel Marvin was assigned by the CIA to assassinate the Crown Prince Nordhom Sihanouk of Cambodia. Marvin refused, and was branded a renegade Green Beret. Rumors were floated that he was almost terminated (along with the rest of his command) by an elite South Vietnamese regiment.

LtCmdr Pitzer's job was to train naval videographers to record medical procedures such as autopsies, as unobtrusively as possible, without disturbing the physicians. Pitzer had surreptitiously filmed the autopsy of John Kennedy from the second floor observation gallery of the autopsy facility at Bethesda Naval Hospital. The still-frame photos that Pitzer developed from the film, and the inevitable arguments between the doctors, senior officers and FBI agents that Pitzer captured on film would have sent shock waves through the American public. Pitzer had intended to sell the film and the still photos to a Hollywood producer.

* * * * * * * * *

On the day President Kennedy was assassinated, Lee Bowers was at his post in the Dallas train yard, located a considerable distance above and behind the pergola of Dealey Plaza. Bowers managed railroad car traffic in the yard from his glass-enclosed lookout tower, high above the train yard. From his vantage point, he had an unobstructed view of the backside of the stockade fence at the top of the grassy knoll, and the parking lot behind the fence.

Another witness recalled, "*...there were tracks and cigarette butts lying where someone had been standing on the bumper looking over the fence behind the station wagon. I expect you could've counted four or five hundred footprints down there. And on the* *bumper, oh about twelve or eighteen inches apart, it looked like someone had raked their shoes off; there were muddy spots up there, like someone had been standing there. They didn't extend further than from one end of the bumper to the other. That's as far as they would go. It looked like a lion (had been) pacing in a cage."*

Bowers had testified to the Warren Commission that he *"…saw a commotion…"* behind the stockade fence, just after the shots were fired in Dealey Plaza. Counsel for the Warren Commission interrupted Bowers before he could add any further evidence to what he saw near the stockade fence. Following his testimony, an FBI agent interviewed Bowers. *"I saw a flash of light and a puff of smoke,"* said Bowers, *"Then I saw two men run from the stockade fence, put something into the trunk of their car, and drive out of the parking lot."*

Shortly after that interview, Bowers disappeared for two days, something he was not known to do. Upon his return, Bowers was missing a portion of a finger.

On August 9, 1966, Roy Virgil Edwards was driving a tractor, repairing fences along Highway 67, just a few miles south of Midlothian, Texas. Bowers had stopped at Madge's Diner, the usual spot for his morning coffee.

"Hey, Madge, this coffee tastes kind of bitter this morning," Bowers complained.

Madge walked over and leaning close to Bowers and whispered, *"Lee, that's because I am trying a new brand from my supplier…it has chicory in it! What do you think?"*

"I think I like the usual brand better. I've been drinking it in here for years, Madge."

"Okay, Lee, I'll have your usual for you the next time you come by. In the meantime, have some more and perhaps you will get used to it."

"Well, I'll just have another cup with breakfast, thank you."

As Bowers left Madge's Diner to walk to his car, he began to feel dizzy. Thinking the sensation would pass, he started the car. It was 9:15 and his shift at the train yard began at 10:00. He could use the bathroom when he arrived at work. Bowers was traveling along Highway 67 at a speed of 55 miles per hour, when he realized that he was suddenly very tired. Bowers fought to keep his eyes open and his head up.

At approximately 9:15, the farmer, Roy Edwards looked up from his fence mending work to see Bower's Pontiac traveling down Highway 67. At one point on Highway 67, a concrete abutment rises up out of the country landscape. A black sedan had been waiting on the side of the highway, and was now accelerating to close the distance between the two cars. At precisely the right moment, the black car veered towards Bowers, forcing him off the road, where he slammed into the concrete abutment in a head-on collision. Bowers' head trauma was severe, but he lived for several hours after the accident. In the ambulance on the way to W.C. Tenefy Community Hospital, Bowers told the ambulance medical technicians that he believed there were drugs in his coffee. Bowers was transferred to Methodist Hospital in Dallas. He was pronounced dead there at 1:30 PM that day. Bowers died a violent death, and had claimed he was poisoned; yet no blood samples were taken, and no autopsy was performed.

In the years that followed, many other key witnesses in the JFK assassination died within days of testifying, either as part of Jim Garrison's investigation of the CIA in New Orleans, or after receiving a subpoena from the House Subcommittee on Assassinations (HSCA). Just a few of the deaths that were proximate to dates for testimony include David Ferrie and his CIA paymaster, Eladio del Valle, William Sullivan, the FBI Deputy Director of Division V, Mafia don Johnny Roselli, mobsters Rolando Masferrer and Rolando Prio Socarras, who assisted in obtaining weapons for the Cuban exiles, George de Mohrenschildt, Lee Oswald's CIA handler, and Regis Kennedy, an FBI agent who knew a lot about Carlos Marcello and Clay Shaw.

Carlos Marcello had cause to celebrate after the death of President Kennedy. Having been persecuted and prosecuted at length by Bobby Kennedy, Marcello was outspoken about his role in the death of the President. Marcello had sworn he would, "...*destroy the tail of the dog [RFK] by killing the dog [JFK]. Then, I will set up a nut to catch the blame, the way they do it in Sicily.*"

Chapter 15
The Assassination of Robert Kennedy

During a televised speech, President Johnson made a surprise announcement that shocked the nation, *"I will not seek, and I will not accept, my party's nomination for President of the United States."* Most Americans had assumed the President would run successfully for a final term of four years, for which he was eligible. He did not run again so he could fulfill his earlier commitment to Richard Nixon.

* * * * * * * *

Robert Kennedy was a fierce competitor. When dirty work had to be done in the Kennedy family, Robert Kennedy would usually be the one selected to do it. He was known to get into fistfights with young neighbors at his home in McLean, Virginia, during touch football games when he was Attorney General of the United States. He would make Ethel join in on these games, even when she was pregnant. Once, Ethel dropped a perfectly thrown pass from Robert Kennedy, as her pregnant form made its way toward the end zone. Robert Kennedy screamed at her for dropping the ball. Observers said his anger was genuine. As U.S. Attorney General, Robert Kennedy's legal pursuit of Jimmy Hoffa and other leaders of organized crime is legendary. A reporter once shouted a question at Robert Kennedy, asking why they were using such vicious personal attacks against Jack's rival in a campaign he was managing. Robert Kennedy retorted, *"Because we can!"*

But there was also a softer, more sensitive side of Robert Kennedy. On April 5th, 1968, presidential candidate Robert Kennedy stood on the hood of a car in Indianapolis to address a predominantly black crowd.

Senator Kennedy began, *"Ladies and gentlemen, I'm only going to talk to you just for a minute or so this evening. Because I have some very sad news for all of you, and I think sad news for all of our fellow citizens, and people who love peace all over the world, and that is that Dr. Martin Luther King, Jr. was shot and was killed tonight in Memphis, Tennessee."*

Many in the crowd instinctively stepped back in horror, covering their mouths, while others fell to the ground. Others cursed and swore revenge.

Kennedy brushed his hair aside, raised his voice and continued, *"Martin Luther King dedicated his life to love and to justice between fellow human beings. He died in the cause of that effort. In this difficult day, in this difficult time for the United States, it's perhaps well to ask what kind of a nation we are and what direction we want to move in. For those of you who are black - considering the evidence - evidently is that there were white people who were responsible - you can be filled with bitterness, and with hatred, and a desire for revenge. We can move in that direction as a country, in greater polarization - black people amongst blacks, and white amongst whites, filled with hatred toward one another. Or we can make an effort, as Martin Luther King did, to understand and to comprehend, and replace that violence, that stain of bloodshed that has spread across our land, with an effort to understand, to show compassion and love. For those of you who are black and are tempted to be filled with hatred and mistrust of the injustice of such an act, against all white people, I would only say that I can also feel in my own heart the same kind of feeling. I had a member of my family killed, but he was killed by a white man. We have to make an effort in the United States, we have to make an effort to understand, to get beyond these rather difficult times. My favorite poet was Aeschylus, who once wrote; "Even in our sleep, pain which cannot forget falls drop by drop upon the heart, until, in our own despair, against our will, comes wisdom through the awful grace of God."*

* * * * * * * * *

On June 4th, 1968, Robert and Ethel Kennedy were monitoring the results of the California Democratic primary election from their suite in the Ambassador Hotel in downtown Los Angeles; the same city in which RFK had overseen the assassination of Marilyn Monroe. The Senator's staff did not want LAPD officers around Kennedy that night, due to their reputation for civil rights abuses. He also did not want to be stigmatized by associating too closely with Mayor Yorty and his police department following their terrible handling of the Watts riots, and other brutal acts by the LAPD that led to racketeering charges being filed against the LAPD. Plus, Mayor Yorty probably never recovered from the disgusting way Bobby had used his police department to murder Marilyn Monroe.

The Kennedys were in the home state of Richard Nixon, preparing a presidential campaign against him, but first they had to win the Democratic primary election. With them that night, working as personal bodyguards for the Senator and his wife were Rosie Grier of pro football fame, the Olympic decathlon champion Rafer Johnson, and George Plimpton, the journalist. The Kennedys were also accompanied by several paid security guards, including Bill Barry, a former FBI agent, and Thane Eugene Cesar, a guard with the Ace Security Company operated clandestinely by the CIA, which had been recommended by the LAPD. Henry Atherton and his photographer were in the audience at the Ambassador Hotel on that fateful night.

Just before midnight, it became apparent that Senator Robert Kennedy had won California's Democratic primary election, giving him significant political momentum going into the Democratic National Convention in Chicago. Just eight years prior, Chicago had delivered the slim margin of victory for John Kennedy in the 1960 presidential election against Nixon, thanks to muscle provided at the election polls by mobster Sam Giancana, and the leadership of the campaign by his younger brother, Robert. Now it would be Bobby's turn to fight Nixon for the White House.

Senator Kennedy and Ethel made their way down to the ballroom where Bobby's adoring campaign workers and supporters were anxiously waiting for their champion to appear. Senator Kennedy stepped to the podium to claim victory for his team.

The adoring audience started to chant, *"We want Robert! We want Robert!"* Robert Kennedy then took a parting shot at Los Angeles Mayor, Sam Yorty. Yorty was a Democrat who had endorsed a Republican from California, Richard Nixon, in the presidential election of 1960, instead of John Kennedy. Having now declared victory in California, Robert Kennedy started to build a bridge toward his nomination as candidate for President of the United States at the upcoming Democratic National Convention; *"Mayor Yorty has just sent me a message that we have been here too long already,"* the triumphant Robert Kennedy smiled. Members of the crowd laughed and resumed shouting, *"We Want Robert. We Want Robert!"*

It was now shortly past midnight, early in the morning on June 5, 1968. Bobby Kennedy thanked the voters of California and his staffers, delivering a brief campaign speech from the platform; *"We can work together despite the division, the violence, the disenchantment with our society, the division between black and white, between the poor and the more affluent, or between age groups or over the war in Vietnam. We are a great country, an unselfish country, a compassionate country. And I intend to make that my basis for running. So my thanks to all of you, and now on to Chicago and let's win there."*

As the chants resumed, there was confusion about which way Senator Kennedy should exit the room. One staffer motioned for Kennedy to move left through the Embassy Room, past a line of adoring Kennedy girls, dressed in red, white and blue. Kennedy's bodyguards started to clear a path for the Senator in that direction. Atherton and the rest of the press contingent began to move toward that doorway as well. Then Karl Uecker, a *maitre d'* wearing a black tuxedo started leading Kennedy off to his right. He was gripping Kennedy's right wrist with his left hand.

The bodyguards and reporters tried to change direction, but found themselves swept up by the crowd that was already headed toward the main door. Uecker took the Senator's hand, parted the gold curtain at the rear of the platform, and led Robert Kennedy directly toward the service pantry.

The pantry is connected to the hotel's kitchen. As the Senator passed, the pantry was packed with over 70 people, consisting of Ambassador Hotel employees and members of Kennedy's entourage. Senator Kennedy felt obliged to shake the hands of hotel employees and campaign workers as he walked. Since the bodyguard friends and reporters had been diverted, they were now pushing through the crowd to catch up with the Senator. Lisa Urso, a high school student, and a waiter named Martin Patrusky saw a dark-haired young man turn and walk toward Senator Kennedy. Vincent DiPierro, another waiter, had noticed the dark haired man speaking with a shapely girl in a white polka dot dress.

Uecker was walking slightly ahead of Robert Kennedy on his right, when he saw a flash and heard two shots, followed by a flurry of overlapping gunshots as a Palestinian named Sirhan Bishara Sirhan stepped forward, faced Robert Kennedy and fired a pistol from a distance of five feet away. Uecker grabbed Sirhan's gun hand, and pinned him to a steam table. But the .22-caliber pistol kept firing across the room, still pointing in the general direction of Senator Kennedy. The crowded pantry was packed like a beehive, and there was not a safe place in the small, tiled room. People were walking directly into the line of fire. The .22- caliber bullets ricocheted until becoming lodged in a bystander, a wall, or the ceiling.

To Atherton, it sounded like a string of exploding firecrackers. Several bystanders were hit by Sirhan's bullets. Rosie Grier had caught up with Ethel Kennedy, and he threw his massive body over her. Witnesses ducked for cover while looking at Sirhan, who continued to fire from the steam table, emptying his pistol of its eight rounds.

Under the cover of this diversion, while Sirhan's pistol fire continued, Thane Eugene Cesar, drew his .22-caliber pistol. Cesar was the CIA operative who had served with Lee Harvey Oswald at the Atsugi Air Base in Japan, where the American U-2 flights over Russia originated. Working that night for ACE Security, Cesar had been walking close behind the Senator on his right. As Sirhan continued to fire, Cesar closed on Robert Kennedy, firing several shots into Robert Kennedy's body at an upward angle.

Cesar used the same type of pistol and hollow point rounds as were used in Sirhan's pistol. After firing the first two bullets into Kennedy's chest near his armpit, Cesar fired a bullet into Robert Kennedy's brain, entering the rear of the skull, just under RFK's right ear. The powder burns and rippling of the cranial skin later proved the gun barrel was less than two inches from Robert Kennedy's head when the fatal shot was fired. Heads were down and eyes were directed at Sirhan while the security guard quickly put three bullets into Senator Kennedy's body. A fourth bullet fired by Cesar had passed harmlessly through Kennedy's jacket at an angle of 80 degrees. The fourth bullet lodged in the ceiling.

To Atherton, it all seemed like a bad dream, transpiring right in front of him in slow motion. But in fact the gunfire was over in just a few seconds. As he replayed the scene in his mind, he recalled hearing as many as thirteen shots fired.

Atherton rushed forward with his photographer just steps behind him. The photographer pushed forward with his large camera to capture on film what was taking place. The *New York Tribune* photographer took the only photos of Senator Kennedy immediately after the shooting. Not thinking about the horror of what he had just witnessed, the photographer acted on instinct, looking down at those who were now crowded around Robert Kennedy. The Senator was sprawled on the floor of the pantry staring blankly at the ceiling, bleeding from the back of his head, as his wife Ethel bent over him. As life began to ebb away from the 42-year-old presidential hopeful, a hotel bus boy named Juan Romero, whose hand Robert Kennedy had been shaking when the shooting began, was holding the Senator's bleeding head.

Knowing that Senator Kennedy was a devout Roman Catholic, Romero pressed rosary beads into the Senator's palm. Robert Kennedy looked up into Ethel's eyes. His last words were, *"Is everyone alright?"*

The powerful Rosie Grier knelt prayerfully next to the steam table sobbing, *"Oh no! Oh no!"*

Images of Dealey Plaza flashed through the minds of Ethel Kennedy and the rest of the Senator's entourage. The time was 12:15 AM on June 5th, 1968.

The shapely woman in a polka dot dress was seen running from the Ambassador Hotel, shouting gleefully, *"We shot him. We shot Kennedy!"*

* * * * * * * * *

Three days later, Atherton's former wife met him at a restaurant a few blocks from his hotel in New York.

"I am glad you're in town, Andrea," Henry began. *"I have some interesting news. I got a call from an aircraft maintenance specialist who was stationed at Atsugi Air Base in Japan while Lee Harvey Oswald served there as an intelligence officer. Atsugi was a base in Japan used by the CIA to launch U-2 spy planes that gathered intelligence in Russian airspace. The maintenance specialist recalled several instances when Lee Harvey Oswald was engrossed in long, hushed conversations with another intelligence officer by the name of Thane Eugene Cesar. I think they were both CIA operatives at the time."*

"Henry, if the airbase in Japan was used for secret intelligence missions, what's so earth-shattering about Lee Harvey Oswald and Eugene Cesar knowing each other?"

"Don't you think it's suspicious that an intelligence officer who worked at a CIA airbase was the man accused of killing President Kennedy? Why else would they have killed him unless he knew too much?"

"You're right, that does seem odd. And I know who Oswald was, but who is this Cesar fellow?"

"Thane Eugene Cesar was working at the Ambassador Hotel as an armed guard for a local security company last night when Robert Kennedy was killed. Cesar was walking just behind Senator Kennedy and to his right at the moment shots rang out in the hotel's kitchen. The autopsy results indicate that the three bullets entering Senator Kennedy's body were fired into the right side of his body at close range. The fatal headshot was fired while the barrel was just inches behind his head!"

"What about all the rounds that were fired by the Palestinian who stands accused of killing Senator Kennedy?"

"The Palestinian was just a decoy; a diversion. The physical evidence proves that none of his bullets hit the Senator. The human cost of that diversion was high. He wounded several bystanders. Did you know that when Senator Kennedy was killed he had been actively involved in the sale American fighter planes to the Israelis?"

"That could help explain why the shooter was a Palestinian. My God! So you think the CIA killed President Kennedy, framed one of their own as a patsy, then did the same with his brother? Robert Kennedy would have been elected president!"

"Yes, that's what I believe. And that's not the worst of it. I believe the orders in both cases were given by Richard Nixon and Lyndon Johnson."

"Henry, when you began investigating these cases, I was concerned about your sanity. Now I agree with you, and I am worried about your safety."

"Just because I don't like the Democrats, that doesn't mean I go around shooting them."

Thane Eugene Cesar

New York Tribune, June 7, 1968
Henry Atherton, Investigative Reporter

Similar to the aftermath of the John Kennedy assassination, there have been many reports of sloppy police work regarding the response to the murder of Robert Kennedy, such as APBs cancelled within minutes of when they were issued, evidence lost, destroyed, or tampered with, and obvious leads abandoned. Despite significant evidence to the contrary, the official story from the LAPD and the District Attorney's office has always been that Sirhan Sirhan acted alone. The following testimonies were given by eyewitnesses who were in the pantry of the Ambassador Hotel the night Robert Kennedy was assassinated;

"It sounded as if there was more than one gun being used at that point."

Booker Griffin to the LAPD, 7/25/68

"After the shots, I saw to my left a guard holding a revolver."

Statement by Richard Lubic in LAPD files

"But the security guard had a gun and I think he went like this [drawing a gun] *or he put it in a holster or something..."*

Lisa Urso to Dr. Phil Melanson

"I'm pretty doggone sure he [a security guard] *fired his gun."*

Don Schulman to the DA's office in 1971,

"Two or three seconds after Kennedy entered the kitchen, he heard 8 or 9 shots in quick succession. He thought there had been two guns."

LAPD interview of Roy Mills, 8/9/68

"We had reports from two of the eyewitnesses that there were two assailants involved."

Larry Scheer, KTLA live broadcast on 6/5/68

"The guy with the gun could have left. No one seemed to pay any attention."

Darnell Johnson to LAPD, 7/24/68

"My God, he had a gun and we let him go by."

Joseph Klein on 7/3/68, referring to a man who left the pantry in a hurry

Although eye witnesses made these statements, this reporter has learned the police have not conducted follow-up interviews with any of these witnesses. There is concrete evidence the CIA has fielded a program codenamed, OPERATION MK-ULTRA. It is an effort to use mind-control to program assassins, brainwashing them regarding every aspect of committing a crime and then covering it up. There is evidence suggesting that both Sirhan Sirhan and Thane Eugene Cesar were involved in the MK-ULTRA program. The Israeli Intelligence Agency, known as the Mossad, acknowledged that the Palestinian known as Sirhan Sirhan has been used by the CIA as part of this special program for assassins.

The gun used by Sirhan Sirhan the night Robert Kennedy was killed carried a maximum of eight .22-caliber rounds. Both Sirhan and Cesar used brass-plated hollow-point bullets. Evidence gathered and destroyed by the LAPD (door jambs were removed and burned) proved that no fewer than thirteen rounds were fired in the pantry. This was determined by bullet holes in the ceiling and between doorposts, indicating that a second gun had been used. Of course, there are inconsistencies in the chain of evidence, the ballistic analysis, the serial numbers of the handguns involved, and the unexplained absence of certain evidence. Sirhan had been the subject of involuntary mind control tests conducted by the CIA at its safe house in San Francisco. During his trial, Sirhan became angry at times and spoke out in court against his attorneys for using the insanity plea. To this day, Sirhan Sirhan remains in a California prison, unable to remember the events of that fateful night in Los Angeles.

* * * * * * * *

For years the CIA attempted to maintain funding for its MK-ULTRA program, even when it came under close scrutiny. In an effort to protect the program from termination, the CIA changed the name to MK-SEARCH. But the program's objective was the same, to control the minds of subjects for use in high-risk operations, such as assassinations. When the MK program came to an end, the program's director, Mr. Gottlieb, wrote an admission that the use of mind alteration was not only difficult, but also fraught with moral and ethical issues. As a result, it was shunned by most CIA operatives.

* * * * * * * *

An autopsy was conducted on Robert Kennedy's body. The autopsy was performed by Thomas Noguchi, the same doctor who had autopsied Marilyn Monroe's body in 1962. Atherton reviewed a published summary of the Robert Kennedy autopsy report;

> *"In his resulting 62-page report, Noguchi stated that the shot that killed Senator Kennedy '...had entered through the mastoid bone, an inch behind the right ear and had traveled upward to sever the branches of the superior cerebral artery.' The largest fragment of that bullet lodged in the brain stem.*
>
> *Another shot had penetrated Kennedy's right armpit and exited through the upper portion of his chest at a 59 degree angle. The coroner*

determined that the Senator's arm must have been upraised (as when shaking someone's hand) when that bullet entered.

Yet another, a third shot entered one-and-a-half inches below the previous one and stopped in the neck near the sixth cervical. This is the bullet that was found intact.

Checking Kennedy's clothing for other telltale signs, Noguchi followed the path between two bullet holes in his suit coat and announced that a fourth bullet had been fired at the Senator. It entered and exited the fabric without touching the Senator.

The autopsy, having clarified what bullet actually killed the public's beloved Robert Kennedy, also created a controversy. Sirhan Sirhan had carried an Iver-Johnson eight-cylinder handgun, the chamber having expended all eight cylinders — in other words, fired all eight bullets. Four of those had been fired at Robert Kennedy — the public accepted that — but there were five others who had been wounded in the pantry. Because there were more victims than accounted for bullets, a second gunman theory was born.

The LAPD responded, reminding the public that some of the bullets passed through their bodies or grazed them. After all, the pantry had been a virtual beehive of bullets. In essence, what the LAPD was telling the public was this: Forget about any 'second gunman' theory. Every one of Sirhan Sirhan's .22 caliber copper-coated hollow-point bullets was accounted for. No less, no more."

Now that the popular Democratic candidate for president had been eliminated, Richard Nixon won the election, succeeding Lyndon Johnson as President of the United States. Thus, Johnson fulfilled his promise to turn the presidency over to Nixon, while Nixon employed the CIA to kill Robert Kennedy, and the LAPD to cover-up the crime. The assassination of Robert Kennedy took place in the same city, involving the same police force, the CIA and the same coroner's office where Robert Kennedy had supervised the murder of Marilyn Monroe just six years before.

When Sirhan Sirhan fired his pistol at Senator Kennedy, it was from a distance of approximately five feet. Most of Sirhan's bullets were fired while Sirhan was pinned to the steam table. The laws of physics say it is impossible to fire bullets into a man's body at an angle of 60 to 80 degrees from such a distance, when the target is standing upright. It is also impossible to fire a bullet into the back of a man's head from a distance of two inches when you are on your back, pressed to a table, several feet away and facing him. The man who pinned Sirhan to the steam cart (but did not prevent him from unloading his pistol in the direction of Senator Kennedy) was the same man who diverted the Senator through the killing zone, Karl Uecker. Uecker thereby shielded Sirhan, keeping anyone else from harming the diversionary shooter until Cesar's mission was accomplished, and Cesar could walk safely out of the room. Just like in Dallas, the assassins in Los Angeles were protected!

Chapter 16
Assassination as an Art Form

Atherton called into the *Tribune* to give Montrose an update, *"Charlie, I've noticed some disturbing patterns in the assassinations of Marilyn Monroe, John Kennedy and Robert Kennedy."*

"Now, Henry, you know very well that Marilyn Monroe's death was a suicide. Your trip to L.A. didn't convince you that she died any other way."

"I'm not so sure about that now, Charlie."

"Okay Henry, tell me what disturbing patterns you've uncovered in these cases."

"Well, the first is destruction of evidence. In the case of Marilyn Monroe, her diary was destroyed, her organ samples disappeared, and the Y incision during her autopsy destroyed the mark of the heart needle that ultimately killed her. Her body was cremated, even though she had bought a gravesite and a casket, and had made previous arrangements for her burial. The cremation covered up a broken rib that was allegedly caused by her psychiatrist's clumsy needle work when he killed her. And her friends all say she was in great spirits, and didn't act depressed at all."

"Henry, where do you come up with all these hair-brained notions?"

"Wait, Charlie, there's more. In the case of President Kennedy's assassination, the FBI immediately washed the telltale blood splatters off the limousine's trunk. The blood splatters were in a V shape, opening up at the back of the trunk. This would have proven the fatal shot came from the front. Forensic evidence was destroyed when the presidential limousine was immediately washed and repaired. Agents recovered bullets in Dealey Plaza that were never entered into evidence. A bullet track in the sidewalk was filled in, since its trajectory didn't point toward the book depository. The casket that allegedly carried President Kennedy's body back to Washington was held in the National Archives until the government drilled holes into it and the Air Force dropped it into 9,000 feet of ocean. To my knowledge, no forensic work was performed to determine if the body that was transported from Dallas to Washington in that casket was the President's. I think John Kennedy's body left Air Force One from Andrews, via helicopter in a plastic military casket, and went to Walter Reed Hospital before entering Bethesda Naval Hospital through the back door. Another body lay in the ornate casket while Jackie Kennedy sobbed alongside it in her blood-soaked dress. The President's body would have been brought into Bethesda Naval Hospital before the motorcade arrived, so no one would have seen inside the ornate casket."

"I don't know what to say, Henry. Please continue." Montrose's mind was conflicted, trying to decide what to do about what Atherton was saying.

"When Senator Kennedy was killed in Los Angeles, the LAPD removed a doorframe from the hotel's kitchen that would have proven the presence of two shooters. The number of bullets fired in those few seconds was more than the number carried by Sirhan's pistol, based on eyewitness testimonies and evidence that has since been destroyed."

"Okay, Henry, now you have my full attention. What other patterns have you been able to discern? And do you have any corroboration of these hypotheses?"

"In the deaths of the Kennedy brothers, the assassins were actively protected! Several of the witnesses I interviewed who had been in Dealey Plaza said the assassins were escorted by shotgun-toting deputies from the train yard to the sheriff's office in the Dal-Tex Building. None of those train yard hobos were booked. When Senator Kennedy was killed in Los Angeles, a maitre d' shielded the patsy while the security guard walking next to Robert Kennedy fired three bullets into the Senator's body at point-blank range."

"I don't know how you are concocting these wild stories, Atherton, but you better come up with some proof, or none of this will ever be printed in this newspaper. You know the rules."

"Yeah, Charlie, I know the rules, but you are not getting it. These people are untouchable. This is some serious shit, Charlie!"

Charlie Montrose hung up the phone and muttered, *"You're right, Henry Atherton, this is some serious shit!"*

Montrose closed his office door, locked it, and pulled a strange-looking telephone out of his desk drawer that he also kept locked.

He plugged the phone cord into a receptacle under his desk, pressed a button and spoke in a hushed tone, *"Montrose here! I just got an interesting call from Henry Atherton."*

"Are you using the scrambler phone?"

"Of course I am. Do you think I'm an idiot?"

"Let's save that conversation for another time."

"So what did Atherton have to say?"

"He claims he has identified certain patterns in the deaths of Marilyn Monroe, John Kennedy, and Robert Kennedy."

"He does, does he? What sort of patterns are we talking about?"

"Destruction of evidence, protection of shooters, falsified autopsies - that sort of thing."

"Pretty interesting stuff! Did you take notes?"

"I always do."

"Okay, I'll need those as soon as you can get them to me. Hey Charlie, thanks for keeping me posted." Then, without another word, the line went dead.

* * * * * * * * *

That night over dinner, Henry Atherton's former wife got an earful and Henry summarized his theories, *"Andrea, it's so clear to me now. All these years I have wondered why Richard Nixon, a conservative Republican would be in cahoots with a Democrat. Kennedy had decided to drop Johnson from his re-election ticket, so Johnson would have never been president. Nixon agreed to stay out of the subsequent presidential race so Johnson could serve a full second term."*

"So you think two men from rival parties who both wanted to be president conspired to kill President Kennedy?"

"It's the very same thing that happened when the Jews and the Romans conspired to kill Jesus."

"What does Jesus have to do with this? Henry, you haven't gone religious on me now, have you?"

"Never mind!"

"With Johnson's clandestine support, Nixon would have easily won the election, except that Robert Kennedy and Adlai Stevenson were two of the most popular political figures in America. Stevenson died of an untimely heart attack in front of the U.S. Embassy in London, a major CIA station, and Senator Kennedy was killed by the guard who was walking next to the Senator as they passed through the hotel kitchen. So the CIA agreed to conduct both murders, Johnson agreed to ignore President Kennedy's executive order to disband the CIA, and Nixon had the most spectacular comeback in American political history. That Nixon is bad news. I wonder what his legacy will be?"

* * * * * * * *

Following the assassination of Robert Kennedy, a disgruntled member of the LAPD Intelligence Division contacted Henry Atherton.

"How did you find me?" Atherton began.

"I am in the intelligence division, remember?" the officer answered.

"I know this is risky for you, so I will listen while you talk."

"Okay, I have read your articles over the years. I know you have investigated the deaths of Marilyn Monroe, President Kennedy, and now Robert Kennedy. When a serial killer is on the loose, detectives look for patterns of behavior, or a modus operandi. *Have you been able to identify such patterns in these deaths?"*

"As a matter of fact, I have detected some patterns, but no one seems to believe my theories, and sometimes I doubt them myself."

"What are those theories?"

"Well, first, my study of U.S. history revealed that our government engaged extensively in assassinations of foreign heads of state during the '50s and '60s. I believe that legacy is what ultimately led to the deaths of Marilyn Monroe and the Kennedy brothers."

"Mr. Atherton, you know that a murder requires the three elements of motive, means and opportunity. What theories have you developed along these lines?"

"Call me Henry. And what should I call you?"

"You can call me Sam." Atherton was certain he had just been given a fictitious name.

"Okay Sam, I believe the President and the Attorney General had Marilyn Monroe killed because she was about to expose them in such a way that their marriages and their political careers would have been destroyed. I believe that Vice-President Johnson and former Vice-President Nixon conspired to kill President Kennedy because his death was required for either of them to become president. As vice-president under President

Eisenhower, Richard Nixon was in charge of CIA operations that resulted in the assassination of several foreign leaders. I believe Nixon utilized his relationship with the CIA and their lethal capability to attain the White House. But I don't know why I am telling you this. You're supposed to have information for me."

"You are telling me these theories of yours because you're looking for validation."

"Yeah, I guess you're right. This job can be pretty lonely, you know."

"Try the intelligence field."

"Amen to that."

"I must say, Henry, that your theories are very intriguing, if not right on the money."

"How can you say that?"

"I had been working in the LAPD intelligence unit for two years when Marilyn Monroe was killed."

"You just said she was killed."

"Yes, I did. I was not a happy camper when that happened, because I saw it from the inside. Now, with Senator Kennedy dead, I just can't continue to pretend I don't know what I know. This interview with you is going to end my career, so the article you write better be good."

"I will do my best."

"All killers leave behind fingerprints. Not necessarily the kind of prints that we typically think about. Sometimes, they are symbolic prints, such as the way a killer leaves his victims, or the way he gains entry to the victim's home. Do you see what I mean? In these murder cases here, the distinctive prints are very unusual. Let me take you through them one by one. The first fingerprint is environmental control. On the night Marilyn was killed, the LAPD intelligence and homicide divisions worked closely with the Attorney General and the federal agents to ensure that the death would look like a suicide, and that no physical evidence would be left behind that might suggest foul play. We wiped the place clean of fingerprints before the night desk officer arrived to investigate."

"You're saying that Robert Kennedy, the Attorney General of the United States, was in Marilyn Monroe's house the night she was killed?"

"Yeah, he came in on a helicopter from Northern California. He supervised the entire operation. It all came together pretty fast. They had Mafia thugs do the actual killing. They pumped liquid narcotics up her rectum, real potent stuff. Our job was to conduct the cover-up operation. Anyway, Kennedy ordered the housekeeper and her son out of the house while the deed was done, and then we went around the house cleaning up. Somebody got the brainstorm that Marilyn's doctor would have to break in to try and save her. But it got screwed up because they broke the window from the wrong side.

The word on the street is that when President Kennedy was killed, the conspirators had the place locked down. The Secret Service had published the motorcade route, they slowed the car, they did not protect the President when the shooting began, the top was off the limousine, and they even had him sitting in an elevated seat. The Vice-President, however, was heavily protected! The FBI and the Dallas Police Department had agents and officers stationed throughout Dealey Plaza, where they tampered with evidence and intervened with witnesses who might have interfered with their operation.

When the accused gunman, Lee Harvey Oswald, was assassinated, he was in the basement of the Dallas Police Department, a controlled environment. Now tell me that a known bad guy carrying a pistol getting into the basement of the Dallas Police Department at precisely the right moment to kill his partner is a fluke!

Now we have the recent assassination of Robert Kennedy. Did you notice during your investigation there were virtually no police officers in the hotel at the time of the shooting? A hotel employee escorted Senator Kennedy through the kitchen, and the guard who actually shot Senator Kennedy was walking just behind him. There was tremendous confusion in that kitchen pantry with about 70 people crowded into it, so while the Palestinian emptied his revolver, the guard was able to step toward the Senator and put several bullets into him before anyone could react. I know for a fact that several of the officers who were supervised by Robert Kennedy on the night that Marilyn Monroe was killed were involved in the planning and cover-up of his assassination."

"Live by the sword, die by the sword," Atherton reflected.

"I couldn't have said it any better. So you see that in each of these cases, the conspirators had full and complete control over the environment when the crime occurred.

The second common element is the use of diversionary tactics. The word is that in the case of the President, a man faked an epileptic fit just before the motorcade entered Dealey Plaza. This enabled the shooters to take up their positions without being seen. Since multiple shooters fired simultaneously at the President, it was virtually impossible for any witness to determine the direction of fire, what with the echoes from buildings that must have been heard as citizens threw themselves to the ground. Before Senator Robert Kennedy was diverted through the hotel kitchen in Los Angeles, his bodyguards were sent off into the crowd, diverted, and then left behind.

The third common element is the protection of assassins. Even though Marilyn's killers were wanted criminals, the LAPD provided them with whatever they needed, and the police guarded the neighborhood in case someone might interfere while the murder was being committed. Officers carrying shotguns escorted President Kennedy's killers to police headquarters. These hobos were protected by the Dallas Police Department and released immediately without any record of their arrests. And when Sirhan Sirhan was shooting in the direction of Robert Kennedy, a conspirator protected Sirhan by grabbing him, shielding him while appearing to be stopping the assassination. Sirhan had to be protected until he unloaded his pistol, giving the real assassin time to do his job. In each case, protection for the killers was a key part of the plan.

The last common element, and perhaps the most important, is the destruction of evidence. In and of itself, the destruction of documentary evidence is the most important aspect of the killer's fingerprint. Who has the power to steal diaries and organ tissue samples out of the coroner's safe? Who can ensure that a grand jury never completes its task in pursuing the truth in the death of Marilyn Monroe? Who has the capacity to perform pre-autopsy surgery on John Kennedy at a military hospital? Who can murder innocent witnesses to the John Kennedy assassination and get away with it?

This is why Jack Ruby was petrified to testify while he was in Dallas. The police in Dallas had led Oswald to Ruby for him to kill, in the basement of their own building. The witness elimination team needed to silence Oswald before he could tell the world about the CIA assassination team in New Orleans that had just killed the President of the United States. How can the LAPD remove a doorway containing bullets, evidence in a murder investigation, from the Ambassador Hotel and get away with it? How was it that in spite of all the testimony and evidence that another shooter was involved, that a barely coherent Palestinian was found guilty of murdering Senator Kennedy and all other leads were abandoned? In each case, there was a rush to judgment.

Finally, in each case there was an impending crisis that provided motive for murder. Marilyn Monroe was going to hold a press conference within 72 hours of her death that would have destroyed John Kennedy and Robert Kennedy. President Kennedy was about to dismantle the CIA and remove American forces from Vietnam. Robert Kennedy was making a successful run at the presidency. The Kennedy/Stevenson ticket would have been difficult for Richard Nixon to beat, and Nixon was not going to let another Kennedy get in his way.

As a concluding note about protection, notice that in both of the Kennedy assassination cases, the degree of personal protection for the victims was reduced on the day of the assassination. Some might say this is a coincidence, and that it was the coincidental lessening of personal protection that allowed the lone gunmen to succeed. The location and timing of the killings negates those arguments, in my opinion. Democracy succeeds only if assassinations of elected officials and candidates can be prevented. Now, Mr. Atherton, I have been talking for some time now. How does this match up with your theories about these murders?"

The reporter had been listening in a state of awe. His new friend, the LAPD Intelligence Officer, was finally providing the validation he had been seeking all these years.

After a long pause, Henry Atherton replied, "You have no idea how much I appreciate your willingness to share this information with me."

Chapter 17
The Reign of Demo-Fascism in America

*"A popular government without popular information or the means of
acquiring it is but a prologue to a farce or a tragedy, or perhaps both.
Knowledge will forever govern ignorance, and a people who mean to be their
own governors, must arm themselves with the power knowledge gives."*
James Madison
Fourth President of the United States

New York Tribune, March 15, 1969
Opinion/Editorial - Henry Atherton, Staff Writer

When Lyndon Johnson was sworn in as President of the United
States, a small, clandestine group of men came into power. I have given
this group a name, OCAAU – it means Out of Control Americans Against
UnAmericans.

The foundation of this new form of government, which concentrated
power into the hands of a few people, was a deal made between Johnson
and Nixon. Nixon agreed to sit out the next Presidential election, enabling
Johnson to be re-elected. The Pentagon would get their war in Vietnam, the
CIA would remain intact, and Nixon would be elected to the presidency,
enjoying the greatest political comeback in American history. Johnson
would, together with Nixon, waste 58,000 American lives while he spread
tactical maps of Vietnam, Laos and Cambodia on the floor of the Oval
Office, selecting targets for his generals to bomb. J. Edgar Hoover would
remain as FBI director for many years beyond his mandatory retirement
age, where, together with his homosexual lover, Assistant Director, Clyde
Tolson, he continued his collaboration with organized crime figures while
publicly denying their existence, and oversaw the continued cover-up of the
assassinations of President Kennedy and Senator Kennedy. If John and
Robert Kennedy had not been killed, Johnson would never have been
president, Nixon would never have been president, Hoover would have been
retired at 70, General Lemnitzer would have been relieved of his command,
and the CIA would have been dismantled.

As a result, our country has found itself under a new form of
government. This new ruling mechanism concentrates power into the
hands of a few powerful men. It promotes ruthless aggression against any
perceived threat of communism, it uses assassination to censor popular
politicians, and it has slowed the progress made in the arena of civil rights.
This form of government reminds us of the practices of fascists like Adolph
Hitler, Joseph Stalin, and Benito Mussolini. Webster's dictionary defines
fascism as; *"A system of government marked by centralization of authority*

under a dictator, stringent socio-economic controls, suppression of the opposition through terror and censorship, and typically a policy of belligerent nationalism and racism."

The Democratic Senator Huey Pierce Long of Louisiana, a liberal who fought to improve the lifestyles of blacks and poor whites as Governor of Louisiana, was once asked if he thought America would ever become fascist. He responded by saying, *"Of course it will, but we'll call it anti-fascism."* Long appeared to pose a threat to the reelection of President Roosevelt in 1936, until September 10, 1935 when he was assassinated in a corridor of the new capitol building of Louisiana he had built in Baton Rouge.

Johnson and Nixon crafted a convenient hybrid of fascism and democracy, which I call demo-fascism. They used this hybrid form of government to pursue their ideologies contrary to the interests and the will of the people. The *OCAAUs* are able to project the illusion that America is a democracy by borrowing many of our democratic principles when it suits their purpose. A prime example is the immediate succession of the vice-president to the presidency upon the death of the president. But they did not have the support of the American people and the Congress to wage war in Vietnam. They did it anyway, in the absence of congressional approval, and without a declaration of war. My hope is that Americans will use the power of democracy to restore our government to its proper state of representing the interests of the people.

Atherton called several of his Capitol Hill contacts. One put him in touch with Jerry Paxson, a historian of sorts in the State Department, who was familiar with American policy regarding Vietnam. Paxson met with Atherton at a Georgetown bar to provide the historical background Henry had requested.

"I have heard differing stories about President Kennedy's role regarding American involvement in Vietnam. Can you help me on this?" Atherton asked.

"Sure, in 1961, President Kennedy sent a team to Vietnam to report on conditions in the South and to assess future American aid requirements. The report, now known as the 'December 1961 White Paper,' argued for an increase in military, technical, and economic aid, and the introduction of large-scale American 'advisers' to help stabilize the Diem regime and to crush the NLF (National Liberation Front) in North Vietnam. As Kennedy weighed the merits of these recommendations, some of his other advisers urged the President to withdraw from Vietnam altogether, claiming that it was a 'dead-end alley.'

In typical Kennedy fashion, the President chose a middle route. Instead of a large-scale military buildup as the White Paper had called for, or a negotiated settlement that some of his advisers had long advocated, Kennedy sought a limited accord with Diem. The United States would increase the level of its military involvement in South Vietnam through more machinery and advisers, but would not intervene whole-scale with troops. This arrangement was doomed from the start, and soon reports from Vietnam arrived in Washington attesting to further NLF victories. To counteract the NLF's success in the countryside, Washington and Saigon launched an ambitious and deadly military effort in the rural areas. Called the Strategic Hamlet Program, the new counterinsurgency plan rounded up villagers and placed them in 'safe hamlets,' constructed by the GVN (Government of Vietnam) in South Vietnam. The idea was to isolate the NLF from villagers, its base of support. This culturally insensitive plan produced limited results and further alienated the peasants from the Saigon regime. Through much of Diem's reign, rural Vietnamese had viewed the GVN as a distant annoyance, but the Strategic Hamlet Program brought the GVN to the countryside. The Saigon regime's reactive policies ironically produced more cadres for the NLF.

By the summer of 1963, because of NLF successes and its own failures, it was clear that the GVN was on the verge of political collapse. Diem's brother, Ngo Dinh Nhu, had raided the Buddhist pagodas of South Vietnam, claiming they had harbored the Communists that were creating the political instability. The result was massive protests on the streets of Saigon that led Buddhist monks to self-immolation. The pictures of the monks engulfed in flames made world headlines and caused considerable consternation in Washington. By late September, the Buddhist protest had created such dislocation in the South that the Kennedy administration supported a coup. In 1963, some of Diem's own generals in the Army of the Republic of Vietnam (ARVN) approached the American Embassy in Saigon with plans to overthrow Diem. With Washington's tacit approval, on November 1, 1963, Diem and his brother were captured and later killed. Three weeks later, President Kennedy was assassinated on the streets of Dallas."

"Did Kennedy order the assassination of the Diem brothers?"

"That remains unclear, but those around the President when the news came, said he went into a rage. The assassinations made him physically ill."

* * * * * * * *

President Johnson and his military advisors conferred during the 556th meeting of the President's National Security Council, which was held in the Cabinet Room of the White House on January 29th, 1966.

"What do you want most to win?" asked President Johnson.

"We need a surge of additional troops into Vietnam," answered Army Chief of Staff, General Harold K. Johnson, and then continued; *"We need to double the number now, and then triple the number later. We should call up the reserves and go to mobilization to get the needed U.S. manpower. This involves declaring a national emergency here and in Vietnam. The bombing should be resumed at once to hold down infiltration. By resuming the bombing, we divert North Vietnamese manpower to repair their LOCs, put pressure on their infiltration and their government, and destroy their equipment, especially trucks."*

Air Force Chief of Staff, General John Paul McConnell chimed in, *"There is nothing unusual in the air effort recommended. It involves 330 sorties weekly, B-52 sorties at the rate of 300 a month, and 1200 weekly sorties into Laos. When we resume the bombing, our losses will rise because North Vietnam now has a greater antiaircraft capability. "*

"Our plane loss is now running 5 per 1,000 sorties," Defense Secretary Robert McNamara interjected.

General McConnell replied, *"We can get better results from bombing North Vietnam than bombing either in Laos or in South Vietnam. Air strikes should be resumed by a sharp blow as soon as possible. POL storage areas should be struck at once. Excuse me, POL stands for petroleum, oil and lubricants. Armed reconnaissance is not enough."*

The CIA Director broke in, *"Our bombing cuts by 50 percent the amount of supplies being trucked from the north."*

"We need evidence for Senator McCarthy," President Johnson replied.

"We have destroyed 400 trucks and damaged 250 since the bombing began in February. The bombing will not hurt the infiltration of men, but it will reduce the number," Defense Secretary McNamara suggested.

Then General McConnell cut to the chase, "Our bombing is ineffective because of the restrictions placed upon the Air Force. We should lift these restrictions and we would then get results."

The President stood up, walked over to where General McConnell was sitting, and placed his face within inches of McConnell's, "Now, General, those are mostly your boys sitting out there as human shields. You might be able to write letters to their wives and families, saying they died heroically, but I have a conscience, and I want to be able to sleep at night. I will not hear of such a thing! That concludes our meeting. Thank you, gentlemen!"

"Thank you, Mr. President!"

* * * * * * * * *

General John Gavin had been known as 'Jumping Jack Gavin,' ever since the young general had parachuted into Sicily and Normandy with his airborne troops during World War II. He was highly regarded throughout the Army, and on Capitol Hill. President Johnson had General Gavin on his short list for selection as his next Chairman of the Joint Chiefs of Staff.

After serving two terms as President Kennedy's Ambassador to France, General Gavin returned to the United States to finish his stellar military career. In 1967 General Gavin took an exploratory trip to Vietnam. He wanted to assess the prospects the United States had for winning the war. President Johnson was eager to hear what this fighting general had to say about Vietnam.

General Gavin entered the Oval Office. The President rose, and shook hands with the American war hero, "Take a seat on the couch, General, I have been anxious to hear about your trip."

"Thank you, Mr. President. It's always a pleasure to brief you, as I know you are deeply interested in what's going on with the war."

"Well, some say I am too involved...but I'll be damned if I am going to sit around here while our boys are dying in rice paddies half way 'round the world."

"I am sure they appreciate your dedication to them, Sir. Mr. President, if you don't mind, I would like to give you my frank assessment of the situation, and my recommendation."

"General Gavin, that's why you are here!"

"Very well, Sir. Mr. President, I have spent a considerable amount of time meeting with our commanders in Vietnam, and I have visited with our troops. I have come to the conclusion they are fighting a war that cannot be won."

"What basis do you have for making such an audacious statement, General?"

"Mr. President, you know that I am not afraid to fight. I have fought alongside my troops when I could have remained in the rear. But I refuse to send men into battle when there is little hope of victory, and when men are likely to die in vain. That Sir, is what is taking place every day in Vietnam. President de Gualle warned President Kennedy that Vietnam would be a quagmire, from which it would be most difficult to extricate ourselves. I'm afraid that prediction has come to pass. My recommendation, Mr. President, is that the United States withdraw from Vietnam, or end the hostilities by any means necessary."

"General Gavin, you know I have stated publicly to the American people that the United States will stand by our allies in South Vietnam, to help them throw off the mantle of communism that is draped over them!"

"Yes Sir, I know."

"And you know that withdrawing our forces would not only make us the laughing stock of the world, it would cause a chain reaction of nations that might fall to communism in Asia!"

"Well sir, I am not as much of a supporter of the Domino Theory as some. But I have firmly decided that this war is not winnable, Mr. President, and I am prepared to take that message to the American people."

"Are you aware, General Gavin, that you are on my list of candidates for the next Chairman of the Joint Chiefs?"

"I am honored that you hold me in such high esteem."

"As Commander-in-Chief, I cannot have one of my top generals going around giving speeches against the war in Vietnam!"

"I am sorry, Mr. President, my mind is made up on this subject. I cannot condone a war where there is no clear objective or means to win."

"General Gavin, as your Commander-In-Chief I am hereby ordering you not to discuss this subject with anyone…anyone, do you understand me? Not your wife, your driver, or your tailor. Furthermore, if you disobey this order, I will run you out of the military and cut off your pension."

"Mr. President, I love the Army, and I respect my Commander-in-Chief. But I refuse to support, for one more minute, your policy, which is tantamount to murdering our brave soldiers. You will have my resignation on your desk by the end of the day, and I will take that message to the people. And I have that right, as afforded to me by the First Amendment to the Constitution. Good day to you, Sir."

"General, you will regret turning your back on me. I will not have this. General!"

A poised but determined General Gavin walked briskly out of the Oval Office as an exasperated Lyndon Johnson collapsed on the sofa in disbelief. The frustrated Texan kicked off his shoes and stared blankly at the plush carpet that bears the symbol of the President of the United States.

* * * * * * * *

Atherton decided he would make it his practice to interview as many soldiers, sailors, airmen and marines as he could when they returned from Vietnam. An Air Force pilot invited Atherton to visit his apartment in Arlington, Virginia, to interview several Vietnam veterans who had recently come home. As Atherton drove up the hill looking for the correct apartment building, he looked out over the Potomac River to the opposite bank. He saw the majestic steeple of Georgetown University's chapel rising above the river, with the C&O towpath running along the riverbank. Further downstream he saw the brightly lit monuments in Washington, D.C.

"Welcome, Mr. Atherton" the host said as he welcomed Henry at the door. *"Please call me Henry,"* Atherton replied.

"Very well then, I would like you to meet my friends. My wife and children are not here, so we can speak freely. The first thing you should know is we would prefer it if you did not know our names."

"It would not be my preference," Atherton answered, *"... since it makes it difficult for me to validate and corroborate my facts, but my experience tells me you will not share your stories with me unless I agree."*

"That is correct," the host replied.

"Okay, then let's proceed. But first, I want to thank you all for serving our country, for the sacrifices you have made, and for being willing to share some of your experiences with me. Who would like to go first?"

The first to tell his story was the pilot of a third-generation gunship, based on the C- class transport aircraft used by U.S. services to ferry materiel and personnel to and from Asia throughout the conflict.

The gunship pilot began, *"First of all, I never believed all that stuff about the Tonkin Gulf Incident. That event was what Johnson used to send us all over there, and I can tell you for a fact, it was provoked.*

I flew missions in South Vietnam and in Cambodia. This was at a time when the public didn't even know we were fighting in Cambodia. We fought there for three years before President Nixon would admit it to the public. My gunship was a modified version of the four-engine Dakota, it was an AC- 47, but we liked to call it 'Puff the Magic Dragon.' I would fly it in a circle, and with its side-mounted mini cannons, it could put down a line of concentrated fire that you would not believe! One of the technologies we used helped to protect our lives, as well as increase our targeting accuracy. By operating at night, it was more difficult for the enemy to attack us when we closed in on a target. We installed an advanced technology device that had been designed by the CIA in the early 1960's. It enabled us to see a truck on the Ho Chi Minh trail in the middle of the night. It was called a Starlight Scope.

Unfortunately, many of the targets that my expensive plane was sent out to destroy, such as a truck here, or a deserted camp there, made me wonder. I have carried a theory about the war. It was a war that, because of the way it was being managed, made us wonder what the real reasons were for our being there. I think it may have had something to do with the oil deposits that were in Asia."

"Believe me, there are many here in America who have been searching for answers to that same question." Atherton turned to address the second veteran, *"And what were your experiences?"*

"I was stationed at a U.S. air base in Thailand. I participated in the bombing of Hanoi in North Vietnam. But what I have always wondered about is, there were only two flight paths to Hanoi from our base that we were allowed to fly. One approach was from the East and one from the West. We always flew these missions, 'milk runs' as we called them, at the same time of day, every day, for weeks on end! The Viet Cong could set their watches by our flights, and we lost planes and men because of this predictability. The result was lots of dead pilots and airmen, and the ones who survived were tortured and are sitting in the most hellatious prison on Earth that we call the Hanoi Hilton. Some of the men sitting in the Hanoi Hilton at this moment are wishing they had been killed. I could never figure out why our commanders would put us at risk like that. At the opposite end of our airfield, there were civilian pilots who were flying large quantities of drugs back to the States. Some of the planes carrying drugs also carried body bags. Even though I carry a Top Secret clearance, I was not allowed at that end of the airstrip. I am certain they were members of the CIA's air force, known as Air America.

Here's another thing that bothered me. I was briefed and trained on a new, top-secret air-to-ground missile system, and these missiles were installed on my aircraft. Our planes would often drop hundreds of bombs on a bridge, for example, and most of the bombs would slip through the girders, falling through the bridge to explode in the river below. This seemed very wasteful to me, and dangerous to our planes and crews when I could have hit that same target from 35,000 feet up with my missile and taken that bridge out! Someone is making a lot of money right now manufacturing bombs.

On one sortie in North Vietnam I had a truck appear on my scope. I had one of the new missiles onboard, so I radioed in to see if I should shoot. The control tower wanted to test the guidance system and the contrast of the tracking screen, so I received an affirmative reply. I launched the missile from an altitude of over 30,000 feet, and I watched the screen as the missile homed in on the truck. I was thinking, the driver of that old truck is dead, and he doesn't even know it. After the truck exploded, my first thought was that my million-dollar missile had just destroyed a $200 truck!

One of my superior officers mentioned to me that the Russian pilots had nowhere to train. We were flying sorties every day, firing weapons and taking out targets, although many of them seemed insignificant to us. I came to the conclusion that one of our primary reasons for being in Vietnam was not to fight communism, but to receive live weapons training!

My most memorable Vietnam experience took place after we came home. When Captain Ernest Medina ordered Lt. Calley to rid a hamlet called My Lai of VC soldiers, his soldiers went in after the VC had vanished into the jungle. Pumped up and ready for battle, Lt. Calley ordered a slaughter of the women, children and old men who remained in the village. When the truth finally came out, and pictures of the carnage were entered into evidence at the eventual court martial, but only Lt. Calley was found guilty of murder. Three days after Calley went to prison, President Nixon ordered that Calley be taken to a comfortable apartment at Fort Benning, Georgia, where he is allowed to have pets, entertain guests, and cook his own meals. Calley is going to be eligible for release from military prison in three years.

As Americans became aware of the atrocities that occurred in several Vietnamese villages, I learned of an act of heroism at My Lai which most Americans do not know about."

"I am aware of the My Lai massacre," Atherton commented. "But do you know something the public does not know?"

"Yes, I do. Hugh Thompson was an American helicopter pilot who witnessed the My Lai massacre from aloft. He was sickened by the slaughter. Thompson saw a child moving among the dead, so he quickly landed his helicopter to rescue her. Thompson ordered Larry Colburn, his machine gunner to open fire on any American soldiers who continued to shoot villagers. Hugh Thompson pulled the traumatized three-year-old girl out of the ditch. Thompson was also able to rescue nine unarmed civilians who were about to be executed. Soon after Thompson described to his section leader the carnage he had just witnessed, Calley received an order to stop killing the South Vietnamese citizens.

When I returned from 'Nam and heard of this story, I got in touch with Hugh Thompson who was living in Louisiana. My friends and I contacted the Defense Department to get Thompson recognized for his heroism at My Lai. We are having one heck of a time getting decorations for these men for their acts of valor. I believe it's because the Defense Department doesn't want to admit that these atrocities occurred. President Nixon has caused this insanity by demanding body counts. He doesn't care if they are combatants or civilians. What I don't understand is, if we are there to save the South Vietnamese, then why have three million of them died and over fifty thousand Americans?"

"Again, these are questions we all have," Atherton replied as he turned to a third serviceman. "What is it about the war that you would like Americans to know?"

"I'm a sergeant in the United States Army," the GI said. "During my tour of duty in Vietnam, I was assigned to collaborate with a particular officer of the South Vietnamese Army. As I worked with him, I began to witness signs that he might have been turned by the Viet Cong, and was spying for the communists in Hanoi. When enough intelligence had been gathered, I was ordered to assassinate this officer of our military ally. So, following my orders, I put a bullet into his brain at the first opportunity. It's something I will never forget."

"So you are saying that we have even assassinated some of the officers in the South Vietnamese army?"

"Yes, I am saying that, and I believe it's justified because they are spies, and have tremendous ability to inflict harm since they know our capabilities and our plans."

"Yes, they are dangerous, but couldn't they have been tried, convicted, and imprisoned?" Atherton suggested.

"Well, you have a point there. But I was just following orders. Anyway, we are in a war, and war brings out the worst in people and governments."

The fourth guest to speak was a U.S. Army intelligence officer who served in the southernmost part of South Vietnam, in the fertile and strategic Mekong Delta.

"I returned from 'Nam with two photographs, one of which was for my son," the Army intelligence officer began. "In fact, it was not a photograph that I took, but one I removed from the body of a young North Vietnamese soldier. This young VC was probably 14 years old and had walked all the way from Hanoi wearing sandals to the southernmost region of Vietnam, where he crouched in jungles and rice paddies, waging war against the rebels in the South. He must've felt much like young Union soldiers in the American Civil War, who were dedicated to the cause of maintaining the union. Draped around the neck of this young Viet Cong, on a stained piece of yarn, was a picture of Ho Chi Minh wrapped in cellophane paper. This young man was on a mission. He was fighting for a cause. I was not, and I wanted to show this picture to my son in an attempt to explain the difference to him, and perhaps to myself as well.

I have often reflected upon the absurdity of it all. The French had brought all the best of their culture to Vietnam, their music, their food, their quality of education. We Americans brought the shallowest elements of our convenient lifestyle. I think about the things that I cherished, that helped me to survive the depravity of my Vietnam experience. Things like taking a jeep into Saigon to get a hot dog and a chocolate milkshake. There must have been some deep, ideological goal for the North Vietnamese, because when they finally won, all they got where things we imported of negligent value, like bicycles, jeeps, milkshake makers and hot dog machines!"

The last veteran stood up to give his testimony, as if he had been called upon by a superior officer to relay an after action report, "I was a crew chief in Vietnam, assigned to maintain Huey helicopters, which are made by Bell Helicopter in Texas. Vietnam is a helicopter war, because that's the only way you can get anywhere. We have a real problem with cannibalization of parts for our helicopters, and more importantly, there are numerous cases of outright sabotage. Soldiers in the battlefield are protesting the war by removing or disabling important parts of our choppers. This has already caused the destruction of helicopters, and the deaths of several crews. By the time I left, crew chiefs were required to fly every mission with the crew. That was the only way our commanders could be sure the choppers were safe to fly. I have to say the policy has worked pretty well!

American civilians are dying in Vietnam as well. One contractor sent about a dozen engineers to test a new technology to suppress ground mortars. The VC terrorized our guys by lobbing mortar rounds into our bases from the jungle. These engineers would set up down range from us, and we would fire inert mortar rounds in their direction. They would track the trajectory of the mortar fire, and develop a firing solution for our bombers by determining their coordinates. These guys lived in Quonset huts adjacent to our landing strip. Well, one day we had a C-130 coming in and the landing went badly. The pilot lost control and the aircraft slid off the runway, taking two of the Quonset huts with it. There were four civilians sleeping in each hut. The C-130 erupted in flames and the crew on that aircraft died as well.

But most of my time over there was spent fighting in Cambodia when we were not supposed to be there. In my opinion, both Johnson and Nixon are pricks for keeping us there so long and for letting so many of my buddies die."

"Do you have an opinion of why the United States is in Vietnam," Atherton asked.

"I'll tell you why we are there," the GI replied, *"The United States wants to be the Matt Dillon of the world."*

"You are referring to the sheriff of the American Wild West?"

"Yep, we just want to run into any country we want and take over. We went in with good intentions, but those intentions didn't last for long. We don't care to learn much about the culture of the people, and what is important to them. We just want to impose our values on them, because we think we are so much smarter than the rest of the world."

Atherton thanked the servicemen for their candor, and gave them assurances their identities would never be revealed. He had agreed to meet two other recently returned Vietnam veterans separately at a Pho restaurant in Falls Church, Virginia. Since these soldiers were obviously nervous on the phone, there was a chance one of them might arrive, get cold feet and leave, so Henry arrived early, claiming a small table at the rear of the restaurant. When the first veteran walked in, he carried himself with the strength and confidence of a soldier, but with the look of someone who had witnessed wartime events that made his face appear much older than his years.

His opening statement belied his fears, *"You know that I should not be here,"* he said.

"I understand your reasons for trepidation," Henry assured him.

"No, you don't..." the vet replied, *"...and what I intend to tell you today doesn't even scratch the surface. So ask your questions now, because you and I will have no further contact after today."*

"Well, first of all, what should I call you?"

"Captain! Just Captain."

"Okay, Captain, there's a reason why you are speaking with me, despite your trepidations."

"Yes, I know you aren't afraid to take a dangerous path to pursue the truth. I admire that in a man."

"Thank you," Henry replied with a half-smile.

"I want the American people to know what's going on over there. I want them to know why their fathers and sons are dying. I want them to know why we are not fighting the war to win. I want them to know how our country is being flooded with marijuana and cocaine."

Henry gave him a confused look, *"I know about the heavy drug production that goes on in Vietnam, Laos, and Cambodia, but what does that have to do with drugs in this country?"*

"Ever hear of Air America?" the captain asked.

"It's the CIA's air force, right?"

"Bingo," the captain replied, "Air America consists of some of the toughest bastards I've ever known. Now I warn you the next chapter of my story is classified. It also reveals illegal acts by our government. Disclosing it to you could get us both killed."

"If you are willing to assume that risk, then so am I," Atherton replied.

"Okay, now because I was part of an intelligence squadron, it was not unusual to be flown to various bases within Vietnam for intelligence briefings, or to evaluate certain intelligence findings. These flights often found us in the belly of a C-130 class transport aircraft, operated by an Air America crew. On one such trip I was standing in the cargo hold of one of these aircraft with marijuana plants stacked up to my hips. I am sure that pot was destined for delivery to the United States. At one point we landed, and as soon as I stepped out of the aircraft, the hilly landscape indicated to me that we were no longer in the flat regions of South Vietnam. When I asked one of the crewmembers where we were, he said he was not allowed to tell me. I just know in my gut that most of the dope manufactured over there made its way back to our country for sale on our streets. That's one reason why you can buy pot anywhere you want in this country today. It really is screwing up American families. I know, because my daughter has been using it."

Atherton was mulling over what he had just heard after the first soldier left the restaurant, when his second interview walked in. Unlike the last soldier, this one wore a big smile which did not belie the incredible story he was about to tell. They exchanged the usual pleasantries.

"I was one of the first to go into Vietnam," he began, in a matter-of-fact way. "I recall going to Fort Bragg, North Carolina, where I was trained as a sniper. One day, my buddies and I were called into a building for a classified briefing. Fort Bragg was buzzing with excitement. Officers were more irritable than usual, phones were ringing on all the desks, and people seemed to be moving faster when they walked. We were herded into a classroom building. A heavily armed Marine was posted at the door with a shotgun, and the door was locked behind us.

The briefing was conducted by the CIA. We were going in ahead of our troops as part of OPERATION PHEONIX, to assassinate targets in both the North Vietnamese and South Vietnamese forces. The funny thing is I don't remember a lot of the training I received at Fort Bragg after that briefing. But we went to Vietnam and we did what we had to do.

When I returned stateside, I went A.W.O.L. through a network that had been established on the West Coast. I escaped to Canada, into British Columbia. There were less than seven people living in a ten-mile radius of my home. It was really strange when one day, a car came up the mountain and pulled up right in front of me. It was a dark sedan with Virginia tags. A guy got out of that car, looked straight at me and said, 'How are things going, Sergeant?' It was really scary. That's when I remembered the chip that's buried under my skin in my left shoulder. Here, would you like to feel it?"

The soldier smiled, raising his shirt sleeve, exposing a small, subcutaneous device that measured approximately one square inch. Atherton reached over to feel the chip for himself.

"Why do you say you don't remember much of your training for OPERATION PHEONIX?" Atherton asked.

"Well, for example, when I came to the West Coast, I volunteered to help in a martial arts dojo. As far as I could recall, I had never been trained in martial arts before. But that was obviously not the case, because I tested out as a black belt. Of course I don't know what else I can't remember, but I often wonder, and it bothers me. There is one other thing..." the soldier reflected as an afterthought.

"What's that?" Atherton asked.

"One time I had to go to a V.A. hospital for a procedure. I don't remember what it was, but these guys showed up and told me the Government had determined I was disabled, and would be receiving a stipend of $ 2,000 per month for life. As you can see, I am not disabled, and I'm sure it's hush money. I don't dare have that chip taken out of my arm. They want to know where I am at all times."

Atherton was in the process of wrapping up his interviews with Vietnam veterans when he received a phone call that prompted him to conduct one more. This soldier had been decorated in Vietnam. He was the only recruit in basic training who raised his hand when an officer asked for soldiers who knew something about gardening. This unique knowledge put him on a fast track of advancement, serving as aide and gardener for several U.S. Army generals. It also brought him into contact with many notable Americans.

"When I was in Vietnam, I was trained in reconnaissance. I was often behind enemy lines, spotting the VC so our boys could smoke them out. The VC lived in underground cities that were connected by tunnels. Frequently I would spot a VC soldier, adjust my binoculars, and he would have already disappeared underground. Damn, they were good!

The Americans were moving lots of drugs in that region. I remember American civilians bringing large quantities of heroin down through the canals. I know for a fact that some of the bodies that have been shipped back to the States had bundles of heroin sewn into their body cavities.

One particular Vietnam memory will always stay with me. I remember escorting my general to a meeting with General Westmoreland at MAC V (Military Assistance Command, Vietnam) in Saigon. My general was eager to end the war and bring our boys home. Westmoreland would hear nothing of it. I was waiting outside by my general's jeep when the conflict started. The voices in Westmoreland's office began to rise. As the argument approached the point of physical violence, I ran into the Supreme Commander's office, grabbed my general by the arm, and hauled his ass out of there!

When I entered the Army, I was 17 and didn't know any better. If I knew then what I know now about Vietnam, I'd have gone to Canada.

My most memorable experience in the Army took place before I ever went to Vietnam. In late July of 1962, I was tending the general's garden when our base was graced by a visit from Miss Marilyn Monroe, the Hollywood actress. She was as beautiful as my gardenias! I escorted her through the garden, answering her questions about her favorite flowers, when she suddenly blurted out, 'I am pregnant, and the Kennedys are responsible! It's okay though, because I am going to tell the world!' *Boy, what a shock that was! I didn't know what to say, and after that we walked together in silence. She thanked me kindly for the tour of my gardens, and left me with an innocent kiss on my cheek. A few weeks later, Marilyn Monroe was dead!"*

Chapter 18
The Legacy of the *OCAAUs*

"I think the impression has arisen that foreign policy is the private property of the President of the United States and that no one - Congress, the press, and the judiciary has a role, they're kibitzers and they shouldn't be allowed to meddle with the president when he's trying to navigate the tricky currents of international politics. This is not what the Constitution intended, nor is it the way it should be done in a democracy, nor is it good for the presidency itself."

Dr. Arthur M. Schlesinger, Jr.

A U.S. Army officer who served in Korea spoke with Atherton about his experiences during the Korean conflict. They met at a crab house on the western shore of the Chesapeake Bay in Deale, Maryland.

"I landed in Korea about the time the heaviest fighting had ended," the veteran began. *"I was involved in the provisioning process, handling logistics for supplies, electronics and food. I distinctly remember an election that took place in South Korea that resulted in murder. The night before the election, the man who opposed the incumbent died suddenly of what was reported as a coronary thrombosis. A fifty-year-old Korean man who worked for me talked about it the next day at work. 'Yeah,' the South Korean said, '…that coronary thrombosis was caused by a .38-caliber pistol to the head!'*

I also got to know a young South Korean man who worked as housekeeper for a friend of mine whose living quarters actually had a shower with hot water! On one occasion while visiting my friend and using his shower, the young man asked me if I would give him 350 U.S. dollars. I told him that was a lot of money and I asked his purpose for the loan. He replied that he had saved $ 50, and if he could raise $ 400 he could bribe South Korean officials to avoid serving in the Korean Army.

Now, I was a married man with several children. I had lost my student deferment, and had been drafted into the Army. Yet, here I was, in a place where democratic elections were negated by assassination, and young men were avoiding military service through the bribery of corrupt officials. I had to ask myself, 'What the hell am I doing here?' I never really came up with a satisfactory answer to that question."

"Gee, I never thought I had an effect on people until I was in Korea."
Marilyn Monroe

Atherton's research determined that President Harry Truman went to war in Korea without a Congressional declaration of war. When a senator challenged

President Truman's authority to wage war without a declaration, Truman replied, *"The situation required that I act like Commander-In-Chief, and I did it!"*

Atherton continued to receive calls from other Vietnam veterans who wanted to have their story told. He met two soldiers for lunch at a Thai restaurant in Chevy Chase, Maryland.

Atherton got right to it, *"What can you tell me about the mission in Vietnam? Was the mission clear to you when you were there? Did you feel you were fulfilling a worthwhile purpose?"*

"It's obvious to me there is no clear mission in Vietnam," the first veteran answered. *"Our strategies and reporting structures are not established to facilitate victory, which would bring the conflict to an end. They were established to ensure that the fighting would continue. We are fighting the mantle of Communist China in Vietnam. It is a war we are not destined to win. But even with the fall of Vietnam to the Communists, I never have believed in that stupid Domino Theory. If it were true, Australia would now be a communist country! McNamara knew this. He cut a deal with Johnson which got him out of the Pentagon, sending him to the World Bank."*

The second soldier was a U.S. Army Intelligence Officer. *"I am told you found yourself in an interesting situation with Secretary McNamara?"* Atherton inquired.

"Yes, I was about to deploy to the Mekong Delta region from the States when I noticed that McNamara was sitting a few rows down from me in a movie theatre in Washington, D.C. I was scheduled to ship out soon. I wanted to walk up to McNamara after the movie, make him look into my eyes and convince me there were solid reasons for shipping me to Vietnam - reasons I could believe in. I wanted him to know me in case I came home in a body bag. Although I fantasized about it, I let him go!"

The frustration and futility of life in Vietnam for U.S. soldiers can be summed up in one word – fragging. The practice of fragging seems to have been developed during the Korean War, the other unpopular, undeclared conflict. There were times when a squad would become disillusioned with their situation, having to go out repeatedly into the jungles and rice paddies, wading through leech-infested rivers, having firefights with the Viet Cong, only to watch their comrades die from landmines, snipers, booby traps, pungi sticks, and by other gruesome means. Such a squad would be joined by a new officer from the States, gung ho to go out and '…kill some Gooks.' Most American soldiers in these situations were focused on only one thing, making it home alive. Resentment toward these fresh, arrogant, cocky officers would result in situations where the officer might be shot in the back by one of his subordinates while on patrol, or allowed to be placed in harm's way during a fight with the enemy, or killed by a 'friendly-fire' accident involving an American hand grenade, also known as an anti-personnel fragmentary bomb – hence the term, fragging.

Atherton interviewed a U.S. Army artillery officer and helicopter pilot who said that fragging often had racial overtones.

"Here's the typical way it happened," the black officer began. *"A white officer would get on the case of a black soldier who did not want to perform a task the soldier was*

bound by orders to carry out. While the white officer was sleeping in his tent, the black soldier would walk up to the officer's tent fly, zip it open, pull the pin on a hand grenade and hold it for two seconds. The black soldier would toss it carefully onto the officer's cot, and then run like hell. If the toss was good, the grenade would lodge between the officer's legs just before it exploded. Other times, the officer would be isolated on patrol and fragged, or shot in the back during a firefight with the enemy. This kind of thing rarely happened in WW II, because in that war, we were fighting for a just cause."

"We must face the fact, that the United States is neither omnipotent nor omniscient - that we are only six percent of the world's population -that we cannot impose our will upon the other 94 percent of mankind - that we cannot right every wrong or reverse each adversity - and that therefore there cannot be an American solution to every world problem."

John Kennedy

Henry Atherton, Investigative Reporter

The primary bombing mission in Vietnam is to disrupt the flow of Soviet-built trucks carrying fuel from Hanoi into South Vietnam, aiding VC troops who conduct combat operations in South Vietnam, Laos and Cambodia. If the U.S. can stem the flow, the determined and aggressive VC troops will not be able to continue fighting. Many innovative methods have been used to locate the Viet Cong under the dense foliage they use as cover. A scientist involved in solving this problem stated, *"We're always trying to find ways to pinpoint where the supply trucks are for our bombers to hit. At one point, we learned that cockroaches along the trail were attracted to human urine. So when the VC would stop their trucks to urinate along the trail, the cockroaches would congregate. We then decided to implant tiny transistors in live cockroaches and distribute them throughout the jungles of Vietnam. We bugged the bugs! It didn't take long for the VC to figure out why our bombing accuracy had suddenly improved, so they began hanging their urine buckets in the trees. This negated our bugging program altogether."*

This reporter recently learned that United States forces were engaged in combat operations in Laos and Cambodia long before President Nixon disclosed those activities to the public. As the number of bombing sorties has been stepped up, so have the number of losses of aircraft and crewmembers.

Many brave American airmen have survived the destruction of their aircraft, only to find themselves as prisoners of war. Back home in the States, Americans wear wristbands bearing the names of these imprisoned heroes. Most of the POWs are being kept in a prison built by the French, which is now ruled by the most notorious group of Viet Cong military police, trained in torture and interrogation. The prison is known to American servicemen as the Hanoi Hilton. The residents there are mostly American pilots. The VC torture their American prisoners continually, due to the amount of information the captured pilots can provide about U.S. capabilities, strategies, and plans. And if a pilot dies during the course of interrogation, there is one less man who might escape and fly aircraft against their comrades.

The VC are constantly looking for ways to secure the Ho Chi Minh Trail, as it snakes its way down through the Golden Triangle, to protect it from bombing. An increasing number of flight crew personnel are being located in smaller, portable prisons which are co-located with supply and fuel depots along the trail. The enemy is using these POWs as human shields, protecting their fuel and supplies from American bombers. A highly classified U.S.A.F. project codenamed BLACK TENT is operating in

Thailand in hardened bunkers, using the fastest computer that IBM builds today. BLACK TENT enables the Air Force to manage all the data required to monitor and select targets for our bombers. As information becomes known about a human shield site, it is added to the program, and colored pegs are placed on maps to prevent bombing in that locality.

When the American public learned recently of the fighting in Cambodia, and how President Nixon has deceived them, an outcry arose. This led to the riots at Kent State University where National Guardsmen fired live rounds at students, killing four of them and wounding eleven others. The outcry caused military leaders to terminate a classified operation that would have sent large numbers of ground troops into Laos. The missions were to destroy the petroleum pipeline being built there, and to rescue American prisoners of war, who were a liability to the President because they should not have been fighting there in the first place.

President Nixon and Defense Secretary McNamara are now taking off the gloves. Several weeks ago, a U.S.A.F. captain strode into the BLACK TENT bunker and ordered his subordinates to pull the map tacks. The stunned airmen said they refused to knowingly place their comrades at risk from American bombs. The White House had anticipated this reaction, and the captain was prepared with his response. With his men standing at rigid attention, he quoted from the Uniform Code of Military Justice, giving specific attention to the section devoted to the penalties for refusing to obey a direct order. The captain stated that replacements would soon arrive for any who disobeyed, adding that beds were reserved for them at the U.S. military prison at Fort Leavenworth, Kansas. When this conflict ends, how will these "fratricide" casualties be explained when hundreds of American prisoners of war, killed by American bombs, do not return home to their families? Will the Pentagon acknowledge these friendly fire deaths, or will these pilots always be remembered as missing in action?

"A war for a great principle ennobles a nation. A war for commercial supremacy, upon some shallow pretext, is despicable, and more than aught else demonstrates to what immeasurable depths of baseness men and nations can descend."

Albert Pike

There comes a time in every war when one side realizes preparations must be made for defeat or withdrawal. As the South Vietnamese and the United States entered into negotiations with the North, a delegation of six American generals was dispatched to Hanoi to work on securing the safe return of the remaining hostages.

As the last American staffers were whisked off the roof of the American Embassy in Saigon by helicopter, with South Vietnamese residents pulling at their heels trying to flee the VC, the six generals were detained against their will by the North Vietnamese. One of the generals was later interviewed by a member of the press.

"Do you think the United States should have fought in Vietnam?"

"I believed when I was deployed here that we were here to help the South Vietnamese. I really did. But as the months turned into years, and I saw how this conflict was being conducted, I formed serious doubts, as have many military officers here. We just did not express them, as we had a duty to perform."

"What about President Johnson's response to the firing on our ships in the Tonkin Gulf?"

"I know what happened in the Tonkin Gulf. The U.S.S. Maddox was sent deep into North Vietnamese waters to provoke an attack. I am not even sure they were fired upon."

"So you even question the event that led to the United States doctrinal shift from an advisory role to wartime?"

"Yes, I have serious doubts about that, and I want Americans to know, because a president might try this again in the future."

* * * * * * * *

As president, Richard Nixon issued many executive orders that his staff did not execute, since they knew the catastrophic impact such acts would have had on the country. They knew their boss was paranoid and instable, and that certain orders should be ignored. Their standard operating procedure was to wait until Nixon was in a different mind state, and he would be asked if he still wanted to follow the severe direction he had previously ordered. Nixon had a chronic sleep disorder. Senior aides to the President would administer his evening sleep ritual by giving him a Secenol and a stiff drink.

In his memoir, reflecting on his years with Nixon, John Ehrlichman noted that Nixon had a drinking problem in two senses. *"First he liked the stuff, and second, he could not handle it,"* Ehrlichman recalled. Before he agreed to work on the

President's reelection campaign, Ehrlichman made Nixon promise to lay off the booze. The promise was not kept.

When former President Lyndon Johnson lay on his deathbed, he made a chilling confession to one of his staff members.

"We did it," Johnson said, *"We worked behind the scenes with the Mob in the early sixties, and were running Murder, Inc. in the Caribbean. The world will remember my civil rights initiatives, but I just implemented the plans that were developed by President Kennedy."*

* * * * * * * * *

"Hello, DC police? This is Frank Wills. I'm a security guard at the Watergate office complex. At about 1:15 AM this morning I noticed our back door had been taped and propped open so it wouldn't lock. I removed the tape, and returned later to see the tape had been replaced. I think you better send some officers to check this out!"

On June 17th, 1972, five men, including three Cuban exiles, were arrested for breaking into the Democratic National Committee headquarters on the sixth floor of the Watergate office complex in Washington, D.C. The men were wearing surgical gloves. They carried lock picks, cameras, and sophisticated listening devices. When President Nixon learned that his Plumbers had been caught, he was concerned about the involvement of the Cuban burglars, which could open up an investigation into the Bay of Pigs, OPERATION FORTY, and the role of CIA-trained Cuban exiles in the assassination of President Kennedy. From that moment on, Nixon could no longer conceal his involvement with the Kennedy assassination and retain the presidency....although he did not go down without a fight.

On August 8th, 1974, in the wake of the Watergate scandal, President Richard Nixon requested air time which was granted by every broadcast network. Only the President's closest advisors knew in advance what he was planning to say. The President had weighed his options in view of lagging support in the Congress.

"I shall resign the presidency," Nixon intoned, *"...effective at noon tomorrow."*

On the day he left the White House, Nixon gave a speech to his staff that many thought was nonsensical.

* * * * * * * * *

In recognition of Henry Atherton's tireless and courageous pursuit of the truth in matters relating to presidential politics, the National Press Club invited Atherton to convene a presentation of views regarding the president's role in times of war. Andrea Atherton was seated at the head table with her former husband. She was proud of her former husband's accomplishments, and how he had persevered in his pursuit of the truth.

Atherton had invited Dr. Arthur M. Schlesinger, Jr., Special Assistant to President Kennedy, and Admiral Gene LaRocque, USN (retired), Director of the Center for Defense Information, both of whom have had academic and real-world expertise in the constitutionality of war.

"Good morning everyone," Atherton began, *"Our purpose here today is to discuss views surrounding the question of whether or not the President of the United States has the authority under the Constitution to declare war. Both of our distinguished guests will make a short statement, and then we will open up the floor for questions. But first, I have a few comments to make.*

Thomas Jefferson wrote to James Madison, describing the conflicts between the countries of Europe at that time. Jefferson said '... they are countries of eternal war.' America was supposed to be something different. Madison stressed that the legislative control over the war power was '...the most important provision of the Constitution.' America was to lead the world to a more peaceful condition. The constitutional precedent is best summed up by Thaddeus Stevens who said in 1867, ' Though the president is Commander-in-Chief, Congress is his Commander.' Dr. Schlesinger, I would like to begin with your statement, please."

"Well, thank you for the opportunity to be here today to discuss this most important topic. In order to answer the question at hand, one must look at it in an historical context. The drafters of the Constitution had just gone through the experience of the war with Great Britain, a war brought about by the decision of one man, King George III, the British monarch. With the war fresh in their minds, our founding fathers were determined that no single person should have the authority to declare war. They believed the country would best be served by a division of powers, not a centralization of authority. To that end, the Constitution, in Article 1, Section 8 gave Congress the power to declare war. The nation's founders, however, also realized that Congress was too large to direct military operations, especially in wartime. Thus, Article 2, Section 1 of the Constitution provides that '...the president shall be Commander-in-Chief of the Army and Navy of the United States and of the militia of the several states when called into actual service of the United States.'

Presidents started to undertake military actions without congressional approval soon after the American Revolution. Presidential historians have noted that once American troops have been deployed to an area of conflict, a president can always make a powerful emotional appeal to support our troops. 'Are you going to send bullets and guns to American boys under fire or are you not?' *And it's an almost impossible situation for a congressman to challenge the president at that stage. That's why unilateral presidential action to commit Americans to war is so dangerous.*

The United States has declared war only five times. Those instances were as follows; The War of 1812, The Mexican War of 1846, The Spanish-American War of 1898, World War I, and World War II. Every other conflict in which Americans have fought and died has been undeclared. Thus, those conflicts may not have been supported by the people, as was the case with Vietnam.

The Founders were determined to deny the American president the sole prerogative of making war and peace. The president's power as Commander-in-Chief, in short, was simply the power to issue orders to the armed forces within a framework established by Congress."

"Thank you, Dr. Schlesinger. Now I have the pleasure of introducing Rear Admiral Gene LaRocque, who also has studied this question quite thoroughly."

"I am delighted to be here today to meet with the members of the press. The Founding Fathers made it very clear that the declaration of war rests with the people; that is, the Congress of the United States. They also made it clear that the president, as one of his duties, would be Commander-in-Chief of the armed forces. Our President today as Commander-in-Chief of the armed forces commands the most powerful military force ever assembled, and we also know that our presidents in the past, in the role of Commander-in-Chief of the armed forces, have shown a certain penchant for using our armed forces whenever they thought it was best. Now here is the question we have to decide as a democracy; Have we allowed too much power to rest in the hands of the president as Commander-in-Chief of the armed forces to decide when, where and how to fight a war? I think all of us ought to get involved in that issue, learn more about it and note again that the President of the United States is only the Commander-in-Chief of the armed forces; he is not authorized in the Constitution to exceed that, to declare war."

Atherton concluded, "Thank you, gentlemen, for your statements. Now our guests would be delighted to answer questions from the audience..."

New York Tribune, July 4, 1970
Opinion/Editorial - Henry Atherton, Staff Writer

The time has come for Americans to peacefully demand redress of our grievances, as guaranteed by the First Amendment to the U.S. Constitution. This must occur now and into the future so that incidents of civil rights abuse and obstruction of justice by elected officials will be properly restricted. Our government can only be managed by constant, diligent oversight by the people and its representatives in Congress. The people must control the government, not vice versa.

The only way we can ensure the future of our children is to hold our elected officials accountable for their actions, to swiftly and fairly try them for their wrongdoings, and to aggressively impeach them when necessary. And in those instances when they use the power given to them by the people to commit treason and suppress legal prosecution, we must rise up with force and remove them from power.

In the meantime, all records held by the government in the assassinations of President John Kennedy and Senator Robert Kennedy must be opened so the people can judge those events for themselves. Future generations can be protected from further miscarriages of justice only by an unmolested democracy under the Constitution.

When John Kennedy was a congressman, he wrote, *"For, in a democracy, every citizen, regardless of his interests in politics, holds office. Every one of us is in a position of responsibility, and in the final analysis, the kind of government we get depends upon how we fulfill those responsibilities."*

"The rise of dictatorships has always corresponded to the abdication by the individual of his responsibility to take an active interest in the function of government."

Victor Solomon

"Treason doth never prosper. What's the reason? For if it prosper, none dare call it treason."

Sir John Harrington

"Patriotism is not demonstrated by allowing our country to be attacked, then sending our troops to fight undeclared wars for undisclosed economic or political purposes and fraudulent motives. Rather, patriotism is defending the rights of all Americans, as guaranteed by the Constitution; especially the rights of our men and women in uniform. Chief among those are the rights to life, liberty and the pursuit of happiness. May God have mercy upon those who knowingly violate this sacred trust."

Victor E. Justice

Epilogue
The Crime of the Century

"Courage is not the absence of fear, but rather the judgment that something is more important than fear."

Ambrose Redmoon

After the simple wedding ceremony in a rustic church in the historical town of Saint Michaels on Maryland's Eastern Shore, Henry and Andrea Atherton returned to their white Victorian cottage a few miles from the church, overlooking one of the many Eastern Shore creeks that flow into the Chesapeake Bay. The reunion he had yearned for so many nights had finally come to pass, thanks to Andrea's compassion and her willingness to see the changes in Henry, and the potential of a loving future with him. They sat on their screened porch, sipping their favorite Sonoma chardonnay, watching the sun set over the Chesapeake.

Henry noticed his wife's faraway look, *"Are you sure you're okay with not jetting off to some island in the Caribbean for our honeymoon?"*

"Why would I want that when I can have this?"

"My thoughts exactly," Henry replied.

"Henry, this is all I ever want for the rest of my life."

"Me too," Henry said as he sat down next to her and took her hand. *"You know, if you want me to, I can quit writing and take a job in a hardware store in Saint Michaels..."*

"Don't be silly, Henry. Telling you to stop writing is like telling one of those Canadian geese out there not to migrate. It's in your blood."

As the California wine relaxed them, the reunited couple sat closely together on the porch swing, which Henry gently rocked every few minutes by pushing off the decking with his foot.

"I really am proud of you. You know that, don't you?" Andrea asked.

Henry leaned over and looked into her eyes, as his own began to show signs of a tear, *"I could not have done this without your steadfast support. Thank you for being there for me."*

"It took a lot of guts for you to travel this road, and you should feel good about that."

Henry looked toward the sunset over the Western Shore, across the Bay. He felt the breeze that swept over the Bay start to subside. The sky was painted with pale red-orange, fading to a light salmon. The groom watched as a solitary male osprey returned to his nest, perched atop a navigation marker post in the middle of the creek that flowed from the nearby marsh into the Chesapeake Bay. The osprey had a fish clutched in its talons, which it fed to the hungry mouths of his offspring.

A blue heron crossed the osprey's path in the opposite direction, his fishing ended for the day, as it headed for its next in a lagoon to settle in for the night.

Andrea noticed again the intense look that often occupied Henry's face whenever he was lost in thought. *"A penny for your thoughts!"* she inquired, leaning forward to observe his face.

"Oh, I am sorry, Honey" Henry replied, *"I don't mean to be distant. This is our wedding night!"*

"Darling, I understand. You've been through quite an ordeal these past years. There have been some scary moments."

"Many scary moments, but somehow a desire for truth and justice has driven me to continue this quest, even when I've been warned repeatedly to cease and desist."

"You've shown a lot of courage, and I am proud of you. But I hope you're getting some closure and resolution about all of this now."

"Ever since Marilyn Monroe was killed, I've been struggling to piece everything together. The death of President Kennedy followed, and the deaths of many witnesses to that crime, then Adlai Stevenson, Dr. King, and finally Bobby Kennedy. There were too many common elements in these murders to ignore the possibility they might somehow be connected. And so we're sitting here on our wedding night and my mind had to drift back into that morass. Damn it!"

"It's okay, Henry, go on."

"We're supposed to have faith in our government. A man named Knowles once said, 'Faith is often the boast of the man who is too lazy to investigate.' Well I want to have faith in my government, and I have been investigating now for almost a decade. It's our responsibility and duty as citizens to investigate and regulate the possible illegal activities of our elected officials. You know people keep referring to the assassination of President Kennedy as 'The Crime of the Century.'*"*

"Yes, I have seen the news reports and the documentaries."

"Well, the assassination of President Kennedy was not the crime of the century! It was just one of several deliberate acts by a few men who violated the Constitution, then imposed a new form of government on the American people. We didn't act when we should have! We didn't investigate and impeach President Johnson when he imposed the Warren Commission on the American public. The Warren Commission was run by several of the guilty parties. They acted as judge and jury - exonerating the beneficiaries of the coup d'etat. And if our efforts to investigate and impeach Johnson had been suppressed, then we should have exercised our constitutional right and responsibility to bear arms and overthrow the fascists who had usurped our government! I'm convinced the administrations of Johnson and Nixon were prearranged, and that these two men acted in collusion with the Secret Service, the CIA, the Mafia, the FBI, and the Joint Chiefs of Staff to murder President Kennedy and to commit the United States to fighting in Vietnam. I further believe the CIA brought large drug shipments into the United States, and the cash sales from those drug shipments were used to fund the CIA's special projects, including several covert and unconstitutional wars. The combination of attacks on the Constitution, the ensuing years of

conflict, the disruption and division in our country, and the deaths of 58,000 Americans in Vietnam and 3 million Vietnamese, in my opinion, constitutes the Crime of the Century."

Henry heaved a heavy sigh, then stood up and walked to the edge of the screened porch. He looked out into the marshes of the Eastern Shore, where he could hear the distinctive calls of redwing blackbirds. The final vestiges of sunset were beginning to fade, and night was falling upon the Chesapeake Bay.

"Well, my dear Henry," Andrea called to him softly, *"that's all over now."* Henry's bride stood up, walked over to him, and tenderly taking his face in her hands, kissed him warmly.

"I would like to think so," Henry replied wistfully, as he looked deeply into her eyes. Then he turned, took both of her hands into his as he gave her a loving look, and said, *"But as long as we have presidents with misplaced loyalties, I'm afraid that history will continue to repeat itself."*

"With a good conscience our only sure reward, with history the final judge of our deeds, let us go forth to lead the land we love, asking His blessing and His help. But knowing that here on Earth, God's work must truly be our own."

John F. Kennedy

Reflective Quotations

"Both Jack and Bobby had much to lose should Marilyn have gone public about her relationships with the two of them. If they hadn't taken her out, she would have ruined both of them. Even when we used to hang around with Johnny Roselli, the gangster, she used to say things to me like, 'Gosh, they actually kill people!' *And I'd tell her,* 'Yeah, like their friends, their mothers and anyone else who gets in their way.'"

Jeanne Carmen
Close friend and neighbor of Marilyn Monroe

"That Bobby (Kennedy) *made life miserable for me and my friends. We shouldn't have killed John* (Kennedy). *We should have killed Bobby."*

Carlos Marcello
Mafia boss in New Orleans

"I told you they could do it. I'll never forget what Carlos and Santo did for me."

Jimmy Hoffa to Mafia attorney, Frank Ragano

Afterword

In order to maintain the historical accuracy of the primary events in this book, I have tried to resist stating my opinions, despite developing some strong views along the way. Of course, some author opinions were stated by means of the opinion/editorial pieces written by Henry Atherton in his newspaper, and in some of the dialog. But now, if the reader will indulge me, I would like to share some further thoughts in closing.

First, when I am asked how to discern the difference between a probable conspiracy and a coincidence, my answer is one simple word…timing. The U.S.S. Maine explodes mysteriously in Havana Harbor and the United States enters the Spanish-American War, under the motto, *"Remember the Maine."* Pearl Harbor is attacked under questionable circumstances, and a fiercely neutralist America is drawn into World War II. Shots are allegedly fired at the U.S.S. Maddox in the Tonkin Gulf, and President Johnson escalates the war in Vietnam. In each of these instances, such provocations provided the catalyst needed by the sitting president to commit U.S. troops to combat. Every American I have asked has said we would not have gone to Afghanistan and Iraq had we not suffered the tragedy of 9/11. How else would the American people have supported a pre-emptive attack on Iraq?

Second, we have much to be thankful for, living in America. We are blessed with an abundance that is unparalleled when compared to other parts of the world. But with that incredible quality of life has come a deep-seated sense of apathy. We know intuitively that something went terribly wrong when President Kennedy was assassinated on November 22, 1963, in Dallas. And despite the killing of witnesses, the destruction and locking away of evidence, and the perpetual misinformation/disinformation campaign, the collective American consciousness is slowly grasping that what happened on that day was not an act of random violence by a lone gunman, but a highly-sophisticated attack in broad daylight, involving many agencies of the federal government. Our indifference is slowly being replaced with the realization that what took place in Dallas was a carefully planned coup, and that the subsequent years of the Vietnam War, the drug culture, Watergate and the resulting loss of trust in our government that followed the Watergate cover-up, were linked directly to the men who seized power and ruled America in spite of the will of the people.

Perhaps the most incredible irony of Dealey Plaza is that JFK would have survived the bullet that lodged in his upper back, which did not penetrate deeply into his body. But it was that James Files, the man who fired the fatal shot, was recruited only two hours before he pulled the trigger on the Fireball handgun. Had Files not played a role on that day, everything else remaining the same, JFK would have survived the assassination attempt, Johnson would have never been president, Nixon would never have been president, there would have been no Vietnam or Watergate, and the Civil Rights movement would have progressed at a faster pace in America. I believe we can predict these outcomes with a high degree of certainty.

What we can't see is how the Cold War might have proceeded, and what impact other Kennedy initiatives might have played in American and world history.

I believe that if JFK had remained faithful to Jackie, he might still be alive today. You might ask, '*How could President Kennedy's fidelity have saved his life?*' It is my contention that the Secret Service was deeply disturbed by JFK's unbridled womanizing, partly because JFK's regular exposure to strange women made their duty of protecting him an impossible mission. President Kennedy's many extra-marital liaisons might have been perceived by the Secret Service as a legitimate threat to national security. I believe those concerns led to the premeditated fallback by JFK's protective detail from the time he left Love Field until his motorcade entered Dealey Plaza. The timing of the dissolution of the most important protective security perimeter, coinciding with a diversion of the motorcade and overlapping fire is highly suspect.

The exceptionally high degree of collusion and cooperation that had to exist between the CIA, the Mafia, the FBI, the Dallas Police, the Joint Chiefs, the Cuban exiles, the oil merchants, the politicians, and the many persons who stood to gain from the death of President Kennedy, almost defies belief. But if you can suspend disbelief long enough to see how they were all brought together to commit this evil act, you are left with wondering how we allowed it to go unpunished.

Why did Chief Justice Warren cow to LBJ, when Warren knew he must resign from the Supreme Court and live out his life with a clouded legacy? Why did the legislative branch not do a better job of investigating the murders of JFK and RFK, as they both affected the management of the White House? It is obvious that our system of checks and balances broke down.

The only conclusion I can draw is that these men had force of personality that drove fear into those around them. It is the same reason why President Clinton failed to take out Osama Bin Laden three separate times when Attorney General Janet Reno recommended strongly against it. So what happens when a president who exhibits a strong personality has misplaced loyalties?

If you believe a *coup d'etat* took place in Dallas, Texas on November 22, 1963, then as Americans, we failed to carry out a duty that is spelled out for us in the Constitution of the United States.

Due in great part to pleadings from Virginia Delegate George Mason, the Founding Fathers included in the drafting of the Constitution, ten amendments we know today as the *Bill of Rights*. George Mason had written *The Virginia Declaration of Rights*. It was the primary source document, not only for the *Bill of Rights*, but also for the *Declaration of Independence*, which was drafted by another Virginian, Thomas Jefferson.

"However you might feel about the Bill of Rights and the Constitution, they make you a beneficiary in perpetuity in principles, ideals, and they place an obligation on you."

John Henry Faulk

The Second Amendment to the Constitution guarantees the right to bear arms, *"A well regulated Militia, being necessary to the security of a free State, the right of the people to keep and bear Arms shall not be infringed."*

When the King of England sent his redcoats from Boston harbor to capture the supply magazine containing the weapons of the colonial militia, it led to the confrontation at Lexington and Concord, the shot heard around the world, and the beginning of the American Revolution. The colonists knew the taking of their guns would make them subservient to the King, and they were willing to die to protect their right to bear arms. So the Founding Fathers wrote that right and responsibility into the Constitution.

And so on November 22, 1963 when Lyndon Johnson retreated to the White House, it was our right and our duty to storm the White House to insist that LBJ be imprisoned pending trial for conspiracy, murder, and treason, along with every other public official who was involved, and there were many. No wonder the CIA sent an official to watch over Bobby Kennedy, who was the highest ranking law enforcement officer in the country. No wonder the phones in the Washington, DC area were shut down immediately after the assassination in Dallas. At the moment JFK died, so did the will of the people. And the aftermath proves my theory. America was adrift during the late sixties and early seventies, floating on a cloud of marijuana and cocaine, much of which was brought into this country by our own government to provide untraceable funding for covert wars sponsored by the CIA.

The riots in Tiananmen Square, China and protests in the Ukraine following two assassination attempts on presidential candidate Viktor Yuschenko, are examples of angered peoples who refuse to live one more day under the boots of those who might use their power to restrict the rights and freedoms of the people. We must always be prepared to follow their example, as they are true patriots, willing to sacrifice for the welfare of their country.

But the advanced quality of life in America has sapped the hungry spirit of independence from us. We are overcome with a sense of apathy, an absence of feeling about what goes on around us, even though we have suspicions that what we are being told might not be the truth. We are indifferent, and we do not take action.

William Somerset Maugham said, *"If a nation values anything more than freedom, it will lose its freedom, and the irony of it is that if it is comfort or money that it values more, it will lose that too."*

Do I propose that we storm the White House? No, I propose we do what our forefathers intended. We must hold our elected officials accountable for their actions while in office. We must make certain they do not send our troops to fight wars that are not in the interests of our nation as a whole, and we must fully understand and fulfill our constitutional rights and obligations.

Impeachment is a powerful constitutional process. It was the threat of impeachment that drove Richard M. Nixon from the White House before he could inflict further damage on America. We may never know all the evil deeds committed by Nixon, but he is the only American I know of who ever received a pardon for crimes he MIGHT have committed.

While completing my research for this book, I read Katherine Graham's Pulitzer Prize winning biography, Personal History. I was impressed at how she, her sons, and her daughter worked through the tragic loss of Kay's husband, Philip, and how Kay went on to have a stellar career while learning the business world, courageously running *The Washington Post*, and playing a major role in bringing down a corrupt president by publishing the investigation into the Watergate case.

Despite Philip Graham's debilitating disease, his brilliant mind and energy enabled him to play a major role in the political lives of both Lyndon Johnson and John F. Kennedy. The fact that Philip Graham knew these men so well, and admired them both, gives one reason to wonder if what he knew about the circumstances surrounding the assassination of JFK had anything to do with the torment that led to his own suicide. Katherine Graham was shocked when Bobby Kennedy announced to her at a dinner party that, *"Philip had appointed Lyndon Johnson as vice-president."* It was not far from the truth, since Johnson would have likely dismissed the offer had Philip not been at the Democratic National Convention in Los Angeles to facilitate the negotiations.

But there is a glaring omission in Graham's story that would give pause to any editor. In her biography, Kay Graham delves into the detailed stories of her friends in Georgetown, her fellow graduates from Vassar, the housewives who supported their cold warrior husbands; husbands whose deeds would later be disclosed to the world. Not once in her detailed descriptions of friendships and personal tragedies does she mention her Georgetown neighbor who was married to the sister of her closest associate at *The Washington Post,* Editor, Ben Bradlee. She never mentions this dynamic and attractive socialite friend who had been married to the Deputy Director of the CIA Special [Covert] Operations Directorate. Graham never mentions her classmate from Vassar days, who had many sexual liaisons with the President of the United States – the woman her husband had ranted about at the editor's conference. Graham did not mention the surreal funeral attended by 200 journalists, spies, diplomats and policy makers that she attended on October 14, 1964 at the National Cathedral, the day when her dead friend Mary Meyer should have received a birthday card from Kay Graham.

The fact that Kay Graham never mentions Mary Pinchot Meyer in her book, and that the CIA has detailed, yet heavily redacted records on the death of Mary Meyer, is worthy of consideration. This combined with the fact that Mary Meyer was assassinated with professional skill on federal property just a few hundred yards from a CIA counterinsurgency training facility across the Potomac from CIA headquarters, and that her brother-in-law, *Washington Post* editor Ben Bradlee, and James Jesus Angleton, the CIA's Director of Special Operations, both scrambled to recover Mary Meyer's diary within hours of her death, raises many questions that have gone unanswered for decades. When you think about the fact that Mary Meyer died at a time when her former husband, Cord Meyer, was the second highest ranking covert operations officer in the CIA, this all translates to a silence on the part of Katherine Graham that is deafening.

* * * * * * * * *

The Constitution of the United States contains a motive for murder. It is highly probable this motive was at work during the assassinations of Lincoln in 1865, Garfield in 1881, McKinley in 1901, and Kennedy in 1963. Those assassinations and even the attempted assassination of President Reagan were allegedly committed by lone zealots, who could be easily manipulated for political purposes. Attempts were also made on the lives of Andrew Jackson, Franklin Roosevelt, Harry Truman and Gerald Ford.
Article II of the U.S. Constitution states;

> *"In case of the removal of the president from office, or of his death, resignation, or inability to discharge the powers and duties of the said office, the same shall devolve on the vice-president, and the Congress may by law provide for the case of removal, death, resignation or inability, both of the president and vice-president, declaring what officer shall then act as president, and such officer shall act accordingly, until the disability be removed, or a president shall be elected."*

Although the first half of that sentence seems to be in conflict with the second, it is meant to be yet one more check and balance of our constitutional system of government. The meaning is clear. If the president dies, the vice-president immediately assumes the office. But Congress (representing the people) has a mechanism to change that assignment of power. A preordained assumption of power is a dangerous thing. It brings out the worst in men, and it should not be allowed in America. Worst of all, it has led to murder and treason, and the people should take corrective action to prevent it from happening again.

Due to the nature of politics and politicians, a vice-president is a likely candidate for corruption is a target for conspirators to involve in the subversion of a president. Some religious denominations have figured this out, as they forbid an assistant minister to replace the rector, as it might foster a revolution within the parish.

What is needed during a national crisis such as a presidential assassination is a fair and level-headed government official who is less likely to have his head turned by private interests, who is governed by the rule of law. Therefore, I would propose a constitutional amendment, making the Chief Justice of the Supreme Court the designee who would immediately replace the president in the event of death or disability, until such time as a proper election can be held. I would imagine most chief justices would not relish the idea of being president. That cannot be said for vice-presidents. Such an amendment would return the presidency to the will of the people where it belongs, and not allow it to fall into the hands of a few, dangerous men, which is fascism.

Videographic evidence at Love Field and subsequent testimony from agents of the Secret Service prove the United States Secret Service pulled protection away from JFK on the day he was killed. Agents were peeled away from the presidential limousine from the time it motored away from Air Force One. Oversight must be provided to ensure the Secret Service protects every president without prejudice, at all times.

The flamboyant Joseph P. Kennedy, Sr. intended to build a political dynasty, beginning with Joe, Jr., then Jack, then Bobby, then Teddy. Instead, the quiet yet powerful oil man Preston Bush fathered the presidential dynasty of George H.W. Bush, and George W. Bush, with Jeb Bush and perhaps even Laura Bush waiting in the wings. One dynasty replaced the other. The fact that George H.W. Bush was director of the CIA should not be overlooked.

Today, we are living in an era when our government tells us each day how scared we are supposed to be. What is the threat level today? Our government says, *"The more control you give to us, the safer you will be."* And just like the shameful days of Joseph McCarthy, who, along with Richard Nixon, promoted the fear of communism as a means of gaining power, and like Adolph Hitler who used radical nationalism and prejudice as means to gaining power, today we are led to believe there is a terrorist behind every bush. The pattern is all too familiar.

The United States has the best intelligence-gathering and special forces capabilities in the world. And we should use them quickly and decisively when they are needed to do the terrible deeds that are required of them to keep us safe from bad people. But they and their commanders must be accountable to the people they are trained to protect.

Finally, there have been many instances in this book when reporters, editors, and publishers found themselves in awkward positions with senior politicians. The establishment and protection of a free press by the First Amendment is perhaps the single most important element in keeping our elected officials accountable for their actions, as well as their votes and their policies. In order to get the scoop, reporters must always cultivate contacts and relationships in the political sphere. But like all areas of potential conflict of interest, a respectable distance needs to be maintained between the politician and members of the press. Too many presidents, including JFK, have successfully manipulated the press to their political ends. In recent history, the abuse has been extended to paying celebrity commentators to espouse the policies of a given administration or party. The public must hold the press accountable to a code of ethics that protects those whom the members of the press are supposed to serve.

I believe the pen is mightier than the sword, and I trust that some of my words have struck a chord in you or have given you a heightened awareness as to how the events of the 1960's have dramatically affected us today.

You possess a weapon that has far greater power than any military in affecting change in the world. That weapon is your vote. Not using that vote, being apathetic and remaining indifferent to the historical patterns of democracy, creates a destiny of continuing the pattern of increased violations of your civil rights into the future. And as President Kennedy said, you should be, "...*unwilling to witness or permit the slow undoing of those human rights,*" which are guaranteed to you under the Constitution. Yes, I do believe that left unchecked, history does repeat itself. What do you believe?

"The difference between coincidence and conspiracy is timing."

Victor E. Justice

Historical Footnotes

Lincoln Assassination Attempts: Although the assassination of President Abraham Lincoln by the actor, John Wilkes Booth at Ford's Theatre is well known, not so well known are the other attempts that were planned and attempted on Lincoln's life. Included in those attempts were a shot fired by a Confederate sniper from 800 yards, while the President visited with his generals at Fort Stephens, that wounded an officer standing next to the President. A bullet fired from the woods not far from the White House as the President rode alone on horseback. The bullet passed through his stovepipe hat. Another planned attack, which was foiled by a chance encounter with Union cavalry, consisted of a black powder bomb that was to have been placed in a basement room of the White House, which would have caused the floor above to collapse, killing the President and anyone else who happened to be in the dining room at the time.

As the Civil War came to a close, there was tremendous political pressure on Lincoln to end the bloodshed. But he held on to the increasingly unpopular view that the Union should be defended. Had an assassination attempt succeeded just months earlier, many historians believe the incoming president would have begun peace negotiations with the Confederate States of America in earnest, creating a possible 'europization' of America, resulting in several small countries. The Emancipation Proclamation would probably have been repealed, continuing the institution of slavery in the South for some time. And most importantly, the powerful nation we know as the United States, would never have reached the potential it has reached today to be a superpower.

One must ask, *"What might have happened if Kennedy and Khrushchev had not kept their generals from launching their nuclear weapons?"* Lincoln's death and its timing provide us with some interesting perspectives on how we might view the historical implications of the death of President Kennedy.

Secret Service Negligence: When the U.S. Secret Service was created in 1865 under Chief William P. Wood, its mission was to suppress counterfeit currency. In 1894 the U.S.S.S. began part-time protection of President Grover Cleveland, beginning its more famous, or infamous, duty. During one of the inaugural parades for President Franklin Delano Roosevelt, news reels show cars of agents surrounding the President, wearing white trench coats, with Thompson submachine guns scarcely tucked away under their coats. This demonstrates why the U.S.S.S. is suspect for relaxing its protection of President Kennedy on November 22, 1963. Such lax protection was highly-irregular, even in 1963.

Assassination by Airline: On February 22, 1974 an unemployed tire salesman from Philadelphia, who had been questioned by the Secret Service for picketing the White House, rushed a Delta boarding gate at BWI Airport in Baltimore, shot and killed a transportation officer, and the Delta co-pilot. The man's name was Samuel Byck. In addition to his stolen .22-caliber revolver, Byck carried aboard a large briefcase with road flares and two large plastic containers filled with gasoline. During the shootout with police, Byck was hit twice, and then he shot himself in the head. When the police discovered Byck's car in the BWI parking lot, it contained detailed tape recordings of how Byck had intended to fly the Delta DC-9 into the White House while President Nixon was there waiting for the outcome of the Watergate investigation.

Restriction of Records: In 1992 the President of the United States signed legislation that restricted the release of certain types of evidence in the JFK assassination, until the year 2017. Although the Assassination Records Review Board legislation released certain documents to the public immediately, the law states that the president can overrule such disclosure because *'...continued postponement is made necessary by an identifiable harm to the military, defense, intelligence operations, law enforcement, or conduct of foreign relations.'* That president was former CIA Director, George Herbert Walker Bush.

Death of CIA Director Colby: President Nixon had rewarded William Colby for his leadership of the famed PHOENIX PROJECT, the assassination program employed by the U.S. in Vietnam, by appointing Colby as CIA Director. On April 29, 1996, during the Clinton Administration, the Associated Press reported that former CIA Director, William Colby had died while canoeing at his weekend home on the Wicomico River, in Maryland. No paddles were found floating on the Wicomico, and the waterlogged canoe miraculously floated from the site of Colby's disappearance to the shore of Colby's cottage. Navy divers and sophisticated radar could not locate Colby's body. When the corpse reappeared one week later in a marsh near his home, Colby's shoes and lifejacket were missing. Forensic testing of his shoes might have proven that Colby was on land when he died. The Director was known to always wear his shoes and lifejacket when canoeing in chilly weather. The press reports that Colby had telephoned his wife to say he was ill, but would be canoeing anyway, were later refuted by Mrs. Colby. William Colby had testified before the Church Committee about the M-1 Umbrella Weapon that was used in Dealey Plaza to paralyze JFK during the assassination in Dallas. At the time of his death, William Colby was writing for a financial newsletter that was decidedly anti-Clinton.

Precursor to War: When the tragedy occurred on 9-11-2001 in New York, Washington, and Pennsylvania, civilian officials and generals appeared on our television screens to say that our country never could have imagined or anticipated someone committing such a crime with a commercial airliner. Tom Clancy's book, <u>Debt of Honor</u>, which describes how a Japanese pilot flies his commercial airliner into the U.S. Capitol killing hundreds of lawmakers, was temporarily pulled from the shelves of bookstores across America after the catastrophes of 9-11.

Many who were glued to the television sets that day came to certain realizations that if conditions had been different, the tragedy would not have been so dramatic. During the late 1980s, I became aware of a metal mesh product manufactured in Germany, which can prevent a gasoline tank from exploding, even if a bullet is fired through the can. The mesh adds little weight to the gas tank, but it compartmentalizes the combustion reaction, suppressing it, so a fire is not created – only a fuel spill. Acting on authority of an American distributor of this fire-suppressing product, I contacted the FAA engineer who worked at the Boeing facility in Seattle. When I had finished describing the product, the engineer explained to me the costs of removing the mesh each time the tanks were cleaned, and the weight they would add, precluded the product from consideration, although he acknowledged it would save the lives of those passengers who would otherwise perish in a fire resulting from a crash at takeoff, for example. Had the 9/11 airliners not burst into flames upon impact, the towers would still be standing, and hundreds of lives would have been saved.

My next 9-11 shocker took place on a domestic airplane flight. Sitting next to me was an American consultant who gave me his business card, showing that his expertise is in advising airports and airlines about air security. The man stated that all indications were the airliners that struck the World Trade Center towers were controlled remotely. Up to that point, I had not thought about how someone with rudimentary training in a flight simulator could reroute an aircraft, fly it into Manhattan to a specific target, accelerating just before impact. If remote control was in evidence, we would certainly want to know who controlled those aircraft. It is possible that the hijackers took the controls for just the last few seconds of the flight in both cases.

Why is this information relevant to _Misplaced Loyalties_? Remember the premise illustrated in this book that what at first seems coincidental, looks more like a conspiracy, when considered in light of the timing of events that immediately follow the tragedy. In reference to previous discussions about the limitations imposed upon presidents by the Constitution regarding declarations of war, I have yet to meet an American who believes we would be fighting in Afghanistan and Iraq were it not for our dramatic losses on 9-11.

Prior Knowledge and Cover-up of 9/11: On May 21, 2002 FBI Special Agent and Chief Division Counsel Coleen M. Rowley wrote a 13-page letter to FBI Director, Dr. Robert S. Mueller, expressing her concerns about how FBI headquarters had stymied efforts by the FBI Minneapolis, Minnesota office to review the contents of the laptop computer that was in the possession of suspected terrorist, Zacarias Moussaoui. French intelligence had informed the FBI that Moussaoui was directly affiliated with Osama Bin Laden. When the FBI Minneapolis office determined that Moussaoui had participated in simulated flight training for large commercial aircraft, FBI headquarters stalled agent's efforts to question Moussaoui, stating there was not sufficient probable cause. An incensed

Rowley lectured the Director in her May 21ˢᵗ memo that the Bureau had developed a *'hindsight rule'* for determining probable cause – waiting for the crime to be committed before apprehending the perpetrator.

Although Rowley went to great lengths to avoid making charges of cover-up by the Director and FBI SSAs (Special Supervisory Agents), she did maintain that at a minimum, the FBI legacy of careerism *(the practice of advancing one's career often at the cost of one's integrity)* was the real culprit for the strong allegations by the Director that the FBI had *"no prior knowledge"* that terrorists might fly commercial airliners into major American buildings.

I doubt that when she wrote her Director, Counsel Rowley had any intention of her memo ever being made public. As good attorneys do, she was advising her boss that his public statements could come back to haunt him in light of the Moussaoui investigation that was being conducted in Minneapolis. Apparently, the memo reached the SAC (Special Agent in Charge) level prior to 9/11, but did not come to the attention of Director Mueller until after the attacks.

When I consider that a senior attorney in the bureaucracy of the FBI took such a risk to her career and her personal safety by writing that memo to Director Mueller, in an effort to ensure that due process and justice was upheld for the protection of the American public, Coleen M. Rowley goes into my book as a patriotic American.

Nixon Ramblings: The Watergate burglary took place on June 17, 1972. When White House attorney John Dean decided to blow the whistle on President Nixon during the Watergate cover-up, he opened the safe of E. Howard Hunt, an operative for the CIA station in Miami. Hunt was an active participant in the Bay of Pigs operation, and an advisor to President Nixon in the White House. In Hunt's safe, Dean found bogus telegrams that were designed to link JFK to the assassination of the Diem brothers in Vietnam. Hunt was convicted during the course of Watergate, as was burglar Frank A. Sturgis, another Miami operative who was involved in the Bay of Pigs. Sturgis was present in Dealey Plaza on November 22, 1963. During one of Nixon's many incoherent moments, often self-induced by way of drugs and alcohol, a Nixon aide heard President Nixon complaining that the Watergate investigation could lead to damaging disclosures regarding the Bay of Pigs...probably a reference to OPERATION FORTY.

Morales/Bush Connection: David Morales was chief of operations of the CIA's JM/WAVE station in Miami, and the Agency's top assassin in Latin America. He was the Cuban sharpshooter on the sixth floor of the TSBD, at the opposite end of the hall from the sniper's nest. Morales appeared at Sylvia Odio's house with Oswald. LHO 2 (Oswald impersonator) whistled for Morales in Dealey Plaza. Morales picked up LHO 2 with the light green rambler station wagon, drove to the Trinity River bed, and flew with LHO 2 and another unsuspecting passenger, USAF Sergeant Robert G. Vinson, to a CIA base in New Mexico. At JM/WAVE, Morales reported to Ted Shackley, who later became deputy director for special operations at the CIA under George H.W. Bush.

Assassination Research: On March 24, 1995, a JFK assassination researcher by the name of Edgar Tatro, presented some interesting evidence and questions to the Assassinations Records Review Board. The following are excerpts from that testimony:

"Okay. I have a record that came through Emory Brown, an excellent researcher who is very little known from the New Jersey area, and the Navy, by accident -- actually, it came through the Air Force. It's a document that puts Oswald in Gulf Port, Mississippi, and he wasn't there, according to the Navy. I have the actual document, and I have all the Navy denials, and I don't know what it means, but something's amiss. Oswald's military intelligence files were destroyed. The House Select Committee called it very troublesome, which is the understatement of a lifetime, but cross-reference files were destroyed. I have a letter from the Navy admitting that."

"I have a letter from the Canadian government admitting they destroyed Oswald files as recently as 1990. So, that's not very good."

"When Oswald came back from Russia, he met with a man they call the travel agent, Spas Raikin, but actually he was the president of the anti-Bolsheviks nation, and I've been able to obtain documents showing correspondence between Hoover in 1959 to Raikin. Raikin says it's all innocent, but there are things blacked out, and even he doesn't know why they are blacked out. So, even he would like to get a hold of those things."

"There are at least five witnesses who said there was a hole in that windshield, forget about the dent, that there was a hole in it, and it's never been resolved, and I have been told that there were five to eight windshields available and they could switch windshields. I think someone ought to try to look into the possibility of a windshield switch. There's a sidewalk scar down there that was stolen by Earl Golz, broken right out of the sidewalk. It's down in a Texas researcher's possession now. It does fit a bullet miss from the other knoll that no one talks about."

"Oswald, it's been alleged, was at the Monterey School in Miami, by one of the Warren Commission members in January of 1964. There are no records. It's called the Defense Language Institute now."

"Allen Dulles' mistress, Mary Bancroft, was also a CIA agent. She was the friend of Michael Paine's mother. Michael Paine and Ruth Paine were taking care of Marina Oswald."

Bush Denial of Kennedy: On June 19, 2000, Governor George W. Bush of Texas penned a letter to recognize the rededication of the John F. Kennedy Memorial Plaza in Dallas. He applauds the group who conceived the concept of the memorial 30 years prior, and speaks of hallowing such tragic sites in American history. Not once does he mention John F. Kennedy, the man, nor does he acknowledge any of JFK's accomplishments during his political career, and the feelings of loss felt throughout the world on that tragic day in Dallas. Researchers have proven that his father, George H.W. Bush was in Dallas on November 22, 1963, and that he was a senior CIA officer at the time.

Bush Suppression of Evidence: *"President George W. Bush on November 1, 2001 signed an executive order that gives all incumbent and former presidents since 1980 full veto authority in perpetuity over public access to documents in their presidential papers."* That statement was made by Professor Hugh Davis Graham, a member of the Department of History at Vanderbilt University. In his article, entitled, *Presidency: The Reagan Papers Runaround*, Graham says, *"Bush is advantaged by congressional unity and bipartisanship following the terrorist attack of September 11, and by Republican control of the House. In the new era of global antiterrorism, U.S. government involvement in clandestine warfare, possibly including political assassinations, is expected to increase, and in the process to intensify government determination to seal off documents from public scrutiny."*

Putin's Demo-Fascism: Russian President Vladimir Putin showed his KGB roots when he crushed regional elections in Russia, and exerted undue and illegal influence on elections in other former Soviet countries, such as the Ukraine, including the obvious poisoning of Viktor Yuschenko, Putin's democratic nemesis in Kiev. Putin, like Johnson, Nixon and Hitler, has used his position which was obtained through democratic processes, to impose demo-fascist rule on his country. A primary example of Putin's brand of demo-fascism is how he wrested control of Russia's largest oil company, Yukos, from private ownership and placed it under the control of his government. Russia is one of the world's largest producers of crude oil, second only to Saudi Arabia. Placing large oil reserves outside the free market economy can have disastrous impacts on the prices paid by customers at the pump. The state control of the Russian oil market is probably one of the many reasons why Americans are paying the highest gasoline prices we have seen in decades. To add insult to injury, Iraqi Dictator Saddam Hussein diverted oil allocations to high-ranking officials in the Kremlin who profited from selling oil which was to have been part of the U.N. Oil for Food Program.

Exhibit A

Autopsy for Marilyn Monroe

Report from the public records of the Coroner for Orange County, California, Thomas Noguchi, on the subject of Norma Jean Baker

[aka Marilyn Monroe]

External examination: The unembalmed body is that of a 36-year-old well-developed, well-nourished Caucasian female weighing 117 pounds and measuring 65-1/2 inches in length. The scalp is covered with bleached blond hair. The eyes are blue. **The fixed lividity is noted in the face, neck, chest, upper portions of arms and the right side of the abdomen. The faint lividity which disappears upon pressure is noted in the back and posterior aspect of the arms and legs.** A slight ecchymotic area is noted in the left hip and left side of lower back. The breast shows no significant lesion. <u>There is a horizontal 3-inch long surgical scar in the right upper quadrant of the abdomen. A suprapubic surgical scar measuring 5 inches in length is noted.</u> The conjunctivae are markedly congested; however, no ecehymosis or petechiae are noted. The nose shows no evidence of fracture. The external auditory canals are not remarkable. No evidence of trauma is noted in the scalp, forehead, cheeks, lips or chin. The neck shows no evidence of trauma. Examination of the hands and nails shows no defects. The lower extremities show no evidence of trauma.

Body cavity: The usual Y-shaped incision is made to open the thoracic and abdominal cavities. The pleural and abdominal cavities contain no excess of fluid or blood. The mediastinum shows no shifting or widening. The diaphragm is within normal limits. The lower edge of the liver is within the costal margin. The organs are in normal position and relationship.

Cardiovascular system: The heart weighs 300 grams. The pericardial cavity contains no excess of fluid. The epicardium and pericardium are smooth and glistening. The left ventricular wall measures 1.1 cm. and the right 0.2 cm. The papillary muscles are not hypertrophic. The chordae tendineac are not thickened or shortened. The valves have the usual number of leaflets which are thin and pliable. The tricuspid valve measures 10 cm., the pulmonary valve 6.5 cm., mitral valve 9.5 cm. and aortic valve 7 cm in circumference. There is no septal defect. The foramen ovale is closed. The coronary arteries arise from their usual location and are distributed in normal fashion. Multiple sections of the anterior descending branch of the left coronary artery with a 5 mm. interial demonstrate a patent lumen throughout. The circumflex branch and the right coronary artery also demonstrate a patent lumen. The pulmonary artery contains no thrombus. The aorta has a bright yellow smooth intima.

Respiratory system: The right lung weighs 465 grams and the left 420 grams. Both lungs are moderately congested with some edema. The surface is dark and red with mottling. The posterior portion of the lungs show severe congestion. The tracheobronchial tree contains no aspirated material or blood. Multiple sections of the lungs show congestion and edematous fluid exuding from the cut surface. No consolidation or suppuration is noted. The mucosa of the larynx is grayish white.

Liver and biliary system: The liver weighs 1890 grams. The surface is dark brown and smooth. There are marked adhesions through the omentum and abdominal wall in the lower portion of the liver as the gallbladder has been removed. The common duct is widely patent. No calculus or obstructive material is found. Multiple sections of the liver show slight accentuation of the lobular pattern; however, no hemorrhage or tumor is found.

Hemic and lymphatic system: The spleen weighs 190 grams. The surface is dark red and smooth. Section shows dark red homogeneous firm cut surface. The Malpighian bodies are not clearly identified. There is no evidence of lymphadenopathy. The bone marrow is dark red in color. Endocrine system: The adrenal glands have the usual architectural cortex and medulla. The thyroid glands are of normal size, color and consistency. Urinary system: The kidneys together weigh 350 grams. Their capsules can be stripped without difficulty. Dissection shows a moderately congested parenchyma. The cortical surface is smooth. The pelves and ureters are not dilated or stenosed. The urinary bladder contains approximately 150 cc. of clear straw-colored fluid. The mucosa is not altered.

Genital system: The external genitalia shows no gross abnormality. Distribution of the pubic hair is of female pattern. The uterus is of the usual size. Multiple sections of the uterus show the usual thickness of the uterine wall without tumor nodules. The endometrium is grayish yellow, measuring up to 0.2 cm in thickness. No polyp or tumor is found. The cervix is clear, showing no nabothian cysts. The tubes are intact. The right ovary demonstrates recent corpus luteum haemorrhagicum. The left ovary shows corpora lutea and albicantia. A vaginal smear is taken. Digestive system: The esophagus has a longitudinal folding mucosa. The stomach is almost completely empty. The contents is brownish mucoid fluid. The volume is estimated to be no more than 20 cc. No residue of the pills is noted. A smear made from the gastric contents and examined under the polarized microscope shows no refractile crystals. The mucosa shows marked congestion and submucosal petechial hemorrhage diffusely. The duodenum shows no ulcer. The contents of the duodenum were also examined under polarized microscope and show no refractile crystals. The remainder of the small intestine shows no gross abnormality. The appendix is absent. The colon shows marked congestion and purplish discoloration. The pancreas has a tan lobular architecture. Multiple sections show a patent duct.

Skeletomuscular system: The clavicle, ribs, vertebrae and pelvic bones show fracture lines. All bones of the extremities are examined by palpation showing no evidence of fracture.

Head and central nervous system: The brain weighs 1440 grams. Upon reflection of the scalp there is no evidence of contusion or hemorrhage. The temporal muscles are intact. Upon removal of the dura mater the cerebrospinal fluid is clear. The superficial vessels are slightly congested. The convolutions of the brain are not flattened. The contour of the brain is not distorted. No blood is found in the epidural, subdural or subarachnoid spaces. Multiple sections of the brain show the usual symmetrical ventricles and basal ganglia. Examination of the brain stem shows no gross abnormality. Following removal of the dura matter from the base of the skull and calvarium, no skull fracture is demonstrated. Liver temperature taken at 10:30 A.M. registered 89 F.

Specimen: Un-embalmed blood is taken for alcohol and barbiturate examination. Liver, kidney, stomach and contents, urine and intestine are saved for further toxicological study. A vaginal smear is made.

T NOGUCHI, M.D. DEPUTY MEDICAL EXAMINER 8-13-62

Author's Note: Notice the sections underlined by the author and those sections in bold print. The notation, *"No nacelle marks"* was scratched in the margin, presumably after the original autopsy was prepared. This was meant to say there were no needle marks evident anywhere on Marilyn's body. The fixed lividity on the front of Marilyn's body proves she died in a downward facing position, and that her body remained that way long enough for lividity to develop.

Exhibit B
Transcript of Author's Follow-Up Interview with John, May of 2004

Author: Did I first interview you in October of 2000, which led me to do extensive research and write *Misplaced Loyalties*?

John: Yes, we had our first conversation at around that time. And I have given you exclusive permission to tell my story in your book.

Author: Why do you think we have not had much contact during that time?

John: Because this is a….a dangerous area. This could be a dangerous area.

Author: Okay, before we get into the specifics of your story, please restate why you chose to tell me this information, and what impact it could have on your life.

John: When I got involved in this situation I was working as a young engineer, in the 20- to 25-year-old group *(between 1960 and 1965)*, doing some very exotic technology work for the CIA. And in there we got involved with some very challenging technical problems, and some very threatening social problems that were concerning to me. And in fact I left my position, because I didn't like to do that work anymore.

Author: So you actually had a moral issue, and that's why you left?

John: Yeah, I…I couldn't do it anymore.

Author: Why did you tell me this in October of 2000?

John: For all my life it has been threatening to me. There is no one I can tell it to. When I did explain it to some people, they didn't believe it. It was too far out. It was threatening. As I have gotten older, I don't care anymore. They can't hurt me anymore. My career is done. They can't hurt what I am doing.

Author: Please talk about your experiences in upstate New York in the early 1960's. Who you worked for, you've mentioned already. What were you doing, and what were people doing around you? What city were you in? Umh…let's start with that.

John: Okay, I worked for *(corporate name omitted by author)* in their corporate research center in Building 37, which is the old Edison laboratory. I worked primarily for the CIA…a lot of work….building sophisticated electro-optical equipment.

Author: And what degrees do you have?

John: I have a bachelor's degree in science, and a master's degree in science. *(Names of educational institutions omitted by author).* I was working on my doctoral dissertation, but my thesis advisor died. So I left.

Author: Do you remember the topic of your thesis?

John: I was looking at using lasers for library readers.

Author: And how would that have worked?

John: Well, that would be using the holographic images from words to recognize the words in a book, and therefore categorize books by what part of the library it goes in. I was an expert at that time in a new form of electro-optics and Fourier transforms. Most people at that time were experts in geometric electro-optics. I was into wave optics.

Author: So you were sort of leading edge then?

John: Yes, leading edge technology in that area. I was involved in the night vision work, the early stuff, like taking pictures of tanks at night at ten mile ranges.

Author: How did you do that?

John: Put a laser pulse out, watch the image on a television and time the return of the echo, you capture the picture, take a snapshot of it, and you can see the tank…or the people.

Author: So you basically synched up the signal coming back with the television?

John: That is correct.

Author: Umh…can you talk please about what you were doing and what people were doing around you in that building?

John: There was a lot of UHF communications that could work on anything. For instance, we built power supplies that you could plug into different voltage sources, from 12 volts to 400 volts, AC or DC, the equipment would operate without any adaptation, so they could go into any hotel room and plug it in. We were building special equipment for the Navy, to do certain, uh… interrogation types of things. Basically a lot of CIA work.

Author: At that time, what did you believe was the purpose of your work?

John: I was really a dumb farm guy from *(location omitted by author)*. I thought we had a very loyal country, and I thought the Vietnam War kept me in my job, because they liked what I did technically. And I thought I was doing things that were good for the country.

Author: And did your attitude change about that?

John: Yeah, I saw us do things like eliminate people who didn't know they were being eliminated. And we had equipment to do that!

Author: And do you think your inventions might have had something to do with that?

John: I know they did…I saw pictures of what I did!

Author: Okay…umh. Did you or your coworkers have code names? Can you talk about that?

John: We all had code names. Nobody knew anything. Everything was done by word of mouth. Everything was handled. How much money do you need? Take what you want. It was…it was a free-for-all.

Author: Why code names?

John: Well, it was supposedly such high security. I mean it was above Top Secret. Nobody knew what you were doing. My boss didn't know what I was doing.

Author: So, you are saying that your work was highly compartmentalized?

John: Highly compartmentalized. It was cell work. Three people would work together here, and three people there. And I had people working under me. Nowhere at any spot, were there more than three people involved. One of my cell members was a Hungarian. He worked for the CIA. I don't remember his codename. But he always had lots of money. He would show up with beautiful girlfriends, and we would go to a bar and we would discuss what we wanted to do, and what equipment he needed me to build.

Author: So, what would happen to someone if they shared information from one cell to another?

John: You weren't there anymore. You lost your job, at the minimum.

Author: Immediately?

John: Immediately!

Author: What was the primary function - you spoke of technical, but what were some of the things the Government was doing with this technology internationally?

John: Well, I built the first night vision television system. The CIA used my invention to go after Che Guevara, one of Fidel Castro's lieutenants. We could tell how many people were down there the night before. The next day the CIA went in there with a team (*of Bolivian police*), and Che's men no longer existed. (*Author's note: A US military technology used in multiple aerial weapon systems and as night scopes for sniper rifles would later be known as the Starlight Scope. All such scopes were based on the wave optic technology developed by John in the CIA lab in Schenectady*).

Author: That was in the forests of Bolivia, yes?

John: Right

Author: And it was at night, yes?

John: We were flying over the forest at night at an altitude of one mile. We could see Che and his men around the campfire, just like daylight.

Author: And were you involved in the development of that equipment?

John: I sure was. Electro-optics was my area of expertise.

Author: How did your night vision scope work?

John: I used an image isoton with an intensifier on it. I basically used starlight to get enough light to see. It just magnified the image on the ground, using light in the infrared region, beyond .6 microns. We had both the firelight and the starlight...

Author: So that's how the CIA located Che Guevara and his team in the Bolivian forest?

John: Yes.

Author: Did you see the film?

John: I saw the film of the night before, and I saw when he was attacked. Every one on our side had night vision equipment. It scares me to think that we killed people without any warning.

Author: So expertise like yours was used to commit assassinations?

John: I think it is still today.

Author: Did one of your co-workers tell you about a plan to assassinate an American citizen? About a woman in Hollywood...

John: I was told how Marilyn Monroe was killed, after that happened. It was the same Hungarian who worked for the CIA, who told me in advance about the Kennedy assassination. He told me how and why Marilyn Monroe was killed, two weeks after it happened.

Author: What was the method used?

John: They got her drunk and forced a condom of intense drugs into her…up her ass.

Author: They used anal insertion of liquid drugs?

John: Yes, they employed anal insertion of the same drugs she was taking orally. The drugs were Nembutal and chloral hydrate. But Marilyn didn't die right away, because she shit it out, even though she had been given an enema earlier that day. There was chaos about taking her to the hospital, or not to take her to the hospital.

Author: Who was involved in the attack on Marilyn Monroe?

John: I know the Mafia and the CIA were involved in Marilyn's death, and others in the U.S. Government. It was so scary, because lots of people were involved in this. They killed her because she had affairs with both of the Kennedy brothers, and one of them had gotten her pregnant.

Author: Did you always get what you wanted, or did you ever get turned down?

John: I never got turned down. I would say this is how much I need, and this is what it is going to take. I would buy high-powered transistors, and I would pick one out of a hundred. I bought the best I could find for technical performance.

Author: Did you invent a device that could kill a man with plausible deniability?

John: It could kill rabbits! It doesn't take much energy to cause a heart attack.

Author: So you designed a machine that could do that?

John: I never tested it on humans, but I built it with that in mind. I knew that's what the CIA wanted it for.

Author: Did you say that once you saw the results of your heart attack machine?

John: It's hard to say, but I saw pictures of two people who had fatal heart attacks in restaurants. We rarely knew who the target was. We just built the equipment and it went out the door. Sometimes the gear would come back looking like a train had run over it, and we would have to try and repair it. Your body uses micro volts or micro amps to control your heart. A pacemaker uses 300 to 400 volts.

Author: How does your machine work? What technologies does it use?

John: It is a 6 x 6 cube, with a dial on the back, so you can set it on a table in a restaurant, and you can tune the frequency. You are going from about 80 to 100 pulses per second. A megatron is just a tube with voltage on it, with an antenna that can aim the energy beam. It's just a microwave that puts out some pulses of energy. If you can direct an intense pulse of energy into a heart, it doesn't take many microns to interrupt the heart, and you can tune the frequency. Then, when you hit the right frequency, the victim would suffer a heart attack and possibly die right there at the table.

Author: Is there a battery built into it?

John: Yes.

Author: How is it triggered?

John: There is a dial in the back. You want to cause arrhythmia, that's all.

Author: Was this machine you built one of the things that caused you to leave the CIA laboratory?

John: It was one of maybe ten similar programs. I felt like I was the German who was tuning the diesel engine to make a lot of carbon monoxide *(to kill victims of the Holocaust).*

Author: Why do you think you were told about Marilyn's death?

John: I was told about it after it happened. I think to this day, they were testing my loyalty. Imagine someone telling you this at midnight in a restaurant, and you are saying to yourself, *'I don't want to hear this!'*

Author: Did the Hungarian tell you how Marilyn died?

John: He told me how she died, and why she died. I heard some things about Fidel Castro and the Bay of Pigs. At the time I thought these methods were silly. Explosives in cigars, and poison in his milk shake. But we were upset because we did not get air support for the Bay of Pigs. I built some night vision equipment and 500 watt, 500 MHZ transmitters that were used in the Bay of Pigs operation that we shipped out in big suitcases. Some of those suitcases weighed 80 to 100 pounds. We built it, drop tested it, and off it went.

John: There were two guys from Africa who came over here, and were being watched by the CIA. They both died of heart attacks in restaurants. My machines were out there when those deaths took place.

Author: How many of your machines were produced?

John: I think I built about five of the heart attack machines, a handful. The machines are out there.

Author: Did you have an extraordinary experience late one night with the Hungarian in an Italian restaurant?

John: About two weeks before President Kennedy was killed, I was told exactly how he was going to die. I thought this was all fictitious. There were going to be shooters in tall buildings and a one shooter in the front. At first my wife said I was nuts, or that I drank too much that night. Then two weeks later he was dead, just the way the Hungarian told me it would happen. And the assassination took place where he said it would happen. I was very frightened. So I took the wife and we left the state!

Author: Did this convince you that the CIA was involved in the assassination of President Kennedy?

John: Well, it was the first real evidence that something was going to happen before it happened! Nobody told me these people were going to die before it happened. When someone says the President of the United States is going to be killed at this spot... Nobody shoots the President of the United States!

Author: And you did not go to your management?

John: No, they thought I was doing great work. Nobody knew what I was doing there. There was no one I could talk to about this.

Author: So it created a great deal of conflict in you, didn't it?

John: All I knew is what I heard. My wife didn't want to hear about it. We were in an upper-class Italian restaurant in Schenectady. Sometime between 12:00 and 2:00 AM when he told me how this was going to happen. The Hungarian was probably 45 with these beautiful 25-year-old girls, and he was fat, but he always had lots of cash.

Author: Did you try to discuss this with anyone?

John: I tried…people just looked at you like you are strange. When you tell people, they don't believe it. I don't think you believed me when I told you this story the first time!

Author: You are saying when I first heard your testimony? You just turned the interview on me….

John: It's a scary story! *(John laughs)*

Author: Well, you know I believe you now. It just takes a while.

Author: Did he tell you anything about the motorcade route?

Yeah, the Hungarian told me they would be using a certain route through Dallas, and there would be special rifles for this.

Author: When you accepted the Hungarian's dinner invitation, did you not know what you were going to hear that night?

John: No one told me Marilyn Monroe was going to die. No one told me that two Africans were going to die in restaurants. But the Hungarian told me that the President of the United States was going to be killed! I thought the guy was crazy. Then, when it happened, I was horrified. That's when I decided I had to get out of that job.

Author: How long have you carried these stories inside of you?

John: Back then I was only 24, and today I am 67.

Author: Why do you think the Hungarian told you these things?

John: People like to brag about their life. Sooner or later, the truth comes out. People tend to talk. Even if they are in cells. It amazes me that even criminals want to tell their secrets. They usually end up talking at some point later in their lives.

Author's Note: The omissions in this interview are for the sole purpose of protecting John's identity.

Exhibit C
Starlight Scopes

Starlight Scope as used by U.S. Marine and Army Snipers in Vietnam

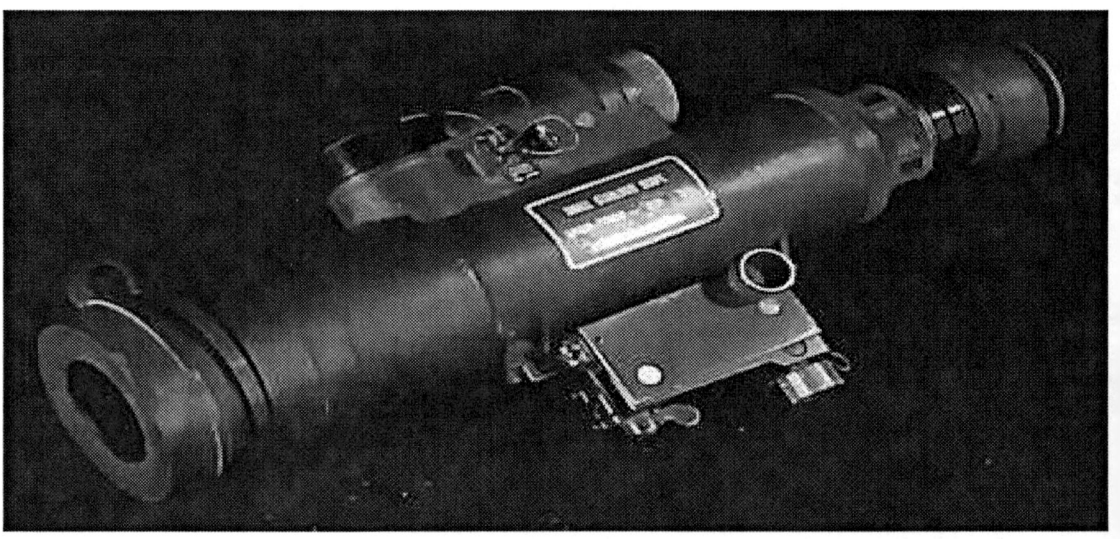

Close Up of First Generation Starlight Scope

Source: Starlight Scope images provided by Fulton Armory in Savage, Maryland

Exhibit D
Sailing with President Kennedy

Pat Newcomb yachting with President Kennedy aboard the *Manitou* off the coast of Main on August 12, 1962 — four days after Marilyn's funeral. *Left to right in the wheel well:* Pat Newcomb (wearing the president's jacket), Paul "Red" Fay, JFK, Peter Lawford, Patricia Lawford (standing). *Robert Slatzer Collection*

What prompted President Kennedy to take Marilyn's publicist, Patricia Newcomb and Peter Lawford for a sail, just a few days after Marilyn's funeral? Several days later, Pat Newcomb was spirited away to Europe for an extended stay, which made her conveniently unavailable for questioning about her possible role in the murder of Marilyn Monroe.

Source: The Robert Slatzer Collection.

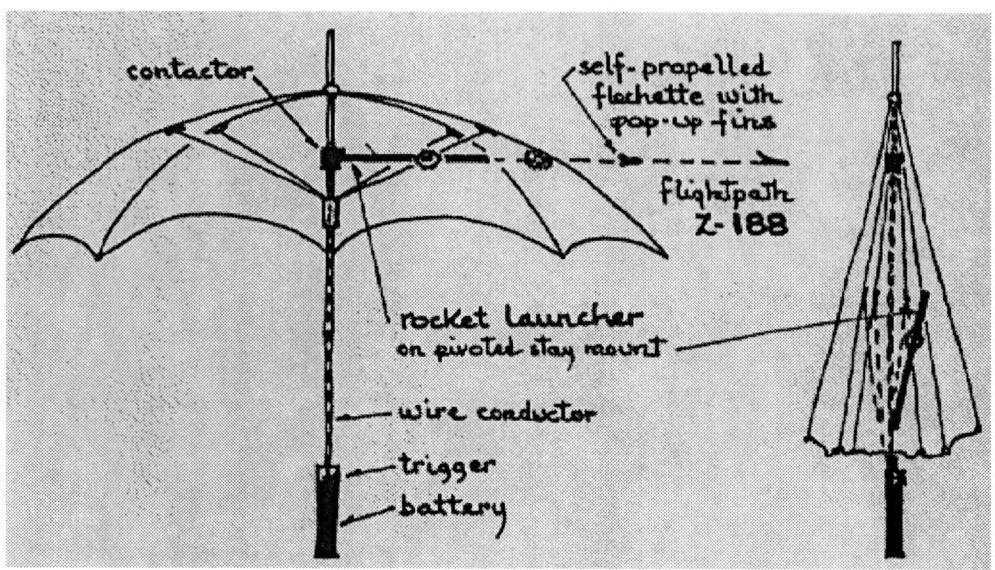

Schematic of the M-1 rocket powered flechette [a self-propelled dart] weapon used by Umbrella Man in Dealey Plaza, piercing President Kennedy's tie, totally paralyzing Kennedy just seconds before the volleys were fired. The flechette darts could either kill or totally paralyze a large dog or human, while the dart dissolved completely in the body, leaving no trace of its presence. The existence of this weapon was disclosed by the inventor, Charles Senseney, former CIA Director Richard Helms, and then current CIA Director William Colby, in September of 1975 to the Senate Intelligence Committee, chaired by Senator Frank Church.

Source: Article by Cutler and Sprague

Exhibit F
The Umbrella Weapon Story – Testimony before the Senate Intelligence Committee, Regarding Development of Umbrella Weapon

<u>TUESDAY, SEPTEMBER 16, 1975. Testimony of William E. Colby, Director of the Central Intelligence Agency</u>.

The Committee met at 10 A.M. in the Russell Building.
Present: Senators Church, Tower, Mondale, Huddleston, Morgan, Hart of Colorado, Baker, Goldwater, Mathias, and Schweiker.
Also present: William G. Miller, staff director, Frederick A. 0. Schwarz, chief counsel, Curtis Smothers and Paul Michel, Committee staff members.

Chairman Church: The particular case under examination today involves the illegal possession of deadly biological poisons which were retained within the CIA for five years after their destruction was ordered by the President. The main questions before the Committee are why the poisons were developed in such quantities in the first place: why the Presidential order was disobeyed; and why such a serious act of insubordination could remain undetected for so many years.

William Colby: The specific subject today concerns the CIA's involvement in the development of bacteriological warfare   materials with the Army's Biological Laboratory at Fort Detrick, CIA's retention of an amount of shellfish toxin, and CIA's use and investigation of various chemicals and drugs. Information provided by him [a CIA officer not directly associated with the project] and by two other officers aware of the project indicated that the project at Fort Detrick involved the development of bacteriological warfare agents--some lethal--and associated delivery systems suitable for clandestine use. The CIA relationship with the Special Operations Division at Fort Detrick was formally established in May of 1952.

The need for such capabilities was tied to earlier Office of Strategic Services World War II experience, which included the development of two different types of agent suicide pills to be used in the event of capture and a successful operation using biological warfare materials to incapacitate a Nazi leader temporarily.

The primary Agency interest was in the development of dissemination devices to be used with standard chemicals off the shelf. Various dissemination devices such as a fountain pen dart launcher appeared to be peculiarly suited for clandestine use.

A large amount of Agency attention was given to the problem of incapacitating guard dogs. Though most of the dart launchers were developed for the Army, the Agency did request the development of a small, hand-held dart launcher for its peculiar needs for this purpose. Work was also done on temporary human incapacitation techniques. These related to a desire to incapacitate captives before they could render themselves incapable of talking, or terrorists before they could take retaliatory action. [Or to prevent guard dogs from barking.]

One such operation involved the penetration of a facility abroad for intelligence collection. The compound was guarded by watchdogs which made entry difficult even when it was empty. Darts were delivered for the operation, but were not used.

Church: Have you brought with you some of those devices which would have enabled the CIA to use this poison for killing people?
Colby: We have indeed.
Church: Does this pistol fire the dart?
Colby: Yes it does, Mr. Chairman. The round thing at the top is obviously the sight; the rest of it is what is practically a normal .45, although it is a special. However, it works by electricity. There is a battery in the handle, and it fires a small dart. [Self-propelled, like a rocket.]
Church: So that when it fires, it fires silently?
Colby: Almost silently; yes.
Church: What range does it have?
Colby: One hundred meters, I believe; about 100 yards, 100 meters.
Church: About 100 meters range?
Colby: Yes.
Church: And the dart itself, when it strikes the target, does the target know that he has been hit and [is] about to die?
Colby: That depends, Mr. Chairman, on the particular dart used. There are different kinds of these flechettes that were used in various weapons systems, and a special one was developed which potentially would be able to enter the target without perception.
Church: Is it not true, too, that the effort not only involved designing a gun that could strike at a human target without knowledge of the person who had been struck, but also the toxin itself would not appear in the autopsy?
Colby: Well there was an attempt--
Church: Or the dart?
Colby: Yes; so there was no way of perceiving that the target was hit.

WEDNESDAY, DECEMBER 17, 1975. Richard Helms' [former CIA Director] testimony:

Huddleston: Mr. Helms, you said you were surprised, or that you had never seen the dart gun that was displayed here yesterday. Would you be surprised or shocked to learn that that gun, or one like it, had been used by agents against either watchdogs or human beings?

Helms: I would be surprised if it had been used against human beings, but I'm not surprised it would have been used against watchdogs. I believe there were various experiments conducted in an effort to find out how one could either tranquilize or kill guard dogs in foreign countries. That does not surprise me at all.

Huddleston: Do you know whether or not it was used, in fact, against watchdogs?

Helms: I believe there were experiments conducted against dogs. Whether it was ever used in a live operational situation against dogs, I do not recall.

THURSDAY, SEPTEMBER 18, 1975. Testimony of Charles A. Senseney:

Senseney: I worked in the Biological Warfare Section of Fort Detrick from 1953. I was the project engineer of the M-1 dart launcher and following on microorganism projectiles and so forth.

Smothers: Is this a device that looks roughly like a .45 caliber pistol with a sight mount at the top?

Senseney: This was a follow-on. It was to replace the M-1 projectile to go into the Army stockpile. It did look like a .45.

Smothers: Did the CIA have, Mr. Senseney, the wherewithal to utilize this dart launcher against humans?

Senseney: No, they asked for a modification to use against a dog. Now, these were actually given to them, and they were actually expended, because we got all of the hardware back. For a dog, the projectile had to be made many times bigger. It was almost the size of a .22 cartridge, but it carried a chemical compound known as 46-40.

Smothers: And their interest was in dog incapacitation?

Senseney: Right.

Baker: Your principle job with the DoD, I take it, was to develop new or exotic devices and weapons: is that correct?

Senseney: I was a project engineer for the E-1, which was type classified and became the M-1. They were done for the Army.

Baker: Did you have any other customers?

Senseney: To my knowledge, our only customer was Special Forces and the CIA, I guess.

Baker: Special Forces meaning Special Forces of the Army?

Senseney: That is correct.

Baker: And the FBI?

Senseney: The FBI never used anything.

Baker: Looking at your previous executive session testimony, apparently you developed for them a fountain pen. What did the fountain pen do?

Senseney: The fountain pen was a variation of an M-1. An M-1 in itself was a system, and it could be fired from anything. It could be put into--

Baker: Could it fire a dart or an aerosol or what?

Senseney: It was a dart.

Baker: It fired a dart, a starter, were you talking about a fluorescent light starter?

Senseney: That is correct.

Baker: What did it do?

Senseney: It put out an aerosol in the room when you put the switch on.

Baker: What about a cane, a walking cane?

Senseney: Yes, an M-1 projectile could be fired from a cane; also an umbrella.

Baker: Also an umbrella. What about a straight pin?

Senseney: Straight pin?

Baker: Yes, sir.

Senseney: We made a straight pin, out at the Branch. I did not make it, but I know it was made, and it was used by one Mr. Powers on his U-2 mission.

Huddleston: Were there frequent transfers of material between Dr. Gordon's [a researcher at Fort Detrick] office and your office, either the hardware or the toxin?

Senseney: The only frequent thing that changed hands was the dog projectile and its loaders 46-40. This was done maybe five or six in one quantity. And maybe six weeks to six months later, they would bring those back and ask for five or six more. They would bring them back expended, that is, they bring all of the hardware except the projectile, okay?

Huddleston: Indicating that they have been used?

Senseney: Correct.

Huddleston: But it could have been used on a human being?

Senseney: There is no reason why it could not, I guess.

Schweiker: Mr. Senseney, I would like to read into the record [from a CIA document] at this point a quote from paragraph nine [exhibit 6, document 67]: *"When funds permit, adaptation and testing will be conducted of a new, highly effective disseminating system which has been demonstrated to be capable of introducing materials through light clothing, subcutaneously, intramuscularly, and silently, without pain."* Now, I just have a little trouble, Mr. Senseney, reconciling your answers in conjunction with this project, when the CIA document makes clear that one of the very specific purposes of the funding and the operation was to find a weapon that could penetrate light clothing subcutaneously, which obviously means through the skin, and intramuscularly, which obviously means through the muscles of a person. And are you saying that you have absolutely no recollection at all that tests or programs were designed to use any of these devices to permeate clothing on people and not dogs?

Senseney: We put them on mannequins.

Schweiker: What's that?

Senseney: We put clothing on mannequins to see whether we could penetrate it. These were the requirements. You almost read the exact requirements that the SDR quoted from the Special Forces there.

Schweiker: I would not expect you to test them on live human beings. I would hope that you did use mannequins, Mr. Senseney. Wouldn't that be directed toward people-usage, though? That is the point we're trying to establish.

Senseney: That is what the Special Forces direction was. You have to look at it this way. The Army program wanted this device. That is the only thing that was delivered to them. It was a spin-off, of course, from the M-1. The M-1 was a lethal weapon, meant to kill a person, for the Army. It was to be used in Vietnam. It never got there, because we were not fast enough getting it into the logistics system.

Schweiker: What was the most-utilized device of the ones with which you worked and supervised?

Senseney: The only thing I know that was really used was the dog projectile. The other things were in the stockpiles. I don't think anyone ever requested them.

Schweiker: How do you know for certain it was for dogs?

Senseney: Well that is what they asked us to test them against. They wanted to see whether they could put a dog to sleep, and whether sometime later the dog would come back and be on its own and look normal.

Schweiker: Of the devices that came through you, which of these were utilized in any capacity other than for testing?

Senseney: That was the only one that I know of--the dog projectile. I call it a dog projectile. We were developing it because the scenario read that they wanted to be able to make entrance into an area which was patrolled by dogs, leave, the dog come back, and then no one would ever know they were in the area. So that was the reason for the dog projectile.

Church: Thank you Senator Schweiker. I think it is clear that the CIA was interested in the development of a delivery system that could reach human beings, since not many dogs wear clothing. And you would agree with that, wouldn't you?

Senseney: Yes.

Church: Okay.

Schwarz: Along the same line, I assume you must agree that spending money in order to make darts of such a character that they cannot be detected in an autopsy does not have much to do with dogs?

Senseney: No, that would not have anything to do with dogs.

Source: U.S. Senate Testimony, reprinted in an article written by Cutler and Sprague

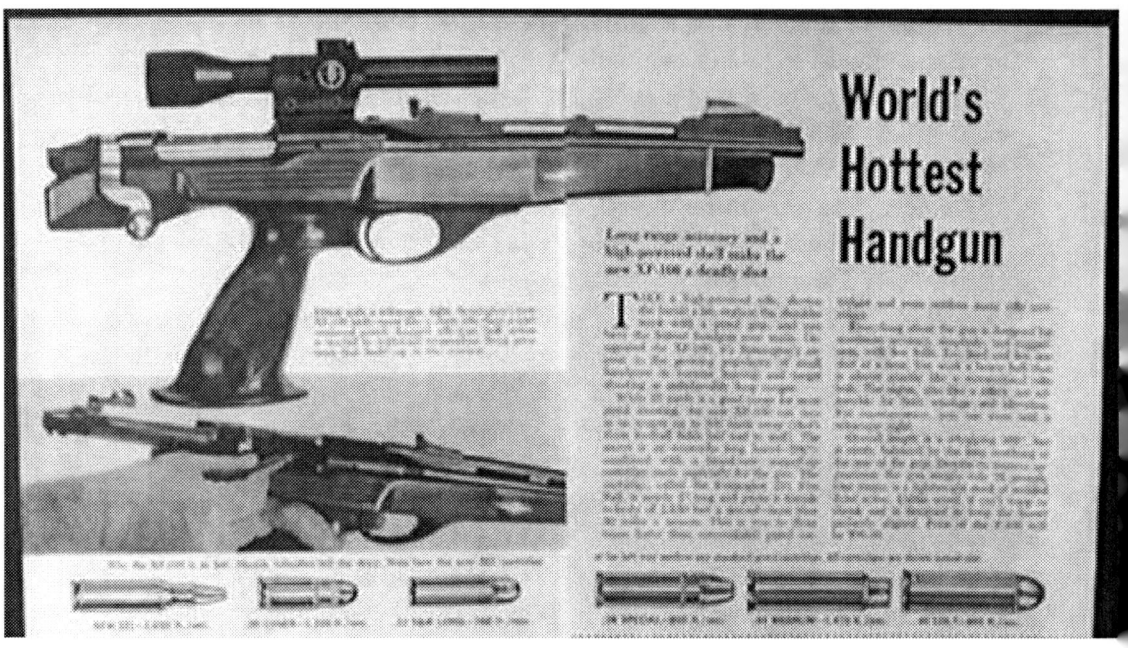

An advertisement for the XP-100 Fireball, the prototype handgun James Files fired from behind the stockade fence on the grassy knoll, resulting in the fatal wounding of President Kennedy.

Exhibit H - Immunity Order for Santo Trafficante

UNITED STATES DISTRICT COURT
FOR THE DISTRICT OF COLUMBIA

In the Matter of the Application of
(UNITED STATES HOUSE OF REPRESENTATIVES) Misc. No. 78-287
(SELECT COMMITTEE ON ASSASSINATIONS)

ORDER CONFERRING IMMUNITY UPON AND COMPELLING TESTIMONY
FROM SANTO TRAFFICANTE

The United States House of Representatives Select Committee on Assassinations
having made written application, and pursuant to Title 18, United States Code,
Sections 6002 and 6005, for an order conferring immunity upon Santo Trafficante
and compelling him to testify and provide other information before the Select
Committee on Assassinations, and the court finding that all procedures specified by
56005 have been duly followed, it is hereby, this 20th day of September 1978,

ORDERED, that Santo Trafficante in accordance with the provisions of Title 18,
United States Code, Sections 6002 and 6005, shall not be excused from testifying or
providing other information before the Select Committee on Assassinations on the
grounds that the testimony or other information sought may tend to incriminate
him.

ORDERED FURTHER, that Santo Trafficante appear when subpoenaed by said
Committee and testify and provide such other information that is sought with
respect to matters under inquiry by said Committee.

AND IT IS FURTHER ORDERED that no testimony or other information compelled
under this order (or any information directly or indirectly derived from such
testimony or other information may be used against Santo Trafficante in any
criminal case, except a prosecution for perjury, giving a false statement or otherwise
failing to comply with this ORDER.

United States District Judge
Dated: Sept. 20 1978 A TRUE COPY
JAMES F. DAVEY, Clerk

Exhibit I
Taylor-McNamara Report

Memorandum from the Chairman of the Joint Chiefs of Staff [General Maxwell Taylor] *and the Secretary of Defense* [Robert S. McNamara] *to the President* [Kennedy] – issued 51 days before the assassination of JFK.

Washington, October 2, 1963

SUBJECT: Report of McNamara-Taylor Mission to South Vietnam

Your memorandum of 21 September 1963 directed that General Taylor and Secretary McNamara proceed to South Vietnam to appraise the military and paramilitary effort to defeat the Viet Cong and to consider, in consultation with Ambassador Lodge, related political and social questions. You further directed that, if the prognosis in our judgment was not hopeful, we should present our views of what action must be taken by the South Vietnam Government and what steps our Government should take to lead the Vietnamese to that action.

Accompanied by representatives of the State Department, CIA, and your Staff, we have conducted an intensive program of visits to key operational areas, supplemented by discussions with U.S. officials in all major U.S. Agencies as well as officials of the GVN and third countries.

We have also discussed our findings in detail with Ambassador Lodge, and with General Harkins and Admiral Felt.

The following report is concurred in by the Staff Members of the mission as individuals, subject to the exceptions noted.

Conclusions

1. The military campaign has made great progress and continues to progress.

2. There are serious political tensions in Saigon (and perhaps elsewhere in South Vietnam) where the Diem-Nhu government is becoming increasingly unpopular.

3. There is no solid evidence of the possibility of a successful coup, although assassination of Diem or Nhu is always a possibility. *(emphasis added by author)*

4. Although some, and perhaps an increasing number, of GVN military officers are becoming hostile to the government, they are more hostile to the Viet Cong than to the government and at least for the near future they will continue to perform their military duties.

5. Further repressive actions by Diem and Nhu could change the present favorable military trends. On the other hand, a return to more moderate methods of control and administration, unlikely though it may be, would substantially mitigate the political crisis.

6. It is not clear that pressures exerted by the U.S. will move Diem and Nhu toward moderation. Indeed, pressures may increase their obduracy. But unless such pressures are exerted, they are almost certain to continue past patterns of behavior.

(Recommendations Followed)

• •

Below is a quotation from former Secretary of Defense, Robert S. McNamara *[his middle name is actually, Strange]* in his eighties while reflecting upon his role in the fire bombing of Japanese civilians in World War II, of dropping the atomic bombs on Hiroshima and Nagasaki, and of his employment of carpet bombing and napalming of civilian targets in Vietnam.

"What makes it immoral if you lose and not immoral if you win?"

Robert S. McNamara

Author's Note: McNamara wondered if he, USAF General Curtis LeMay and others who made those decisions, would have been found guilty of war crimes by the Japanese and the Vietnamese.

Exhibit J
N.S.A.M. 263

Author's Note: President Kennedy had Bundy issue this memo just 42 days prior to JFK's death. He was pulling the United States out of Vietnam. The result would have probably been the saving of 58,000 American and 3,000,000 Vietnamese lives. The bureaucrats ignored the memo long enough for Kennedy to go to Dallas.

• •

National Security Action Memorandum No. 263

Washington - October 11, 1963

TO: Secretary of State

Secretary of Defense

Chairman of the Joint Chiefs of Staff

SUBJECT: South Vietnam

At a meeting on October 5, 1963, the President considered the recommendations contained in the report of Secretary McNamara and General Taylor on their mission to South Vietnam.

The President approved the military recommendations contained in Section I B (1-3) of the report, but directed that no formal announcement be made of the implementation of plans to withdraw 1,000 U.S. military personnel by the end of 1963.

After discussion of the remaining recommendations of the report, the President approved an instruction to Ambassador Lodge which is set forth in State Department telegram No. 534 to Saigon.

McGeorge Bundy

Source: Department of State, S/S-NSC Files: Lot 72 D 316, NSAMs. Top Secret; Eyes Only. The Director of Central Intelligence and the Administrator of AID also received copies. Also printed in *United States-Vietnam Relations, 1945-1967*, Book 12, p. 578.

Exhibit K

J. Edgar Hoover Memorandum

Author's Note: Below is an excerpted portion of a memo from J. Edgar Hoover to the State Department, dated one week after the assassination of JFK.

November 29, 1963

From: Director, FBI

To: Director, U.S. Department of State - Bureau of Intelligence & Research

Subject: Potential for Unauthorized Raids on Cuba

Our sources and informants familiar with Cuban matters in the Miami area advise that the general feeling in the anti-Castro Cuban community is one of stunned disbelief and, even among those who did not entirely agree with the President's policy concerning Cuba, the feeling that the President's death represents a great loss not only to the U.S. but to all of Latin America. These sources know of no plans for unauthorized action against Cuba.

An informant who has furnished reliable information in the past and who is close to a small pro-Castro group in Miami has advised that these individuals are afraid that the assassination of the President may result in strong repressive measures being taken against them, and although pro-Castro in their feelings, regret the assassination.

The substance of the foregoing information was orally furnished to **Mr. George Bush of the Central Intelligence Agency...**

****
Author's note: This memo from J. Edgar Hoover provides credence to the theory that former President George H.W. Bush was intimately involved with the CIA activities concerning the Cuban exiles. Other evidence indicates that George H.W. Bush was most likely the lead CIA agent who oversaw the Bay of Pigs operation.

Exhibit L
Transcript from the Nixon Tapes

Author's Note: During this conversation, recorded as part of the 'Nixon Tapes,' President Nixon is making vague references to the break-in at the office of Daniel Ellsberg's psychiatrist in California. Ellsberg was the government contractor employee of TRW who exposed the documents that became known as 'The Pentagon Papers,' which first disclosed the realities about the conflict in Vietnam to the American people. Nixon's plumbers broke in to gather psychiatric evidence they thought might discredit Ellsberg. The same Plumbers were later caught breaking into the Democratic National Headquarters at the Watergate complex. At least one of the Plumbers was Cuban, a holdover from the Bay of Pigs operation, and E. Howard Hunt was the CIA operative who helped run the Bay of Pigs operations.

• •

APRIL 26, 1973:
> THE PRESIDENT AND KLEINDIENST,
> 12:16--12:21 P.M.,
> WHITE HOUSE TELEPHONE

Nixon: I forgot to tell you, please give me a call on any development on that California thing.

Kleindienst: Yes sir, I will.

Nixon: On the decision, so that we'll know how to react here.

Kleindienst: I'll keep you posted.

Nixon: We've done the right thing, and these clowns get out and do such stupid Goddamn things as that, we've got to take the blame for it. You know.

Kleindienst: Yes. Well, I think we can obviate a lot of that in this situation, though.

Nixon: How?

Kleindienst: Well, I think the fact that, you know, when it came to our attention, that is yours, mine, you know, we made an immediate disclosure.

Nixon: Oh, yeah, that, of the event. But I mean the fact that it was done, you know.

Kleindienst: Oh.

Nixon: The fact that it was done. As you know, it was not authorized. This is a case where these guys had the responsibility when they were at the White House to conduct an investigation of the Ellsberg thing due to the fact that Hoover would not. And so they go out and do this sort of thing.

Kleindienst: Right. Well, we've just got to live with that.
Nixon: Yeah. Just say this was totally unauthorized.

Kleindienst: Right.

Nixon: Dean is basically what the problem is. I mean, here's a desperate man who has misled and so forth and so on, and there's an old story: **you don't strike a king unless you kill him.**

Author's Note: Although Nixon is making reference to John Dean's relationship with himself, he may also be reflecting on his own role in the assassination of President Kennedy. The conspirators agreed that JFK could not leave Dealey Plaza alive.

Exhibit M
Quotes from CIA Personnel Regarding Lee Harvey Oswald

On the afternoon of the assassination, Seth Kantor, a Dallas reporter, was provided with detailed biographical information on Oswald. This was before Oswald's name was broadcast on radio or TV. The information was supplied to Kantor by Harold Hendrix, whose job it was to leak information from the CIA to the press.

Donald Deneslya was a CIA employee who read reports of a CIA agent who had worked at a radio factory in Minsk and returned to the US with a Russian wife and a child. Oswald had returned from Minsk with Marina, and his child, June. Oswald had been working in a radio factory.

CIA officer David Atlee Phillips provided the Warren Commission with information that Oswald was at the Russian and Cuban embassies in Mexico City. Phillips later recanted, admitting that he had given falsified information to the Warren Commission.

Donald Norton, a CIA agent, said *"Oswald was with the CIA, and if he did it, then you better believe the whole CIA was involved."*

Joseph Newbrough, a retired CIA agent, said *"Oswald was an agent for the CIA and acting under orders."*

James Wilcott was a paymaster for the CIA. Wilcott said he had furnished money for the Oswald project, which bore the code name: RX ZIM. Wilcott said that among his group, it was common knowledge that Oswald was an agent of the CIA.

John Garrett Underhill was a CIA agent who talked with friends about the JFK assassination just before he died. Underhill said, *"Oswald is a patsy. They set him up. They've killed the President. I've been listening and hearing things. I couldn't believe they'd get away with it, but they did."*

Exhibit N
Photos of Oswald and Ferrie

Photo of David Ferrie's Civil Air Patrol Unit – Ferrie is pictured far left in the helmet. On the far right is, without question, a young Lee Harvey Oswald.

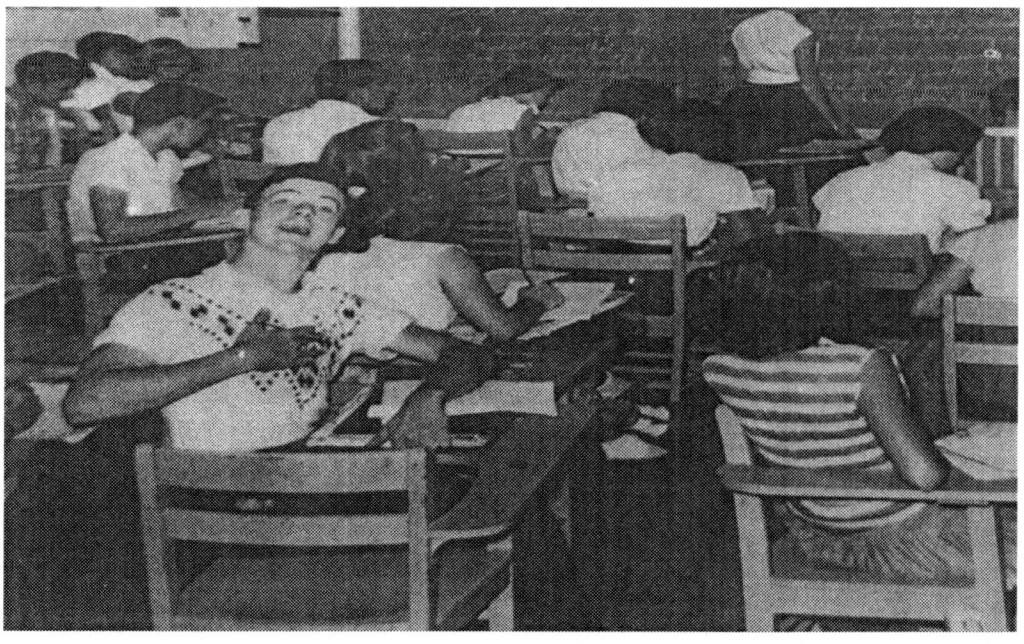

Lee Oswald showing off his missing tooth, after Robin Reilly punched him in the mouth during the 1954 - 55 school year at Beauregard High School in New Orleans.

Exhibit O
Rostow Memo re: Che Guevara

Author's note: The sanitized sentence may have read something like, "*After displaying Che's body for several days, the Rangers severed Che's hands from his body and delivered to CIA headquarters for absolute identification.*"

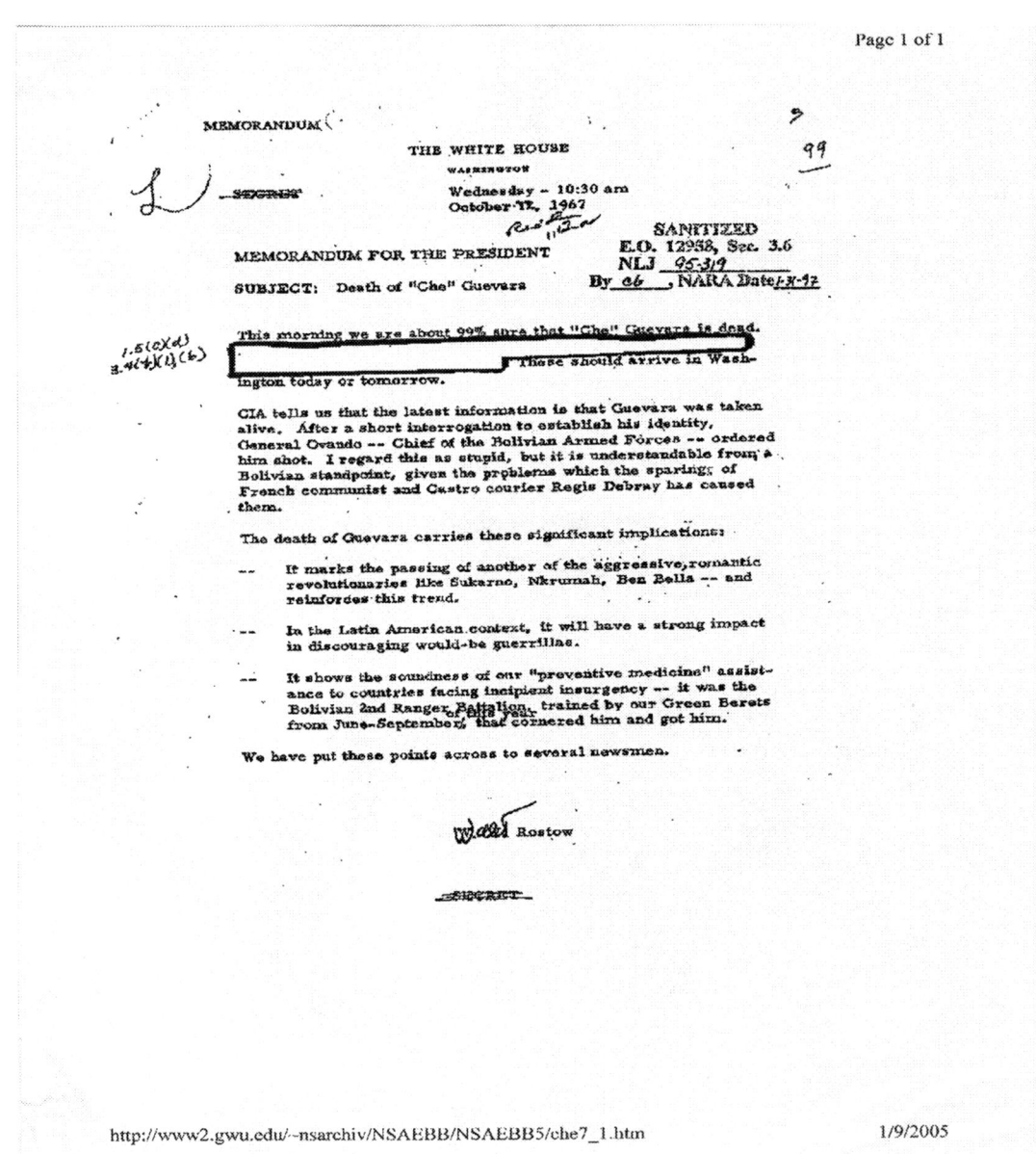

MEMORANDUM

THE WHITE HOUSE
WASHINGTON

Wednesday -- 10:30 am
October 17, 1967

SECRET

SANITIZED
E.O. 12958, Sec. 3.6
NLJ 95-319
By cb , NARA Date 1-8-97

MEMORANDUM FOR THE PRESIDENT

SUBJECT: Death of "Che" Guevara

This morning we are about 99% sure that "Che" Guevara is dead. _____ These should arrive in Washington today or tomorrow.

CIA tells us that the latest information is that Guevara was taken alive. After a short interrogation to establish his identity, General Ovando -- Chief of the Bolivian Armed Forces -- ordered him shot. I regard this as stupid, but it is understandable from a Bolivian standpoint, given the problems which the sparing of French communist and Castro courier Regis Debray has caused them.

The death of Guevara carries these significant implications:

-- It marks the passing of another of the aggressive, romantic revolutionaries like Sukarno, Nkrumah, Ben Bella -- and reinforces this trend.

-- In the Latin American context, it will have a strong impact in discouraging would-be guerrillas.

-- It shows the soundness of our "preventive medicine" assistance to countries facing incipient insurgency -- it was the Bolivian 2nd Ranger Battalion, trained by our Green Berets from June-September of this year, that cornered him and got him.

We have put these points across to several newsmen.

Walt Rostow

SECRET

1/9/2005

Exhibit P
FBI Memo re: Jack Ruby

Author's note: If this poorly reproduced memo is to be believed, then it provides proof that Richard Nixon was collaborating with and protecting Jacob Rubinstein, [aka Jack Rubenstain],[aka Jack Ruby], the man who murdered Lee Harvey Oswald, as far back as November 24th, 1947.

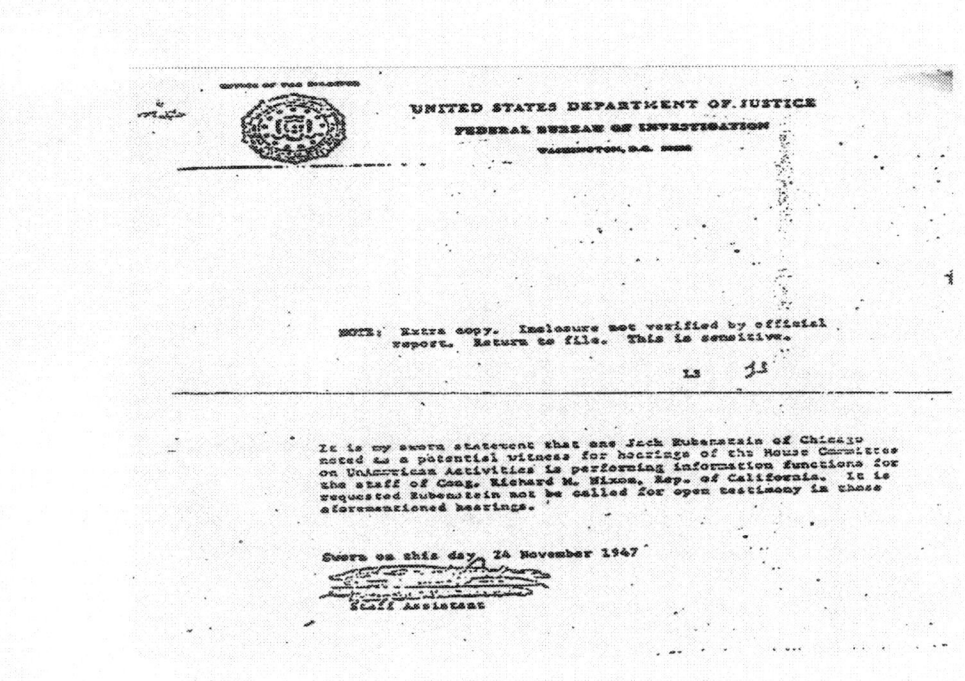

Cast of Characters

The following listing of key characters is provided to assist you in separating fact from fiction while reading _Misplaced Loyalties,_ and to give you a deeper understanding of how each individual fits into the overall framework of history. In order to form an accurate interpretation of the historical events, you must know the who actual characters are, who are actual persons with fictitious names, and who are fictitious characters I created to facilitate the storyline of this book.

Adlai Stevenson – Mr. Stevenson was a prominent and beloved leader in the Democratic Party during the time of John F. Kennedy. Stevenson spoke to the multitudes gathered on the Mall in Washington, D.C. on the centennial celebration of Abraham Lincoln's signing of the Emancipation Proclamation. President Kennedy appointed Stevenson as U.S. Ambassador to the United Nations. On July 14, 1965, Adlai Stevenson suffered a fatal heart attack on the grounds of the U.S. Embassy in London. Legally speaking, and from a jurisdictional perspective, Mr. Stevenson died on U.S. federal government property.

Carlos Marcello – Known as the _Big Daddy in the Big Easy_, Carlos Marcello was the ruthless Mafia boss in New Orleans. His strip joint, known as the 500 Club, was a night spot frequented by Lee Harvey Oswald and his lover, Judyth Vary Baker. Marcello was assisted frequently in New Orleans, by David Ferrie, who was also his personal pilot. In March, 1961 Attorney General Robert F. Kennedy had Marcello deported to Guatemala, on the basis of having a forged birth certificate to prove U.S. citizenship. Marcello was soon back in New Orleans, protesting his 'kidnapping' by RFK.

Charles 'Chuckie' Nicoletti – The primary hit man for Sam Giancana in Chicago, Charles Nicoletti assisted in the assassination of Marilyn Monroe, and was the shooter from the second floor of the Dal-Tex Building in Dealey Plaza. Charles Nicoletti was the mentor of James Files, the 21-year-old who fired the fatal headshot from behind the stockade fence on the grassy knoll. Nicoletti was murdered in 1977 just prior to his scheduled testimony before the House Subcommittee on Assassinations, regarding his role in, and knowledge of, the assassination of President Kennedy.

Cindy Ackerman – Cindy Ackerman is the fictitious name of an actual person. This law student, an intern during the Kennedy administration, witnessed the events on Air Force One during the return flight from Dallas on the day of the assassination. Her story was relayed to the author by a woman who attended the meeting portrayed in this book, who was working as a secretary in the history department of a major university.

Dwight David Eisenhower - Born in Texas, Dwight David "Ike" Eisenhower was the 34th President of the United States. He had served as the Supreme Commander of Allied Forces in World War II. Eisenhower's crowning achievement was OPERATION OVERLORD, the invasion of France on the beaches of Normandy, otherwise known as D-Day. When Eisenhower left the White House, he televised a speech warning the American people about the dangers of nuclear weapons, and the power of America's military-industrial complex.

Francis Gary Powers - A Virginian, Gary Powers is known for the fact that his U-2 spy plane was shot down by Soviet surface to air missiles (a Soviet plane chasing Powers also exploded) on May 1, 1960, while flying a surveillance mission, photographing ICBM sites on a track over Russia from Pakistan to Norway. Presuming that Powers was dead and the plane destroyed, the U.S. vigorously denied the existence of Powers, and President Eisenhower had a U-2 painted with NASA markings to position it as a 'weather plane.' After America issued its denials and photographs of the recently painted plane, Khrushchev brought out the processed film from the U-2, as well as Gary Powers, tried him as a spy, and cancelled the superpower summit on May 16, 1960. Power's survival kit included 7,500 rubles and jewelry for women.

George De Mohrenschildt – George De Mohrenschildt was known as *The White Russian*. He was Oswald's CIA handler and his closest friend the last two years of his life. De Mohrenschildt had worked for Preston Bush and Clint Murchison in Texas. George Herbert Walker Bush had known De Mohrenschildt since 1942. In 1977, the House SubCommittee on Assassinations (HSCA) called on De Mohrenschildt to testify. As HSCA investigator Gaeton Fonzi prepared to interview De Mohrenschildt on March 29, 1977, the *White Russian* died of a shotgun blast to the head.

Jack Ruby – Born Jacob Rubinstein, [aka Jack Rubenstain], Jack Ruby was the operator of the Carousel night club in Dallas. Ruby ran drugs and guns for the CIA. He had been protected by Richard Nixon and the FBI in 1947, while he was working as an informant for Congressman Nixon. Then, on November 23, 1963, Ruby was allowed into the basement of the Dallas Police Department, where he shot Lee Harvey Oswald, the accused assassin of President Kennedy, before Oswald could testify publicly about what he knew about the JFK assassination. Ruby pleaded with Chief Justice Warren to allow him to testify for the Warren Commission in Washington. His request was refused. While Ruby was incarcerated in Dallas, he unwittingly received an injection of virulent lung cancer cells, as part of a CIA operation in New Orleans that was meant to be directed against Fidel Castro. According to the death certificate, the cause of Jack Ruby's death was lung cancer.

Jacqueline Bouvier Kennedy – Jackie was First Lady of the United States. She married John F. Kennedy while he was a congressman from Massachusetts, and the couple had two children together, Caroline and John, Jr. Not long before the fateful trip to Dallas, Jackie had given birth to a second son, Patrick, who lived only a few days. The trauma reminded President Kennedy and his wife of their mortality, and JFK was obsessed with the possibility that he might be assassinated. Despite previous marital difficulties, many observers claim that on the day of JFK's death, the King and Queen of Camelot had never been closer. Jackie fled from the United States and married the wealthy shipping magnate, Aristotle Onassis, and lived on his private island in Greece.

James E. Files – Born James E. Sutton, James Files is the man who, at age 21, fired the fatal headshot that killed JFK from behind the stockade fence on the grassy knoll in Dealey Plaza, using a mercury-loaded .222 slug from a preproduction Remington Fireball handgun with a 3X scope. Files was trained at Fort Leonard Wood, Missouri, for Army basic training, then went to Fort Bragg, North Carolina, to join the 82nd Airborne Division. He was trained in explosives and mechanical ambushes, then sent into Laos. He had honed his shooting skills as a child by shooting squirrels and rabbits. While he was in Laos, Files witnessed the illegal drug trade in the Golden Triangle. He was fighting there in a covert war that was not known to the American people at the time. James Files got the attention of the CIA when he shot two of his own men in the head while they were running away from him. Files executed the American soldiers to endear himself to his Laotian counterparts. Upon his return stateside, Files was recruited into the CIA by David Atlee Phillips, who was his CIA controller on the day of the JFK assassination. Subsequent to the JFK assassination, after surviving multiple assassination attempts on him by federal agents, James Files was convicted of attempting to kill a police officer who had tried to kill him. Witnesses testified the undercover cops were in an unmarked car, and had fired at least fourteen shots before Files and his partner defended themselves. On March 22, 1994, James E. Files gave the first videotaped interview during which he detailed how he had fired the shot at President Kennedy's right temple that killed JFK. When Files contacted 'Wolfman,' his associate who had prepared the six mercury-loaded Fireball rounds for the JFK assassination, Wolfman said he wanted to check into some things before deciding to be interviewed by the private investigator who had located James Files. One week later, Wolfman died of a heart attack. The premature deaths of both Wolfman and the private investigator, both from heart complications, motivated Files to confess his participation in the assassination of JFK, so he could tell his story before he ended up like his two friends. As of the date of first publication of _Misplaced Loyalties_, James E. Files is doing prison time in Joliet, Illinois.

John – John is a physicist who worked in a CIA assassinations lab in upstate New York during the early 1960's. John heard the details of the plan used to kill Marilyn Monroe two weeks after she died. John was told in detail of the plot to assassinate JFK two weeks prior to the event in Dallas. John invented a microwave device that could noiselessly stop a man's heart with pinpoint accuracy in a crowded restaurant from a distance of 50 feet. John also developed the first wave optics night vision Starlight Scope, which was used by the CIA to capture and kill Che Guevara and his men in the forests of Bolivia. John's astounding testimony forms the basis of this book, and he has given the author the exclusive right to tell his story.

John Fitzgerald Kennedy – John Kennedy was the 34th President of the United States. He pre-empted a nuclear holocaust by leading his country through the tenuous thirteen days known as the Cuban Missile Crisis while standing against the Soviet Premier, Nikita Khrushchev. Kennedy also prevented what might have become a nuclear war with Russia by not allowing the Bay of Pigs invasion by Cuban exiles to escalate into a full scale invasion by the United States. JFK suffered from a degenerative illness of the adrenal glands, known as Addison's disease, which he hid from the American people. His marital infidelities, known by Capitol Hill insiders and the press were not known by the general public until decades after his death. President Kennedy was assassinated in Dallas, Texas, on November 22, 1963. The *coup d'etat* of that tragic day marked the beginning of years of rule over the populace of the United States by a group of powerful men. This fascist form of government, which governed contrary to the will of the American citizenry, remained in power until the electorate regained control several elections after JFK's death.

John Roselli – Johnny Roselli (aka Filippo Sacco) was a former lieutenant of Al Capone in Chicago. Roselli had served as bodyguard for Harry Cohen, the president of Columbia Pictures in Hollywood. Roselli was the top Mafia man in Los Angeles and Las Vegas, representing Sam Giancana of Chicago. Roselli was the liaison between organized crime and the CIA during such operations as the attempted assassination of Fidel Castro, and the murder of JFK. Roselli was the lead assassin in the murder of Marilyn Monroe, and was the spotter for Chuckie Nicoletti as Nicoletti fired at President Kennedy from the second floor of the Dal-Tex Building in Dealey Plaza on November 22, 1963. Roselli was scheduled to testify before the House Subcommittee on Assassinations (HSCA) in 1976. But before his appearance in Washington, his dismembered and decomposing body was found in a 55-gallon drum, floating in Dumbfounding Bay, Florida.

Judyth Vary Baker – Although the fact is not well-known, and many have worked to discredit her story, Judyth Baker was a lover of Lee Harvey Oswald. Vary Baker was a contract employee of the CIA, engaged in the development of a virulent form of lung cancer for use in an assassination attempt against Fidel Castro. Although the attempts by the CIA and the Mafia against Castro failed, there were subsequent, suspicious deaths by cancer, related to the JFK assassination. Two men who died of rapid onset of cancer are Jack Ruby and the Cuban exile leader, Manuel Artime.

Lee Bowers – The train switching yard manager who was working in the control tower behind Dealey Plaza at the moment of the assassination. Bowers testified he saw, *"smoke and a commotion,"* on his side of the picket fence at the top of the grassy knoll, which is where James Files claims to have been located when he fired the fatal shot. Bowers died following his testimony to the Warren Commission in a single-car accident on a deserted Texas highway. Minutes before he died, Bowers told the ambulance medical technicians he thought he had been drugged.

Lee Harvey Oswald – Lee Oswald was a career agent of the CIA with a TOP SECRET clearance. Oswald served in the Marines at Atsugi Air Base in Japan where the U.S. launched U-2 surveillance flights over Russia. During that time, he conducted counter-intelligence (spying) operations, monitoring the activities of U-2 pilots who consorted with prostitutes in Tokyo and the surrounding region, particularly at the Queen Bee club. During that mission, Oswald contracted, and was treated for, a minor venereal disease. Oswald was later sent into Russia with the classified "Vest Pocket" designation, while he had multiple covers and misinformation tags by NSA to cover his intelligence activities. The CIA sent Oswald into Moscow on an undercover mission to give information to the Soviets which enabled them to shoot down, on May 1, 1960, the U-2 reconnaissance plane flown by Francis Gary Powers. This event cancelled the nuclear summit between President Eisenhower and Nikita Khrushchev, and increased the tension between the nuclear superpowers. While Oswald was in Minsk he married the niece of a Russian secret service operative. Marina had been sent by the KGB to keep an eye on Oswald while he worked in a radio factory, in close proximity to a Soviet spy school in Minsk. Upon his return from Russia in 1962, Oswald was interviewed at length by FBI Special Investigations Agent, John Faine. Lee Oswald served with David Ferrie in the Civil Air Patrol. Oswald worked with David Ferrie and Judyth Baker to develop the lung cancer cells to be used against Castro. Oswald spent the five days leading up to the assassination of JFK, driving Chicago Mafia hit man James Files around Dallas, assisting Files as he test fired and calibrated the scopes on the Mannlicher-Carcano carbines and the Remington Fireball handgun that were provided by the CIA, and were used to kill Kennedy. Oswald had told his lover, Judyth Baker, that he was being framed for the upcoming assassination of JFK in Dallas, but he could not tell anyone about it. Oswald maintained silence and waited patiently for his CIA superiors to gain his release from the Dallas jail, while he was tried and convicted in the court of popular opinion. Although few people, other than immediate family and reporters attended Oswald's burial, there were many armed federal agents surrounding the casket, until they were sure Oswald's body would not be exhumed for forensic testing. The drugs used to expedite and ensure Oswald's death would decompose with the body, causing future exhumation to be of little concern.

Lionel Grandison – Lionel Grandison was the Los Angeles Deputy Coroner's Aide who refused to sign Marilyn Monroe's death certificate due to *"faulty handling of autopsy evidence."*

Lyndon B. Johnson – Lyndon Johnson was the 35th President of the United States. He was under suspicion for criminal links to Bobby Baker and Billy Sol Estes at the time of JFK's assassination in Dallas. Texas was Johnson's home state. Johnson appointed the members of the Warren Commission who investigated the assassination of President Kennedy. Johnson's private airline ferried troops to Vietnam, and he authorized the bombing campaigns that contributed to the deaths of three million Vietnamese. LBJ did not seek reelection in 1968, when he stepped aside to be replaced by Richard Nixon. During his presidency, Johnson enacted many of the civil rights and other reform acts that were drafted during the Kennedy administration. On the night before the JFK assassination, LBJ emerged from a private meeting at the home of an owner of the Dallas cowboys, walked over to the table where his lover, Madeleine Duncan Brown was sitting, and said, *"After tomorrow, those goddamm Kennedy's will never embarrass me again...that's no threat...that's a promise."*

Marilyn Monroe – Born an orphan, Norma Jean Baker fashioned herself into the most famous woman in Hollywood, using her sex appeal to open many doors. She took the stage name of Marilyn Monroe. She was married numerous times to such notables as the playwright Arthur Miller, and the baseball sensation Joe DiMaggio. Marilyn never realized her two lifetime dreams, to be a mother and a respected actress. She died in August of 1962 under suspicious circumstances, in her bungalow located in the Brentwood suburb of Hollywood, California.

Mary Pinchot Meyer – A contemporary of Jackie Kennedy, Kay Graham, and other future Washington notables, Mary Meyer was the former wife of Cord Meyer, a senior covert operations director at the CIA. Mary Meyer lived in Georgetown near her sister, Toni, who was married to Kay Graham's senior editor at *The Washington Post*, Ben Bradlee. An adventurous, artistic soul, Mary Meyer was without question the favorite mistress and confidante of President Kennedy.

Nikita Sergeyevich Khrushchev - Political Commissar of the Russian Army during the Battle of Stalingrad (present day Volgograd) during which he lost his eldest son, Leonid, Khrushchev rose to become the Premier of the Soviet Union. He denounced Stalin, then stood against Eisenhower and Kennedy in the Cold War. When the Soviet Union shot down the U-2 spy plane flown by Francis Gary Powers over Russia on May 1, 1960, the incident resulted in repeated denials by the U.S. and, ultimately, the cancellation of the summit by Khrushchev on May 16, 1960. His second son, Sergei, is an American professor at Brown University's Watson Institute for International Studies.

Richard Nixon – A member of a devout Quaker family, Richard Milhouse Nixon was the 36th President of the United States. Nine years transpired from the time he lost his first presidential bid to John Kennedy in 1960 until he gained the White House when Lyndon Johnson did not seek reelection in 1968. Nixon was responsible for the destruction of career government employees, such as Alger Hiss, when he sought the political spotlight by accusing Hiss of being a communist. Nixon later ordered the breaking and entering into the office of the psychiatrist for Daniel Ellsberg, the government contractor employee who broke the story first printed in *The Washington Post* that would come to be known as *The Pentagon Papers*. Despite President Nixon's attacks, Ellsberg was vindicated by the Court. When President Nixon authorized the Plumbers (some were Cubans) to break into the Democratic National Headquarters in the Watergate office complex in Washington, DC, he started a chain of events that ended his presidency. To this day, few people know what was said (and by whom) during the several minutes of phone recordings Nixon erased before handing them over to the Watergate investigation team. During the presidential transition period, Johnson briefed Nixon on a plan to open relations with China.

Robert Fitzgerald Kennedy – Bobby Kennedy was JFK's campaign manager, and his closest advisor. On the insistence of Joe Kennedy, Sr., JFK appointed Bobby as U.S. Attorney General. He was indispensable to the President during the critical days of the Cuban Missile Crisis, and the Bay of Pigs invasion of Cuba. Bobby double-crossed the Mafia when he launched relentless attacks on Sam Giancana, Carlos Marcello, Santo Trafficante, and Jimmy Hoffa, to name a few. It is well accepted today that both JFK and RFK had affairs with Marilyn Monroe. Bobby Kennedy had won the California presidential primary, and was headed for the Democratic convention in Chicago, when he was assassinated in the pantry of the Ambassador Hotel in Los Angeles. Richard Nixon won the election. California, the state in which RFK died, was Nixon's home state.

Robert Strange McNamara – Robert McNamara was Secretary of Defense during the Kennedy and Johnson administrations. The conflict in Vietnam was fought on McNamara's watch. McNamara played a pivotal role in the destruction of the ornate coffin that allegedly carried the body of JFK to Washington from Dallas. Strange is the actual middle name of Robert McNamara.

Sam Giancana – Gilorma "Momo" Giancana was born on May 24, 1908. Sam Giancana was first charged with murder at age 18. He worked for a while for the gangster, Paul Ricca. When a mobster put out a contract on the life of Joseph Kennedy, Sr., Sam Giancana was able to quash it. In exchange for saving his life, Joe Kennedy promised to take care of Giancana when one of his sons entered the White House. Giancana delivered Cook County, Illinois, illegally to John Kennedy which assured his election as President of the United States. Giancana harbored a plan to make the Dominican Republic the 'next Cuba,' to restore a haven for money-making and money-laundering enterprises, such as gambling, drug running, and prostitution. Using their shared lover, Judith Campbell Exner as a go-between, Kennedy agreed to the assassination of President Trujillo of the Dominican Republic, who was leaning toward Moscow. Afterward, when Bobby Kennedy realized that Giancana planned to turn the Dominican Republic into another Cuba, he had Giancana tracked so closely by the FBI, that Giancana had personal confrontations with the FBI agents in public places, such as airports. Giancana knew the names of the FBI agents who were tailing him. Exasperated by the Kennedy double-cross, Giancana played a major role in the execution of JFK that took place just down the street at the Adolphus Hotel in Dallas, where he was staying at the time of JFK's death. Giancana was scheduled to appear before the HSCA committee in 1976. But while fixing a sandwich at his home in Oak Park, Illinois on June 19, 1975. Sam Giancana received a fatal gunshot wound, from a large caliber pistol, in the back of his head. When the body was discovered, there were six, smaller bullet holes forming a ring around Giancana's mouth. The implied meaning was obvious for those who were scheduled to testify.

Santo Trafficante, Jr. – The son of a Mafia boss, Santo Trafficante cooperated with Lucky Luciano, Frank Costello, and Meyer Lansky in setting up gambling operations in Cuba during the reign of the Cuban dictator, Fulgencio Batista. Batista received large graft payments from the mobsters until he was ousted by Fidel Castro. In 1961, Johnny Roselli convinced Trafficante in Tampa, to help Roselli and the CIA murder Fidel Castro. The mobsters cooperated with the CIA in return for protection from prosecution for their criminal behaviors. In 1963, Trafficante told his associate, Jose Aleman, *"Mark my word, this man Kennedy is in trouble, and he will get what is coming to him. Kennedy's not going to make it to the election* [in 1964]. *He is going to be hit."*

LAPD Detectives Edwards and Calvert, Malika, Captain Martin [the Navy Captain], and the veterans from Vietnam and Korea are actual persons with fictitious names.

Henry Atherton, Andrea Atherton, Charlie Montrose, John Faulk, Professor Thomas White, Jerry Paxson [the State Department Historian], Senator Mark Andrews, and the LAPD Intelligence Officer are fictitious characters, created by the author to tie the facts and the storyline together.

Sources & References

Personal Interviews

Several meetings in late 2000 – Multiple interviews with John, a former CIA scientist, who heard the plan to assassinate President Kennedy two weeks before the assassination in Dallas. He also heard the plan to kill Marilyn Monroe two weeks after she died. John invented the heart-shocking machine for the CIA, and was aware of the methods designed to kill Fidel Castro. He also developed the first night vision scope, which was used by the CIA to capture Che Guevara.

Fall of 2000 – Conversation with an employee at an antique emporium regarding an event he witnessed involving Jacqueline Kennedy at a horse racing event in Middleburg, Virginia.

December 2000 – Interview over lunch in suburban Virginia with a Vietnam veteran who was ordered to assassinate his allied South Vietnamese counterpart. The Vietnamese officer had been suspected of spying for the North Vietnamese.

April 23, 2001 – Conversation with a decorated Vietnam veteran who gave Marilyn Monroe a tour of his general's garden just days prior to her death. She admitted to him that she was pregnant with either JFK's or RFK's baby at the time of their meeting.

March 1, 2001 – Conversation with a Vietnam veteran, now living in the U.S. with his Vietnamese-American wife, who spoke about the lack of purpose in the war, and the frailty of the Domino Theory.

May of 2001 – Conversation with a Korean war veteran who recalled how a Korean boy avoided the draft with a payment of only $400. That interaction made the American soldier question why he was required to leave his family to serve in Korea.

June of 2001 – Conversation with a newsman who served in several White House press corps. He described the moment when he heard the news of President Kennedy's death while driving his father's car.

July of 2001 – Conversation with a former US Navy gunboat skipper who served in the CIA's secret war in El Salvador, regarding the Bay of Pigs invasion.

December 2002 – Conversation with a former US Army officer who served in Germany following WW II. Most of his U.S. Army friends died in Vietnam.

April 2003 – Conversation with a former Huey helicopter side-gunner in U.S. Army who served in Vietnam. He also served in Cambodia years before the American public knew that U.S. troops were fighting in Cambodia.

April 2003 – Conversation with a former chopper pilot in Korea and Germany who described the practice of killing commanding officers by 'fragging' in Vietnam.

May 2003 – Conversation with former (Bell Helicopter) Huey crew chief who talked about the cannibalization of helicopters by U.S. soldiers.

June 2003 – Conversation with retired military official regarding hostages in Vietnam and our reasons for being there.

July 2004 - Terrence McGarry Interview. Conversation with Terry McGarry, a UPI reporter who was in Dallas on 11-22-63. McGarry witnessed the assassination from one of the follow-up cars in the presidential motorcade, as well as the shooting of Lee Harvey Oswald by Jack Ruby in the basement of Dallas Police headquarters.

August 2003 – Conversation with a retired U.S. Coast Guard captain, regarding the purchase of the U.S.C.G. headquarters building from Richard Nixon's friend, Bebe Rebozzo. Nixon and Rebozzo were caught in other uncomfortable real estate deals, such as Nixon's private properties, and questionable investments in the Caribbean.

September 2004 – Conversation with a retired U.S. Army enlisted man who was one of the first fighting men to be inserted into Vietnam. He was a marksman, trained in assassination and martial arts. He participated in the PHEONIX PROJECT, and to this day has a microchip embedded in his left shoulder, which he allowed the author to verify.

October 2004 – Conversation with a retired U.S. Marine enlisted man who had trained in Puerto Rico, preparing for the U.S. invasion of Cuba following the Bay of Pigs operation.

October 2004 - Conversation at an American university with a department secretary, regarding the law school student who was on Air Force One during the return flight from Dallas to Washington, D.C.

December 2004 – Conversation with a former U.S. Navy pilot who witnessed Air Force One make a hasty take off from the taxiway at Andrews A.F.B. on November 22, 1963 while flying overhead in an F-8 Crusader.

Throughout 2004 - Correspondence and phone conversations with Wim Dankbaar of the Netherlands, and Judyth Vary Baker, a credible JFK assassination researcher who was of great assistance to the author, and a former CIA scientist who claims to have been the mistress of Lee Harvey Oswald, respectively.

July 2005 – Conversation with a retired U.S. Air Force officer who was detailed to NSA (National Security Agency) during the Cold War. He was familiar with the capabilities of the American U-2 spy plane as well as the Soviet surface-to-air missiles (SAMs) that brought down Francis Gary Powers while Powers was flying over Russia.

Resources Quoted

Adlai Stevenson and the World, Doubleday Publishing [Anchor Books], Copyright © 1978, by John Bartlow Martin

"*America's Defense Monitor*" Copyright © 1992, Center for Defense Information.

America's Queen: A Life of Jacqueline Kennedy Onassis, by Sarah Bradford, Viking Press

An Oral History of the Cuban Missile Crisis, by D. Gordon, February 3, 1999

An Unfinished Life; John F. Kennedy, 1917-1963 by Robert Dallek, Published by Little, Brown & Company

A Thousand Days; John F. Kennedy in the White House, by Arthur M. Schlesinger, Jr., Mariner Books, Copyright © 1993

A Very Private Woman; The Life and Unsolved Murder of Presidential Mistress Mary Meyer, by Nina Burleigh, Bantam Books, Copyright © 1998

Battlefield Vietnam, Public Broadcasting System

Blood, Money & Power; How LBJ Killed JFK , The legal evidence that proves Lyndon Johnson had a role in the death of President Kennedy, by Barr McClellan, Hannover House

Coleen M. Rowley [Special Agent and Chief Counsel for Minneapolis FBI Division] *Memo to FBI Director Robert Mueller*, written on May 21, 2001 and published by *TIME Magazine* on the Web, regarding the inaction on the part of the FBI relative to handling of intelligence information in the Moussaoui case, which might have averted the 9-11 disaster.

Covert Action Quarterly, Fall of 1993

Cutler & Sprague: Article that includes testimony before the Church Senate Intelligence Committee regarding the CIA developed [M-1]Umbrella Weapon used in the assassination of President Kennedy.

Dead Center; A Marine Sniper's Two-Year Odyssey in the Vietnam War, Ballantine Publishing [Ivy Books], Copyright © 1999, by Ed Kugler

Eyewitness to Power, Simon & Schuster. Copyright © 2000, by David Gergen

Falling for Marilyn; The Missing Niagara Collection. Friedman/Fairfax Publishing, Copyright © 1996, Photos and narrative by Jock Carroll

Files on JFK, a DVD produced by Wim Daankbar, available for purchase on the Web at www.jfkmurdersolved.com, Copyright © 2003

First Hand Knowledge, by Robert Morrow, Shapolsky Publishers, Inc. Copyright © 1994

Flawed Giant; Lyndon Johnson and His Times, Oxford University Press, Copyright © 1998, by Robert Dallek

Flight from Dallas, by James P. Johnston & Jon Roe, 1st Books, Copyright © 2003. The story of Sargeant Robert G. Vinson, a NORAD officer who unwittingly found himself on a CIA flight from Andrews AFB to Dallas on 11-22-63 to pickup CIA personnel who participated in the assassination of President Kennedy.

"Friendly Fire" by David Ruppe, www.abcnews.com article entitled, "U.S. Military Drafted Plans to Terrorize U.S. Cities and to Provoke War with Cuba."

Grace & Power by Sally Bedell Smith, Random House, Copyright © 2004

Headliners & Legends, an MSNBC special, Copyright © 2003

High Times, by Jorge Mas Canosa, Copyright © 1999, Trans High Corporation

"History and Politics Out Loud" Robert F. Kennedy eulogizes Reverend Martin Luther King, Jr.

Inside the CIA; Revealing the Secrets of the World's Most Powerful Spy Agency, by Ronald Kessler, Simon & Schuster [Pocket Books], Copyright © 1992

JFK, the motion picture, Oliver Stone, 1991

JFK Revisited, an article by Dr. Arthur M. Schlesinger, Jr., reprinted by *Cigar Aficionado Magazine* in 2004.

Jim Garrison's New Orleans Photo Gallery

"Johnny, We Hardly Knew Ye" Little, Brown & Company, Copyright © 1970 & 1972, by Kenneth P. O'Donnell & David Powers, with Joe McCarthy.

"Justice For John Kennedy" by Robert D. Morningstar, [details the death of Dorothy Kilgallen].

LIFE Commemorative, John F. Kennedy Memorial Edition, Fall of 2003.

Marilyn Monroe Photo Gallery, CMG Worldwide & Marilyn Monroe, LLC

Minority of One, Sylvia Meagher, an independent researcher of the John F. Kennedy assassination, wrote a review of the book by Epstein, which focuses on the Warren Commission Report.

National Security Council Notes, Johnson Presidential Library, 1966

NATION, August 13, 1988 – disclosure of the Hoover memo regarding the briefing of George Bush of the CIA in Miami.

President Kennedy Has Been Shot, by the Newseum with Cathy Trost & Susan Bennett, Sourcebooks, Incorporated - Copyright © 2003

Profiles in Courage, Harper & Brothers, 1956 [Harper Perennial, 2000], by John F. Kennedy

PT-109; John Kennedy in WW II, McGraw-Hill, Copyright © 1961 and 2001, by Robert J. Donovan

Six Seconds In Dallas, by Josiah Thompson, Ph. D., Bernard Geis Associates, New York, Copyright © 1967

Someone Would Have Talked, by Larry Hancock, JFK Lancer Productions and Publications, Copyright © 2003

<u>Texas in the Morning</u>, by Madeleine Duncan Brown, ghost written by Harry Livingston, The Conservatory Press, Copyright © 1997

The Constitution of the United States of America, and the *Bill of Rights.*

<u>The Death of a President</u>, by William Manchester, Galahad Books, Copyright © 1967

<u>The Enemy Within</u>, by Robert Fitzgerald Kennedy, Da Capo Press, Copyright © 1960

<u>The Fifties</u>, by Douglas Miller & Marion Nowack, Doubleday Press, Garden City, New York, Copyright © 1977

<u>The Imperial Presidency</u>, by Dr. Arthur Meier Schlesinger, Jr., Houghton Mifflin Company, Boston, Copyright © 1973

<u>The Kennedy Men</u>, Perennial Books [Harper Collins] Copyright © 2001 by Laurence Leamer

The Kennedy Tapes, Harvard University Press [Belknap Press], Copyright © 1997 & 2000, edited by Ernest R. May & Philip D. Zelikow

<u>The Last Days of Marilyn Monroe</u>, William Murray & Company, Copyright © 1998, by Donald H. Wolfe

The Library of World History by Diodorus, 336 BC

The Marilyn Files – a videotape documentary by Robert Slatzer, KVC Entertainment, Copyright © 1991

"The Men Who Killed Kennedy," a British television documentary

<u>The New Big Book of Presidents</u>, Running Press [Courage Books], Copyright © 2000, by Marc Frey & Todd Davis

The Strange Actions (and Inaction) of Agent Emory Roberts, by Vincent M. Palamara, Copyright © 1999

The Top Secret Second Autopsy of President John F. Kennedy, by Bjorn K. Gjerde, Copyright © 2004

The Umbrella System: Prelude to an Assassination, by Richard E. Sprague and Robert Cutler

The Untimely Death of LtCmdr. William B. Pitzer: The Physical Evidence, by Allan R.J. Eaglesham and R. Robin Palmer, Copyright © 1998

The Warren Commission Report, U.S. Government, Copyright © 1964, 26 volumes of evidence and testimony pertaining to the assassination of President John F. Kennedy

United States versus Clay Shaw, transcripts of the case brought against CIA operative and JFK assassination conspirator Clay Shaw, by District Attorney Jim Garrison in New Orleans, 1964

Printed in the United Kingdom
by Lightning Source UK Ltd.
129651UK00001B/47/A